## AUTHOR'S NOTE

*Home Is The River* is a work of fiction. All characters, places, issues and events are fictitious or are used fictitiously, and any similarity to real people, places, issues or events is purely coincidental. In other words, I made the whole thing up and don't you believe a word of it.

### Also by M. H. Salmon

~ ~ ~ ~ ~ ~

Non-fiction

*Gazehounds & Coursing*

*Gila Descending*

# DEDICATION

To the Western Myth, - the real one -
and to the myth makers and the
keepers of the myth, coast to coast.


~ ~ ~ ~ ~ ~


*"Faith in wildness or in nature as a creative force, has
the deeper, possibly the deepest, significance for our
future. It is a philosophy, a faith; it is even, if you like, a
religion. It puts our ultimate trust, not in human
intelligence, but in whatever it is that created human
intelligence and is, in the long run, more likely than we
to solve our problems."*


Joseph Wood Krutch


*"If there is still magic left upon this planet, then it is
contained in moving water."*


Loren Eiseley

# PROLOGUE

*Even now, hardly anyone goes there. The flow
remains free, if sometimes meager - a creek when it's
dry season, a river when it's wet season, mostly just a
stream on its own. Horse tracks and man tracks are
sometimes seen in the sand between the rocks along the
river's edge where the waters enter the canyon and the
rough, sun-lit hills for the long descent. Occasionally,
these same tracks are also seen in the rough hills
themselves and beneath the cliffs along river's most wild
interior flow. But catfish don't draw the numbers, nor
do unusual birds that few can identify. Nor do coyote,
bobcat, gray fox and raccoon which are so common
elsewhere. Javelina and Coatimundi are much too
peculiar and little known to be popular here. Black
Bear, Cougar, deer, elk and Bighorn Sheep can be sought
more easily elsewhere in the forest. The truly rare
animals that are found along the river and nowhere else
in the great Southwest remain difficult subjects. They
are so seldom seen that only those with true afición for
the wilds will ever try to find them. The region is far
away from any settlement, a unique blend of cactus and
Ponderosa Pine, cottonwood and piñon, where running
water has formed a declination in the desert; but even
those who have documented the river's rarity and
loveliness now, once familiar, do most of their studies
from afar. Even now, hardly anyone goes there. Even
now, hardly anyone really cares.*

# PART I   THE OLD MAN

*"Only those able to see the pageant of evolution can be expected to value
its theater, the wilderness...But if education really educates, there will,
in time, be more and more citizens who understand that relics of the old
West add meaning and value to the new."*

Aldo Leopold

# HOME IS THE RIVER

*Chapter 1*

NOBODY KNEW THE COUNTRY like the old man. From the lofty headwaters rich in Canadian zone forests through the craggy descent of the river to Chihuahuan grasslands, no one knew so much of land, water and the wildlife therein. Here where the mountains yielded to more mountains, where the canyons with names yielded to more canyons with none, where the grass rolled on to an empty horizon, the old man was home. This was a legend who was still alive. He had wintered at the headwaters, trapped the streams and packed the pelts out when spring thawed the snow. Where rock canyons fingered off the streams into a labyrinth of canyons beyond, he had scrambled after the yelping hounds and shot the bobcat, lion and bear they'd treed or brought to bay. He knew the elk from the grassy highland parks, the deer from their secret visits to mountain springs; the bighorns from the cliffs and the antelope from the desert below. He knew the fish and could catch them - cold water trout, cool water bass, warm water catfish. And where the Big Canyon finally took the last of the feeder streams and blended the desert with the big timber with the chaparral inbetween, the old man knew the country best of all.

~ ~ ~ ~ ~

Up on the south rim looking down into the canyon the river looked slim enough to step across and any descent appeared impossible on foot let alone horseback. But the old man spit a long stream of tobacco juice, took a well considered and copious drink from the bottle, replaced it in the saddle bag and urged his horse over the edge. Without urging Harley's horse followed, followed in turn by an old, flop-eared, redbone hound.

Magically, little by little, a rough trail appeared before the old man, allowing them a circuitous descent to the river. They side-sloped, rimmed around bluffs, lost sight of the river for a time in a side canyon. They brushed through the scrub oak, piñon and juniper, yielded to the occasional ponderosa that grew in the path. At times, to Harley, the trail disappeared entirely, but when it came back the old man was always right on the route. And then there were the rocks - loose rock slopes where their horses sat on their haunches for short slides till they could regain their footing; and boulders bigger than the horses that the brutes picked their way around; and rock ledge drop-offs where a couple of times they stepped off to lead their animals down. The old man complained about the animals.

"Damn horses are picky. Damned slow. Mules would have us to the bottom by now."

But a good riding mule, as the old man always said, was hard to come by.

1

# HOME IS THE RIVER

They'd broken camp that morning a day's ride from town midst a light frost. It was late morning when they'd started down into the canyon and it had warmed up. It got warmer still as they descended, there was a good breeze, and the buzzards rode the thermals rising between the cliffs, racing their shadows over the rocks. Most of them had soared below as they looked off from the top, they passed them on the way down, and when they got to the bottom Harley looked up and saw the buzzards where you'd expect them to be, high in the sky. They crossed the stream twice going down river and made camp in a mixed grove of cottonwood and sycamore and there was plenty of grass for the horses. The water was blue/green and clear. It pooled calmly against a rock ledge right by camp, turned away and funnelled into white water before dropping into a roily backwash pool below. Then it split into several channels as it wound on down and around some large boulders at the next bend.

"No better stretch of water for catfish than this," the old man said. "Get down and unsaddle your horse."

It was a tall horse and Harley slid off the saddle, held briefly to the horn and dropped to the ground.

Following the old man's lead, Harley unsaddled his horse and staked him out on plenty of rope where there was grass and shade. Harley knew his horse, Leo, was not a great horse. He was a little bit lazy when he was young and he wasn't young anymore. But he was steady, sure-footed, and he got you there. If he ever absolutely balked, it was for a good reason. He was also a deep blood bay color that was fine to look at, especially when his head was clean of the bridle and outlined by one of the colorful halters the old man braided himself. Leo went to his back and rolled, got up and began to eat.

The old man was spreading everything out on the grass, the bedrolls, food, the traps and fishing poles. Then he hung the traps by their chains over his shoulder and without speaking started upstream. Harley and the old hound followed. Every few hundred yards they were bluffed by the canyon walls and had to wade the stream. Harley had just begun to pack a wallet like a grownup, but he was till a head shorter than the old man and he worried that he would wet his several dollar bills and the picture in his wallet of the old man, himself and a big trout the old man had caught. But the old man picked out riffles and the heads of rapids where it was shallower and Harley kept the water below his pockets.

They hiked a couple of miles and came to where a big cottonwood hung to the edge of a bank. The river undercut the bank and several of the roots of the tree hung like claws in the air. In the shallows under the bank was a muskrat house and, nearby, holes in the bank showed where they had been active. The old man set a #1 1/2 trap in the shallows in front of one of the holes that was near the house; his hands were large and gnarled, deft and artful, making the set. He made another set where he could see the rats had been going under to get into the house. He staked the chains to alder brush, then, upstream at a beaver dam, he kicked a hole in the edge of the dam. He pulled a Conibear trap part way open, then stepped on the spread and sprung it out. He set the Conibear in the shallows in front of the flow where it leaked through the dam. He pounded a stake into the mud in the shallows through the ring on the end of the chain.

"Tell me what happens," he said.

Harley said, "The beaver comes to fix the dam, and springs the trap."

"That trap will crush down on a fifty pound beaver, but in a few years you'll be able to set your own."

"Yes sir," Harley said, though he had no confidence he would ever be strong enough to do it.

Upstream another half mile the old man set the two coyote traps on a bench of sandy soil just off the river in a jungle of riparian growth. He made dirt sets, digging out a place for each #3 trap with a stick and then sifting the dirt back over the steel till it just covered the pan; and the way the old man did it Harley knew if he looked away for just a moment he wouldn't be sure anymore where the trap was set. Near each set the old man squirted some nasty smelling fluid that he said was "mostly coyote piss" from a small plastic bottle onto bushes and the bark of a small piñon. They hiked back to camp and the old man started a small fire for the noon meal.

"When you come here, always trap upstream. Don't trap downstream where the otters are."

"Why don't we ever see the otters?"

"You cain't never tell when you'll see the otters, but since our luck is due to change I think maybe we'll see the otters tomorrow," the old man said.

~ ~ ~ ~ ~ ~

They fished on into the night. Harley yawned and shivered and circled the fire. The old man checked the lines and, except when he needed a drink, kept his bottle in his coat pocket. They had spent some time that afternoon before supper searching through the rocks in the riffles for crawfish and they picked up plenty; some thumb-sized, a few looking like small lobsters. They had divided them up back at camp, the old man went downstream, Harley went upstream, and they fished the pools and channels. Using a light sinker, Harley lofted the bait upstream into the currents and let the currents take the crawfish down into the pools, naturally, like the old man had taught him to do. He tried to concentrate, to be always ready for the signs of fish. But as the sun began to set, a moving array of tone and tint graced the rock walls of the canyon all around him - a fluctuating admixture of colors and shadows - the buzzards kept their easy flight above, and he had to stare for a time at a small herd of Bighorn Sheep scattered up the side of the south face, standing it seemed on nothing at all; the slimmest of ledges was home to the bighorn. The one ram in the bunch stood impassively by a scraggly ponderosa growing obliquely and improbably out of a crack in the rock. They all stared back at Harley but none seemed to mind that he was there.

At one pool Harley saw the quick, dark green Smallmouth Bass cruising in the shallows, then disappearing into the depths. He put his bait into the pool, then drew it into the shallows. A couple of bass made passes at the crawfish. Whimsical, they would not take.

At another pool he hooked and landed a Channel Catfish of several pounds. The fish struggled well for a time, then gave it up and came to the shore on his side. Harley hooked a finger through his gills and took him back to camp. The old man had caught a bass of a couple of pounds and a Flathead Catfish two feet long. He had the fire going. The grease was heating in the pan and he was rapidly turning his fish into filets. The old hound, who always followed the old man, sat patiently by the fire. Harley's fish went on a stringer near camp; the bass and larger catfish were fried crisp. They ate them wrapped in tortillas toasted over the flames and there was plenty left for the redbone hound. Then, sharing a pot of coffee, they hugged the fire, doing what the old man perhaps loved best of all - waiting into the night for big fish.

~ ~ ~ ~ ~ ~

Harley had dozed off on his bedroll when he heard, it seemed simultaneously, the click of the reel letting out line and the old man hissing, "That's yours!"

Harley moved quickly to the edge of the river and picked the rod up off the forked stick. The old man said, "He's big; that crab would scare a small fish. Let him run yet."

Harley let several more feet of line off the reel, then the line went limp.

"He's crushing that crab; when he moves again, nail him," the old man said.

As if by order the line went taut and Harley reared back and struck the fish. The rod bent like a hoop. And immediately Harley was forced to give line as the fish moved slowly off downstream.

The old man got the flashlight as they left the light of the fire and followed the fish. Once, walking, Harley came abreast of the fish and was able to regain line. The fish moved off again, down to the first set of rapids where he turned, still deep. He started back upstream, back up the long channel towards the deep pool where he'd taken the bait. He came abreast of Harley again and this time he made a run, spinning the reel handles into a blur as he sprinted upstream through the whitewater and into the pool.

4

The fish fought a dogged, deep fight in the pool, bending and pumping the rod, while Harley, at the old man's constant urging, kept pressure on. Then the fish showed himself as he left the pool to run upstream through the riffle into the channel above. Slicing up through the shallows of the rapids, the old man's light showed a fish longer than Harley's leg, a mottled body of brown, green, with a yellow belly, a grotesquely flattened head, and mouth that could swallow a grapefruit. He powered up through the fast water into the slack water in the channel and kept going. Soon Harley was bluffed up and had to cross the river, the old man shining the way with the light.

In the next pool upstream the fish went deep and dogged again. Harley's arms and wrists had begun to ache badly. But the fish had begun to tire, too. Twice he came near the surface, showing whiskery and ugly in the light, then powered back to the bottom. The third time he came up, the old man told Harley to lean back on the rod; as he did the fish came over on his side, his yellow belly half up, and drifted in towards shore. The old man went in to his knees, held the flashlight in his mouth with the beam on the fish, preparing to slip his hand under the gill cover. But the big flathead had one more move, rolled upright and made a strong run downstream. There was a sharp report as the line snapped in front of the old man's nose.

Crossing the river walking back to camp Harley slipped in the current and got the rest of himself wet. The old man helped him ashore.

"You cain't never point your rod at a big fish," the old man said. "He won't break that line if he's pulling on the rod. You pointed your rod at the fish."

Harley didn't respond. He didn't feel like fishing any more and the old man knew it. At camp, he reset Harley's bedroll closer to the fire while Harley stripped down. The old man helped Harley dry himself, then helped him into the bedroll. Harley turned on his side, his head away from the fire; he could hear the old man chunking up the fire, felt the fire's warmth on his backside while a chill breeze felt icy as it met the tears on his face. He was still awake when the old man lay his coat over Harley's shoulders. Then Harley fell asleep.

It was well past dawn when Harley awoke. Sun streaks decorated the rock walls above; it was still dim and very cold at the canyon floor; Harley's bedroll was covered with a light, silvery frost. The old man and the hound were gone. Harley dressed quickly and started upstream, noting as he left camp a fresh coon hide rolled up by the old man's saddle. He found the old man at the second set, by the beaver dam.

"We're not doin' worth a damn," the old man said.

"You didn't catch the beaver?"

"Or the muskrat either one. The beaver was here; the trap was sprung. But we didn't catch the son-of-a-bitch."

"You caught a coon. I seen the hide."

"Rufus caught him. Caught him on the ground. He struck the cold trail about a half mile below camp, jumped him a quarter mile below there and pushed him down river. Crossed the river twice on the trail - really was a-bellowin' in the canyon; when he sighted him he went silent. Fooled that old coon and it sure was a scrap. I had to help kill him."

Rufus stood in the water now, watching the old man retrieve the Conibear. His old scarred muzzle had fresh cuts that would further map his face.

"I wish I was with you," Harley said.

"Sure was a race. That was some kind of sound, him pushin' that coon down canyon...just a bellowin'; I was afraid it would wake you up; I didn't want you to get wet all over again."

~ ~ ~ ~ ~ ~

Up river the last coyote trap was gone. The old hound circled twice, took the backtrack once, then began to bay in a deep hound squall as he galloped upstream on the trail. He swerved into a side canyon and located the coyote 100 yards up the draw where the trap drag had hung the coyote up in the brush. He'd been there awhile; all around him in the dirt and brush were the signs of his struggle through the night. But the coyote was quiet and nearly motionless as the old man sprinted like a youngster up to the catch. The old man waited for Harley who, too, ran as fast as he could. For a moment they watched the little wolf who leaned away from the trap that held his front foot; he pulled his lips back showing his teeth; he snarled silently and without hope at the hound who squalled in his ear.

The old man pulled the hound back by the collar and gave him to Harley. Harley held the hound and watched as the old man took a stick and struck the coyote high up on the muzzle. The little wolf slumped silently, stunned. The old man put one boot down on the coyote's neck and placed the heel of his other boot on the coyote's heart, pressing down on the brisket just behind the shoulder. Soon the coyote was dead.

The old man hung the coyote by his hind feet from a nearby oak limb. He cut around the heel of one back leg, then cut down the leg to the base of the tail, then he peeled the hide off the leg. He did the same with the other leg then cut, pulled and peeled the tail bone out of the tail. Then he pulled the hide down off the body of the carcass like peeling a shirt off a man hanging upside down. The hide came easily off the warm body of the coyote. The red meat glistened as the hide peeled away. The old man made many quick deft cuts with the knife while peeling the last of the hide off the head of the coyote. The head was pop-eyed, toothy and grotesque after the hide was gone. The old man cut the carcass down and threw it into the brush. Then he knelt with the hide across his knee and ran his fingers through the fur.

The hide of the coyote was a mosaic, with white belly fur and silver, grey and black blended down the sides and back. Beautifully patterned, but blended in such a way that no one word could describe the color. The silvery guard hairs over the shoulders, down the center of the back and over the hips, stood out from the rest.

"These guard hairs are just coming in," the old man said. "This is a 20 dollar coyote. In a month he'd of brought more. He's not prime, but he's furred out good for this early in the fall."

The old man turned the hide inside out, revealing the skin inside.

"He's still a little blue," the old man said.

Harley said, "He'll be white inside when he's prime."

"You're learnin'!"

"He's a pretty one."

"They're all pretty when they start to prime," the old man said. Then the old man reversed the hide, so the fur was up, and he started to run his fingers through the fur and he said, "Don't ever take fur that's only good to throw away. You got four maybe five months out of the year when you can take fur. There's plenty of other things to do the rest of the year. Whatever it is you want to do, this is the country for it. These are wildlands and they're some of Mexico and some of the Rocky Mountains. There's no place else you can see an elk and a javelina, a Red Squirrel and a coatimundi, all on the same day. There's nearly as much fur and game in this wilderness as when the Apaches and the mountain men had it. And I believe there's fewer hunters and trappers. You wouldn't think that but I believe it's true, at least once the weather sets in. Anymore, men are too lazy and too soft to pack in here once it turns real winter. You take any place in this forest. Where there's roads they'll drive them, but most guys won't get far off the road. Where they ain't any roads, like in here, they's fewer people, and the ones come in here won't get far off the trails. That leaves a lot of country for a few guys like us who are willing to follow hounds or game wherever they go. That's good, 'cause we may not have this life forever."

"Why not?" Harley said.

"There are people think the fur trade is wrong. They don't approve of trapping or hunting of any kind and they sure don't like the idea of people killing animals and skinning them and selling pelts and then other people wearing them for clothes. Some of them even think that fishing is wrong. I don't see it in my lifetime, and I hope not in yours; but ever' year they's more of them and fewer of us and the day will come when the life I have and the life you will have will be something historical, like something you read about in the history books, like we read about Jim Kirker and James Ohio Pattie."

"They were mountain men," Harley said.

"Yes they were. And this was their territory. Them and Ben Lilly and Montague Stevens and a few others left a heritage, and me and you and a few others keep it alive. And we'll hold on to what we can until it's all against the law. Or until they find another use for this river and take this country away from us."

"They couldn't do it," Harley said. "They're too soft and too lazy to come in here and do it."

The old man smiled. "They're not soft or lazy when it comes to building roads and damming up rivers," he said. "I couldn't have been much older than you when I first started hearing about it. They even taught it to us in school. They told us how all the water in the Río Jalisco comes from rain and snow that falls in the Mondragón Range and what a terrible shame it is that it all rolls on down through the canyons and on down out of the mountains and across the desert into Arizona without hardly anything being done with it. To hear them tell it, that water, the water that runs right by our camp, that's all wasted water. A river that flows like it always has, some people can't stand that. It eats on them day and night and they won't rest till they do something about it. Water in the stream is wasted water, they say. To keep that water from going to waste, what they do is build a dam and put that water to use. Their kind of use."

"Do you think they'll do it?"

"There's no good reason why it should ever happen, and I haven't heard much about it lately. But, since the war, they's a lot of dams been built, and they wasn't much reason for most of them either. At least not that I could see. They see things different. And, like I said, they's more of them than they is of us. No use worrying about it. If they ever get to it, there isn't any way people like you and me can stop it. We'll enjoy all this while we have it. And as long as we have it, we'll show some respect. Don't ever kill anything that carries a valuable hide when the hide's worthless. Don't ever kill anything you can't use. Nothing's so useless you can kill it and just leave it lay. And don't ever kill anything that's almost gone."

"Like the otters?"

"That's right. They're awful scarce. They's about as many of them left as they is of us. I hope they'll be around a while longer. I hope it'll all be here a while longer."

Harley said, "I hope I grow up fast, before it's all gone."

"You'll grow up soon enough. Meanwhile, this country, this river has as much to offer a kid as a grownup. I know it's hard for you sometimes, 'cause there's so much to learn. But it'll be just as hard later, only different. You've got to be a kid first. That's when you learn how to do it right. If you don't get the right ideas now, you'll be just like the rest of them later."

"Yes sir," Harley said.

The old man rolled up the coyote hide, gathered up all the traps and they returned to camp. There, the old man revived the fire, then he went over to the edge of the river. There was a rope stringer in the water and the old man bent over and pulled a huge catfish up out of the water. Harley thought it might be the fish he had struggled with in the night, only it was a different kind of catfish than he had ever seen.

"I got him a little downstream about the time the birds started to wake up," the old man said. "This is a Blue Catfish. There's very few of them in this river. The biologists claim there's none at all, but we know better. I wanted you to see him."

Harley ran over to the edge of the bank as the old man released the fish. The big catfish with the snow white belly and high, silver/blue back settled momentarily in the pool, then swam calmly back into the depths.

"Now we'll eat your catfish for breakfast," the old man said.

After breakfast Harley rinsed out all the dishes with gravel and river water while the old man gathered up all the gear. Then they saddled and packed the horses. Harley had to stand on a rock to saddle Leo. As usual, after everything was loaded, the old man came over to inspect. He immediately began to loosen the cinch and reset Harley's saddle.

"Christ sake, get the fork of this saddle up on his withers where it won't wallow from side to side," he said. Then he boosted Harley up into the saddle. They were ready to ride and while Harley sat there in the saddle fidgeting with the reins in his hands and shuffling his boots in the stirrups the old man stood beside the horse with his hand on the saddle horn, and when Harley had quit fidgeting he knew another lecture was coming and, sure enough, the old man took a fresh chew, reset his Stetson on his head, looked up at Harley and started to talk.

"Now you're going to have to do this all yourself one of these days and if you want to spend your time in this wilderness without getting killed or caught you better learn to do it right. That means you got to be able to ride as well as you can walk and walk as well as you can ride. You get a horse or mule that you can depend on and that can go hard all day and when you get into places a horse or mule can't go you got to be able to go hard all day a-foot. Don't ever buy, borrow, steal or ride one of them goddamn fifty pound roping saddles that'll have a good horse thinking he's carrying a fat man. This saddle don't weigh half that and it's all you'll ever want and you can use the pounds you save to carry something you need, like food, or traps, or a crippled hound. Don't wear those pointy-toed, high-heeled cowboy boots 'cept Saturday nights when you're out honky-tonkin. You stay with these boots that have a heel and lace up and you can walk or ride either one. Remember, you're not a cowboy. That's honest work and it's still better than being cooped up with a town job but I think you're old enough to know by now they's nothing dumber in this world than a herd of cow brutes and what does that make the man that spends his life following them around? I ought to know, I spent enough of my life following them around. The only thing dumber is what we have nowdays that imitates those that follow them around. It wasn't cowboys ever really knew how to live in this country, it was the Apaches and mountain men. Oh a Stetson's a good kind of hat except in the winter, but you're not a cowboy, you're a hunter, and to be a real one you got to be as tough and as smart as the critters you're after and the more you run bear and lion and bobcat and trap coyotes and the like the more you realize they know how to live in this country. They have a spirit that goes with this country and if you're lucky, someday you may have it too. Remember when you head into the wilderness, if you're packing so much stuff you need a pack horse, you're packing too much stuff. Inside of a week, you and your horse and a couple-three hounds can get along. And for Christ sake get the fork of your saddle up on his withers where it won't wallow side to side."

"Yes sir," Harley said.

The old man turned away, stepped up on his horse and they started downstream.

~ ~ ~ ~ ~ ~

The river was never the same from year to year, even Harley knew that. The old man had not brought him to the river since June and now in October he could see that high water from the heavy rains in September had left their mark. In places the channel had changed course and several large trees that had stood tall and seemingly secure were now torn from their roots and upturned into slash. But Harley knew that new growth would replace the old and that whatever the changes from year to year, a pattern retained. He knew it because he had seen it in just his own few years along the river. And he knew it because the old man told him so...

Deep pools would form where the water ran up against abrupt rock walls, and rapids would be followed by slack-water channels, and opposite the sheer walls where the water swirled would be broad beaches of sand and gravel; and up on the benches away from the river seep willow would grow and then young cottonwoods and sycamores would spring up, and there would be hackberry and walnut and stolid Emory Oak and stringers of Ponderosa Pine up the side canyons; and Alligator Juniper in the shade with prickly pear, cholla and ocotillo, scrub juniper and piñon clinging to the sunny slopes, however steep. It was all there just as it always had been even though, since June, some of it had changed.

Harley watched the old man moving easily with his horse at a trot up ahead. There were no clouds and it was warm in the sun now and the sun felt good. Then they would ride under steep walls where the canyon narrowed; here sunshine never lingered for long and here it was cool, even through a summer day. Periodically, they crossed the river, and Harley listened to the muffled clip-clop of the horse's hooves striking rocks under water. The old man was up ahead watching all there was to see and Harley hoped he was taking him to see the otters.

~ ~ ~ ~ ~ ~

10

# HOME IS THE RIVER

There came the place where the river bottom widened out into a green meadow with lots of grass on both sides of the stream and there was a large grove of cottonwoods. And below the canyon narrowed up again and the river dipped into a small waterfall and just below the waterfall Ocotillo Creek came into the flow from Engelmann Peak to the south. They left their horses with the reins loose on the ground in the meadow under the trees. The old man tied the hound and led Harley on a short climb up into the rocks where they could see downstream to the waterfall and beyond. They sat on a flat rock in the sun well above the river.

"Just sit tight and keep your eyes peeled," the old man said.

Harley sat on the flat rock and looked downstream. Then he lay down on the flat rock, felt its warmth from the sun on his back and looked downstream. Then he fell asleep.

To alert whomever he was with, a hound or a horse or Harley, the old man would hiss like a snake. Harley awoke to this sound and to the old man's hand on his knee.

Harley turned over on his side and looked downstream to see the first otter come out of the stream and into the sun on the beach. It glistened with wetness and looked like a big, black weasel. A second otter came bursting out of the water and the two raced in circles around the beach, wonderfully quick and swift as they tagged and leaped over each other in a frolic.

"About nine o'clock," the old man whispered, indicating direction. Harley looked to his left and a third otter was swimming upstream, coming much closer, below them. This third otter swam up through the rapids and took the waterfall like a spring salmon, then moved easily into the slack water above. The two otters on the beach were quick and animated but this third otter was at home in the water. Then without a splash and scarcely a ripple he was under the water and he disappeared. When Harley looked downstream again the other two otters were also gone.

"They winded us, or more than likely the horses or ol' Rufus," the old man said. "You won't see them again, not today anyway."

They returned to the horses and the old man led the way back up-stream. Then they began to climb out of the canyon up to the north rim. It was a difficult climb for the horses who had to be led part of the way. They topped out and then rode upstream, overlooking the river far be-low, till ascending to a large park, open except for a scattering of Ponderosa Pine. Again they dismounted and dropped the reins. Over by the edge of the rim was a big Alligator Juniper, fire scarred by lightning but still making cedar leaves high above.

"This old Alligator Bark Juniper is the place," the old man said. "Don't forget any of what I'm going to show you, but don't never tell anyone either."

The old man led Harley on over the edge and down the slope. They were still well above the river when a narrow path appeared from nowhere and promptly rimmed around a bluff into a jumble of boulders scattered over a flat outcrop. A seep spring trickled water from high up on the bluff down on to the outcrop, forming a small pool in a depression and making grass grow amongst the boulders. And where the bluff met the outcrop a small cave went into the side of the mountain, the opening perhaps large enough for a man to crawl through. The hound began to nose the opening of the cave. The old man called the hound back. Then the old man said, "You cain't see this cave from anywhere along the far rim or from above or from down below in the canyon. The only place you can see it is from where we're standing. That's why the last of them survived here so many years after all the other wolves were gone."

"What happened to the wolves?" Harley asked.

"They killed them off because they were killing cattle. Fact is, they never found this den, but they finally got the last pair just the same. The bounty had built up on that pair to where it would tempt any man. They was two trappers full time after 'em over the last year. I knew them both. One night ol' Kenny Padgett followed me out of the Copper Palace...we were both pretty drunk...says he's gonna kill me if I didn't tell him where the den was...and he pulled his gun. I told him to go to hell. He looked me right in the eye and threw a round out of that .357 straight up into the sky, turned and walked away. Sure was loud right there downtown. Jimmy Gabaldón was the other one. He got 'em both that spring, north of the river somewhere. There hasn't been a wolf in New Mexico in twenty years."

"Were they really killing the cattle?"

"A pair of wolves can kill anything that lives in this country. Damn straight they were killing cattle. You put cattle in a wolf's range, he's gonna eat some of them. But the response was, the smartest critter ever lived in this country was killed off to save the dumbest. It wasn't control, it was extermination. Oh I trapped wolves myself when they was plentiful. And I ran 'em with hounds. Nobody else around here ever ran wolves with hounds. That was the toughest hunt in these mountains. I quit hunting them when they started showing up scarce. Wished I'd quit sooner. Not that it would have made any difference."

"I'd like to go on a wolf hunt," Harley said.

"So would I, "the old man said. "We'd hunt them together. They never was a reason to kill them all off."

They returned to the horses and continued on upstream on top of the north rim and as always it didn't seem to Harley that there was any way down. When the old man finally picked a spot it didn't look promising to Harley. But riding and leading their horses, the old man got them to the canyon floor and the river. Then they had to ride downstream a mile to find an ascent to the south rim which, with its north-facing slope, was better wooded than the south-facing slope across the canyon. It was the toughest yet; the horses puffed and lathered up the slope and grunted as they topped out over the rim. It was early afternoon. The old man got out sandwiches from his saddle bag and they ate as they rode south towards home.

It was good going at first through the grasslands with the higher country and timber still ahead. Harley liked the look of the desert, the grama grass, the occasional yucca, cholla and mesquite bush, as they rode through the park. The old man rode at a long trot that he used whenever the going was good and he was headed for home. Across the grassy park, scattering the half wild cattle that grazed there, Harley watched the old man, relaxed and slouched in the saddle up ahead. For a while, before he had enough hours and days in the saddle to ride comfortably, Harley thought it was the horses the old man rode, and once he had complained to the old man that Leo was a "rough horse" and that he should be allowed to ride an "easy horse" like the old mans'. The old man had smiled and they changed mounts. The old man was slouched and relaxed at a long trot riding Leo while Harley alternately bounced and stood in the stirrups to ease his pain riding the "easy horse." Now Harley could smile himself, thinking about it. He already had more hours and days in the saddle than most grown men and while not a rider like the old man, still he could ride all day and not be sore.

They began to climb into the hills, headed south towards the Continental Divide. Up in the zone of piñon and juniper, Harley looked back down at the grasslands far below, yellow-brown and shiny in the sun, all the way to where it all stopped and disappeared at the canyon rim. Then they ascended into Ponderosa Pine. These were tall, arrowy, red-barked trees and some of them were very large. The big ones were without branches at the eye level, with shocks of limbs and needles and cones far above. A Tassel-eared Squirrel crossed in front of the horses and sped across through the pines, its white tail flashing; the hound loped baying after the squirrel and soon had it treed. They rode over there. The old man dismounted, pulling an old single shot .22 iron sighted rifle from the scabbard. He steadied the rifle against a nearby pine and shot the chattering squirrel off a high limb. As the old man retrieved the squirrel, the hound moved off down the slope, worked his nose in the air, and began to bark treed once again. Harley and the old man walked down there.

The old man said, "Well son-of-a-bitch! I've seen ol' Rufus tree a lay-up coon, but I've never seen him tree a lay-up squirrel. I've never seen any hound tree a lay-up squirrel."

"I don't see any squirrel up there," Harley said.

"Neither do I, but sure enough Rufus has winded one."

The old man circled the tree.

"There he is."

The rifle cracked again and a second squirrel dropped and bounced a little on the carpet of pine needles. A third squirrel appeared in the same tree, scampered along a limb, leaped and grabbed the trunk of another ponderosa. The squirrel was a long way up and the hounds' tree bark was a bawl chopped off at the end.

"I want to," Harley said, as the old man loaded the rifle.

Harley steadied the rifle and sighted as the old man had done. He squeezed the trigger as he was taught to do, shot low, and the scattering of bark kicked the squirrel off the trunk. The hound grabbed the squirrel as he hit the ground.

"Nice shooting!" the old man said, smiling, and he took the squirrel from the hound. "Not every hunter can bring down a squirrel with no bloodshot meat!"

The old man quickly dressed out the three squirrels.

"Don't never get down to using a scope on a rifle," he said, peeling hide. "I don't care what the caliber is or what you're hunting, you get close enough to knock it down with one shot and a naked eye. Don't ever let hardware take the place of your skill."

"Yes sir," Harley said.

They rode south and kept climbing. The Ponderosa Pine forest yielded to a thicker forest of Limber Pine, Douglas Fir, aspen and even a few Engelmann Spruce. The aspen were turning the various colors of yellow they do in the fall and some of the crisp leaves were falling as they rode on through.

They rode a ridge and dropped of on a game trail into the upper reaches of Ocotillo Creek where trout held skillfully, finning in the current; they were gone in a flit as the horses splashed upstream.

They took a trail out of the creek, up the north slope of a Canadian zone forest, the last long climb to the divide. Harley started to think about the following day - they would ride in about noon to the adobe house and his own hound dog puppy would run out and grab him by the leg even before he'd stepped off his horse. He wanted to go home and play with his puppy and he wanted to lay in the hot tub and feel warm and clean. But he didn't want to go back to school and he was already starting to miss the river. He didn't feel so badly anymore that he'd lost the big fish. But he wanted to go back and try for him again. He wanted to go back and this time hear ol' Rufus run a big boar coon down the canyon. He wanted to saddle his horse right and shoot a squirrel with one shot. But it was time to go home and, really, Harley was glad he didn't have to decide; he would follow the old man home and the next day the old man would wake him up early and get him ready for school.

They reached a saddle in the Continental Divide an hour before dark. There was enough of an opening in the fir and aspen for a little grass to grow and there was a three-rock fireplace in the middle of the clearing; this was a place where they and others had camped before. Harley went to unsaddling and staking out the horses while the old man built a fire. The old man put grease in the fry pan and seared the squirrels; he added a bit of flour and water and made a gravy from the grease, cut up two potatoes and put them in. He covered the pan and said, "one hour till supper."

Harley and the old man sat by the fire, waiting for supper and watching the sun go down. They could see everything, it seemed, from the Continental Divide. Far to the north, the Mondragón Range that fed the river was blue/black with heavy trees; waves of mountains off to the horizon, some of them already snow covered, two thousand feet higher than their camp on the divide. And looking to the south from the last of the high country of the Mondragón Mountains their vista was of foothills descending away and finally leveling off into the grasslands of the Chihuahuan desert. As the sun set they could see clearly the outlines of the land falling away into Mexico; and over toward Arizona, to the west, where the sun set on the even lower Sonoran desert, a perfect scarlet reflected off a dry land and rose into the dry air to meet and blend with the deepest blue sky color in the world. The sun went down and the colors in the air yielded to stars in a dark moonless sky. They all ate well by the fire.

When the coffee was done, the old man went to his saddle bags and got his last bottle and poured the whiskey into the dark brew. Harley had coffee in a tin cup too; they chunked up the fire and watched the lights of Del Cobre sparkle in the dark.

The town was in the foothills far below, to the south and east, centered in the basin and fingering off into the ridges and draws. The lights of the town were yellow and sometimes red or blue, some of them moved along the roads and streets, and the glow of all these lights as it rose through the haze over the town was almost orange. The haze came in over the town from the big stack to the south at the copper mine; at night an impressive silhouette that towered over the town even when seen from the Continental Divide. The stack belched smoke and prosperity day and night. Harley watched its rich plume froth from the stack into the night sky, then settle into an orange haze over the town.

The old man finished his coffee but stayed with the bottle. Harley knew the old man was going to drink it all before he slept. The old man had not been drinking heavily on this short trip to the river. Harley knew the old man didn't drink as much when he went to the mountains as he did at home or in town. But the old man was almost home now and they were within sight of town and Harley knew the old man was going to take his time and drink the whole bottle. Yet it was worse, it would be worse, when they got home. The old man would get him off to school and then the old man would do his chores. He would feed the hounds and horses, curry the horses and perhaps trim their feet or reset a shoe. He would scrape and stretch the coyote and coon hides. He might sit in the sun on the porch for a while. Inevitably, he would go to town to the Copper Palace, drink hard, stay late, and hunt women. It was not unusual for him to bring one home. Often Harley would see these women in the morning, in the kitchen or coming from the bathroom, and he would not know what to say to them and he knew he'd never see any one of them again. And though he missed the old man when the old man went to the mountains for weeks or even months at a time, he almost preferred it. Then he would stay with the widow Hidalgo who lived just across the creek. She was kind to him and he was learning Spanish from her because she didn't know English, and while he was there the old man was off in the wilderness someplace, and there he didn't drink so much. Or if he did, Harley didn't know it; he didn't have to watch. And the old man had not been drinking heavily on this trip but he was starting to drink heavily now and Harley knew he wouldn't stop until the bottle was gone.

"We'll butcher a deer at Gavilán Spring in the morning," the old man said.

"You only brought the .22," Harley said.

"When I hit him in the head, that will be plenty," the old man said.

Harley didn't say anything. He didn't care if the old man still poached a deer now and again. He didn't worry about that.

Harley sat by the fire and watched the lights of vehicles moving slowly off to the east and south on the highway from Del Cobre to Cooke City, a town the size of Del Cobre and just a glow on the horizon, far off on the desert. He watched another line of moving lights on the highway going off to the southwest, towards the town of Tobosa, not far from the Arizona line. He watched lights move off into the desert until they disappeared. He watched them disappear for a long time. Then he said, "Where's my mother?"

The old man held the bottle in both hands and stared into the fire. He said, "Son, I have no idea where your mother is."

"We could find her," Harley said.

The old man was tall and thin, bearded, bald on top of his head but with dark curly hair growing from the sides over his ears; and in response to Harley he took his Stetson off his head and slapped it against his leg as he turned to Harley with hard blue eyes, and Harley knew that he was angry. Then the old man put his hat on his head and looked back into the fire. Finally, he smiled. "No," he said, "that woman is long gone."

Harley climbed into his bedroll and soon he fell asleep. Long before dawn he awoke, the moon had come up to give some light, and he looked up into the big fir trees, rolling and groaning in a high wind; a norther had come down and now reached the south end of the Mondragón Range. It was a cold, fearsome wind and it had the beginnings

16

of winter behind it. The horses stood off to the side, under the trees, sleeping on their feet, their heads drooped and their rumps turned against the wind. By the remnants of the fire, the hound was curled tight against himself. His father still snored like a drunkard. And the lights of Del Cobre never went out.

## PART II  PROTAGONISTS

*"...he was of a strong constitution, spare-bodied, of a common visage, a very early riser, and a lover of the chase."*

Miguel de Cervantes
*Don Quixote*

*Chapter 2*

**HARLEY SIMMONS SAT ON THE PORCH** in the early morning sun with his new home pretty much in order. A week ago, the old man's horse and two hounds had come in alone after the late winter blizzard abruptly shut down. Mounted officers trailed them back to the old man's body, frozen dead and frozen drunk in the mountains. Harley arrived from out of state in time for his father's funeral. Then he came to the old house, now his new home. The old adobe house needed some work but was sound. Harley had worked two days, arranging the old man's personal effects, patching the roof and corral, replacing a window. He kept the old man's veteran mountain horse. He sold the two veteran hounds that were definitely slowing down, to a hunter who could use such hounds to train pups. Harley refurbished the corral and secured possible escape points in the dog pen. Then he spent a third day on a round trip over the state line, returning with all his belongings. His own three hounds rode in the bed of the pickup with all the gear. His horse and mule rode in the open, two-horse trailer behind. Except for one of his hounds having run off the evening of their arrival, he was well set up, the morning of the fourth day, sitting in the sun on the porch of the old house. He owned it now. And he expected the hound would show up.

Harley had left Del Cobre the spring before, in part because of the old man. They had fought, on occasion physically, over the old man's drinking.

"You're a constant drunk!" Harley would yell in his father's face, grabbing the old man and pushing him up against the wall.

"Pot calls the kettle black!" the old man would come back while pushing Harley away. "I don't drink any more than my son!"

There was something to that. But with Harley it was a periodic blitz; for Alvin H. Simmons, it was whiskey for breakfast. And Harley was saved to some extent by his relative youth. His father was aged by liquor well beyond his years, surviving only because the corpus remained unaccountably tough as a boot. Nearly a year ago Harley had despaired of living in the same town with a father whose life was ineluctably washing in amber to the grave. He left town.

Harley had left town for other reasons, too. He had despaired of living in the same town with his own son, whom he had essentially lost, and with his wife, or former wife, who had come to want nothing to do with him. Both were sequestered from him by a complex legal apparatus. Following a lengthy and erratic separation, the divorce had been a nasty business. During the divorce proceedings, her most positive and perhaps most revealing comment about Harley had been verbal: "He's an educated man, but you'd never know it!" She also noted: "He talks more to his dogs and that mule than he does to us." There was also the matter of his having one night, during an interplay of bad feelings and passion, broken her nose. She mentioned that, too. Then she got serious. Through her attorney, Bonney Simmons alleged that her husband, Harley Simmons, was a binge drinker, bar-room brawler, flagrant adulterer, and a latter day mountain man, river rat and desert scoundrel who consistently neglected his family while roaming the wilds killing things. All this of course was true. The local paper had diligently covered the demise through divorce of such a well known character, but no one who knew Harley and read the accusations could have called the information news. Harley's attorney had suggested early on certain procedures for rebuttal, until Harley allowed as how some of the worst of himself hadn't come out but, pressed into investigations, could be discovered. Harley bit his lip and took a licking. The court order, in sum, was that he was not to bother his ex-wife. He was granted one weekend per month with his son, so long as he stayed sober during the time provided by the court, and did not introduce the boy to guns, hunting, honky-tonks, or the perils of the wilderness. The relationship, so arranged, proved worse than none at all for Harley. Drawn from the bosom of an urban mother and her ordered life in town, the boy was left increasingly bewildered one weekend a month by a man whose rented bachelor shack on the desert south of town lacked indoor plumbing, whose hounds howled at improbable hours at the moon, and who tried too hard during those precious hours to interest his son in what the court had allowed of the rural life. Harley left town.

But a year is a long time and now, sitting in the sun on the porch of the old house where he grew up, Harley was definitely back, and he had no intention of leaving again. Not for any length of time. Harley knew now he could never live anywhere else. The old man had raised him here; it was right that he should take his place in the old house, and in the wilderness. His wife (for Harley, she was still his wife) had at one time thought enough of him to marry him. And years ago he had been close to his son. Harley had plans that they were going to be a family once again. Harley was back. Harley was home. A. Harley Simmons was going to make a stand.

~ ~ ~ ~ ~ ~

The old man had chosen well in building the adobe home just where he did up Gavilán Road, along Gavilán Creek, in the foothills above Del Cobre that flexed and grew up into the high peaks of the Continental Divide. And he had built the porch where he wanted it, to catch the morning sun and afternoon shade. Seated on the porch, leaning back in the chair so it set against the wall, Harley realized for the first time there was no where around there that you could put a house that would offer a comparable view. He could see the Mondragón Range to the north, white capped peaks where the remnants of the latest blizzard were going fast on the south slopes, gradually showing more green each day as the melt inched up to the top. The north slopes he couldn't see.

He knew that they would hold mighty drifts for some time to come. The snow melt would turn the tributary creeks into freshets that would turn the river into a flow worthy the name. Bringing his eye down into the foothills of his own locale, Harley's new house was set in rolling grasslands that descended slowly into the desert; placed nicely in the roll of grama and tobosa grass, while the occasional piñon, juniper, scrub oak and yucca warted the ridgelines.

In the basin below, south and east, not far, Del Cobre centered itself, and grew into the draws and ridges. Harley could see most of the town, picking out the familiar landmarks - the big Felps-Dodd Corporation stack to the south; the college closer in, its neat, white buildings amongst the small hills at the west end; the historic downtown and older neighborhoods; the newer shopping and business areas, and trailer parks, out along the Cooke City Highway - the strip - to the east. Growth outward left the old downtown looking small. And some of that growth was coming north up Gavilán Creek. Harley could see two double-wides and one real house that he couldn't remember from a year ago. But if growth was coming on up, there would be limits to where it could go. The north boundary of what was now Harley's property was the south boundary of the Jalisco National Forest. And Harley himself now owned 160 acres along Gavilán Creek that he could say with confidence that they would never get.

Del Cobre, it was often said, couldn't stay small and quaint forever. Maybe not. But its population, about 10,000, hadn't changed much in 40 years. For while it was growing out, the downtown and some of the old neighborhoods were dying. When the old El Sur theater folded up, replaced by the new Cinema Twin out on the strip, the exodus reached its zenith; the bank, department stores, grocery stores, the realtors, all soon left the downtown for greener pastures out on the strip. The business community, the boomers and boosters, the shakers and movers, all of whom had led the exodus out to the strip; they had no use for the empty shell of the El Sur. The quality-of-life community - artists, a few writers, some college folks, conservationists, the true conservatives - they had a use for it, or at least a plan. The El Sur, an architectural classic and historic landmark, could be revived as art cinema and melodrama. It could not only revive the El Sur, they said, it could also revive the downtown and help establish Del Cobre as an arts community, a sort of latter day Taos in the southwest part of the state. But it would take a community effort. The quality-of-life types were for it. The college community liked the idea. The business community, the boomers and boosters, did not. An arts colony, they said, would attract the wrong sort. Furthermore, as one of the boosters was quoted in the Del Cobre *Region*, "Art cinema is really just a fancy name for dirty movies!" The El Sur stood empty for a while, till one of the boomers picked it up and used it as a warehouse. The downtown Copper Palace

Hotel had died too, though the Copper Palace Bar still drew a certain clientele. The hotel died when the passenger trains quit coming in. The demise of the trains proved the demise of the old adobe train depot as well. It died harder than the Copper Palace, or the El Sur. The depot had seen the last of the Indian wars; the entire history of the town had passed through its adobe walls. Again, the quality-of-life types had a plan. Following restoration to the original, the historic adobe train depot would be the perfect building to house a proper town museum, something the town had always lacked. "Our History is our Future," the conservationists said in the petition that went around town; "SAVE THE DEPOT!" That would cost a bundle, the boomers said; the money would be better spent out on the strip where prosperity was assured. The boomers won; the "eyesore" came down. With their eyes always on growth and expansion, rather than restoration and conservation, the boomers won most all the battles in Del Cobre; but because the town, overall, refused to grow, they remained frustrated, though hardly discouraged, in the war. The conservationists, too, remained frustrated, and doubly discouraged; depressed by the aesthetics, or lack thereof, of the new growth out on the strip, yet lacking the money, business acumen and political power to save "old town." The result was that while Del Cobre refused to boom, and remained small, it did grow, little by little, less quaint. It survived because the big stack south of town employed thousands and continued to belch smoke and prosperity day and night.

Harley Simmons could only recall one battle the boomers had lost. He was still in school when the boomers decided to try and change the name of the town, Del Cobre, to Copper City. It had been Del Cobre since the first settlers, Spaniards and Mexicans, opened the mines and thereby established the town in the first decade of the 19th century. But settlement in the deep Southwest was limited and delayed by the constant threat of the harrier Apaches. It was the Anglos who finally defeated the Apaches, opening the region to a brief flurry of settlement, circa 1900. Since then the Hispanic/Anglo populations had rather balanced each other in Del Cobre. But the Anglos, for the most part, were the business community, the business community were the boomers, and the boomers owned the town. Del Cobre, the boomers said, was a problem. Only the Mexicans could really say it right, and the tourists didn't know what it meant. Del Cobre was archaic. Copper City would be progress, it would boost business, it kept the original meaning, more or less, and everyone could say it and knew what it meant. The boomers circulated a petition calling for the change from Del Cobre to Copper City. The quality-of-life types, finding Copper City prosaic next to Del Cobre, dug in to hold on to history. And the Hispanics, the quiet community, seeing a threat to the language, for once got involved. They came out of the barrios, hills and small ranches, joined the conservation-

22

ists, and a rare coalition was formed. The coalition circulated their own petition, calling not only for the retention of Del Cobre, but as well for a change in the county name, from Arthur County to Geronimo County, in honor of the Apache warlord and horse thief who was born at the headwaters of the Río Jalisco and raised holy hell in the nearby mountains. "Geronimo County," the petition said, "IN MEMORY OF THE FIRST DEFENDER AGAINST UNSAVORY DEVELOPMENT!" The boomers saw the numbers and petitioned for compromise. They gave up any quest for Copper City. They got to keep Arthur County, named for the former President, Chester A. Arthur, a contemporary of Geronimo and one of many U. S. Presidents who has never been within 500 miles of the place.

Harley Simmons had always shied away from local politics. But it was certain that no one had ever called him a boomer.

~ ~ ~ ~ ~ ~

Something just slipped by the porch! Harley Simmons, brought from a reverie wherein he was anticipating his return both to the town of Del Cobre and the nearby wilderness, was sure something sizeable just sneaked by the porch. He set the chair down on four legs, stood and leaned over the porch railing, looked out to the south and west into the nearby scrub oak that cloaked the hillside. Nothing. He sat down and leaned back in the chair.

There it goes again! There was something slinking around out there all right. Harley remained seated, the chair leaned back against the wall, but he directed his vision to the south. Then Harley could definitely see something moving, skulking low in the brown grass and up close to an oak patch. It was a large animal, it was flat to the ground, skulking, sneaking, slinking, hiding, and its eyes were yellow. It was alive all right...it was moving...it was wagging its tail!

"Lurk, you son-of-a-bitch! Goddamnit. I see you Lurk. Get over here."

Lurk stood up. For the moment he quit wagging his tail. He was a big dog, leggy as a Greyhound, but thicker in the neck and quarters, heavily muscled and lop-eared like a foxhound. His eyes were yellow, like a wolf. His dark gray coat was close to black; faint, lighter, brindle stripes running through it, and it was long, rough, wiry and shaggy, like that of the big British coursing dogs. The rough, wiry hair extended back onto the long tail, and up over the long heavy muzzle, forming a dog beard and mustache. A big, lank, rough-coated hound.

Lurk broke into a long lope; gaining deceptive speed as he approached the porch, he leaped up and over the rail and landed in Harley's lap, sending the man and his chair ass-over-applecart across the porch. Harley came up with a hammer lock on the hound. He kept it as the two wrestled across the porch and crashed down the steps into

23

the yard. Finally, Harley pinned the hound. He looked the hound in the eye. "You ran off again, Lurk," he said. Lurk said nothing.

Indeed, Lurk had run off again. When Harley pulled in the evening before, he put his horse and mule in the pasture with the old man's horse, and put his three hounds - Lurk, a tri-color Walker gyp named Geraldine, and a stout Saddleback with an odd white patch named White-eye - into the dog pen. In anticipation of Lurk, he had strung the fence higher, from five feet to six feet. After the gate was shut, Lurk eyed the fence knowingly, but made no move to escape until Harley went into the house. After that it didn't take long. Harley watched from the window as the hound took three bounds to gain speed and then cleared the fence without touching a strand. Harley had just time to race to the porch and holler, "Lurk! Goddamnit!" as the hound, already pushing it into high gear going uphill, disappeared over the rise. Once, Harley awoke during the night and heard Lurk pushing a track with a long, frantic squall that was not pretty but carried all over the mountains. Then the hounds' bay faded into the far hills and was gone.

Harley let Lurk up. For a moment they each in their own way paced and pawed and shook themselves back into form. Lurk was limping on his right front foot. Harley lifted the foot and found that Lurk had run a pad off. There was dried blood on the hound's mouth and when Harley ran his hand under the hound's muzzle he came away with hairs on his palm that were not Lurk's. Deer possibly. More likely coyote.

"You sorry trash-running hound."

Lurk said nothing. He stood on his hind legs, put his paws on Harley's shoulders, and nearly looked a tall man in the eye. Harley took hold of Lurk's paws and set him back down on all fours.

"Lurk, we need to go to town. Get in the truck."

Lurk loped over to the pickup and leaped through the open window on the driver's side into the front seat. Harley got in, said, "roll over you mother," and turned the key. The truck coughed, cleared its throat, and came to life. Harley drove out of the yard, across the creek, slowed for the chickens in the road as he went past the widow Hidalgo's place, and turned on to Gavilán road headed for town. He wore, because it was still winter, "longhandles" under his clothes. Over his long underwear he wore faded Levis, a wool shirt, an old brown canvas coat faded to the dead grass color by the weather, and an impossible old Stetson, stained with sweat. His truck was old, red, bent and dented in a variety of ways, but the engine and transmission were newer than the truck. The engine had six cylinders and a competent sounding chug. The transmission had a low "granny" gear that would pull a horse trailer through a mud hole, and it was geared high enough in fourth that it got pretty good mileage on the road. And there was enough range in second and third gears to get it from first to fourth. Harley wasn't in any hurry as he went down the road. On the passenger side the hound held his head out the window, sniffing the cool breeze that went past the truck. Harley's window was open too and, like the hound, Harley turned his head from time to time to sniff the breeze. He also from time to time expectorated a brown stream of *Red Man* into the air. Some of this landed on the dirt road. Some of this didn't get that far and landed far back on the driver's side of the truck, forming the characteristic "rally stripes" of a true countryman. And Harley's eyes were working, too. He noticed as he hadn't before that the two double-wides he had seen from his house were part of a pattern, a plan. A dozer had marked off square tracts in the grassy hills and here and there in another kind of pattern were sticks set in the ground, each with an orange streamer fluttering in the breeze. Harley eyed all this as he went by. Then he sent another stream out the window, pushed a cassette in the tape deck, waited a bit, and then Willie Nelson started to sing:

> *"Miracles appear in the strangest of places,*
> *fancy meeting you here..."*

Nelson's mellow, dusty, east Texas voice that carried so well, and peculiar pace and phrasing, always pleased Harley. In five minutes he was working his way downtown. He drove down Ballard Street and parked across from the Cafe Luera. It was warming up nicely now as the sun rose and it was warmer in the lower elevation of the town than it had been up in the hills. Behind the cafe where Gavilán Creek ran through town the cottonwoods along the creek were just showing some little green buds. There was no breeze, at all, and it was almost spring. Harley got out, got rid of his chew, and crossed the street. In front of the Cafe Luera he put a quarter in the machine and got a copy of the Albuquerque *Times*. He went inside, got a table and sat down. He greeted Lupe, the long-time waitress at the Cafe Luera, and when she finally got done telling him how sorry she was about his father, and asking him where he'd been and what he'd been doing, he ordered coffee and asked for the menu. Then he opened up the paper. Harley had not seen a New Mexico newspaper in nearly a year and had seen very few newspapers at all for several months. As he perused the front page it didn't appear that much had changed concerning all the bad news in the world. There were people fighting and people starving and the politicians were bickering and on the streets of America's larger cities there were sad souls with very little competence and no homes. Nothing he saw surprised him or caused him to read past the headlines till he turned to the State Section where there was a short piece that had news closer to home. This story he read word for word. And then he read it again.

# HOME IS THE RIVER

## GREANE PLEDGES STATE SUPPORT FOR DAM

SANTA FE  - *The State of New Mexico is ready and willing to contract with the Department of Interior for the proposed Río Jalisco Dam, Governor Garner Greane told Bureau of Reclamation (BOR) officials here Monday.*

*Speaking at a regular meeting of the State River Commission, Greane said, "It will be a major expense, but Arthur County is ready to contribute and I have determined we have the support we need in the state legislature. The time for this badly needed project has come."*

*Commission Chief and State Engineer Sterling Roberts added that the River Commission was unanimous in support of the project and said that the state's share of the one hundred million dollar construction costs would total about twenty five million dollars, with a repayment schedule stretching over a span of 40 years.*

*Roberts said that a dam for the Río Jalisco in northern Arthur County was first proposed some fifty years ago. However, Congressional authorization was not achieved until last year, Roberts said.*

*"An engineeringly feasible site has been identified at a remote point along the Río Jalisco," Roberts said. "I see no reason at this point not to proceed."*

*BOR project planner Joel Smithers said that the repayment contract by the state was the key issue and that based on the pledge by the governor, "we appear finally to be on a schedule we can keep."*

*Smithers added, "Certain environmental procedures must be adhered to and this puts our first access into this remote area about one year away."*

*Roberts said, "The Federal (U. S Fish & Wildlife Service) biologists and those of our own agency (State Department of Wildlife) have assured me that there are no serious environmental conflicts with the dam."*

*Greane emphasized that the cost of the project would be easily justified by the benefits the dam would bring to economically troubled counties in the state's southwest quadrant.*

*"You add the consumptive uses of the water to the recreation benefits associated with a 20 mile-long lake and this is responsible water development," Greane said. "This will be the boost to economic growth and de-*

*velopment so badly needed by our southwestern counties."*

*Greane added that the construction of the Río Jalisco Dam would fulfill a campaign promise he made in Arthur County last November.*

*"I told the citizens of southwest New Mexico that the Río Jalisco Dam would be a priority of my administration," Greane said. "The Secretary of the Interior is a personal friend of mine and it is my commitment to our people down there that this dam will be built while I'm governor."*

*Garth Bilker, president of the Jalisco Rod & Gun Club, a local support group, praised the Governor for his involvement in the project.*

*"The only thing our dam proposal has ever needed is a governor who believes in water development," Bilker said. "All we got from the others was excuses; Governor Greane gave us a promise."*

Harley was sufficiently intent on reading this news story that he didn't hear the door open behind him. He did however feel it when a huge hand gripped his shoulder and when he turned around he saw something akin to a Cinnamon Bear: the frame was very large and ursine in shape; awesome strength was apparent; reddish blonde hair curled from underneath a Stetson and there was a full beard to match. Unlike a bear, however, the eyes were blue, the cheery, dimpled face was smiling, and the man wore a khaki uniform complete with a badge and a shoulder patch that featured the head of a wolf and said New Mexico Department of Wildlife. He also was wearing a gun.

"Hey!" Harley said. "Ted Beeler!"

"Sorry to hear about your old man, partner."

"Well, I guess he lived longer than he had a right to."

"How old was he, Harley?"

"Seventy four."

"That's a full life for a rounder."

"You bet. Sit down, Ted. By golly, sit right down."

Lupe brought the coffee, said, "Looks like old home week around here," and took two orders for breakfast. Directly she brought them each a plate of *huevos rancheros*. There never was *huevos rancheros* like they served at the Cafe Luera. The eggs laid out on a homemade corn tortilla and the green chili was lavish and hot but not so hot that a Southwest gringo couldn't eat it. There was plenty of beans and meat swimming in the sauce and a flour tortilla on the side with a pat of butter and salt. They both had plenty to say to one another but there was plenty of time to say it so they just kept their eyes on the food and went after it. Harley was hungry as a spring bear himself and Ted looked up just once and said, "God a-mighty," and went back to his plate. They both mopped up the last of it and got a refill of coffee. Then Ted said, "I know why you came back, but where have you been?"

"Arizona. Over by Clifton. I drove a truck in the mines for a while last summer. I hunted fur through the fall and winter up in the Blue Range and did a little guiding. I was formulating this plan to go to Mexico, to the Sierra Madre, with no plan at all as to what in hell I would do when I got there, when I got word about the old man. Clifton is too close to Del Cobre. I figured once I crossed the international line, rather than the state line, I could finally cut myself some slack. That was probably wishful thinking. Anyway, now I'm here and I've got my own place. Never really owned my own place before. It's looking like a bigger chore to leave and start over than to stay and start over. I'm going to stick around and see what happens."

"Have you seen Bonney? Or little Billy?"

"No. Other than the funeral, I've been at the house or on the road the past week. I'm guessing she knows I'm in town. Word of that would have run the road ahead of me and reached her before I even crossed the divide."

"I talked to her the other day, for a few minutes at the Quik-Stop. She'd heard all right."

"Yeah?"

"There's still something there, Harley."

"Sure. Me for her."

"And her for you. I could tell. That's not any recommendation. The best thing you two can do for each other is leave each other alone."

"Right. I've heard that one before. What I'm gonna do is, wait a few weeks and let her swim in it awhile. Then I'll hunt her up and see if she'll let me take Billy fishing. Then I'll let her swim in it awhile more. I'll know when it's time, and I'll be ready. She's got some banker hanging around the door, I've heard that."

"I've heard the same. Only he's not *hanging* around the door, he's *in* the door. Name is Bruce something. Or something Bruce. I think it's Bruce something. Business Manager at the bank. Supposed to be a whiz with computers."

"A banker shouldn't be too much."

"Depends on the banker."

"If he *was* much, he wouldn't *be* a banker!"

Ted took off his Stetson and swatted Harley on the shoulder with the hat. "Goddamn Harley!" he said.

"Well if the shoe fits, let the son-of-a-bitch wear it. Now, what are you doing back in the old home town?"

Ted waited while Lupe poured more coffee. Then he said, "Harley, that news story you were reading pretty well says it; we're going to get that dam. I'm down here from Santa Fe to document the environmental loss and work with the Fish & Wildlife Service to develop a mitigation program. Sharon and the girls are here; they got in last week and we're still moving in. We'll all be here for the next year, at least. They're going to build it Harley ; I don't see anything to stop it."

"Christ, they've been talking about that thing for longer than we've been around. When you and I were knee high to a short duck they said, 'this is the year for the dam.' That project was a dog then, it's a dog now."

"Maybeso. It makes sense to the people promoting it. As you know, the Feds subsidize these water projects through loans. The interest rates on the loans have no connection to the real world of finance but the loans are made nonetheless. Some of that loan has to be paid back by the locals and the only way they can come up with their share is by selling water to lots of people. The subsidy keeps the water artificially cheap. The cheap water and the recreation that comes with the reservoir are used to promote the area and bring in all those people they need to buy the water and pay off the project. So, the project is subsidized, and more than that, it's used to subsidize growth. It doesn't just serve growth, it promotes it. Once the project is begun and the contract with the Feds is signed, bringing in lots of new people is more than a goal; it becomes a necessity. That's how the West was won. And a lots' happened in the past year to put this project on the front burner. Our Governor, my boss, got himself elected lamenting the fact that New Mexico lagged behind Arizona, Texas and Colorado in growth and development."

"I do remember reading something about that; said, 'the sunbelt is booming all around us.'"

"Exactly. Above all, Greane is the consumate booster. His idea of a Department of Wildlife is a bunch of game wardens who set seasons and bag limits, arrest poachers, and otherwise do not allow the needs of wildlife to get in the way of progress, booster style. And he was an old hand in Washington before he came in to make the governor's race. He knows how federal water projects get from the drawing board to reality. And the administration in Washington is sympathetic to any western states water project. The West elected him."

"He got elected promoting himself as a fiscal conservative, just like Garner Greane."

"Sure. But we haven't seen a fiscal conservative yet who wouldn't roll over for a western states water project. Here in the state it's a matter of priorities. This is the last river in New Mexico without a dam on it. This river is *the* priority now. They can focus all their attention here, and to get this last river damned will be the final victory for water development in this state. Every promoter in the state who's even remotely involved will put a feather in his cap when the last free flow comes to a halt. And I think they're all involved. But I'm seeing the worst of it in the local promotion."

"Don't tell me...there's Garth Bilker and the Rod & Redneck Club."

"Right."

"And Dirk Johngood and the Río Jalisco Dam Builders."

"Of course."

"And Stew Mayfair is whipping up the City Council and Morey Solís is whipping up the County Commission."

"Yup, and don't forget Stan Baer."

"Stan Baer? Ol' Bubba?"

"You bet; Bubba Baer. Baer Contracting is working hard for the dam."

"I thought he about went under...wasn't he caught with both hands in the cookie jar?"

That's true. But there's going to be a lot of local contracting work once construction begins, starting with some major road building to open up the forest and get the crews and equipment and tourists into the damsite. Bubba Baer is at the head of the line for some big contracts and you may know who is setting him up."

Jim Bo Moreland?"

"Yes sir. Do you know him?"

"I talked to him a few times, before I left. I feel like I know him well enough. Seemed like he would go to the top of the local heap in a hurry."

"He has. You'll remember when he arrived he took over as President of the Arthur County Bank. He's since moved up to Chairman of the Board. Meanwhile, he's got subdivisions going up here and there, he's picked up the radio station, and he's gotten himself elected mayor. He's the catalyst that's gathered up all the shakers and movers in town and got them all pointed in the same direction. Every project of this kind needs a core group of local supporters. Jim Bo has put that group together. He came in here from Phoenix, but he's nonetheless well connected in Santa Fe, and in Washington. He's the king pin and I'll say it, he's done a hell of a job."

"Ought to be some way to stop it. They stopped that dam up on the Río Grande gorge."

"The gorge is a weekend excursion for all sorts of people in Albuquerque, Santa Fe and Taos. It's one of the most popular whitewater river runs and trout streams in America. Every sportsman, river runner, and environmentalist in the state felt violated by that project. Sure, they stopped it. But this dam is set for a little ol' river in the middle of nowhere that you can wade across ten months out of the year. Very few New Mexicans know anything about this country, let alone folks from elsewhere."

"And down by the dam site, there's not much except a bunch of big catfish. I haven't met a sport yet who'd pay me to guide him to a catfish."

"Our little river has never paid its way, Harley."

"So now they figure to turn our little ol' river into a big ol' reservoir and, finally, put Del Cobre on the map."

"That's the motto!"

"What?"

"You damn right. PUT DEL COBRE ON THE MAP! That's the little feel-good message they've tacked on to this project. They've got a brochure out, in color, and you open it up and it spreads out into a map and there's the river turned into a big long lake and just over the divide is Del Cobre all swollen up four times normal size like a bloated tick and it says, PUT DEL COBRE ON THE MAP!"

"Catchy."

"Sure. Who could resist it?"

Harley turned around. There was some activity over at the door and he heard someone mention his name. Two locals that Harley recognized had evidently been accosted by an out-of-towner who was pointing to the map he had in his hand. Directly one of the locals pointed to Harley. The stranger came over to Harley and Ted as the two locals walked out. The stranger had a red, sun-burned face, blond hair, and he wore shorts and a short-sleeved shirt with a little green alligator over his left tit.

"Ed Harmon, El Paso," the new man said. He smiled when he said it.

"Harley. And this is Ted," Harley said.

They shook hands all around. Then Ed Harmon laid the Forest Service map out on the table. He talked to Harley.

"Those guys told me you know all about this area."

"My old man did," Harley said. "I'm still learning."

"Well, I'm up here for a few days with my wife and boy and we want to find some nice water and catch some trout and relax. I was looking at these creeks on the map. They said there's lots of trout in these creeks but they said the biggest ones are in the river."

"They're right."

"Well that's a lot of river. Where are the big trout? Those guys weren't sure but they said wherever they are you can't get in there."

"You can get in there," Harley said. "That's all National Forest...public land."

"But there's no roads on this map."

"You have to walk or ride a horse. These little single dotted lines are trails."

Harmon frowned. "Where can we drive and fish for trout?

"Over the state line, in the White Mountains of Arizona."

"I've been there. Every place you can go there's a crowd of people."

31

"There's a reason for that. The White Mountains are full of roads. If this country was full of roads it would be the same."

"All right. But I can't see having all those big trout and then you can't get in there."

"You can get in there," Harley said. "You have to walk or ride a horse."

"I'm traveling with my wife and son."

Harley smiled. "Has one of them got a broken leg?"

Harmon frowned. "Those two guys said the dam would be built right here" - Harmon pointed at the map - "and it would be about twenty miles long and stocked with bass and trout."

"Maybeso."

"We'll bring our boat and stay a month and catch a bunch of big trout when they build that dam and make it so you can get in there."

"You can get in there now," Harley said. "You have to walk or ride a horse."

Harmon scowled. "Thanks for the info," he said, and he picked up his map and went for the door.

Harley finished his coffee. Then he said: "Maybe when his wife or son, one, gets over that broken leg we'll see them in there along the upper Jalisco trout fishing."

"They'll be in there catching big trout and living off the land," Ted said.

"Come to think of it, I haven't been in there myself in over a year."

"It's been a lot longer than that for me. I'll be in there plenty this summer. That's going to be a big part of my job. After I get settled in and my office set up I need to go in there. I did drive over the bridge at Gunsight the other day. Walked down and got my feet wet. Felt good."

"Should be a good run-off."

"Oh there's plenty of water this spring."

"Ted, let's run it."

"Sure. I was going to wait till the water went down and pack in. But now that you're here, let's run it. I've never run that stretch. There's parts of that lower canyon I've never seen."

"My canoe is still in Arizona. There's nothing wrong with it. We'll wait a couple of weeks. The water will clear some and the trout and bass will see a fly. And it will warm some and those big cats downriver will start to feed. We'll catch all the fresh meat we need and you can start to document the beginning of the end of it all."

"Let's not be morbid. They're only going to inundate 20 miles of the river."

"The best 20 miles as far as I'm concerned. And it sounds like they're going to road-in the whole south end of the drainage."

"They are. But not before you and I have some fun in the next year. We'll run the whole canyon. You tell me when it's right and we'll go."

Harley and Ted stood up and they both reached for the check. Harley got it first but Ted quite decisively took it out of his hand. Harley left the tip and went outside to his truck while Ted paid for breakfast. Ted came out and they stood in the sun by Harley's truck. Ted got out his can of *Skoal,* tapped the shiny cover to clear the lid, lifted the lid and reached in. He grabbed a good pinch between one thick finger and one large thumb and tucked it away in his mouth. Harley removed his pouch and took a large, loose pinch of *Red Man* between two long fingers and one long thumb and tucked it away. They each worked the stuff down and lofted a brown stream on to the street between passing cars. Then Lurk sat up in the truck.

"What the hell is that? Ted said.

"That's Lurk."

"What is he?"

"Well, this ol' kid down by Las Cruces had a staghound/blue-tik cross. Wanted more speed for those night hunts coon hunters all want to win these days. He got all kinds of speed but the hound couldn't smell a warm biscuit. But I've always liked the idea myself. I figured he just didn't go far enough. So I crossed that dog with Geraldine - you remember her...that little Walker gyp - and one pup came with a rough shag coat. He was also the leggiest and the most aggressive."

"Pretty good hound?"

"Sorry, worthless, trash-running son-of-a-bitch. Lurk will run anything that leaves a scent. He's got a nose all right, but he won't tree. All he wants to do is run. You remember that Saddleback I was working with, the one I call White-eye?

"Yeah, he was coming along good."

"Well, he's come along great. A complete hound. He can strike, cold trail, run a hot trail with his head up and driving, work out a loss, locate, he's straight, and I'm mean he'll starve at the tree. He's taught Geraldine everything she knows and except for the strike she's nearly as good as he is, and she's faster. Now Lurk, he's learned some things, but he acts like he'll never learn some others. He can strike too, and trail, and I've never known a hound can move a track with his speed. He beats them to the tree every time. Then he'll mill around the tree for a few minutes and if I'm not right there, off he goes. Pretty soon he's got another race going and you can hear him all over the mountains. He'll pull Geraldine off the tree with him, sometimes, but he won't pull White-eye. Son-of-a-bitch might be gone for days, particularly if he gets on a coyote. He loves to run a wolf. And you can't keep him in a pen. But I'm going to work him through another year because if I ever get him broke off trash I'll have the best hide dog in the Southwest. I've never seen a hound can move a track like Lurk."

"Well if big and ugly counts, you've got yourself a hound. I'd tree if he was after me."

Inside the cab, Lurk panted with a big, red tongue, stared with yellow eyes, and fogged up the window.

"He's a charmer," Harley said.

Ted put out his hand. "Harley, I've got things to do at home. We're getting settled."

"I'll help you," Harley said, shaking Ted's hand.

"Oh we're moved in, we're just not settled. It's busy work. You and Lurk go on, and stay out of trouble."

"Lurk's in trouble already. I'll be all right. I'm coming around. I'm going to get it together."

Ted sent a brown stream on the pavement between his feet. Then he looked at Harley. "I'll watch for that," he said.

## *Chapter 3*

FRIDAY NIGHT IN DEL COBRE and the southwestern town was beginning to cut loose for the weekend. But in the hills above town, up Gavilán Creek, it was so quiet in the house that Harley Simmons could hear his wrist watch tick. He had always had very good hearing, could hear the hounds treed over the next mountain when others could not, but when he could hear his wrist watch tick Harley knew it was very quiet indeed. The only other sound in the house was the occasional crackle of the piñon burning in the wood stove and the faint rustle of the smoke going up the pipe. Sitting by the wood stove, Harley could look out the window and see there was a fair breeze rolling the barren top branches of the cottonwoods along the creek. There was just enough light left in the evening sky that he could see the wind in the trees. But he couldn't hear the wind at all. It was the way the old man had built the house - a double thickness of carefully wrought adobe brick. And all windows and doors were carefully crafted; they wouldn't rattle in a bad storm. Harley had forgotten, but now remembered, that living in the house one was so ensconced in silence it was like living underground. And indeed the house was made of dirt. There was a radio in the house but Harley seldom played it. There was no television and Harley didn't want one. There was a telephone but no one called. And the one person he really wanted to talk to, he wasn't ready to call.

He had spent the day puttering around the place. He alternately put his saddle on the horses and the mule and with each he took a little ride. He slapped together a rough lumber dog house for Lurk and there he staked him out on a chain so he wouldn't run away. He crossed the creek and made a visit to the widow Hidalgo, who had looked after him when he was young, and looked after the old man towards the end. They spoke in Spanish and the old woman cried when they talked about the old man which made Harley feel things he hadn't felt at the funeral. As evening came on Harley made some supper, did the dishes, and then sat by the stove with a book, listening to his watch tick, hearing the fire in the stove, and watching the wind silently move the cottonwoods down by the creek. He kept expecting the old man to come out of the kitchen, where he would roll and smoke a cigarette after supper, and say, "I'm going to town." In the silence of this evening Harley would have relished that, and even the argument that would have followed - shouts and mumbled words and mutual accusations concerning what might happen to either one of them should they go to town. Harley had decided he wasn't going to town himself. He wasn't going to do that anymore. He was going to stay home and stay out of mischief. But he'd entirely lost interest in the book, and the stove rustled with a slow burn, and his wrist watch ticked plainly, never missing a beat, and down by the creek the barren cottonwoods waved silently in the breeze. He watched them till the darkness took them from sight.

Harley stood up, got his coat and hat and went to the porch. From the porch he could see the lights from the town. And he could see Lurk, curled up on the roof of his new dog house; he would never use the house, always sleeping on the roof, impervious to the weather, whatever it was. Lurk was chained and he knew it. And he knew Harley wasn't going hunting, at least not in the woods. Lurk stayed curled on top of the house, eyeing the man. Harley said, "Lurk, I'm going to town."

~ ~ ~ ~ ~ ~

As usual the teenagers were cruising south down Ballard Street, making the U-turn at the deadend by the creek, then cruising back up Ballard before completing the circle at the Heidi-Ho drive-through hamburger joint. Harley got in line and began the stop-and-go drive down Ballard. Every vehicle was full of people and someone was honking their horn it seemed like all the time. In the line of cars coming up the other lane one guy took his can of beer off the dash and tucked it between his legs when Harley looked his way. Harley thought: I guess I don't look like a kid anymore. He felt better when a girl shouted,"Hey baby!" and when he looked at her, gave him the finger. Then she shrieked and sped ahead. He looked in the rear mirror and she flipped him the bird again. And another one, better looking, pulled over close, heading up the other lane, reached over and offered him a number. "Get loose cowboy," she said.

Harley waved off the joint and said, "Ride with me; we'll drive around and kiss."

She laughed, stuck out her tongue and was gone.

Directly, Harley reached the corner of Ballard and Main and as he turned out of the cruising lane on to the much quieter Main Street he said to himself: "Who says you can't have fun in a small town?"

At the bar, inside the old Copper Palace Hotel, Harley joined an assortment of mine workers, cowboys, office workers, businessmen, folks from the college, women, lonely hearts, burnt-outs and the unemployed. As his eyes adjusted to the dim he saw some faces he recognized, a surprising number he didn't, and a few people he knew. One of them bought him a beer, for when the barmaid brought the draft he'd ordered, she walked away from the dollar bill he'd laid on the bar.

"Hey Harley."

Harley looked across the U-shaped bar, and there was Eddie Deming.

"Eddie, what's happening?"

"Nothing yet. But there's plenty of time. Where you been?"

"Clifton."

"That town will starve you out."

"I did all right. Even saved a little. But I got lonesome for the home folks."

"Sure. We've all been away. But we always come back. Good to see you Harley."

Harley raised his mug to acknowledge the purchase and the conversation came to a close.

As he drew down on the brew, Harley noticed there had been some changes in the Copper Palace Bar. For one thing, the place looked and smelled clean; that was a big change. The walls, that a year ago were chipped and peeling paint, had been paneled over, it looked like with real lumber, tongue-in-groove paneling. Decorating the new walls was a variety of western art and some nice, large format, photographs, properly framed. All the art and photographs showed off local scenes and landscapes and Harley recognized the works of local artists and photographers. The odd assortment of metal framed tables was gone, replaced by substantial wooden tables, round in shape, that looked like something out of a western movie. They were of an old style, but were obviously new. Clearly the entire motif of the Copper Palace had been redone. The Copper Palace Bar now resembled what Harley figured it looked like at the turn of the century when it was built. What remained from a year ago was the massive mahogany bar, that reportedly dated from the turn of the century, and the impressive hide and head mount of a wolf that covered the wall behind the bar, that Harley knew for a fact dated from the 1930's. He knew because his father had killed the wolf, and had been photographed with the wolf and a mule and a pack of hounds shortly after the hunt. Harley looked at the wolf over the bar and recalled the story of the hunt that he had asked his father to tell him, so many times. The race, the old man said, had begun early in the morning at Engelmann Peak and went north to the rim of the canyon. Then east along the rim and during the afternoon the wolf led his pursuers down into the canyon, then upstream, then south up Brush Creek to that awesome expanse of jungle and canyons known as Brushy Mountain. Past midnight, the old man always said, the hounds brought the wolf to bay. "To this day there's parts of Brushy Mountain no white man has ever seen," the old man used to say, recalling the hunt. "That's where that wolf went, to one of those places. I left my horse and crept in by moonlight and that's where I shot him. Everyone in the chase was run down." Harley had heard the story so many times, it was like he had been there himself. Now the hide and head mount of the wolf was still over the old mahogany bar and it seemed the rest of the bar had been redone to match the old mahogany and the pelt. Harley was pleased with the way things had been done.

Harley drained the draft, ordered another, and once again was unable to pay for it. Leo Silva stepped up beside him, gave him the two-part Chicano handshake, and paid for the beer.

"I seen you in town yesterday, man. You were walking into the Luera. I didn't have time to stop. What do you think of the new Copper Palace?"

"Pretty classy. Whoever did it, did it right. What are you doing out tonight, Leo?"

"Just getting away from the old lady. There's some nicer stuff coming in here now."

"I imagine. Nicer place, you get some nicer stuff. It's not going to help me any. I'll be lucky if I can make out with the old hides."

"You'll make out good, man. You always make out, Harley. Well, I'll see you, Harley. You wait till the dance starts and watch what comes in. You'll like what comes in here now, man."

"I'll watch for it," Harley said.

They exchanged another two-part Chicano handshake and Leo Silva returned to his place at the bar. Harley promptly consumed his second beer, ordered another for himself, and for Eddie and Leo, and paid for all three. At the Copper Palace Hotel the dance hall, called the Copper Room, was across the lobby from the bar and Harley turned on his bar stool and watched couples and singles of both sexes come into the lobby. Some of them came into the Copper Palace Bar which was now nearly full, but several already were turning into the Copper Room which was just across the lobby and where the band was tuning up. Directly the band clipped into a solid two-step beat and a number of people in the bar got up and filed out of the bar, across the lobby, and into the dance hall, although some stayed. Harley stayed for awhile until it became evident that little by little most of those leaving for the dance hall were women and couples and that pretty soon the only thing left in the Copper Palace Bar would be the burnt-outs. Harley had never been so much of a burnt-out that he ceased caring where the women went on Friday night; he finished his latest beer and left the bar and crossed the lobby. He paid the one dollar cover charge to Shirley and went into the Copper Room.

# HOME IS THE RIVER

The Copper Room was a good dance hall. Big enough to hold a crowd sitting at the tables and a bunch more dancing, but not so big you couldn't stand at a strategic spot and see who-all was there. There was a bar in the Copper Room, too. Harley got a bottle of Coors and leaned against the wall that all the men on the watch leaned against while they looked things over. He noticed that the Copper Room had been refurbished, too, in the same motif as the Copper Palace Bar. There was the wood paneling, the work of local artists on the walls, new tables; and what had been retained - the stage and the box seats that lined the walls above -   that dated from the days before moving pictures, was what was right to start with. The new had been done to match and enhance the old.   Again, Harley felt the refurbishment had been done right and he was pleased. The band up on the stage pleased him too. The banner behind the group said "Desert Wind." There was a fiddle player and the lead singer had a good deep voice that carried without strain and Harley could feel the beat was tight and clear - good clean licks - and would be easy dancing. They were already into their second song:

> *"They took my saddle in Houston,*
> *broke my leg in Santa Fe,*
> *lost my wife and a girlfriend*
> *somewhere along the way..."*

And the room was full of predators. Little by little the boys began to line the wall, slouched against the wall much like Harley with a beer in one hand and the thumb of the other hand hung in a denim pocket. A few others stood around the bar. A few of the single women stood around the bar too, but most were seated in twos, threes and fours at the dance tables. All the couples were seated at tables too, when they weren't dancing. The single women never stood against the wall like the boys, and the boys seldom sat at tables together unless they found some women to sit with. And down the wall to the right of where the boys stood was the women's bathroom. This was a good deal for the boys. Every woman in the place who stayed for any length of time made the walk to the bathroom and went by the boys lined up against the wall. Being one of the boys, Harley watched them go by; they were seldom alone, usually in pairs; it was a tough walk alone. Like the boys they wore tight jeans. But where the boys wore tight jeans and hung a thumb in a front pocket and set the beer bottle on the corner of the hip to draw attention to the crotch, the women wore tight jeans with a design or two sewn onto a back pocket to draw attention to the ass. And of course it worked. Harley and the boys watched them walk by on the way to the rest room and got another look when they came back. The women looked straight ahead, seldom acknowledging the boys; a little uptight but they liked it. Back at their seats they stole glances at the boys against the wall, and those at the bar, and watched the couples dance. The room was now full of people, including couples, and there were also a bunch of predators, hunters. The women were at the tables hunting, and hoping for, Mr. Right. The boys were hunting too, leaning against the wall and standing around the bar, hoping one of the women would take them for Mr. Right, if only for the night.

Harley leaned against the wall and watched it all. Of the women he looked at he saw some familiar faces but no one he knew well. Mostly they were new women to Harley; there had been quite a turnover in just a year. But Harley liked looking at them. Most of the men were new faces, also. But the pattern was familiar. Some of them were white collar types who looked like they worked in offices and wore their white collars to the dance. And there were miners and construction workers, most of whom wore jeans and work boots and tractor caps on their heads and hung their keys from a leash snap attached to a belt loop. But the majority of the boys wore jeans and cowboy hats and cowboy boots. For most of them it was an act. A few of them were genuine. Like old Junior Prine, seated at a table with a woman half his age. Junior was a tall, fat, ageing rancher whose wife rousted him out of the house for good a few years back, leaving him to buy drinks at the Copper Palace for women half his age, what he wanted all along. Junior had been a friend of his fathers', reminded him of his father, and dressed like what he was. He was okay by Harley. And J. D. Ancheta looked right to Harley. J. D. was a rodeo man. He rode bulls and he rode them very well. He was short, stocky, with an oversized hat and belt buckle. He was cocky, strutted when he walked, and he was a mean drunk, but he looked like what he was. He was okay by Harley. And probably most in character was Bruno Bursum, on his way across the room to shake Harley's hand. Bruno wore greasy denim coveralls over an even dirtier flannel shirt and a hopeless non-descript hat; he was black-bearded, long-haired, and looked like a cross between a prospector and a turn of the century trapper. Except for the time frame, that's just what he was.

"Harley, you back here hunting fur or women?"

"Bruno, fur's started to rub; practically worthless; women are prime all year. You struck it rich yet?"

"Well not exactly. The price of furs' been good, but you know that. And I been sloshing out a *leetle* gold on occasion and I'm not telling where. But that's recreation. Mostly I'm coming out good on antiquities. I've been poaching this site in the wilderness nobody knows about. Can't even tell you about it, Harley. I got three Mimbreño pots intact and an *olla* about the best I've ever seen. Big *dinero* once I found the market and slipped it through."

"I know the cave."

"Hell you do!"

"About a half mile up Jackson Canyon, east side, fifty feet below the rim and well hidden. The *olla's* got jackrabbits painted around it."

"Well hell, you could have had them all!"

"Years ago."

"Well, I couldn't let a pile of money like that just sit there."

"Bruno, that Mimbreño pottery is one of the few good things the human animal has ever done in this country. They got the clay from that river bottom somewhere, formed everything by hand and even the paint that decorates it was made from scratch... I don't know how. And it lasted a thousand years."

"Harley, you're breaking my heart."

"For a few bucks, that's a lot of history to take out of the country, that's all."

"It was more than a few bucks, you can bank on that. That's the only reason I know of to go after it at all. I mean that was a pile of money, Harley, and it was just sitting there."

"That's the same reason they give for putting a dam on the river - there's a pile of money to be had, and that river, it's just sitting there."

"Sons-a-bitches will, too; you know they will, Harley. And there's caves there yet with stuff in them that even you and I don't know about. There's a thousand caves and more in that canyon country. When it all goes under behind that dam, that's it. We just as well get it out now and do some good with it."

"If they dam it."

"Sons-a-bitches will, Harley. You know they will. Ignorant mountain men like you and me can't stop it. Sierra Club and those other daisy sniffers won't even be able to stop it. We might just as well go in there and taken it out while we can. What say you and me go in together this summer? I know there's sites and caves nobody's touched since those Indians folded up the tent."

"I'll pass, Bruno. There's other ways I can make a living. And I don't think they're going to build that dam."

"Sons-a-bitches will, Harley. You know they will. I'm gonna get what I can before that river's gone. I'll see you, Harley. You let me know when you want to go in there and get those antiquities."

Harley watched Bruno Bursum head on out of the dance hall, headed for the Copper Palace Bar. He'd been in the woods for a while and his habits were well known and as he passed through the crowd headed out the door the women gave him plenty of room.

Harley got himself another beer (he was starting to get a pretty good buzz on) and returned to his place of perusal along the wall. He didn't like what Bruno Bursum was doing, but he liked him just the same. Three of the boys slouched against the wall to Harley's right weren't doing anything, yet, but already Harley didn't like them. He didn't like their type, a type that was becoming all too common in the

New West to suit Harley. They were dressed like him, like westerners who spend lots of time outdoors, but Harley knew they didn't. Harley knew for a fact that the one sold "western" clothes at the local "western" store and the other was the parts man at the Ford garage. He'd never seen the third one, who was a big guy, but Harley would have bet a good mule that he, like the other two, was a truck jockey who belonged to the local jeep club, had soft white hands and wouldn't know a curb bit from a snaffle, or a coon print from a beaver track. The two men he knew a little bit had 4-wheel drive pickups with big tires and they raised the frame way up over the wheels. They cheated, driving those trucks all over the countryside, wherever they could find or make a road, where an honest man walked or rode a horse; and, with luck, they shot game from out the window. They were dress up cowboys, urban cowboys, and Harley preferred miners and construction workers, businessmen and young urban professionals, burnt-outs and even Bruno Bursum to what was slouched against the wall just to his right.

Harley was so intent on checking these three out that he hadn't noticed what they were looking at, but now he did. They were looking at two women, singles it would appear, who had come in and sat down at a nearby table right on the edge of the dance floor while he was talking to Bruno Bursum. They were both young. One had short hair, a hard, pretty face, and she smoked cigarettes. She carried the cigarette pack in a little purse holder along with a slim, cheap lighter and Harley summed it all up and knew right away he didn't want her. The other girl had long brown hair, a soft face, full, soft body; she didn't smoke and, Harley thought, looked like someone he'd like. Harley knew he'd take her home if he got the chance. Harley waited, the next song was a waltz, and Harley saw the parts man to his right nod to the salesman of "western" clothes and they stepped over and asked the two women to dance. The third urban cowboy waited, against the wall, impassive, and then for the first time gave the slight indication that he'd noticed Harley; he shifted his weight to the other foot.

It was a good waltz song and the band played it well. The lead singer even sounded a lot like Don Williams:

> *"I've held it all inward, Lord knows I've tried,*
> *it's an awful awakening in a country boy's life,*
> *to look in the mirror in total surprise,*
> *at the hair on your shoulders and the age in your eyes.*
> *A...m...a...n...da, light of my life..."*

Harley watched the show. The long-haired girl had a wonderful ass. The parts man was plug-ugly but a pretty good dancer. Harley didn't think he'd ever be able to dance well enough to make up for how ugly he was. The salesman was a handsome man in his new "western" clothes.

41

But when he wasn't stepping on the feet of the short-haired girl he was stepping on his own. He sure couldn't waltz. Harley had known lots of women at the Copper Palace to go home with plug ugly men and men who couldn't dance but, still, these two guys looked vulnerable. Harley watched them through the dance; when it ended the boys brought the girls by the hand back to their seats. They sat down with the women and ordered a round for the table. Harley watched all this and so did the third guy, the big guy, who appeared to be well acquainted with the parts man and the salesman; he still leaned against the wall, just to Harley's right.

Harley got another beer, returned to the wall and watched the pursuit as the parts man and the salesman took the two women through another waltz, a two-step, and then an old timey rock and roll. The parts man was still plug-ugly and the salesman still couldn't dance. They changed partners once but that didn't help; the two women refused to dance any closer to the men then they had on the first dance and it appeared certain to Harley that they had ceased to be flattered by all the attention and would be happy for some variety. The band went on break. The boys ordered another round and Harley went and got another beer for himself. He was now in that realm where he knew he had already had one too many and he was going to keep drinking beer until he'd had way too much and that one way or another before the night was through he was going to make something happen.

Harley leaned back against the wall and watched the parts man and the salesman make conversation with the two women during the break. The girls were polite and they smiled. They were not intrigued. When the band came back to the stage and slung their guitars back into position Harley didn't move but he was ready. When the group went into a brisk two-step Harley took two long steps himself; he set his beer on their table with one hand and tapped the long-haired girl on the shoulder with the other just as the parts man turned around in his chair to ask her to dance. She looked up at Harley and reached up with her hand at the same time. Harley took it and they stepped onto the dance floor and fell quickly and easily into the rhythm.

The step was one...two...one-two. A simple step, the two-step; anyone but a salesman of "western" clothes with an urban cowboy hat could learn it easily enough, but there were any number of ways you could hold your partner and step and twirl and with a good band and a good song and a good partner Harley figured the two-step to be the best dance step there was. Harley had a good partner. Every way he stepped, every way they twirled, she was right there. She was long-haired and pretty, firm-bodied and yet soft, she could dance and she had a wonderful ass. With all that they stepped: one...two...one-two through the song as the fiddle whined and the lead singer strung out the words to an old Hank Williams song:

*"The news is o...u...t,*
*all over t...o...w...n,*
*that you've been s...e...e...n,*
*a-runnin' r...o...u...n...d."*

She settled in against him nicely, not resting her head and lovely soft hair against his shoulder - not yet - but settling in just the same - relaxed, enjoying herself, not taut as she'd been with the parts man. Harley looked over her shoulder as they danced. He watched the salesman who was doing his best out on the dance floor with the short-haired girl. Harley caught the name on the back of her belt - Kim! Harley also eyed the parts man, seated at the table, plug-ugly, watching, doing a slow burn. Harley winked at the parts man.

The song ended. Harley held her hand as they walked back to the table; she gave it a squeeze as he let her go. The band promptly kicked into the next song. The parts man quickly grabbed the long-haired girl. The salesman was as slow as he was clumsy; Harley took the hand of the short-haired girl. Once away from the salesman she proved she, too, could dance. They covered the floor as the band played another two-step. Harley danced with the short-haired girl, looking all the while over her head at the long-haired girl with the wonderful ass. She danced and twirled with the parts man, looking over his shoulder every little while at Harley. When they made eye contact, she smiled. As she twirled away he read the name on the back of her belt - Ellen!

The song ended. The women were returned to their seats. The band was slow in getting into the next song so Harley got his beer and went back to his place against the wall. The third guy, the big guy, was definitely noticing Harley now. When the band finally kicked into an old Chuck Berry tune the two guys at the table turned to the two women for another dance but the women turned to each other, stood, excused themselves with polite smiles, and headed for the ladies room. They went by Harley and the big guy on the way. The long-haired girl smiled at Harley on the way by; Harley smiled back and watched her wonderful ass go down the wall and around the bend into the ladies room. They were there awhile, and when they came back by the long-haired girl smiled at Harley again and Harley said, "Ellen!"

She turned to him and momentarily fingered one of his belt loops, right by the buckle.

"I like you're belt man, but there's no name."

"Name's Harley."

"Hi, Harley. This is Kim. I'd ask you to join us but..."

Harley was aware that the parts man, the salesman and the big guy were all giving him the evil eye.

"Ellen, let's dance."

He took her hand in a way that no one who was interested could miss it and led her to the dance floor. The band was now into a Mexican *cumbia*:

> *"Para bailar La Bamba. Para bailar La Bamba,*
> *se necesita una poca de gracia. Una poca de gracia,*
> *y otra cosita, arriba, arriba..."*

Harley and Ellen fell easily into the odd, quick, step-step of the *cumbia*. Kim went back to her seat. Harley enjoyed looking at Ellen while they danced, and he watched over her shoulder. The salesman looked like he wanted to ask Kim to dance but was not up to risking *La Bamba*. If you can't do the two-step, *La Bamba* is way too much. When the *cumbia* ended the crowd dispersed as always to the tables but a few couples including Harley and Ellen stayed on the dance floor waiting for the next dance. Harley put his arm around her and she came in against him. The band picked their way through a waltz, then a two-step - one of Harley's favorites. The lead singer even sounded a lot like Tex Ritter:

> *"I told my heart I didn't love you,*
> *that I'd be happy if we'd part,*
> *lonely days of tears and sorrow,*
> *I told a lie to my heart."*

Harley and Ellen never missed a beat. Then the band played another waltz, then another two-step. Harley and Ellen stayed on the dance floor and did them all. The salesman was out on the dance floor again, doing his best with Kim. He wasn't doing very good. But Ellen snuggled in very nicely now. Harley could feel her very well; he could feel what she would be like. Harley hooked his thumb in the middle belt loop right between the two l's in Ellen and let his hand rest on the base of her spine, with his fingers resting on the upper part of her wonderful ass. He could tell she liked it. Harley watched the parts man watch all this. Harley watched the parts man squirm and burn.

Halfway through another two-step Harley said: "Is Kim with you?"

"No," she said, picking it up right away, "she drove."

"Can she get home by herself?"

Ellen looked up at Harley. "She doesn't want to go with him. When this dance is over I'll take her with me to the restroom. I'll tell her. She's ready to leave now anyway. Then we can walk her to her car, so she can get away from him. Then I'll go with you."

She tucked her head in under his chin, against his shoulder. He pressed his hand against her wonderful ass and she allowed her hips to rest her crotch against his thigh while they danced. He knew now before the night was through he was going to peel her jeans down and away from her wonderful ass, then her panties, and they were going to fuck. The only distraction to this juicy anticipation was the parts man over at the table; he was burning and giving Harley the evil eye and as much as anything else, Harley wanted to bust him in the face.

The song ended and the band, with a "short pause for a good cause," announced a break. On the way back to the table Ellen gave Kim the sign and they broke off for the restroom. Harley did not avoid walking right by the parts man as he passed the table, headed for the wall. The parts man put out his foot just enough to trip Harley as he went by. Harley saw this as it happened and came down hard with his boot heel on the parts man's pointed toe. The parts man winced as he felt the pain and started to come up out of the chair in violent response and then Harley chopped him back down with a hard left just before the salesman came across the table with a hard right on top of Harley's right eye. The women - it sounded like every one in the dance hall - began to scream and the men began to holler as Harley spun away from being hit with the blood squirting off his eyelid as the big guy came off the wall, lunged across the table and tackled him around the waist.

The parts man was down, groggy and feeling his jaw, but Harley and the big guy and the salesman were rolling around amongst several tables that a bunch of people had just vacated. The veteran honky-tonk band, seeing their cue, regained their instruments and promptly went into a snappy number...

> "*Well the race is on and here comes*
> *pride up the backstretch,*
> *heartaches going to the inside...*"

...as Harley tried to get out from underneath the big guy who was pounding him on the ear. Folks had started dancing again and Harley could hear ol' Junior Prine and J. D. Ancheta cheering him on but nobody was helping him any as the salesman regained his feet and started kicking him in the back and ribs. Harley whipped one leg around and upset the salesman who hit the floor and piled in again and the big guy was still pounding him on the ear. Harley rolled in under a table that fell over on them all and he broke away from the big guy and started swinging, still on the floor, and kicking at either one he could get at. He got in some good shots with both fists and feet but so did the big guy and the salesman and Harley thought: these guys are pretty rough for having soft white hands and riding around in pickup trucks all day long. The cops were never far from the Copper Palace on a Friday night and Harley and the salesman and the big guy were still rolling around and swinging and kicking when two deputies came in and ran across the floor, dodging through the dancers, and broke up the fight before anyone got killed. They hauled all the combatants out of the dance hall, through the lobby and into the street as the band finished out that old George Jones classic:

*"My heart's out of the running,*
*and the winner loses all..."*

On the street in front of the Copper Palace the squad car was parked with it's red light on top going round and round and round. Under the streetlamp on the sidewalk between the squad car and the Copper Palace the sergeant examined the parts man's jaw. It hung slack and wobbled and looked funny. Harley's eye and ear were starting to swell and they both looked funny too. Harley took out his bandana and pressed it against his eye. He'd closed the split above the lid and the bleeding was already starting to staunch when the corporal reached up to look at the wound and Harley said, "It's all right, goddamnit!" The salesman of "western" clothes was bleeding out of the mouth and nose and the big guy's chin was split wide open and was bleeding profusely as well. Shirley came out to announce what the officers had already assumed - it was all Harley's fault.

"I seen Harley throw the first punch when this one tried to get up out of his chair," she said. "He hasn't changed a bit."

"Son-of-a-bitch was fixing to trip me," Harley said.

"So you had to break his jaw," the sergeant said. The parts man mumbled something about his version of what happened but his jaw was badly broken and nobody understood what he said. Then the sergeant said: "Okay, you two idiots take this idiot to the hospital so they can wire his jaw up. Then you get your chin stitched and you have someone look at your front teeth." Then the sergeant turned to Harley and said: "Harley, do you want your eye stitched up?"

"No."

"We don't want you bleeding all over the jail"

"It's about quit, Ernie."

"Okay mountain man, get in the car."

The two idiots helped the third idiot across the street to where a four wheel drive all-terrain bigun' stood on enormous wheels with the body raised well above the tires, while Harley got in the front seat of the squad car. The sergeant drove and the corporal sat behind Harley in the back seat. They were just pulling away when the long-haired girl and the short-haired girl came out of the Copper Palace. They glanced at the police car but didn't stop as they quick-stepped down the street and around the corner and the one with the long hair had a wonderful ass and then she was gone, gone.

∿ ∿ ∿ ∿ ∿

"He's back," the clerk behind the desk said as Harley was booked for a night in jail. "We've been expecting you, Harley."

46

"Nice to see you again, Celia."

"What's the charge, Ernie?" She started to type on a form.

"Drunk and disorderly," the sergeant said. "And maybe assault."

"He won't do that," Harley said. "He won't advertise that he got whipped."

"We'll wait on the assault till the sheriff is in on this," Ernie said.

"Drunk and disorderly, *y nada mas*," Celia said, typing. She typed very fast and Harley noticed that on the line of the form marked "name" she had typed: (Crazy) Harley Simmons (is back).

"Celia, that's clever," Harley said.

"I'm through," Celia said, looking up at the sergeant, "I've got the rest on file."

"Let's go mountain man," Ernie said.

Harley followed Ernie and the big .357 magnum hanging from his hip down the hall to a big plain metal door with no door handle. A buzzer sounded and Ernie pushed the door open. He took Harley through the door where another deputy picked him up. To the right of the door the jailer sat at a desk underneath a bare bulb, bent over some paper work. He looked up briefly, saw who it was and rolled his eyes, then went back to his paper work. Automatically, he reached underneath the desk and the buzzer sounded again. Ernie went back out the door. Harley followed the deputy further down the hall, which was dimly lit beyond the big metal door, until the hall opened up into a room lined with cells and the first cell was the drunk tank. There were four guys in the drunk tank. The drunk tank smelled very bad. Two guys were snoring like drunkards on a couple of cots. Another one was slumped against the wall by the commode. He had tried to barf in the commode but it was all over the floor, too, and down the front of his shirt. Now he was sleeping in it. The fourth guy didn't want anywhere near the commode and Harley watched as he began pissing in the corner against the wall.

"Don't do that," the deputy said.

"Clean that shitter up and I'll piss in it," the man said. He continued to piss against the wall until he was done. Now the drunk tank smelled even worse. Harley was still pretty drunk himself; his head was swimming and the smell didn't help. He knew if he went in the drunk tank, he'd barf too. He hadn't decided where.

"Let me see that eye, Harley." It was the jailer. The jailer gave the deputy a look and the deputy left and then the jailer pushed Harley aside a couple of steps until Harley stood under one of the lights.

"I said let me see that eye, Harley."

Harley dropped his hand away from his eye. His bandana was stuck to the eyelid and the jailer carefully peeled the bandana away from the eye.

"Looks pretty ugly right now. We'll clean it up and it will look a lot better. Anymore, goddamn prisoners will sue us if we don't provide proper medical care."

"Pete, you guys are all heart," Harley said.

Harley followed the jailer down a hall to a washroom. The jailer got a pan of cold water and a rag. Then he led Harley down past a row of cells. At the end of the row was an empty cell.

"This is where you're father used to stay," the jailer said.

"That wasn't necessary, Pete." Harley said.

"It's here or the tank."

Harley stepped into the cell. The jailer gave him the pan of cold water and the rag.

"Clean your eye, soak that ear, and sleep it off," the jailer said. He stepped out and closed the cell door part way. "Don't run off," he said, and then the jailer walked away.

Harley sat on the edge of the bunk and wet the rag. Using both hands and moving very carefully he held the wet cloth against his eye and ear. He held it there for a long time. Then he lay down on the bunk. His head was swimming. So he sat up on the bunk and leaned against the wall. He sat there like that for a long time, soaking his eye and his ear. Then he lay down again. It took a while because his eye and his ear both hurt and he felt sure the salesman had cracked some ribs when he kicked him, but he finally fell asleep.

In the morning there was sunshine coming through the tiny window high up on the wall of the cell. Harley was awake looking up at the sun spot on the wall when he heard a tin cup tapping against the bars. The jailer pulled the cell door open as Harley sat up on the edge of the bunk. He hurt all over.

"Here's some coffee," the jailer said.

Harley said, "Thanks Pete," and took the big tin cup and sipped some of the hot coffee. It was some of the best coffee he'd ever had.

"Take your time with that," the jailer said. "Then come by my desk. You may be on your way home. But the sheriff wants to talk to you first."

~ ~ ~ ~ ~ ~

Henry Bustos, the graying, squarely built, duly elected sheriff of a county the size of the state of Connecticut was in his office bright and early Saturday morning holding a magnifying monocle to a strip of negatives. Though technically off duty on weekends, he was in his office bright and early most every Saturday morning. His interest was photographs. Sometimes police work photographs, some of which he still took and developed himself, but generally, on Saturdays, it was his own photography, his hobby, that brought him to his place of work. Here he had access to the excellent darkroom facilities, and on Saturdays he usually had the dark room to himself and could concentrate on photog-

48

raphy that pleased him. Looking at the strip of negatives that hung from the clip attached to the wire in front of the window of his office, there was not much that pleased him. This was not unusual. The last two frames looked like they had possibilities, however. He cut the last two negatives off from the rest of the strip and put them in an envelope. Then he drew a large wooden match from his shirt pocket and struck it with his fingernail and held the match to catch the flame. Then, slowly, smoothly and expertly, he drew the flame up the strip hanging from the wire. Without causing a flame he scorched each negative into oblivion. He was almost as pleased by the final removal of those negatives that weren't right as he was by the saving of those that were. He opened the clip and the ruined negatives dropped into the empty waste basket.

"What's wrong with those, sheriff?"

The sheriff's office door was seldom closed and the sheriff looked up at Celia, standing in the doorway.

"I only keep the ones I like," the sheriff said.

"I'm sure I'd be happy to take any one of the pictures you throw away," she said.

"Maybe right now. The hardest thing in photography is being able to tell the good ones from all the rest. When you come to see that damned few are really any good, you're starting to make a photographer. In time, you would come to see that too, Celia."

"I don't know. For me, if it's in focus, it's pretty damn good. Henry, crazy Harley is ready to see you."

"*Bueno*, I'm ready to see crazy Harley."

"Henry, can I go home now?"

The sheriff looked at his watch. "You're already an hour past your shift."

"I know. I thought you might have something else needs doing."

"Hell, go on home. Max will be lonely."

"And horny."

"That too, I'm sure."

"He doesn't like my working the night shift...because of that."

"Celia, I wish you could work every shift. Then you wouldn't have to straighten out every thing that goes wrong while you're gone. Carla's here; you go on home to Max. Send that outlaw in and we'll see you on Monday."

The sheriff was relaxed, smoking his pipe in his swivel chair with his feet up on the desk, when Harley walked in. Harley was carrying his coffee in the big tin cup. He set it down on the desk and sat in the chair across from the sheriff. Then he tilted the chair back and put his feet up on the sheriff's desk and waited. The sheriff waited, too. He took the time to re-light his pipe. Finally, the sheriff said: "Harley, you look like you lost a rake fight."

"You ought to see those guys, Henry. That one, I broke his jaw."

"I heard. I heard all about it. What would you think about a charge of assault?"

"That asshole wouldn't sign the complaint. That would put it in the papers and tell the whole town I whipped him with one punch."

"Are you sure you know what he would do?"

"No."

"Are you sure that the district attorney, based on the evidence supplied by this office, won't file a charge of assault."

"I guess not Henry."

"There won't be an assault charge, Harley. Not this time anyway. I took care of it. But I'm going to tell you, you've got to be the most self-serving bastard in this whole self-serving town."

"Self-serving?"

"You know damn well what I mean; don't play the dumb bumpkin with me. You're a horse's ass, Harley, and you know it. But you're also a likable guy in your way, and you know that too. So you take advantage of it all over town; you figure, no matter what you do we'll all say, 'oh that's just crazy Harley,' and it'll all blow away. It doesn't always blow away. You ought to know that by now. You lost that lovely wife and a fine son by being a self-serving horse's ass."

"I haven't lost them yet. I'm going to patch things up."

"Now that you're back, I'm sure Bonney will be impressed to hear how you got drunk and got in a brawl and spent your first weekend in town in the county jail."

Slowly, Harley set his chair down on four legs and removed his feet from the sheriff's desk. He took a gulp of coffee and looked away from the sheriff.

"One of these days, Harley, you're going to break the wrong man's jaw, or you're going to run someone down driving drunk, or you're going to punch a cop, and there won't be a thing I can do to help you. What's more, I won't even try."

Harley took another gulp of coffee. And he wouldn't look at the sheriff. The sheriff waited awhile. He took some time to puff on his pipe. Then he said, "I was sorry to hear about your father."

"Thanks," Harley said.

"But you're going to be just like him, Harley. Exactly like him."

"What's wrong with that?"

"I admired you're old man, Harley. He was the last of his kind, unless it's you. But he got to be a pretty pathetic old man. Like any town drunk, he got to be a joke. I found him after the blizzard. Ernie was with me and he said it was fitting that your old man died in the mountains. I figure it was pretty pathetic that you're old man died in the mountains. I figure it was pretty pathetic that a man with the skills and knowledge your father had could get caught in a blizzard in the mountains and not be able to take care of himself. But he was drunk. He didn't die because he was old. He died because he was drunk."

"That thought has occurred to me," Harley said.

"You can be the same, Harley, or you can be different. It's up to you."

Harley drank down the rest of his coffee. Then he set the cup on the desk, stood up and went to the wall of the office where some of the sheriff's prints were framed and on display. They were all prints taken in wild country, up in the mountains or down on the desert. There were no people in any of the pictures. All the prints were in black and white.

Harley said, "How come you never work with color?"

"Anyone can take a pretty color picture," the sheriff said. "It's much more challenging to take a picture worth saving in black and white."

"How do you get that life in the sky and the water? How come you make me see all the colors in these pictures, even though they're black and white.?"

"The life is there, the color is there; it's all there naturally. The trick is not to lose it when you release the shutter. And then, with black and white, you can do a lot with developing. You can bring things out in the dark room...if you got something to work with when the shutter released. Black and white is like a good book that has you read between the lines."

Harley went to the end of the wall where there were two of the sheriff's pictures he'd never seen before. The first one was a photograph of a Desert Bighorn Sheep, a ram like many Harley had seen along the Río Jalisco canyon - a full-curl picture of nobility and competence in an environment of cliffs where your first slip was your last. Harley had never seen one slip. And he'd never seen one this close.

"You must have been near enough to spit in his eye," Harley said. "How did you do that?'

"I was clear across the canyon when I took that," the sheriff said.

"Some lens!"

"Five hundred millimeter. That's about a ten-power magnification."

"Must be hard to hold that still enough."

"I always pack a tripod when I take that lens."

"You caught him, Henry. Goddamn, you caught that bighorn like he really is."

Then Harley looked at the other photo. It was a picture of the river, taken from high up on the rim, looking downstream past a small waterfall to where the flow disappeared around the bend. A creek came into the picture, and into the flow from the south, just below the falls.

"When did you take this, Henry?"

"Last fall. But I just hung it up this week. Like it?"

Harley looked at the photo. Then he said, "You're the best, Henry." Harley looked at the life and the shadings of black and white and the composition of the photo for several more minutes. And then he said, "That's where Ocotillo Creek comes in."

"*Sí Señor*. And that's the box just below where the river hooks to the southwest. That's where they're going to build the dam."

"That's the place?"

"*Es cierto*. At the foot of the box. I had to have a picture of that before it's gone."

"You're the sheriff...stop them."

"I didn't get elected three terms as sheriff involving myself in local political hassles."

"Henry, I'd give anything if I could take a picture like that."

"Give it a try. You're out there enough. In the meanwhile, would you like a print?"

"That would make more sense than me trying to do it. That's the river you have there, Henry. That's the Río Jalisco. You got it, right there in that one picture. I've got to have one of those. I'll pay your price, Henry."

"Come by some day next week. I'll make a print for you. Don't pay me, Harley. Just stay out of my jail."

### Chapter 4

"**SORRY** mister, you're barred." It was Shirley, in no mood for nonsense.

"Barred? What the hell does that mean?" It was Harley, and he still hurt all over.

"It means, Harley, that you can't come in. The new boss has some new rules - no fights."

"Barred! Who has this place now?"

"Pearlmann."

"Sidney?...so that's why this place is done over. I know Sidney; he'll let me in."

"He told me, anyone who starts a fight is barred. You started a fight last night, mister."

"Sidney will let me in. Bet ya'."

Shirley took four dollars and checked four people into the Copper Room. Then she said, "Wait here Harley," and went around the corner and across the lobby and through a door marked Office. She came back with a small, bespectacled, balding and bookish looking man who nonetheless approached Harley with a firm and steady gaze.

"Harley, there's been some changes here."

"I see that. Looks pretty nice."

"In regards to you, the big change is, we no longer allow fighting on the premises. The only way to enforce that is to bar those people who precipitate any sort of violence."

"I've been out of town for a year. I didn't know this was your place."

"I can appreciate the fact that you were unaware of the new policy."

"Also, I promised the sheriff I was going to stay out of mischief."

"I'm going to let you in, Harley. But the first sign of any trouble and you're gone, and you won't come back."

"No trouble, Sidney."

Shirley said, "You got a dollar, Harley?"

Harley gave a dollar to Shirley. His sore ribs made it difficult to stand, so he went and sat down at a nearby table. He watched as Sidney Pearlmann went to the stage and spoke briefly to the Desert Wind band. Then Sidney Pearlmann came over to Harley's table and sat down. He signaled one of the waitresses, held up two fingers. She brought two bottles of a dark, rich, foreign beer, two glasses, and left. Sidney Pearlmann filled Harley's glass first, then his own. Then he turned to Harley and said: "Sorry if I sounded a bit like a school principal. Part of that was for Shirley's benefit. I don't want her getting soft on the policy here."

"I don't believe you have to worry about that, Sidney. She's got to wake up each morning rough as a cob."

"She's just what I need - a female bouncer. I had a big goon here for awhile. He started more fights than he stopped. Shirley gets right in their face and tells them to get out. And they do."

"Over the years, she's thrown me out of every place in town. I wouldn't argue with her for very long. How do you do this and teach business at the college at the same time?"

"I don't. This is it now. I taught business for 12 years and it dawned on me one day I'd never been in business. I'm in it now, up to my neck. I intend to make this a nice place once again. And I intend to make money. Probably not a lot, but enough."

"Where's the M-TV they used to have in the bar? And the heavy metal bands? This place had gotten to be a rock and roll club."

"No M-TV. No hard rock. I lost a few when I changed the format, but nobody I really wanted. And I picked up a lot more. Before I bought this place, I researched its history. The Copper Palace was built in 1897. It was frequented by horseback cowboys, hard-rock miners, a literate college clientele, and travelers that came in on the train. At the college museum I got the old photos of the place. I know now what the bar looked like, the restaurant, the rooms, lounge and dance hall. I'm working to recreate that. What you see here is very close to the original Copper Palace. The cafe is almost ready and we're renovating the rooms; then we'll have it."

"Sidney, I'll bet in 1897 there were lots of fights in the original Copper Palace."

"No doubt. That's one concession I'm making to the modern era. In that sense, this will not be a Wild West hotel."

"I like this band."

"We're going to play traditional country music here, some of it *ranchero* music from south of the border. On Sunday afternoons we let local musicians jam, so long as they don't play anything hard on my traditional ears. You'd be surprised at the jazz musicians, folk singers, and even classical musicians who have come out of the closet since we started that. There are people around here that can play and read music. Some of them quite good, too. We're going to encourage local artists and photographers to decorate our walls with their work. We're going to serve good food. We're going to present an ambience that's in keeping with the history of a fine old building. And we're going to have people coming downtown for their evening's entertainment once again. If I don't go broke first. As I said, I'm in up to my neck."

"That's good for you. If you don't go in deep, you won't hustle."

"Perhaps. Indeed, I have an entrepreneural theory along those very lines." Sidney Pearlmann raised his glass and took a healthy swallow. Then he said, "Harley, that magnificent wolf on the wall over the bar...do you know anything of the history behind that?"

"Some. My father killed him."

"I'd heard that. And I asked him about it. He was evasive on the subject. He said that was before his time."

"That *was* his time. He killed that wolf by himself. Had hounds of course, and a good horse to run the race. He started him at the headwaters of Ocotillo Creek. About sixteen hours later he killed him on Brushy Mountain. I think I've still got the old photo at home of the old man - he was young then - with that wolf slung over his shoulder. He was over six feet tall and that wolf made him look like a little kid. He talked around it later because he got to feeling bad after they were all gone."

"I know Brushy Mountain...at least I know where it is; you can see it from town. I've heard of Ocotillo Creek, but I can't place it."

"It's that steep canyon all over-grown in spruce and fir at the upper end that forms up on the north side of Engelmann Peak...you can see that from town too. The creek drops over four thousand feet by the time it gets to the river. There's quite a bit of desert vegetation at the lower end. They named it for what grows at the confluence, not the headwaters."

"Engelmann Peak is that prominent mountain just to the north that virtually watches over the town."

"That's right. It's not quite the mountain that Brushy is but it looks bigger because it's so close. You've got to get *into* Brushy to appreciate it. And it seems the further you get into it the bigger it gets."

"It's hard for me to conceive of a wolf living that close to town."

"This was all wolf country, right onto the desert. And Grizzly country too, till they drove them all down."

Sidney Pearlmann hesitated briefly and looked away while he recaptured a thought. Then he turned to Harley and said, "I recall now where I've heard of Ocotillo Creek. When they build the dam, the pipeline that will bring the water to town will run up Ocotillo Canyon. There was an article and a graphic in the paper to that effect last month."

Now it was Harley's turn to take a long swallow of beer. "I suppose," he said, "if they're going to build a pipeline to town it's got to come up one canyon or another. But they didn't have to pick Ocotillo Creek. Above five thousand feet, that's a wonderful trout stream. Those are wild trout in there; they won't stand that activity."

"The trout will be displaced, Harley. That was acknowledged in the article. But the dam and the reservoir and the pipeline and the water will put Del Cobre on the map. The Chamber of Commerce says so."

"Are you a member of the Chamber of Commerce?"

"I most certainly am. Now that I'm the proprietor of this hotel, commerce is my business, so to speak. As a member I didn't hesitate to voice my firm, albeit diplomatic, objection to the dam. I told them that Del Cobre's absolutely unique setting literally in the shadows of the wilderness was in the long run its greatest attraction and should not be compromised."

"And you're still a member of the Chamber of Commerce?"

"Oh yes. In as much as I'm the only member with such an opinion, they can afford to be indulgent."

"Sidney, is there a Chamber of Commerce, anywhere, that's ever any different?'

Sidney Pearlmann refilled his glass with a dark, rich foreign beer and considered it carefully before taking another swallow. Then he said, "You have touched on a subject very much in my thoughts the past few years. I have a theory on the matter which I used to incorporate into my lecture schedule at the college. To little avail, I might add. But you are a man who might find this pertinent. In summary form, the lecture goes something like this... As a town or city matures, it is not unusual for quality of life to become a concern of that communities' citizenry, and even to an extent its Chamber of Commerce. It's not unusual in the eastern states to find Chambers of Commerce which are quite progressive. Unfortunately, by the time that sort of enlightened viewpoint takes over, much of the quality, if you will, is gone. You end up preserving the remnants, rather than the essence. Within the town itself, restoration can often restore and remedy some of the loss. Many towns are happily at work trying to save or recapture some of their history. When the loss involves mountains, trees, wildlife, clean air, or, say, a wild river, it's often permanent. Here in Del Cobre, the business community is still very much in the grips of the Western Myth. It has nothing to do with cowboys and Indians, or the mountain man mystique, or wild rivers and wilderness, or wolves and Grizzly Bears. That part of the myth has evolved into something known as the Old West. Chambers of Commerce of course are in love with that crap. They promote it *ad nauseam*. If fact, most of what they promote is destroying what little of the Old West that remains. The Old West, if you will, has become a fantasy. The real Western Myth has been sadly distorted. It has been aberrated, and in its aberrant form it is still very much with us. You can see it, vividly, right here in Del Cobre; and that is the belief in unmitigated, unapologetic, unrelieved economic growth and development. That's the Western Myth today. You know what I mean, Harley. It's incredible what they've done to our regional heritage. You read the history books, and the accounts of the people who were there. Life on the frontier was essentially enterprise for the sake of adventure. Just being out there, being a part of it, was the prize. It was that sense of adventure that that era gifted to ours. Yet today, enterprise in the West is, with few exceptions, entirely for money. The Western Myth is off on a tangent. I'm continually distressed by the attitudes fostered by my colleagues in the business community here in Del Cobre. But I find it very hard to become truly angry. They're good folks. They're honest - most of them - they work hard, and they're hoping for a long and prosperous life, both for themselves and for the town. In that, they're a lot like us. The main difference is, they have no taste. End of lecture, in summary form."

"Sidney, you're a flat-ass genius. Such brilliant perceptions should be put in book form."

"Perhaps."

The Desert Wind band began to play. It was a good song and the lead singer even sounded a bit like Merle Haggard:

> *"The first thing I remember knowin',*
> *was a lonesome whistle blowin',*
> *and a youngin's dream of growin' up to ride,*
> *on a freight train leavin' town,*
> *never knowin' where I'm bound,*
> *no one could change my mind but mama tried..."*

Sidney Pearlmann said, "Harley, there are some things I have to do. We'll talk again."

"I believe we will."

Sidney Pearlmann wound his way through the incoming crowd and back around the corner to his office. Harley sat and nursed his beer and his sore ribs and his sore ear, and peered from behind his dark glasses that hid his sore eye, looking for single women. He had made a promise to the sheriff about fighting and, since talking to the sheriff, had made a promise to himself about getting drunk. He wasn't ready to make any promises to anyone about running women. There were some single women at the dance, though not as many as last night. Harley did not see Ellen and her wonderful ass. After last night, Harley did not figure he'd have much chance there again, whatever night it was at the Copper Palace. Harley drank his beer slowly through the first set, seeing little of interest and lacking the usual initiative of pursuit. At the break he went up to the bar, made some small talk and stood around while waiting in line for another beer. He took a bit of teasing about the fight, his dark glasses and his swollen left ear, and returned to his table.

Harley hadn't found anything by the time the band began their second set. He knew now he had no interest in being at the dance at all this night. But then he didn't want to go home, either. He was about to finish his second beer and he could feel just a little bit of a buzz coming on. He was a long way from drunk but he knew he was at the point where he was either going to stop, or he was going to drink till they shut the place down. Harley finished his beer with a long swallow and with considerable resolve got up and headed for the door. He was going by the bar when someone grabbed his hand and swung him around.

"Hey man!"

Harley recognized the face - a bit plain but always pleasantly animated, and the form - long and lean - but was slow with the name.

"Come on Harley. I let you copy off my chemistry final or you never would have graduated from high school."

"That was a lot of years ago."

"Well I remember."

"I remember too. It's all there except...Louise!"

"Lois; nice try."

"That's what I said...Lois. How's it going, Lois?"

"Should be great. I'm celebrating; my divorce came though this week. Me and my girl friends were planning a night out on the town but they all pooped out on me. So I'm getting drunk alone, and looking. You're the first interesting man has come in here." She reached up and removed his dark glasses. "Oh wow man! No wonder you're wearing dark glasses in the middle of the night. And look at your ear! I heard you gave it all back though."

"There were four losers in all. Lois, let's dance."

"Go for it, Harley."

He took her hand and led her to the dance floor and she immediately wrapped him up like she was a four-limbed vine. They slowly two-stepped around the floor.

"I'm pretty drunk," she said.

"That's all right. This would be the night for it."

"I hope so," she said. She was almost as tall as he and when she talked to him she could whisper in his ear and she clung tighter. Then she said, "You should be home nursing your wounds, honky-tonk hero."

"Honky-tonk fool. And I get restless evenings."

"Want some company?"

"Yes."

"Harley, let's get out of here, and go somewhere."

With a twang from the lead guitar and a deep low moan from the fiddle the band finished the song. She unwrapped her long limbs (Harley could already feel it; what she would be like) and hooked her arm through his as they left the dance floor, the lobby, and stepped out into the street. It was very cold and she clung close.

"There's two kids and a sitter at my place," she said.

"There's a fire in the wood stove and clean sheets at mine," he said.

"Let's go man."

She climbed into the drivers side of his truck and sat in the middle, her legs astride the four speed shift. He had to scrape some frost off the windshield to see to drive, then he got in.

"You got anything to drink?"

"I think there's a bottle of wine behind the seat."

"Well let's get it."

She leaned forward and he pulled the back of the seat up and reached behind the seat and pulled out the bottle of wine - red, cheap, and nearly full. She held it between her legs and he drove through town and every little bit she pulled the cork and took a short slug. Twice she passed him the bottle and said, "Go for it Harley," and twice he turned it down. Then she said, "I'm glad you're driving." The heater was warming up the cab of the truck and she was leaning against him as they left town and started up Gavilán Road.

"Harley, you know what I told my girlfriends?"

"What's that?".

"I told them I was due. I told them it was time for *me* now. I told them I was going to find the right man at the Copper Palace and I was going to get laid. They were going to come with me and help me pick one. Then they all pooped out on me. And then I was afraid I wouldn't find one, till I saw you. It's been months for me, Harley. I didn't dare. He was trying to get the kids. He would have used it against me in the divorce. He kept threatening me. He was vicious. Christ, I could write a book - *Ten Years With A Prick!* Every married woman in America would read it and it would be like I was telling her story. Think of all the women who would buy that book."

"A bunch, I imagine."

"You ain't shittin'. I guess I'd have to change the names and stuff. But it would be true fiction. I feel good; it's gonna be worth the wait. And there's nothing he can do. He didn't get the kids, and there's nothing he can do to me anymore. You're just the man to make me forget that bastard. My girlfriends, they'll all want to know who I got. And I'm going to tell them."

She began kissing his neck and she started to unbutton his shirt. She was working on the buckle of his belt when he drove into the yard. The headlights swung through the yard and briefly shown on Lurk, the hounds in the pen, two horses, and a big red mule leaning over the fence.

"This looks like your place, Harley"

He buckled his belt going up the steps and inside. The house had cooled down. There was enough light from the kitchen bulb that he found the wood stove in the living room and began to stoke it up. She stood beside him with one hand on his shoulder for balance and she started with her boots. One by one they thumped on the floor. Her pants and her panties came down while the wood went in and her sweater and blouse came up and off while the stove door was shut and the damper set. He turned around and she had come out of everything long and lean and white and she reached and started to unbuckle his belt. He took her by the hand and led her into the bed room; there he let her have the buckle, and the rest. And then they stood, facing off, and she had a hold of him with her long, slim, thoroughly expert hands.

"Harley, it's been such a long time for me."

"Yeah?"

"Really; it's been months. Has it been a long time for you?"

"Sure has."

"How long?"

"About a week."

"I bet that is a long time for you."

Her expert hands were working and she knelt down to them with further skills. He could hear what she was doing when she wasn't telling him all about it."

"Ah...that's a baby..."

"*Jesus!*"

"Comin' up...fast..."

"*Jesus H...*"

"Ah baby...nice one...you should be...proud!"

"*Christ!*"

She stood and took his hand and put it to the confluence of her lengthy thighs, already wet.

"He beat me, but he wouldn't fuck me. I need to fuck. You fuck me, Harley..."

Later in the night he came out of a deep sleep, aware of a restless bedmate.

"Harley?"

"Uh huh."

"You awake?"

"Sort of."

"Guess what...I think I could go again."

"Yeah?"

"Really. It's been a long time for me. What do you say?"

Harley didn't say anything.

"You're pretty tired, huh?"

"I didn't sleep much in that jail last night."

"It's okay. I'll get you again in the morning."

"That'll be nice."

But long before the sun came up he awoke once again. She was moving, and when she sensed he knew it, she stopped.

"Harley?"

"Uh huh."

"I really do need to go again. One more, just like the last one. What do you say?"

He rolled over onto one elbow, looked down at her and slowly stroked a finger along the bone between her small, hard breasts.

"Sure," he said. "That's what we're here for."

## Chapter 5

THE STREETS OF DEL COBRE were quiet. No one was cruising Ballard. The Copper Palace was closed. The businesses out on the strip would not open for another eight hours. You couldn't even buy a hamburger at the Heidi-Ho. Everyone it seemed was laying in on a Sunday night, getting a breather before Monday morning. Only the mines would be going now, and Harley, driving slowly and without firm motives through the streets. For the third night in a row he was unable to stay home alone.

It had started out a good Sunday. He had taken her home. She had said she would always remember their night together. He said he would always remember it, too. She said, "Call if you ever get lonesome," and ran across the street to her house. Home he showered and dressed in clean clothes and then he stepped out onto the porch. It was sunny and warming into a spring day. "Lurk, goddamnit!" Lurk sat on top of his house, waiting for a hunt. Harley sat in the sun for a while, on the porch. His ear felt better, his ribs felt better, and his eye felt better. His wounds *looked* a lot better, too. He sat and let the sun soak in. He recalled the urgency of Lois in the night. And in the morning she had gotten some healing creme from his medicine cabinet and had rubbed it into his sore back and ribs. She was grateful, and he was grateful too. He knew he would never be with her again. The sun felt good and he thought with some satisfaction that for the first time since he could remember he had gone out on a Saturday night without getting drunk.

The barn was a mess. Cleaning, sorting, arranging all the tools and the horse and mule paraphernalia that had accumulated from a time before he was born; that was a chore he had been putting off. He sorted all the tools, put them in a semblance of order so he'd have a chance of finding what he wanted when he needed it. He got the pack saddles and the snowshoes up off the floor. The pack saddles were okay but mice had gotten the old man's snowshoes. Harley hung them up anyway, just because they belonged. The old man's riding saddle had been left on the floor, too. It was a classic, a custom gem built strong and light for a hunter and of a turn of the century style, with a flat seat that put you right over the stirrups, and a high cantle. Harley took it out into the yard, hung it over the pasture gate, and worked saddle soap and then oil into the leather. With oil, the leather still had life; in the coming months he would work it again and again and it would come back. Harley knew he was going to ride it sometimes. But the old man had started to let things go; he wasn't even taking care of his saddle at the end which means he wasn't taking care of anything. And there were horse and mule shoes and all the farrier tools scattered around. Harley sorted them out and hung them up. Toward the end the old man just didn't care anymore. In the bunkroom at the back of the barn things were not so bad. Harley swept the floor in the bunkroom and picked the cobwebs off the window and out of the high corners. Sweeping under the bed he found the cardboard box full of letters and photographs. He took it inside and there went the rest of the day.

He went through everything though he knew what it all was - he'd seen it all before - but he couldn't help looking and remembering things from a long time ago. There was the stack of letters, the exchange of letters between his mother and his father after she had left. He could never bring himself to read them before and couldn't now. But he thumbed through them, looking at the addresses and the dates. His mother's address kept changing, and the dates got further and further apart. Finally, they just stopped. There was the picture of the old man with the big wolf. The old man was tall and young and strong. The wolf was slung over his shoulder just as he'd remembered and was wonderfully furred out and big enough that even a strong, young man would have a job hefting him like that. Two running Walkers and a big staghound were standing around in the photo and a horse that looked like he could run was looking into the picture from behind the old man. He found the photo of the old man and the big grizzly, the grizzly that was now the head mount and rug that covered most of the floor in the living room of his house. There was the old man - even younger then - with the bear, and the hounds, and a mule. The bear - just his hide and the head - was draped over a pack saddle and absolutely blanketed the mule. It had taken another trip with the mule and a horse to pack the meat out, the old man always said. In another photo his father stood with his arm around his mother and he was a little tot in her arms. She was a pretty Anglo woman, but with dark curly hair, brown as an Indian. She was pretty, and she was looking bewildered with her wide eyes going way beyond the camera, out to the great beyond. You could tell looking at the photo that she was going to run. She was a trick rider; time came and she went with the show. And the old man had saved a copy of the photo he had taken of Harley and Bonney and little Billy. They stood in the driveway of the house they had bought, that Bonney had wanted so much, in the Juniper Hills development (three acre "ranchettes" just five minutes from the IGA!) east and north of Del Cobre. Harley had lived there too, for a time, but it was never his home. In this picture Billy was just a tot. Harley held him, his son smiled, happily it seemed, and Harley was looking beyond the camera, out to the great beyond. You could tell he was going to run. Bonney was beautiful. These three photos were not in frames, but some of lesser interest that were also in the box, were framed. Harley removed those photos from the frames and put the wolf picture and the grizzly picture and the picture of his father and his mother and himself as a tot in frames and put them on the wall in the living room. There they joined other photos, all the old hunting pictures, of himself and the old man and all the hounds they'd owned and hunted with through the years, and the bear and lion, elk and deer, and other trophies of the hunt. The photo of his wife and his son he saved, but not where he would see it. He'd put that photo on the wall when it was time. He'd been all day dreaming through the afternoon as he went through everything in the box and by the time he hung the pictures on the living room wall it was supper time. There was always venison in the freezer and he fried a steak and potatoes and eggs and later in the evening with his father and mother and the wolf and the grizzly and all the hounds watching him from the wall he left the house and drove without clear motives through the town.

Inevitably, ineluctably, he was drawn from the downtown streets into the new roads and terraced landscaping of the Juniper Hills development. He turned back once. Then he came around again and finally made the turn up the long oval cul de sac, already within sight of a house where he had once lived. The porch light was on and also the light in the master bedroom on the southeast corner of the house. Everything else was dark in the house. The porch light showed that Billy's bicycle was parked at the foot of the porch steps. He recognized his wife's car, parked in the driveway. Another car, that he didn't recognize, was parked out in the street in front of the house. But he could figure it out. He drove slowly by and went to the end of the loop, stopped, turned around and came back. The porch light was still on. The light in the master bedroom was out. He drove slowly back to town, and drove around. In time, he parked across the street from Lois's home, turned off the engine, turned out the lights, and waited. There was no porch light here but someone was still up in one room, the front room to the left of the front door. Her children were young; they would not be up this late, not on a Sunday night with school in the morning. The light behind the shade was in Lois's room and Harley could see now that a television was on. Harley knew he could go to the window, tap lightly, say her name, and she would come to the window, scold him and then happily bring him in for the night. Harley turned the key and started his truck. He pulled slowly away from the house, then turned on the headlights. He slowly worked his way into a different neighborhood and began to climb the steep hill, driving up Mimbres Street. He had to shift down to top this hill in the old part of town. The old adobe and brick homes were dark. Near the deadend of Mimbres Street, at the top of Sonora Hill, he stopped in front of an old adobe, newly plastered in a white stucco with a fresh, dark coat of paint covering the trim around the windows, doors, and the porch. Here, too, only the porch light was on. He was quite sure no one was home but when he got to the front door, he knocked. He was quite sure, too, that the door was not locked. Getting no response, he opened the door and walked into the kitchen. He waited for his eyes to adjust to the dark and looked around. Everything was as he remembered it. The kitchen was neat as a pin, and the kitchen table was covered with the same bright print tablecloth, just like always. He stepped around the kitchen table, turned left and stepped down one step into the living room. At the far end of the living room the low blue flame of the space heater gave off a modicum of warmth and light. The full couch lay along the front window and as always there was a couch pillow and a large, wool Indian blanket at the end of the couch. Everything was as he remembered it. He sat down on the edge of the couch and took off his boots. He unfolded the blanket and lay down on the couch underneath the blanket with his head on the pillow. He watched the warmth and the blue glow of the heater at the far end of the room until he fell asleep.

*Chapter 6*

IN THE DARK of a moonless night, at the end of her shift, at the end of her week, the only light was provided by the machinery and the workings of the mine, which never shut down. She got used to working in the dark, and the harsh, artificial light, when she was on the night shift; she never, day or night, got used to the engine noise, the loud and constant and terrible whirring from her own machine, the big, Euclid haul truck. Suzie Navarro stepped out of the cab of the haul truck and started to back methodically down the ladder steps, the engine noise even louder now that she was out of the cab. She carefully and steadily stepped and gripped and stepped her way down. She was aware that the cab of the truck was nearly twenty feet off the ground and that she was sufficiently tired that she could fall. But her shift was over and she wanted it done. Below, the van waited at the Que-point; the next driver, ready to begin his shift, was at the foot of the ladder steps, waiting to take the truck. She knew he was watching her. She knew all the men in the van, coming to or leaving their shifts, were watching her; watching her strong, full figure - breasts and hips that even coveralls could not hide - as she descended. Usually, she hated their predatory eyes in the dark. But there were times when, weary to her bones, she could no longer care what they saw or thought. On the ground she left her haul truck to the next driver, walked over and got in the van. She took a seat by the window and dropped her hard hat between her feet on the floor of the van, bent over and rested her arms and her head on her knees. Her thick black hair fell over her face and knees, hiding her from the men, the mine, the world.

"*Qué pasó*, Suzie?"

"Don't worry about me."

She stayed hidden until the van had taken them to the gate. At the gate she left the van, checked out, and went out through the gate to her car. She drove out of the lot and up over the hill, as always with a parting glance at the pit as the road curved away towards Del Cobre. The pit had over the years swallowed a small town - Santa Clara - and the yawning gouge in the earth made the big Euclids working at the bottom look like the toys of a tot.

Suzie Navarro drove into Del Cobre, turned up Sonora Hill, going up Elder Street, and stopped in front of a dark, plain, brick house. She went to the door, quietly stepped inside, and walked to the front bedroom. She stopped at the open door and listened for the child, breathing in sleep. Satisfied, she stepped to the bed, sat on the edge of the bed, and put the back of her hand to her child's cheek, then her forehead. In time, the child opened her eyes.

"Mommy?'

"Yes."

"I been sleeping all night, mommy."

"Good. You're feeling better tonight."

"I think so. *Quiero agua.*"

Suzie went to the kitchen, got a glass of water, and brought it back to the bed. She helped the child sit up. Stopping several times to catch her breath, the child drank all the water, then lay back down on the pillow.

"Are we going home now, mommy?"

"No. You stay and sleep. Grandma will get your breakfast in the morning, then you can walk home."

"Last night I could hardly breath, mommy. Tonight I'm better."

"I know. You're breathing much better now. No more flu for you."

"Not till next winter, right mommy?"

"That's right. Now you go back to sleep."

She covered the child up with the quilts and waited until she was once again breathing in sleep. Then she returned the glass to the kitchen. Her mother called to her from the back bedroom.

"Suzie?"

"Yes."

"Jessica is much better. The fever is gone."

"I know. There's nothing to worry about now."

"*Qué hora es?*"

"Past midnight. You can send her home in the morning after breakfast."

"But you need to sleep. She can stay with me until the afternoon."

"Okay. But send her home right after lunch. I need to do some shopping in the afternoon and she can go with me. *Ya me voy.*"

Suzie Navarro left the house, got in her car and drove up Elder Street one block, turned right and went two blocks. As she turned left on to Mimbres Street, she saw Harley Simmons' pickup parked in front of her house. She pulled in behind the truck, set her car in gear, set the brake on the hill and killed the engine. Then, very quietly, she started to cry.

~ ~ ~ ~ ~ ~

He awoke and in the glow from the heater he saw her standing over him.

"Why have you come?' she asked. Before he could answer she said, "You can't be here anymore."

"I've always come here, whenever I wanted."

"That was before. I don't want to go through any of that again."

"I had to come here. Will you talk to me?"

"I'm tired, Harley...I'm so tired. I don't have anything for you. I don't have anything to say to you. I can't; I'm so tired. I want you to leave me alone."

"No you don't."

"Please, Harley..."

"Please what?"

"Damn you! I know why you're here. You've only come because you're having trouble with you're wife. I know that's why you've come. Like always."

"We're not having any trouble. We're not having anything. She's busy."

"So you want me as a replacement. Like always. I suppose I should be flattered I'm still her replacement. One of them anyway."

"You sound so wounded. It's not like you; you're always so strong."

"I'm not strong right now, not in any way."

"Sit down, Suzie. Talk to me."

She sat down then on the floor by the couch. She turned her back to the couch, leaned back against the couch, raised her knees and rested her hands and head on her knees. Her thick black hair fell again over her face. He reached and, briefly, put his hand on her bare neck.

"You're all in knots."

"So would you be, *señor*, working that truck for ten hours."

"Why do you do it?"

"How else can a girl with a college education make ten dollars an hour in this town? It's for Jessica, not for me."

"I know it. But it's got to be the last word in a horseshit job. How do you sleep, coming home from work all in knots?"

"Sometimes I don't."

"I don't sleep well either, since I've been back. I can't seem to be in that house, alone at night."

"You come back and you're father is dead and Bonney is with another man. So it's not surprising how you feel."

"I need to go to the mountains."

"You won't escape you're father in these mountains. He's been everywhere you could ever go. And you won't escape Bonney, being with me. I can't make you forget her. I've tried. You'll just get through all this, or not. Didn't you know she was seeing someone?"

"*Seeing* someone? You're too kind. She's *fucking* him; that's the thing."

"I'm sure she is. What did you expect?"

"I didn't know what to expect. But I had hopes. Still do."

"Fat chance, *señor*."

"Maybe. I suppose I'm lucky you're not *seeing* someone."

"What makes you so sure?"

She got no response to this.

"Since you're wondering, the answer is yes. But I stopped it. I have a daughter, and a job, and my free time - what there is - is for working on my house. I can't have a man in my life now. And that includes you, *señor*."

"Now you're sounding like yourself...strong, and tough."

"I've never been strong, or tough, where you're concerned. Or very smart either. If I was smart, nothing would have ever happened between us."

He reached over and put his hand on her bare neck. He began to work his fingers into the tight muscles of her neck. She stiffened; then, little by little, he could feel the tension start to go out of her neck.

"If we sleep together Suzie, we'll both sleep well. Like always."

"I can't sleep with you."

"Neither one of us has ever slept so well as with each other."

"It's true for me. But we can't."

"Yes we can."

He got up from the couch and came around and knelt before her. He began undoing the laces of her heavy, lug-soled work boots. He loosened the left boot and began to work it loose from her left foot. She did not object. And for the first time she smiled.

"Service," she said, her left foot now free.

"*Al servicio de la mujer*," he said.

"*Que bién*," she said.

"I want to spoil you."

"You want to go to bed with me."

"Is it working?" He slipped the other boot off.

"Maybe. It's nice. Feels good. You don't know how good that feels." She worked her ankles, stretched her feet and flexed her toes. "What are you going to do with my dirty socks?"

"Take them off."

"*Son feos.*"

"I don't mind; anything that's you is good to me." One by one he removed her socks and held her ankles in his hands. Then he massaged her feet with his hands. He took them one at a time and used both hands. She did not object. Then he stood and gently helped her to her feet.

"You could at least have picked a night when I'm not working. I haven't seen you in a year and now you see me in these filthy coveralls and all the dust in my hair and on my face."

He gently stroked a finger along her forehead and down her nose and the removal of the fine dust from the mines left a mark where his finger had been. He smiled at her.

"*Pareces bien*," he said.

"Do not! I'm the ugly duckling."

"I don't think so. Anyway, we can take these off." He began to unbutton the heavy metal buttons down the front of her coveralls. He opened them up, let them drop, and she stepped out of them. Then he helped her remove the heavy wool shirt and baggy jeans and, finally, her long underwear.

"It must be like undressing a man," she said. "I hate having to dress like a man. I would like to be pretty for you."

Then she was naked and he said, "You are pretty for me. And you sure don't look like a man."

He touched her ample breasts and she watched and then she looked up at him.

"Why didn't you write to me, Harley? I missed you so much! You could have written something, just once, so I could know if you were even alive."

"I didn't write to anyone. I didn't want anyone to know if I was alive."

He got the big Indian blanket off the couch and spread it out on the rug in front of the fire.

We can't make love yet," she said. "I need to take a shower; I've been sweating."

"*No le hace*," he said. "You're ripe; you're beautiful."

He took her hand and lay her down on the blanket. Quickly, he took off his clothes and then he knelt over her. He rolled her onto her stomach. Then he spread her legs and knelt between them. He reached up and began to work strong fingers into her neck, shoulders and back. He took his time, feeling for every muscle, not moving on till he'd taken the tension out of each. Slowly he moved down, taking the tension out; he could feel the muscles relax - her neck, shoulders and back; her magnificent ass, hips and thighs; her calves and feet.

"You *are* pretty for me."

"Thank you," she said.

"How do you feel now?"

"Like a pile of pudding. Like a horny jellyfish."

He rolled her over. He kissed her. First her mouth. Then all of her, coming down. He took his time; he missed nothing. At the last she raised her legs, spread, her knees to her breasts, offering everything he wanted to his lapping tongue and he wouldn't quit till he'd stretched her come to the very last; fluttered, dissolved, all gone. Then he was on her, in her, she wrapped him up as he pumped and quivered, groaning as he let everything go from a long way off within her supple brown thighs.

In the night when she awoke she realized that's how they had fallen asleep.

"Harley, lie beside me now."

He took his weight from her, never leaving her. She reached and pulled the flap of the big blanket around them, making their cocoon. Holding closely to their warmth, they finished the night in perfect sleep.

In the morning, sunlight came through the window and the cocoon began to unfold.

"Oh Harley, the things we do! I've never been so open with anyone."

"*Igualmente*. One of these mornings we're going to wake up and we won't be able to look each other in the face."

"Like that time down along the river.

"Yes."

"I was ashamed the next morning."

"But you liked it."

"That doesn't matter. It wasn't right. It wasn't what we did; I could do anything with you, more than your wildest dreams, if it was right between us. But part of you isn't with me. When I know you're all with me, then you'll see."

"We slept well."

"Yes. Like always."

"I could lie around on this blanket with you for the rest of the day."

"No you're not. I am going to take a shower. Now."

He watched her stand and walk to the bathroom. Then he followed.

~ ~ ~ ~ ~ ~

In the kitchen, he made the coffee and she made the breakfast: chorizo sausage, and fiery salsa covered the eggs and with quick practised hands she flopped the hot tortillas over the burner until, browning but not quite crisp, she added them to their plates. He poured the coffee and they sat down to breakfast.

"Harley, have you seen Bonney?"

"No."

"Have you seen your son?"

"No."

"Well?"

"There's plenty of time."

"Time for what?"

"To put it back together."

"And meanwhile you expect to sleep with me whenever you feel like it."

"Not if you don't want me to."

"Of course, leave it up to me. That way, if she takes you back and I'm left in the night with empty hands, it's my own fault. *Qué no?*"

Briefly he looked up from his plate, but he didn't answer.

"Do you ever wonder why I put up with it?"

"Yes."

"Why don't you ask me why?"

"I don't like to delve into things."

"Well I'll delve into this for you. I know what you're doing, because I did it too."

Again he looked up from his plate without comment.

"I held on to David...tried at least...long past when I knew there was no hope. He would come by sometimes at night and I would let him in. Because we'd been happy once. And because of Jessica. He was her father. He's not anymore. That's why I took my name back, and gave that name to Jessica. I insisted. But for a long time, I hoped something would work out for her sake. Children needs parents; not just one. Some of my friends have told me not to worry about her. They say there's school and day care and what they call *shared parenting* and *quality time*. I don't even think they believe it. Because it isn't true. Children need a mother and a father; they need parents. *Necesitan los dos*, and they need to spend time with them, as much as possible. But it seems there is no one to show us how to live anymore. My grandparents were together to the end. For them, there was no doubting that. But my father left my mother. Your mother left your father. David left me and Jessica. You left your wife and son. Where is there an example today, of how it should be done? I can't believe it should be done the way we do it now. I know that Jessica should have a father. So I tried with David. I made a fool of myself trying. I was a fool because I knew myself we weren't right. It just wasn't there. The difference is, *señor*, that I didn't keep someone else on the side to help me over the bumps."

"*Es que tu quieres.*"

"I want to be with you. With you it feels right. It makes sense. I want you to be with us. I want to be with you, Harley."

"I want to be with her."

"You don't even like her. You're obsessed with her."

"Maybeso."

"And she doesn't like you, either. You're perfect opposites. Whatever it is that attracts you two to one another, is founded on conflict. That's not love. It's not even friendship. It's hardly normal."

"Could be. I can't change what I want."

"Because, of course, you don't want to change...did you know that I knew her before you did?"

"No, I didn't know that."

"She was in one of my psychology classes at the college. I didn't get to know her well but I talked with her a few times. I was envious. Later I was jealous. She was always so beautiful, and slender, and she always dressed so nice. She really does know how to dress. I always felt like such a peasant. And she was so...unto herself. They said she was stuck up. She was friendly to me. She certainly knew she was the attraction wherever she went. She will never want a man as much as the man will want her. That's the way she likes it. A woman like that will drive a man mad. You'll never have her, Harley. Not like you want. But you'll always want to try."

"And I want my boy."

"I can understand that, more than the other. When I go to pick up Jessica, I see him sometimes in the school yard."

This time when he looked up from his plate he said, "Tell me."

"He remembers me. But he's very shy. He looks for me, but when he sees me he won't wave. I wave and then he waves back. And he has a big smile. He's a fine looking boy."

"He's in the third grade now."

"Yes, one ahead of Jessica. She's shy too, at school. But around here she never stops chattering."

"We're like a couple of housewives at the laundromat, talking about their kids."

"It's only natural."

"I hope he's doing well at school. He was before."

"He *is* doing well, Harley."

"How do you know?"

"I know his teacher, Mrs. López. I asked for you. She says he's very studious."

"Studious? I don't want him too studious. He needs an education. But there's another education, outdoors, he needs too. He ought to have that opportunity. Who's going to teach him that?"

This time she had no response. She gathered up the plates, slicked off the table and did the dishes. Harley went to the living room with his coffee and when she was done she came to the living room and took him by the hand and said, "Harley, let me show you what I've been doing with my house."

She led him by the hand through the house into the back yard. There was a room under construction coming off the master bedroom and the beginnings of a wall around the yard. The room was nearly completed. The room was quite large, constructed of adobe bricks and the *vigas* spaced along the ceiling were in place and enough of the beehive fireplace was completed that it was clear what it was going to be. The ambience of the room had been established. Harley walked the room and the yard and went to the outside wall of the house and put his hand on the new plaster.

"This stucco makes the whole house look new," he said. "Nice job. But I had no idea you were building."

"The plaster was the easy part. Not much trick to that; just hard work. But building is all learning for me. This room will be like a den, but it's going to be my little home within the house. It's solid as the earth, just like the rest of the house, and sound and warm with the fireplace and the vigas to make it feel right for me. And it will be bright with sunlight with nice windows looking out onto the *placita*. At least it will be a *placita* when I finish the wall and plant the desert plants and lay the brick walkways."

"I didn't know you knew how to do this. I'd be hard pressed to start a beehive fireplace myself."

"My uncle knows. He gets me started, then I go till I get stuck, then he gets me started again. There are so many old homes like this in the old part of town. They could be restored. And new ones could be built in the old way. That's what I'd like to do. And someday I will."

They returned to the kitchen and sat down again at the kitchen table.

"Well?" she said.

"I'm impressed," he said.

"Thank you. When the mines play out, or when I play out at the mines, I hope to be ready to do this. Do you think I can ever do it well enough to make a living, enough for me and Jessica?"

"Sure you can."

"Then I could stay here. I don't want to ever have to leave."

"You can't leave here, anymore than I can. And I tried."

"I knew you'd be back. *Es su querencia.*"

"*Querencia?*"

71

"I don't think it has an English word. It's like your home. Only it's more than a home...it's like the place where you have roots."

"*Raices.*"

"*Sí. Tu tienes raices aqui.* Harley, do you remember when you left I asked you, I said, 'Harley, will you promise to come back?' and you said, 'Will you promise to be here when I come back?', and we both made that promise. Well, I believe someday we will say those things to each other and it will mean something, it will be more than just something sweet that we say."

"Maybeso. Suzie, can I come and see you again?"

"*Es que tu quieres. Aqui tu tienes un amigo.*"

He got up from the table and went to the stove, poured her another cup of coffee, then himself, then returned the coffee pot and sat down.

"I know it," he said.

## Chapter 7

MONDAY MORNING and in spite of himself Harley Simmons was on his way to the bank. Like Alvin H. Simmons, A. Harley Simmons never had much use for banks. He did like having money in his pocket. Cash money. The more the better. Most enjoyable were those times, increasingly common, when the bills would come in the mail saying, "Send check or money order; DO NOT SEND CASH." Of course, Harley Simmons always sent cash. No one had ever turned it down. As well, Harley Simmons preferred to be paid in cash. He always asked to be paid in cash, but sometimes he got a check anyway. Then, like it or not, he had to go to the bank.

Monday morning there were lots of people in the bank and Harley got in line for one of the bank tellers. When his turn came he handed the check to the teller and said, "Stacy, I need to cash this."

The teller gave the check the once over and said, "Harley, we'll need to send this for collection."

"What for?"

"It's a personal check, it's an out of state check, and it's for forty one hundred dollars. We'll have to send it out."

"It's a good check. That guys' the most honest fur buyer in the Southwest. Probably the only one. It'll clear."

"Sorry Harley. A check like this will have to go for collection."

"How long will that take?"

"A week to ten days."

"That's too long. They'll be after me by then. Call the bank. Check it out."

"We might be able to do that. I'll have to ask one of the officers."

"Go ahead. I'll pay for the call."

Harley watched as Stacy turned around and headed for one of the offices behind the counter. Behind the glass partition was a man behind a desk and the sign on the desk said Executive Vice-president. Stacy had just handed the Executive Vice-president the check when Harley heard the teller at the next window say "Bruce," and she turned around and waved a piece of paper in the air. In response, a man came out of the office next to that of the Executive Vice-president and approached the teller. Through the glass partition the sign on this man's desk said: Bruce Billings Jr. - Business Manager. He was a slim young man of middling height, wearing slacks, a slim tie and white shirt; well groomed, well dressed, longish hair precisely coiffed. He was immaculate. More than that, he appeared to Harley to be very clean. Harley thought he had to be one of the cleanest men he'd ever seen. He took the sheet of paper from the teller and, despite his obvious youth, took a pair of horned-rimmed glasses from his white shirt pocket and put them on. He briefly considered the sheet of paper before quickly flourishing his initials across the bottom. Then he handed the sheet of paper back to the teller, smiled pleasantly, returned his glasses to his shirt pocket, and returned to his office. Harley was still watching as the young man sat down in a swivel chair in front of a screen on his desk that looked to Harley a lot like a TV set. He began to rapidly punch a keyboard that sat in front of the screen. As if by magic, a graph appeared on the screen. The young man considered the graph for a time and then began punching the keyboard again. His hands were very fast. The graph, slightly altered, appeared again. Then the young man hit several more buttons on the keyboard and, as if by magic, a sheet of paper came pumping out from a square, flat-topped box next to the screen and keyboard. The paper landed in a little tray and the young man picked it up, put his glasses back on, and looked it over. Faintly, he smiled the satisfied smile of one who has just gotten a good response from a user-friendly machine.

"Harley." It was Stacy.

"Right."

"Mr. Staman made the call. It's OK. Now, you want this cashed?"

"Right. Twenties."

"Twenties? I'll give you what I can."

It held up the line for a while but the teller went through the bank and came up with a pile of twenty dollar bills plus a few fifties and hundreds that made forty one hundred dollars.

"How much for the phone call, Stacy?"

"That's all right, Harley."

"Sure?"

"That's perfectly all right."

Harley left the bank, got out into the traffic on the Cooke City Highway, and headed for downtown. He parked his pickup downtown in front of the Copper Palace and walked across the street to City Hall. Having discovered that while he was gone for a year the town of Del Cobre had lengthened its boundaries north up Gavilán Road to the forest boundary, Harley was now due to pay the city property tax. The tax, so far, wasn't much different from the county tax that preceded it. And Harley had the money in his pocket to pay the tax. He used a few of his twenties and paid in full. As he turned to leave he noticed the large display of the Río Jalisco Dam and Reservoir set up in the middle of the lobby of the City Hall. It was a relief map with raised mountains and indented canyons and it displayed the south end of the Jalisco National Forest and surrounding countryside, including Del Cobre. The reservoir centered the map, filling the main canyon of the Río Jalisco and fingering up into all the side canyons along the way. The reservoir was bright blue, the mountains were green. The proposed roads, to the damsite, and to the marina, campgrounds and resort at the Ocotillo Creek confluence, and the pipeline up Ocotillo Canyon, were there. Harley noted that the road to the marina, campgrounds and resort was an extension of Gavilán Road, and that, deep in the mountains, a spur off that road went west, out the Gunsight Trail to civilization.

"You have to admit it, Harley Simmons, it's pretty impressive."

"So was Trinity Site, Jim Bo Moreland, but do we want it in our back yard?"

Harley turned and shook hands with a middle-aged man who was as tall as himself. Unlike himself, the man was portly, by way of being somewhat pear-shaped, with a face of a pink complexion topped by a thick shock of well manicured gray hair. His eyes were a noticeable bright blue; and, if you were observant, you noticed they seldom blinked. Some other people that Harley knew were behind Jim Bo Moreland, filing out of the mayor's office and headed out the door. With a wave or nod Harley acknowledged: Garth Bilker, paunchy and pugnacious; Dirk Johngood, elderly, quiet and competent; Stew Mayfair, essentially a follower, always wanting to be liked and not always succeeding; Morey Solís, much the same, being Mayfair's Spanish speaking counterpart on the County Commission; Stan "Bubba" Baer, Stetson, boots, and a smile of overweening self-confidence - the quintessential good ol' boy. The men were soon out the door, leaving Harley with Jim Bo Moreland.

"This is what I want to talk to you about, Harley." Jim Bo pointed his finger at the marina, resort and campgrounds at the Ocotillo Creek confluence. "Come on into the Mayor's Office."

Harley followed Jim Bo and his creme colored polyester slacks, beige polyester sport coat and bright print shirt into the Mayor's Office. Harley took a seat. The Mayor poured them each coffee and sat down on the other side of the desk. Then he looked across his desk at Harley and smiled. His blue eyes, which seldom blinked, never left their target.

"Harley Simmons," he said. "Last of the mountain men."

"That was my daddy."

"That *was* your daddy. Now it's you. They all say it Harley - you know the out-of-doors."

"I make a living at it."

"I know you do. That's what impresses me. You hunt, fish, trap, and you're a guide and outfitter. There's a few others who are something like you, but they don't have your style. They're pretenders. You're successful. You've got some money, Harley, I know damn well you do. It's not in our bank...wish it was...but I know you've got some money put away."

"I usually manage to stay a little ahead."

"I believe it. And you've got a hundred and sixty acres that's prime, brother; I mean prime. You've done good Harley, but I'm here to let you know you can do better. A lot better. Now what I'm going to tell you, I know you won't say yes. Just don't say no. Just hear me out. You'll have a year to think it over and respond. Harley, we're going to build a dam. Like it or not brother, it's gonna be there. I've got the option on that resort and campgrounds and marina. I've got money waiting to spend and I've got backers. We're holding nothing back. It's going to be *the* place in southwest New Mexico. The easy part is finding some wimp to run the lodge and restaurant, some faggot to sweet talk the old folks and manipulate the tourists and steer the help around. The hard part is finding the right man to run that marina and the stables and all that goes with it. Someone who can guide the fisherman, and the hunters, and lead the pack trips and trail rides. And who can train others to do it. There will be bass and trout tournaments on that lake; someone who knows what they're doing has got to run the show. You're the man Harley. You're my man. I'll pay you good. Just don't say no."

"No."

"Harley, I think you're smarter than that. Now some of the boys, they were telling me that you're going to line up with those bleeding hearts trying to stop the dam. I told them you were too smart for that."

"I'm not going to line up with anybody. I don't much like those people. But I don't much like you either, Jim Bo; I don't like what you're trying to do."

"All right Harley, let's dust this one off. I'm the mayor of this town. That means I'm in a real sense responsible for the welfare, and the future, of ten or twelve thousand people. And more to come. I don't feel like I was elected to try and build a wall around Del Cobre. Believe me, there isn't a town in the Southwest with the potential of this little town. And with the lake and the water, there's no limit to what we can do. These mines have twenty, maybe twenty five years at most. Then what? Do we let this town just dry up and blow away? Water is the key to growth in the Southwest; you know that. Now is the time to plan a future that will allow us, and our children, the opportunity to stay here, to live and grow with the town. The Río Jalisco Dam is the key to that future. And for me, it's a personal challenge. Harley, I grew up in a little ol' West Texas town. That town prospered with a short term oil and gas boom but by the time I was twenty, the boom was over. And there was nothing to take it's place. I had to leave my own home town to find work. I went to Phoenix and I got in on a boom that will never end. Because Phoenix is always looking ahead, planning for growth. It's soon to be one of America's great, great cities. I was essentially retired in Phoenix; I'd made my fortune. But I could never be satisfied with that. So I came here, and I couldn't believe what I'd found. This community has advantages of climate and location, for tourism and retirees and new industry, that no town in the Southwest can match. And yet it's stagnated for generations. Again, the dam is the key. We get that and then we go. I'm all for conservation, Harley. Hell, I'm a conservationist, too. I used to hunt some. And I still like to fish now and again. I love the outdoors. When I see wildlife, a deer or an eagle or something like that, I get as big a kick out of it as anyone. I'm well aware what a wonderful country this is, and of all the wildlife around here. That's one reason I came here. But, in this case, the needs of wildlife are going to have to give some to the needs of people. Harley, there's half-a-million acres up around the headwaters that will always be there. Congress designated that a wilderness and even I wouldn't want to change it. But below, in the lower canyon, that's a no-man's land. So we provide some access into what?...a few hundred thousand acres that nobody even knows about and fewer still have ever visited. And a no-man's land becomes a recreation area. What's wrong with that?"

"If it's water you want, Jim Bo, why not go after Felps-Dodd? Everybody knows the mines have more water than they know what to do with."

"Harley, let's not be naive. Everybody also knows that this town is not going to take on the corporation that employs half the people in the county. And that's ground water. You don't promote growth with ground water. Not like you can with a lake. Felps-Dodd has got their water, now we're going to get ours. I repeat: what's wrong with that?"

"I guess I haven't got a routine to match you, Jim Bo. I'm not practiced at this. Frankly, I don't spend much time worrying about the human race, other than to worry about what they're doing to the rest of the world. Judging from the way the population is growing, here and elsewhere, the human animal is doing pretty well. People can look after themselves, and there's plenty like you who think they're helping them. Meanwhile, there's one piece of territory left in the whole Southwest that's big enough and wild enough that it's worth calling a wilderness. And now you're telling me we ought to be pleased to see the best part of it sliced away. Sure, you're a conservationist. I've never heard anyone stand up and say outloud they're not. Certainly not a politician. And then comes the disclaimer. And there goes another mountain, or river, or some critter that we'll never see again. The history of the depletion of wild country in this century is littered with the caveats of living room conservationists like you Jim Bo, who love the outdoors but love money more. And what's left of the wild goes down, piece by piece. But what's the choice? Either you guys get it, and it's dams and roads and four-wheel drives and power boats, or it fills up with birdwatchers and environmentalists and yuppie backpackers and all their flossy ways. One way, it's a playground. The other way it turns into some kind of park. It's a horse apiece. Either way, it's a long way from the frontier."

Jim Bo was smiling, and his blue eyes were still on target. "That's not bad Harley. I'd be lying to you if I said you didn't have a point. But I'll say again, we can't build a wall around the place. It's coming Harley, and a smart man is going to get in on it. With me, you'll have an outdoor job. And those environmentalists will never pay you what I can. I'm talking bucks, Harley. I'm talking about paying a man who can do the job. Just don't say no. Once they start construction, about this time next year, I'll take you out to lunch and we'll get down to business. We can even talk about giving you a piece of the action. Just don't say no."

"I have nothing to say to you, Jim Bo."

"That's fine. That's just fine, Harley. Don't say anything. I knew you wouldn't be easy. I'd be disappointed if you were. Time comes, we'll talk some more."

Harley finished his coffee, stood and shook hands with Jim Bo Moreland. He left City Hall, went across the street and put a coin in a pay phone.

"Ted...we need to run that river."

"I'm with you partner."

"You-all settled in yet?"

"We're closing in on it."

"Me too. There's a few things yet. I've got to make one more trip to Arizona and get the rest of my stuff. Mostly that canoe. How about a week from today? During the week there's likely nobody going to be in there."

"I'll be ready. We'll go Monday week and we'll come out when we damn well feel like it."

"That could mean we'll never come out at all."

"Whatever. I'll see you, Harley, next Monday morning. We'll run it."

## Chapter 8

THE OLD PICKUP rattled, bucked and groaned over the meager forest road, growling with real strength in the lower gears going up the steep slopes, brakes squalling coming down the slopes, the early morning sun sifting through the pines and a bluebird early morning sky above. Harley Simmons artfully steered, shifted gears, and drank coffee as they went along. A small, lithe, tri-colored hound lay sleeping, in spite of the racket, on the seat, her head in his lap. At the other window Ted Beeler poured from the big thermos jug whenever either man got low.

"Nice of the Forest Service to help us with the shuttle," Harley said.

"I told them this was a working trip, which it is, and that you're helping out as part of the biological team, which you are. Sometime tomorrow they'll pick your truck up and they'll leave it downriver at Gunsight for whenever we get out."

Ted picked up the newspaper that lay in his lap and between gulps of coffee looked again at the feature story that covered the top of the fold. The editor of the Del Cobre *Region*, Rich Pennerman, had written the article himself. The headline across the page read: ALVIN H. SIMMONS - LAST OF THE MOUNTAIN MEN. Under the headline, an underlined subheading read: *Local Legend Passes On.*

"Pennerman did a nice job with this, Harley."

"Yeah, he did...got to hand it to him. When he's not just a shill for Felps-Dodd, he can put words together. Pennerman could write a good book, if he wasn't so busy waving the corporate flag."

"Says here that A. Harley Simmons, the mountain man's son, was unavailable to comment on his father's career."

"Pennerman's being nice. Fact is, I had no comment. But I did loan him the photo."

The photo was below the fold. It was the picture of the old man, the hounds, and the big wolf.

The old truck rattled to a stop at the trailhead that led off down a long slope to Mondragón Creek. Harley placed the keys under the mat and got out and helped Ted unload the canoe. All their gear, except their fishing rods, was stowed away in two large, heavy backpacks. Harley shouldered his pack, picked up his fishing rod and prepared to get under one end of the canoe. But Ted, who had shouldered his pack too, squatted down by the center of the canoe and, moving smoothly and with the great power of a Cinnamon Bear, hefted the canoe and turned it over his head where it came to rest, upside down, on his shoulders.

"You carry the fishing rods," Ted said.

It was nearly a mile down the switchback trail to the creek. About halfway there Harley said, "Ted, you want me to take that for awhile?"

"No."

The creek, swollen with snow melt, announced itself with the sound of rushing waters and then they could see the flow in the canyon below bouncing white and winding smoothly over and around the rocks. At streamside they placed the packs for and aft; the hound hopped into the middle. Ted took a paddle and balanced his way out to the front seat.

"Let's see if this thing will float us all," he said.

Harley pushed off, swung into the boat and put his paddle quickly into the flow to grab control of the current. Even with the good spring run-off the creek was marginal for floating. They got out twice to ease the boat over the shallows. But three miles from the put-in they were carried from Mondragón Creek into the main flow of the Río Jalisco. The flow was ever swift. The paddles were required for steerage, not to make time. The rapids, nicely spaced, came every few hundred yards, rushing white whenever the course narrowed, providing sport for canoeists and absorbing oxygen for catfish, bass and trout. Neither the quantity of the flow nor the hydraulics of the rapids were awesome. The treachery for the canoeists was in the boulders that rose just above, or held just below, the waterline, and the twisting course of the river. Meanwhile, the mountains rose on either side, the slopes came down to the beaches. Ponderosa covered the shady slopes; piñon/juniper the sunny sides; oak, walnut and hackberry fingered up the side canyons; and then they slid swiftly and silently under and through a canopy of cottonwood and sycamore, just leafing out.

"Jesus!" Ted said.

"Jesus Christ!" said Harley.

Several miles below the Mondragón Creek confluence Ted motioned with his paddle to a level, grassy, well shaded bank on the north side. Harley levered the canoe over; Ted hopped out and pulled the boat ashore.

Ted said, "I'm going to have to inventory everything I can see, hear or find, every few miles. Especially, this first stop; after this there'll be lots of repetition. Anyway, we might just as well make our first camp here."

The hound, Geraldine, hopped out and began to nose her way upstream. Harley hauled the packs over to the shade of a big cottonwood while Ted opened the cap of the metal rod case and slid his fly rod out into his hand.

Harley said, "I thought you had work to do?"

Ted smiled. "Just one trout and then I'll be fine."

Ted got a streamer from his fly box. He tied it on, went to the bank, stripped out line and with considerable grace worked the line out into a series of false casts. The line went out and came back in large, flowing loops with a complimentary *whisk whisk* sound in company. In control, Ted finally lofted the streamer out into the current. He waited, then drew the fly back up and through and across a stretch of whitewater and promptly came up tight to a fish. Meanwhile, Harley was assembling his own fly rod, not with a fly but with a hook which he skewered into a big, nasty looking helgramite he had just got out from under a rock. He lofted the live bug out and let it drift naturally down through the white water and into the pool below the rapids. By the time Ted's fish had fought the line down out of the fast water and into the upper end of the pool, Harley, at the lower end of the pool, was into a fish of his own.

Ted's fish flashed all the colors of the rainbow. He leaped three times before he came peacefully into the bank. Harley's stout green fish jumped twice, then bored in under the overhanging bluff at the far side of the pool. It was still working the whippy fly rod as Harley worked it ashore.

Ted put the Rainbow Trout in a small pool off the river. Then Harley's smallmouth went in there too.

Ted said: "I'm satisfied...for now."

"I'm not," Harley said. "I've been too many days in town."

"You go ahead and fish. I won't be needing your help with anything until maybe late in the day."

Harley went off downstream, followed by the hound. Ted went to work.

He walked upstream and periodically worked from the streamside back across the benches through the riparian to the edge of the slopes. He crossed the river twice, using a staff to help balance and picking his crossings carefully. The flow was icy and strong and he could just make it. He entered two side canyons and went well up these defiles. He took his time wherever he went, jotting down every species of plant that passed his eye. He took pictures of several. At times he raised his binoculars and recorded the sighting of birds. He recorded the presence of many other birds by sound. He noted tracks on the beach and where patches of sand spotted the floor of the rock canyons. When he got back to camp there was a large channel catfish in the pool with the bass and the trout and Harley Simmons and his hound dog were asleep under the cottonwood. Ted untied the seine that was strapped to his pack and Harley woke up.

Ted said, "You still like your *siesta*."

Harley said, "It lets me stay up late and wake up early; an hour's sleep in the afternoon is worth a lot."

"Take one end of this seine; we're going to find out what lives in this river."

They waded upstream, taking the warm sun on their backs and the cold water on their legs, and drew the fine mesh net through pools, riffles, over rocks and sand, periodically drawing the bow of the net ashore to check the catch. Larger fish escaped but the young of Brown and Rainbow Trout, Smallmouth Bass and Channel and Flathead Catfish appeared at different times in the seine.

Harley said, "Where else can you find this variety of game fish in one stretch of river?"

80

"No place else that I know of."

They also recovered carp, several kinds of suckers and a variety of minnows. Recalling those days when he casually sought an education in wildlife, Harley put each type of minnow in his hand one by one, before tossing them back in the stream. Some he could identify; others he'd forgotten. Ted made notations of everything.

"What are we looking for, Ted?"

"Whatever's here. What I'd like to find is something that's not supposed to be here. Something really unusual."

"As in rare and endangered?"

Ted smiled but otherwise did not respond.

An hour later, with most of the river bottom now in shade, they rolled up the seine and walked back to camp.

At camp Ted said, "We've got just enough sunlight left here that we can dry off before it gets really cold."

Harley said, "How long's it been since we ate?"

"Seems like we forgot lunch. I'm hungry. Skin those fish and I'll get the fire going."

They fried the catfish and the bass and the trout and ate big; there was plenty left for the hound. They drank coffee for an hour afterwards; it got cold and the fire was the only light in the canyon and the flowing river was a continual music in their camp. Then Ted reached into his pack and pulled out a bottle. He poured a first class liquor into the cups, giving the coffee some bite.

"Well," Ted said, "I can tell you we haven't found anything really unusual yet."

"What are the chances?"

"Don't get your hopes up. Paul Thurman and his crew from State did this whole drainage not five years ago. *The ecological diversity is without parallel*, is what he wrote in his report. But he didn't find anything in particular that would make the papers."

"I imagine Moreland and them are aware of that. He's drooling anticipation; he can see it happening, like it was already here."

"You talked to him?"

"Yeah. And he offered me a job."

"The hell you say!"

"The hell of it is, I didn't absolutely turn the son-of-a-bitch down."

"Don't. If that dam goes in, you might just as well learn to get along with it. Moreland is crude, mercenary and slippery, but he's not cheap. That might not be a bad job."

"I suppose I should be flattered. It's not every day an anachronism is offered a salaried job. But I've had this thought Ted, that what I'd really like to do is strap on my single action .357 some morning, saddle my horse and ride into town and call Moreland out into the street. He'd be armed, I'd give him the jump, and when the smoke cleared, we'd know if that dam ought to be built, or not. Only something tells me I missed that fantasy by three generations."

"At least. And it wouldn't do any good. There's a shitpot full ready to take his place, funded by the government, whipped on by politicians like Garner Greane. You could just as well take that tin cup over to the river there and try to scoop it dry."

"We're outnumbered."

"Not necessarily. But for whatever the reason, we tend not to be in positions of power, economically or politically." Ted tossed a stick on the fire. Then he said, "Are you doing okay for money, Harley? There will be some recompense for your help here."

"I'll take it. But right now I've got a pocketful. And when that runs out I know how to get some more. I've already got some fishermen lined up for the summer and one bear hunter coming in late next month."

"How much do you lack for your degree?"

"Nine hours."

"I didn't know you were that close. How about going to work for the Department? This part time job could become a full time job. In one semester you'd have your degree. I know I could get you on. You'd have to work some in enforcement to start with. But with your experience you'd be under me in biological services before long and you'd only have to be a game cop every now and then. Pays not bad. Good vacations. All kind of benefits."

"I might," Harley said. "But in any government job I'd be under orders. Your orders would be okay. But who knows who'd be above us ordering us both around? I'd almost rather work for Moreland. He knows if he hired me he'd have to let me pretty much run the show. I think you're thinking that I'm eventually going to have to start living different than I do now. You may be right."

"If you've got any hopes of getting Bonney back, you're going to have to change your ways. How's it going, with Bonney?"

"It isn't. She's got company all right."

"And Billy?"

"Haven't seen him yet, either. I'm thinking now, I'll wait till school's out. He'll have more time, might be less confused...having me step back into his life. And she'll be less likely to throw a fit."

Ted took the time to refill his cup with coffee and he dropped a dollop into the brew. Then he did the same for Harley. Then he said, "Suzie's still around."

"I know."

"I can tell you what I'd do."

"That's what you think. You've got a family. Intact. It's just going to take more time than I thought. And when it's time, I'll break the ice."

~ ~ ~ ~ ~ ~

In the night Harley lay deep in his sleeping bag, looking up at the stars. It was a moonless night and the stars came sparkling down to the desert Southwest as nowhere else. And too, there was always the sound of the river. A river never sleeps, and, for a long time this night, neither did Harley.

Nearby Ted snored contentedly. The hound breathed the slow breathing of sleep between his feet at the foot of the bag. And Harley could see others, far away, who no doubt also slept...

Lucy, the girl in Clifton, who had simply said, "all right, go then," when he'd announced he was going back to Del Cobre. She knew he wouldn't return, so didn't ask. She would not have slept alone for long...no longer than he; Harley could see her curled in sleep with her lean, tawny back turned to a new man, the way she always slept when she was done.

Lois, so urgent and grateful in the night. She would sleep these nights filled with erotic dreams of himself, and other new men, each a fresh new pleasure after "ten years with a prick." Harley knew what she looked like asleep. He could see her now, asleep, and he could imagine her dreams.

Suzie, on day shift these days, she would be asleep now, too. With him she always slept close, knowing all the while that he was there. Alone she curled closely unto herself, yet with an ear ever alert for the sounds of the child, her body rich, brown, fulsome, and filled with love and need.

And his own child would be asleep. His son would be in the deep sleep of a young boy, his tousled red/brown hair, his mothers hair, partially covering his freckled face. Harley hoped his son slept without dreams.

And surely the boy's mother would be asleep now. He knew what she liked in bed, and by this time someone else would, too. But once it was over she would not be touched. Surely it was over by now. She would sleep separately now, her body pale, leggy and perfect.

Later Harley came out of his own sleep, awakened by ragged, obscene, tormented dreams. There was no sign yet of dawn but a few birds knew and Harley could feel that it was not far away. He climbed out of his bedroll and, cursing the feel of it, pulled on the canvas shoes, still cold, clammy, wet, and half frozen with the frost that covered the ground. The hound lifted her head to watch as he put on his coat and when he strapped on his revolver she got up, stretched where she stood, and waited. When he was ready they walked off quietly down river.

When Ted Beeler awoke it was light in the canyon and he recalled that he had been dreaming of the sound of a baying hound. Then it was not a dream; there was a hound baying on the run down river. Ted did not have to roll over and look to know that Harley and Geraldine were gone on a hunt. He got up and did last night's dishes. Then he got his

83

rod and worked up stream, fishing. It didn't take him long to catch a couple of trout for breakfast. He returned and shortly Harley and the hound walked in to camp. Harley was carrying a raccoon and a Gray Fox. He was wet to the waist and was in good spirits.

"Ted you ought to see this hound work! She's faster than White-eye and nearly as good when that goddamn Lurk's not around to lead her astray. Whenever this coon crossed she just knew what he'd done and she'd swim over and pick up the track. I ran down and I had the light on her as she tightroped across on this little slim cottonwood that had fallen across. She was booing all the way. She got some good going and lifted her head up and started to drive and pretty soon that coon had to go up. I got there and she sniffed the bark where the track went up the tree, then she circled the tree in case he tapped it; then she was sure he was up there and went to her tree bark. I'll bet she chops 100 times a minute. She lets you know what she's done and where he's at. Earlier we picked up this fox in a side canyon. The fox is rubbed a bit but he'll sell. The coon is still prime. How come a coon or a bobcat will stay prime well into spring where a fox or coyote is already rubbed out?"

"I don't know. I doubt if anyone does. I heard the race with the coon; I could follow it."

"I mean she runs to catch," Harley said. "What's for breakfast?"

"Trout. Go ahead and skin those and I'll get us something to eat."

While Ted put the breakfast together Harley hung the coon and fox and skinned their hides. He cut seep willow saplings and fashioned two stretchers and strung the hides over the stretchers inside out. Breakfast was ready when he finished. Harley stood shivering by the fire and ate standing up.

"Cold?" Ted asked.

"Damn straight."

"How do you stand it?"

"It's never too cold as long as you keep moving. But there always comes time when you have to stop. I wish that sun would get up over the mountain and dry me off."

After breakfast they broke camp, loaded the canoe and pushed into the current. Harley took the stern paddle once again so Ted could concentrate on the natural history of the trip and take notes when need be. Every few miles they stopped so Ted could look around and Harley would help him with the seine and he would comment on what he saw or heard. By the fourth day there were no longer any trout showing up in the river but the Smallmouth Bass continued to slam helgramites and Ted's streamers and they caught catfish on rod and reel and on set lines they left out at night. Each morning Harley awoke early and he and Geraldine left in the dark to work the river banks until they had a coon chase going. One of those mornings Ted went with him and while Harley held the light Ted shot the coon. They roasted coon meat whenever they wanted it and fried catfish and bass and had little use for the several packages of freeze dried food they'd brought along. And little by little the mountains that surrounded the river's winding course crowded in closer to the flow and became more precipitous until many of the inclines were sheer rock cliffs. The bighorns started to show up and as the altitude dropped with the flow of the river downstream the days warmed a bit and wildlife of the *Sonoran* zone began to dominate. Ted noted the changes and the new life in his notes, but it was Harley that noted the impressive congregation of buzzards and ravens up Loop Canyon as they perched on the bluffs and periodically disappeared in descent. Ted followed Harley's look and had spotted them too when Harley said, "There's something big and dead up there; let's go see what it is."

The canyon, going south off the river, soon became a jumble of huge boulders. Harley topped out first on a high rock and as the big black birds scattered on big slow wings, he said, "there's something unusual."

Ted got up there where he could see, too, and said, "Jesus, who is it...or was it?"

"Can't you tell?"

"Who could say; they've nearly picked him clean."

"Yeah, but look at those goddamn greasy coveralls and that son-of-a-bitchin' hat. That's ol' Bruno."

"Bursum? What happened?"

Harley looked up to where the canyon topped out on the mesa above. "You see that little scrubby juniper sticking out kind of funny, just below the rim?"

"Yeah."

"There's a cave back of there; if you're up-canyon you can even see it if you look careful. Bruno had to be climbing for that cave and he was a long way up when he slipped. There's pots in there, there's an arrow shrine, there's a bunch of stuff in there. What I wonder is, did Bruno slip before or after he got there? I sure hope it was before. I'm going to find out."

"Don't *you* fall."

"It's easy if you come down from the top. We need to go back to the river and rim out."

Ted followed Harley back down the canyon to the river. They climbed up to the rim above, and when they got over the canyon Harley suddenly went over to the edge and disappeared over the side while Ted kept hold of the hound. Directly Harley was back and they stood on the rim looking down to where the Turkey Vultures and ravens were once again hard at work on Bruno Bursum.

"He slipped before he got there," Harley said. "All the stuff's okay. You can even see where the rock let loose. He was almost there and then the rock went and I'll bet he got to the bottom even before the rock. Dumb son-of-a-bitch; it's just a walk from up here. I'm sure glad he didn't get the stuff."

"I'll let Henry know," Ted said.

"What for?"

"Well, he must have family, kin...parents."

"Parents? Bruno? I doubt it. I figure Bruno just came out from under a rock one day and he was already Bruno - grownup, real dirty, and scratching around for stuff."

"I can appreciate your lack of concern, Harley, but I'm still a cop, of sorts. I can't discover a body and not report it. I"ll let Henry know. And I'll let the State Archaeologist now about this site."

"Let's just leave it, Ted. I don't care what you do about Bruno. Neither does he anymore. But let's leave that stuff where it is. That's where it belongs."

"I know what you're saying, Harley. But the reservoir may cover it."

"Way up here?"

"At flood control levels, the water could very well come up this far. I'll have to check the topo maps to see for sure. But even if it doesn't flood this far, someone else will get to this site. Bruno's not the only pot hunter that's working this wilderness. They'll sell these treasures, and the pots will go underground. The other way, the State Archaeologist will give everything the best of care. It will be on display at the museum in Santa Fe, or maybe even here in Del Cobre, and it will be in a setting that will carefully recreate just what was here. They're really very good at that. Everything will be protected and preserved and the public will benefit. Do you know of any other sites like this?"

"Sure. I've been in every cave and site I could ever find. And there's always new ones that turn up. I just like to see those things, and imagine how it was. I've never touched a thing."

"Could you map out what you know for the State Archaeologist?'

"I suppose."

"You'd be doing a public service if you'd work with that office so they can clear some of that out before they close the gates on the dam."

"I'll do that, when I'm sure they're going to build it."

"Fair enough. But I've got to let Henry know about the body."

"You'll agree there's no hurry."

Ted took one last look to the canyon floor where the black flapping mass of Turkey Vultures and a few ravens covered the remains of Bruno Bursum. "There's no hurry at all, Harley," Ted said.

They returned to the river. They cut up slices of cheese and wrapped them in tortillas and sat by the river and ate them for lunch. The hound waited patiently for treats. Harley let her take a piece of cheese from out of his hand and said, "Ted, I don't feel so bad for Bruno."

"No?"

"Not at all. That last second and a half must have been pretty awful but he had a life up till then. He got to see a lot...more than most. You know he was past fifty?"

"I would have guessed ten or fifteen years younger."

"I'm sure he was fifty, at least. He hid behind that black beard, and the beard and his hair stayed black so it was hard to tell. He was old enough to have known when there were still wolves in the county, and grizzlies and even a jaguar now and then. He and my old man saw it when it was a better country than it is now. A lot's been lost. And we've lost a lot along with it. I went into the Blue Range this past November for six weeks, me and the hounds. We treed some nice cats and a bunch of fox. Got one lion, the limit. I called some coyotes in and ran a trap line. I did pretty good and could have stayed but after six weeks I was just putting in time. I was already thinking about town and this girl I knew there in Clifton, and a restaurant meal and a hot shower and soft bed. I came out after six weeks and they were already starting to call me the *mountain man* over there. When he was my age my father used to go in for six *months*. When he came out he was walking because he needed two pack animals to carry all the hides. There's not much wilderness left Ted, and what's left, a lot of the wild has gone out of it. The wolf, the grizzly, and this river. That's what made this country wild. The wolf and the grizzly are long gone and the river's looking death in the face. And a lot of the wild has gone out of us, too. You can't maintain those skills, or even the attitude that will let you use them, unless you get out there and stay. When you start to lose track of what month it is you're starting to become an outdoor man. Then your old calendar is gone and you start to watch the tilt of the sun and the set of the stars and you start to smell the breeze to know the weather or the season and your real education begins. My old man, and even Bruno maybe, knew some things that we may never have the chance to learn. Here in the Southwest there's only one place big enough where you can pack in and lose yourself. They want to cut the heart out of it. Maybe it's inevitable. I know what I'm trying to hold on to is just a romance. But I'm in love with the romance. I have a romance with the wilderness. But anymore, when you go into the wilderness, it's a little bit of make believe. You have to be creative. And you have to kid yourself a little. But just think, Ted...imagine if we could have broke trail in this country!

The hound crawled between the two men and then squirmed into Harley's lap. The men petted and scratched the hound. Her ears were very long and softer and silkier than anything else you could ever feel in your hands. Ted pulled one hand away and picked up a flat stone and skipped it across the stream. Then he said, "Harley, follow me. I want to show you something."

They left the canoe and walked downstream and picked up the first side canyon headed north. They walked up the side canyon through trickles of spring water. Then Ted led them on a steep climb up out of the side canyon to the mesa on the north side of the river. They picked up a game trail that wound through a scattering of piñon trees with a little bit of a roll to the country to where a rock outcrop came off a hill, and where it jutted out the game trail wound around it. Ted stopped well back of the rock outcrop and said, "Harley, take a look at that and tell me what comes to mind."

Harley said, "Looks like it was made for an ambush."

"Good eye. This is where Jimmy Gabaldón bushwhacked the last wolves in New Mexico."

"I always heard he wouldn't talk about it."

"That was generally true. But he not only told me about it, he brought me here in the spring and described the whole thing. He was an old timer then and I was just starting out with the Department and he was hired to help me pack a base camp into the G-Bar Mesa for an elk roundup. He sure could pack a camp on a mule. And he knew the country, so I was learning a lot and was glad for the company I had. This isn't the shortest route to the G-Bar Mesa but he brought us this way and we stopped here for some lunch and he just started telling me the story. He said he'd been after them for more than a year and he kept hunting for the den. He couldn't find it but he had this runway figured out so he live trapped a jackrabbit and strung him out alive over by that piñon there and made three dirt sets where he figured a wolf would have to trip one if he came to that hare. He said that pair of wolves had turned away from every other bait, lure or scent he'd tried but when the female came by she couldn't say no to that jackrabbit jerking around on the end of a string. When he found her she'd tripped all three of the traps and she tore that jackrabbit to pieces without eating any of it. Well, he left her there with number 4 1/2 Newhouse traps on two of her feet and hid downwind in those rocks and, sure enough, the next morning the male came from the river looking for her and he shot him. Then he shot the bitch. He said the bitch was carrying a bag so he knew she had pups. He tried to trail them back to the den so he could collect on the pups too, but he never could find the den. The pups would have been just a handful at that time of year and couldn't have made it. I asked him, I said, 'How do you feel about it now, Jimmy?' and he said, 'How do you think I feel?' After that he wouldn't talk about it any more."

Harley looked over to where the ambush took place. There was just the rock outcrop and a few scattered piñon trees and a game trail making a line through the high country grass, with no sign at all that the last of anything had died there. Harley said, "Ted, follow me, I want to show you something."

Harley led the way back to the rim of the canyon and then downstream along the rim, above the canyon, to where an enormous Alligator Juniper stood overlooking the river far below. Harley led the way down the steep bank to where the trail appeared from out of nowhere, then down around the big boulders to where the seep spring dripped water onto a flat outcrop right by where a small cave went back into the mountain. The hound started to sniff her way into the cave and Harley called her back.

"Your dad show you this?"

"Yes. I was just a kid. He told me never to tell anyone, but he didn't know you back then. And now, what difference does it make anyway?"

"I can see why they never could find this den. You can't see it till you're right here. But what a view! I wouldn't mind living here myself."

"Ted, when this goes under water, it may be time for guys like you and me to pack it in. I mean, forty years ago they got the last wolves. This cave ought to be some kind of memorial. People ought to come here to pay their respects. Instead, it's going under behind the dam. They re going to drown the last home of the last wolves in the state as if..."

"...as if to be sure that nothing so contrary to progress will ever get in their way again."

"Something like that. I used to come by here a lot over the years. Just sit here and look off into the river. I remember I was sitting here once in early summer. The water was down and was running real clear. I saw this big dark something come swimming upstream. I thought it was a big catfish and then it climbed out on a rock and it was one of the otters. Pretty soon they'll be gone, too."

Ted looked for a long moment at Harley to be sure he wasn't kidding. Then he said, "What otters?"

"The otters. The otters that live in the Río Jalisco."

"Harley, the last certified otter in New Mexico was trapped up river near Mondragón Creek in 1953. Officially, there hasn't been one taken or even seen in the state in over twenty years. The species is considered extirpated from New Mexico."

"Well I'm not certified for anything but I've seen plenty of otters since 1953."

"How recently?"

"A couple of years. But remember I've been away for a year."

"Where have you seen them?"

"At different times, from about where our canoe is parked on down through the Gunsight Box. But mostly near the confluence of Ocotillo Creek."

"You're serious?"

"Sure. I knew they were scarce, but it never occurred to me that anyone thought they were gone because I knew they were here."

"You think you can show me an otter?"

"I wouldn't say. They didn't get to where everyone thought they were extinct by showing themselves to people. But I'll guarantee I can show you some tracks."

"That'll be a start. Let's go."

They climbed away from the wolf den up to the rim, hiked along the rim over the river to the side canyon, slid down into the canyon and walked back to the canoe. They loaded up and shoved off. Increasingly, the river course was narrow and twisted and curved back on itself and the white water was livelier all the time. Ted had to work hard now in the bow to help them through the rapids where a mistake meant a cold swim and a scramble not to lose any of the gear. They floated on without a mishap making real good time and they didn't stop, and then the river funnelled up into a pretty good waterfall right before Ocotillo Creek. They whooped and took on a good deal of water as the canoe took the falls and dipped into the deep pool below. Harley immediately levered the canoe around to the north bank, right opposite the creek. They took the packs out and set them in the sun to dry, and dumped the water out of the canoe. Harley said, "You take this side. I'm going to look up the creek."

Harley and the hound had to swim to cross the pool below the falls, then he wasn't fifty yards up the creek when he found a fair set of otter tracks in the gravel along the creek. A little upstream another set of tracks joined in and then in a patch of mud were the picture perfect prints of two otters. Harley held the hound back and whistled for Ted. The big man was already swimming across the pool, holding his jacket over his head with one hand to keep it dry. He came up the creek and before he got to Harley he dropped to one knee. Then he walked up to the little mud flat and dropped to one knee again. "Those are otter tracks," he said.

"Right."

Ted took his field guide out of his coat pocket, found the page depicting otter tracks and juxtaposed the page with the living print.

"There's nothing in this world that could make those tracks but an otter."

"Right, Ted."

Ted had his camera rolled up in the coat and he took it out and shot a roll of film of otter tracks. Then he stood up, looked up the creek, then gathered up his jacket and headed for the river. He swam across as he had before, followed by Harley and the hound. Ashore on the north side, Ted took a pinch of Skoal and said, "Harley, don't let's talk about these otters for a while."

"I wasn't fixing to say anything."

"I need to think."

"Think, Ted."

Ted went over and sat down in the sun, leaned back against a cottonwood. He took his pen and note pad out of his jacket pocket and started to write.

Harley dried out comfortably, taking his afternoon siesta in the sun on the beach. Toward evening Ted took his note pad and binoculars downstream. Harley broke into the freeze dried food and worked up some beef stew. And he found in his pack a two pound can of creamed corn and he poured it into the stew. When Ted came back they ate supper and brewed coffee and finished the last of the bottle. But through the evening and the night and the following morning there was nothing said about otters. Ted had the last of his work done by noon and they were ready to break camp.

Ted said, "I hear the Gunsight Box is pretty wild."

Harley said, "It's a challenge in a canoe."

"You've done it?"

"Yup."

"You make it?"

"For the most part."

"Well let's get it."

They loaded everything up and tied everything down. The last thing Harley did was put that empty two pound can of corn under the seat between his feet. The Gunsight Box was a notch in the mountains five miles long where the water raced through sheer rock walls that went up hundreds of feet over their heads and in places not more than the width of their outstretched arms between the cliffs. Time and again the roar of whitewater came up the canyon to meet them. They worked the paddles hard and whooped and hollered and swerved through the rocks and bounced off the walls and bucked through the spray of white water and everytime the current slackened Harley bailed like a madman with that empty two pound can of creamed corn. Pretty soon the hound caught on; she'd hear the whitewater coming and start to howl. And then they shot through the last of the defile and the Gunsight Box opened into a pastoral scene where the hills gradually fell away and farms and ranches began to appear along a gentle river. Harley went back to work with the empty corn can and Ted turned around and said, "That was it."

"That was what?"

"That last narrows; that's the dam site."

Harley turned and looked back at the notch of the Gunsight Box. You didn't need to be an engineer to see it was a natural place for a 300 foot tall block of cement, if you were inclined that way.

They drifted on, easily and gently, and just below the highway bridge Harley's pickup truck was parked where it was supposed to be. They loaded the canoe, changed into dry clothes and made the short drive into Gunsight. The got a table at the Gunsight Bar & Cafe, ordered beer and T-bone steaks. When they were done eating they ordered more beer. Harley looked at Ted who was starting to relax and then Ted looked at Harley and said, "Partner, I think we've got something."

"You're thinking about those otters but I don't get it. The otter may be scarce in New Mexico but it's not an endangered species."

"The otter is on the list of State Endangered Species. But you're thinking that's not worth much and you're right. There is no legal apparatus wherein a State Endangered Species could stop anything from happening. I was stumped too; that's why I had to think. The bell rang when I got to thinking about what you said about having to be creative when you go into the wilderness nowdays. Got me to remembering ol' Doc Kersey. You ever take any wildlife management from him?"

"No. But I know who you mean. He was that odd, old bird that used to make the other professors nervous."

"That's him. Doc went beyond population trends and feeding patterns and the like. Next to him, the other professors were stodgy, and they knew it. Anyway, Doc was involved in a lot of issues over the years, and helped pull the rug out from under a number of unsavory projects, including a bad dam and a really gross clear cut. More than once in class he told us, he said, 'a wildlife biologist is a scientist who uses the scientific method, and if he *cares* about wildlife he also knows how to think and be creative on their behalf.' Of course someone would always ask him what he meant by that and he'd always say we'd understand when we'd learned to care about wildlife and to think and be creative. I think I'm beginning to understand what he meant. What ol' Doc meant was that it's not enough to gather the information and program data and establish trends; you've got to know what to do with the information so it's put to use on behalf of the wildlife you think you know so much about."

"In other words, you've got to be just as enterprising as the opposition."

"Right. Now, these otters. As a State Endangered Species they don't amount to a tinker's cuss, but as otters they may count for a good deal more...if we care and can think and be creative in their behalf. Harley, what you've discovered in the Río Jalisco is not some bizarre species of plant, or some odd minnow or tweety bird; you have discovered what is probably the most engaging, charming, and likeable animal in the natural world, living in the last free-flowing river in the state, just above a proposed dam site."

"A man could lose a lot of votes extirpating such an animal by drowning out their home and habitat."

"Beautiful; you're way ahead of me Harley."

"So, by the end of the week we ought to see the headlines in the Albuquerque *Times*, El Paso *Journal*, and Del Cobre *Region* that the New Mexico otter lives after all, but is threatened by an ugly dam."

"Not yet. I don't want you to say a word about these otters to anyone. We're going to use the press to rouse the troops all right, but to start with, I've got to have more evidence than some paw prints in the mud. I don't want our otters to just sort of slip out of the bag. I want them to make a big splash. I'm going to wait a couple of months till their kits have got a good start in life and are looking real cute, then I'm going to pack in there for however long it takes and I'm going to make a video."

"Ted, you're a flat-ass genius."

"Creative Harley; you've got to be as enterprising as the opposition. The Department has the equipment and I know how to use it. I'm going to make a video on the unique ecology and great beauty of the Río Jalisco Canyon and featuring the heretofore extirpated and utterly charming and entirely loveable New Mexico otter. If the chief will turn me lose on it, and I believe he will."

"Harvey Olmsted still the chief?"

"Yes. And I know he doesn't care for the dam. In his position he has to be the picture of impartiality, especially with Garner Greane the governor, but Harvey's no dummy. He knows how to be creative, too. And we're not making these otters up. I'll just be doing my job."

Harley turned his bottle upside down and finished his beer. "What are the chances?" he said.

Ted's beer was already gone. He looked at the empty bottle. "In truth?...not real good. It's a long shot at best. But it's a chance. And being a good biologist and hopefully a little bit creative too, I can say for sure it's the best chance we've got."

Outside the cafe, Harley handed Ted the keys, pulled his pack out of the back of the truck and called the hound, who promptly jumped over the side.

Ted said, "You're going back in."

"I've got to," Harley said. "There's just ten days left in the fur season and that's about how long it will take me to work up Ocotillo Creek and hunt out all the side canyons along the way. There will be plenty of coon in the creek and cats up in the rimrocks and, anyway, I haven't traveled the length of that creek in years."

"You haven't got food for ten days...not nearly."

"There's trout up the creek. And a man will never go hungry with a hound like Geraldine around. Coon and cats are meat as well as hides. You can leave my truck at your place and I'll ring you up when I get out. We'll go out and have a couple and I'll tell you some hunting stories and you can tell me what you're doing about the otters."

"We can cross the bridge and I'll give you a ride part way up the river road."

"No, I'll just cut across here to the river and me and Geraldine will pick up a coon track in this farm country. Then we'll swim across and pick up the Gunsight Trail. That's the short cut into that country. The main thing is to keep moving. You keep moving and you'll never get cold."

Harley stepped away from the lights of the building and was gone.

## Chapter 9

IN SOUTHWEST NEW MEXICO, spring was now master of the land. The last of the late snow storms were now warming into rain hundreds of miles to the north, and falling as sparse cooling showers on the Mondragón Mountains and Chihuahuan desert. Mostly the sun shone, rising earlier, rising higher, and staying longer to lengthen each day. The yuccas were ready to bloom their great white flowers, the cholla had blossomed out in red, yellow and purple, the ocotillo would soon make the world's loveliest pink flowers and the agave were turning that odd red tinge. The grama grass and tobosa grew in the desert grasslands and on up in the foothills approaching the forest. The grass responded to the warmth and sun and waited on the rain, greening briefly after the occasional shower, fading into shades of yellow but still growing into spring. On the farms along the streams the farmers opened the gates by the diversion dams that gave water from the streams to the *acequias*. Then they cut the water from the *acequias* into the fields - oats, alfalfa, chile, and orchards of apples, peaches and pears. On the ranches, the ranchers hunted calves and hoped the real rains, the summer rains, would come early this year. In town the girls had begun to show their arms, legs and sometimes mid-drifts to the sun, warm air, and the boys. Newcomers, visitors and tourists, marvelled at the sun and warm air and said there was no spring in southern New Mexico. Natives and semi-natives said that the season would seem very much like spring once the true heat of June had captured the land.

In the foothills above Del Cobre, along Gavilán Creek, Harley Simmons, a man whose life very much followed the seasons, sat on the front porch contemplating a spring ritual. The old garden plot along the creek had been neglected, though not abandoned, in recent years. It badly needed refurbishing. It deserved better care. Harley knew that given care, and proper tending, the garden would produce. A hard day's work in spring would yield sustenance, nature's bounty and the best of eating for the rest of the year. He knew all he had to do, and the first thing was to catch Ruby the mule.

The hounds watched with curiosity as Harley walked by the pen to the barn, got a halter and a bucket with a scoop of oats in it, and went through the gate into the pasture. He came back leading Ruby, a monster sorrel mule, draft horse size; she would have pulled a plow or skidded logs in times past. She had a head like a suitcase and ears of such a wonderful length and ability to express that whatever they were doing

94

they told it all. Coming down the slope to the pasture gate those ears were up, forward, alert and expectant. The hounds too were expectant; starting to whine in hopes of a hunt. But when Harley came out of the barn with harness instead of a saddle Ruby's ears went back and the hounds quit talking and lay down.

Ruby allowed herself to be harnessed and hitched to the rusty cultivator. Harley climbed on the springy, metal seat and drove the mule through the yard and down the hill to the field along the creek. He drove the mule across the bridge over the ditch into the field. He set the tines into the dirt, hupped the mule and began a slow pass working parallel with the creek, working up the dirt as they went. There was barely 3 acres to the irrigated land, two of it in fruit trees. Harley looked over the one acre vegetable plot and noted that the old man had planted but a few rows during the year that he was gone. But he could also tell that the old man had plowed the whole acre down and worked it up after the fall harvest. Harley circled the mule at the far end of the field and as he came around he could see La Señora Hidalgo waiting at the other end of the field. Harley made another pass back and stopped to talk.

*"Buenos dias, señora."*

*"Buenos dias, mi hijo. Tengo las semillas, maiz, frijoles, chícharos."*

*"Que bién, pero hay semillas en el granero."*

*"Estos son mejor."*

Harley knew that the old widow was a better farmer than he would ever hope to be; it was now certain that there would be good seed in the ground and that his little farm would be well tended and he was going to get a lot of help. He circled the mule for the next pass and started back up the field. The old woman went to the edge of the field along the creek and sat in the sun. She waited patiently till he'd finished the field. She watched as he drove Ruby back to the first pass and started over. Again, rich, darker, moister earth from underneath was pulled up into the sun and the remnants of the clods broke up as they worked through the tines. As Harley looked back he saw the old woman already working the hoe behind him, backing down the field behind him, working the hoe with a practised rapidness in making the first row for the seeds.

Together they worked through the day, right up through the sunset - working the dirt, hoeing out the rows, planting the seeds. They broke for dinner which she prepared for them at her house, then after a short *siesta* in the shade, for it had warmed to a summer-like day, they worked till evening and finished planting the field. The old woman, who was of the same vintage as his father, outworked him all day long. The pace she set in the morning was the same pace she held through the afternoon, while his own back, arms and hands increasingly demanded rest. With the sun down behind the west hills he turned the metal wheel, shutting the gate, cutting the water into his own ditch and from there down the rows to wet the seeds. The water crawled slowly, alive and benevolent, down the rows, offering life to the seeds. They left the water to gently flood the field and walked up the path and across the creek to the widow's house. By lamplight, for she had no use for electricity, the old woman warmed frijoles and braised meat which she wrapped in tortillas with chile for their supper.

"*No es un hogar, sin la jardín,*" she said. "*Ahora, tu tienes su jardín, y su hogar, y tu no puedes salir.*"

"*No voy a salir, señora. Nunca.*"

## Chapter 10

AND IN THE SPRING a man turns his thoughts to bear - big bear, black phase, or brown, or cinnamon, or even blonde, coming out of their winter dens in prime fur, lean and hungry from hibernation. The oak and piñon mast that was the main diet providing fat for the long winter's sleep is mostly gone and in the spring the bears in the Southwest mountains roam widely for food. They graze the greening slopes, cropping grass like cows. They reach for juniper berries and dig for ground squirrels. The tear into the homes of unsuspecting ants and bees, lapping up life by the thousands and honey by the pound, oblivious to bites and stings. They wind a hidden fawn or jump a yearling calf, turning life into meat. In the morning hours of a southwestern spring Harley Simmons had turned his thoughts to bear, when the phone rang. It was a bear of a man.

"Harley?"

"Ted, where you been?"

"Santa Fe. I'm still here...be back the end of the week. We got some action, Harley."

"What did Olmsted say?"

"Well, I got the photos of the paw prints developed and wrote a report that included a proposal along the lines we talked about and then I dropped it on Harvey's desk yesterday morning. This morning it was back on my desk with one word written on it...Go!"

"All right! What's next?"

"I've got plenty to do for a couple of months with the inventory we did and I'll be huddling with the federal wildlife people and in June I figure to pack in with the video. But I've got something for you right now. Have you been bear hunting yet this spring?"

"No. I've got a guy coming in end of the month."

"Well I've got a guy will come in for a hunt tomorrow if you can take him."

"Paying customer?"

"You bet, and that's not all. You heard of Ben Wetzel?"

"One of those outdoor writers."

"Right. But more to our uses, he's the editor of *American Gunner* magazine."

"That's one of the big ones."

"It's very big - circulation over two million. Anyway, I was in talking to Tanner of Big Game yesterday and this Wetzel walks in...a little older than us - not much - not very tall but wiry, dressed in camo with his pants tucked into these lace up boots and stands at attention all the time. All he lacked was a swagger stick. Says he wants a bear hunt for a fall issue. Says he's bored hunting bear over bait, which isn't surprising, and wants to try a hound hunt and could we recommend a guide. Well Tanner starts mumbling about the Sangre de Cristos and Lucas and Lara and some of those guys and first chance I got I butted in and said of course the northern mountains were filling up with hunters and yuppie backpackers and who knows what sort of riff raff but there were lots of bear in the Mondragón Mountains because the country was too rugged for the average hunter. Well that easily I had taken the conversation away from Tanner and had Wetzel responding to a challenge and looking southwest. I went on to say there was a dam and other developments planned for the last great wilderness in the Southwest and this might be the last chance for a man to see that country as nature made it and get in on a real old style hunt. He said a controversy like that always helped to make a good story; and the short of it is, Harley, he's heard of your dad and he wants to meet you and go on a bear hunt. He's coming in here this afternoon...what should I tell him?"

"Send him down."

~ ~ ~ ~ ~ ~

They left Harley's home early in the morning with a rich blue sky high over the desert and a few light pearly clouds roaming over the mountains, and they lined out on the trail and climbed for the divide. Lurk was necked to Geraldine to keep the big hound from running off. White-eye, who wouldn't run anything he shouldn't, namely a coyote, elk or deer, was on his own - the strike dog. Harley led the way, riding a small strawberry roan gelding who was a good mountain horse. Wetzel rode the old man's bay mare, who was long in the tooth but still sound and was not going to do anything stupid, even with a dumb rider aboard. Ruby packed their camp, carrying everything Harley thought they might need, for a week if necessary. The mule was not overloaded. What Harley thought they might need was minimal and many a mule in the West carried more for an overnight pack trip than Ruby carried for a week. Harley watched the Saddleback hound. He trotted up the trail ahead of the horses and other hounds and his nose told him more in passing than a team of biologists could have discerned along the same route in a week of scrupulous study. Where a coyote shit on the trail, White-eye stopped for an inspection. Directly he knew what it was that shit, how old, what sex, what it had been eating, where it was coming

97

from, where it was going, and how long ago it passed by. Where a deer crossed the trail, he checked that out too. Directly he knew as much about the deer as about the coyote. He also knew neither animal was for him, and went on. At the crest of the divide, however, he found something he liked and Harley could tell. Off the trail White-eye put his nose into a small clump of pine needles, snuffled his nose, whipped his tail around, stopped his tail as he stuffed his nose deeper into the clump, whipped his tail around again and let go with one deep base squall. Harley stepped off his horse and, followed by Wetzel, went over to the hound.

"What is it?" Wetzel said.

"Cat scratch."

"Big cat?"

"Big bobcat. It's not a lion."

Wetzel kneeled down to look at a clump of pine needles put into a small pile next to a scrape of bare dirt.

"Cat scrapes with his hind feet," Harley said. "Generally away from the direction he's traveling - so this cat's headed west along the ridge."

"Shall we take him?" Wetzel asked.

"It's out of season for fur, legally and otherwise. And this scratch is from yesterday, at least. A bobcat doesn't leave much scent to begin with and we're losing humidity fast with this sun getting high. White-eye is a cold trailing hound but we'd be real lucky to ever turn this cat track into a race."

They rode over the divide and down the north slopes, through the Canadian forest into groves of Ponderosa Pine, heading east as well as north, still well away from the river, with the headwaters, the higher mountains of the Mondragón Range, blue/black in the distance. Mid-afternoon Harley reined in by a small spring creek in a grassy meadow with big pines scattered here and there. "Camp," he said. Then he stepped down and began to unsaddle his horse. Then he took the saddle off Wetzel's horse and the pack saddle off the mule. He staked the animals out with rope and put leash chains on the hounds. Then he stretched out on the grass with his saddle for a pillow and went to sleep, leaving Ben Wetzel to the scenery and his thoughts.

~ ~ ~ ~ ~ ~

"You a gun nut like me?" Wetzel asked. They had eaten well on meat the first night out, and now they sat by the fire with tin cups filled with spring water and a shot of booze.

"I like guns well enough," Harley said. "A well-made gun is a fine thing. But I own five that suit me and haven't bought a gun in years. So I guess I'm not really a gun nut. What about you?"

"I've got over thirty, most of which I haven't fired in years. That's a gun nut. That revolver suit you?"

"It's just right for what I do."

98

"It's a Ruger .357 Blackhawk with a seven and a half inch barrel, weighs 42 ounces. I can tell; you don't even have to take it out of the holster. That rifle suit you?"

"Just right."

"It's a Browning lever-action in .308, twenty inch barrel, has a quick release clip and weighs a shade under seven pounds. I can tell; you don't even need to take it out of the scabbard. That and the Savage are the only levers with a lockup that will produce accuracy in the modern sense of the word. But with my bolt action here in 7mm Remington magnum, and a scope, I'll outshoot you."

"Others have tried that Wetzel; out to two hundred yards we'd be splitting hairs."

"All right Simmons, I'll believe that you can shoot. You might even outshoot me at two hundred yards. But beyond two hundred yards Simmons...without a scope?"

"If you can't get within two hundred yards of what you're hunting, you're not hunting at all. You're just shooting."

"But you hunt with hounds, Simmons. That makes a difference. What kind of a gun does a houndman really need?"

"You have something there, Wetzel. A houndman needs good hounds. After that a bow or even a spear could get you by. And someday, I may go that route."

Wetzel got up and went over by the spring creek and filled his cup and came back to the campfire and laced it as before. He pulled off his boots and slid into his sleeping bag. He held himself up on one elbow with the tin cup in his hand.

"I like your country, Simmons," he said. "We came over the divide and down through the fir and spruce and across those grasslands with aspens rimming the hills and we could have been up in Colorado. I didn't know there was country like this along the Mexican border. But Beeler says there's trouble. What's coming down, Simmons?"

"There's a block of roughly four million acres of National Forest taking in the Río Jalisco drainage. Some of it's across the line in Arizona. About one-fourth of that four million acres is wild country. A big chunk of that wild country, the best of it in my view, won't be wild anymore if that dam is built."

"You're talking about a dam on the Río Jalisco."

"Right."

"You're talking about roads."

"Right."

"Logging."

"Right."

"Mines, tourists and a ski resort."

"No doubt."

99

"And the people promoting this, they're talking about growth, economic development, jobs, money, new people, tourism, a boom."

"You know all about this, Wetzel."

"Oh yes. It's happening all over, Simmons. And I'll tell you the truth, I'm not sure who's side I'm on. I'm in the outdoor business. Sportsmen buy our magazine. The truth is, most of them haven't got the time or the inclination for a place like this. That's why bear baiting is so popular. It's quick. It's easy. They haven't got the time to hunt bear with hounds. Or the energy. For most of them they'd rather camp out by a dead horse and let the bear come to them. Myself, I like a challenge. But I've got to keep our readers in mind. A million acres, two hundred miles from the nearest city and hard to get into once you're there; that doesn't generate much business. For you or me. But don't bother to argue with me, Simmons. I know the other side of that argument just as well. I could just as well take the other side. Often I do. I know this - the issue of wilderness versus development is going to help the story. And that will sell magazines. I need to see more before I know how I'm going to write it." ·

"You'll see more, maybe more than you want to once the race starts. Once he's on the run, the bear goes where he pleases. The hounds go to the bear. We go to the sound of the hounds. The houndman is part of the chase, so he sees country he never would otherwise."

"Well I'll be ready in the morning, Simmons. Beeler says you're the man for a *real* bear hunt. But I've got to tell you, I've caught you on one thing already."

"What's that?"

"You forgot the tent."

"I didn't forget it. I didn't bring it."

"No tent?"

"It's not raining."

"Not right now."

"I brought a couple of ponchos if it does. And if it really starts to rain I'll find us a cave we can hood up in."

"I've been wondering why you charge about half as much for a bear hunt as anyone else. Now I know why. Goodnight Simmons."

"Goodnight Wetzel."

~ ~ ~ ~ ~ ~

They rode out in the morning and on down to the rim of the Río Jalisco. "Okay Simmons," Wetzel said, looking off into the canyon at the river below, "you've made your point. And they want to dam this·up?"

"That's the plan."

"Okay Simmons," Wetzel said again, on the ground now taking pictures, "you don't need to say anything to me about this river."

They hunted west that first day, and then south, climbing to the headwaters of Ocotillo Creek and then back to camp. The second day they circled Englemann Peak and the third day they hunted along just under the rim of the divide, working east and then north before circling west back to camp. Harley led the hunt at a trot wherever terrain permitted and each morning Wetzel was more stiff and sore climbing into the saddle, and wherever they went they were unable to find fresh bear tracks. The morning of the fourth day Harley was up very early indeed. He had breakfast ready and the horses saddled before Wetzel had crawled out of his sleeping bag. Wetzel was very saddle sore but he ate breakfast standing up in the dark and climbed into the saddle without commenting on how he was moving or how his entire body was feeling. At a high trot, they rode east and a little north at first light towards the highest, most massive mountain along this stretch of the divide; the mountain took the sun's first orange streaks along it's blue/black convolutions and Harley said, "You see that big black monster waking up over there?"

Wetzel spoke as the pace of the trotting mare permitted. "I've been...watching it...for three days...ever since...we crossed...the divide...and I feel like...it's been...watching me."

"That's Brushy Mountain. It looks like one big rolling peak but there are mountains within mountains there, and canyons within the canyons. It's a jungle and it's a maze and it's a son-of-a-bitch to try and catch a bear in there but that's where they've got to be 'cause they're damn sure not anywhere else we've been."

They rode for two hours then put their mounts in a walk as they entered the first heavily wooded canyon ascending to Brushy Mountain. It was shaded in the draw and the humidity was high, the air moist, almost dank. The men could smell the humidity, smell the juniper, pine and spruce, smell the horse sweat; the hounds could smell more than that. Lurk and Geraldine began to whine and pull at the swivels that held them together and the Saddleback was swinging back and forth across the canyon up ahead and working his tail in circles as he ran.

"They smell bear," Harley said. "There's a dirt tank up ahead and if one didn't come in there to water this morning I'm going to give you your money back."

The dirt tank was full of water and it was all roily and the surface of the tank was still moving though there wasn't a breath of wind; and then the Saddleback had circled the tank and gave first cry. He booed a long, drawn out yelp, followed by another, then headed away from the tank on up the canyon.

Harley rode around the tank and saw where a very large bear had left a perfect hind footprint, looking very much like the barefoot track of a man, in the mud. Harley said, "He heard us coming Wetzel; we just rolled a big one out of here," as he galloped up the canyon, jumped off the mule and grabbed the two hounds necked together. He held them while he waited for White-eye to line out. He heard the Saddleback booing intermittently on the track; the hound momentarily confused by the overpowering scent. Then he took the line and squalled...ooooo! ooooo! ooooo! as he went to the bear. Harley unnecked Geraldine and Lurk and sprang into the saddle.

"Let's get it Wetzel; we've got a race!"

For several hundred yards they were able to gallop up the canyon, dodging and bucking the brush. But the canyon narrowed down and the brush grew thicker and they were reduced to walking their mounts and picking there way through the brush. The hounds had already topped out over the rim and were out of sound.

"We've got to get out of here," Harley said. "We've got to get out of here, get up top and stay above the race."

Wetzel was standing in his stirrups. "You should have thought of that before," he said. "We'll never get out of here, unless we go back."

"You're getting ornery because you're hurting on that horse. But you're in luck, Wetzel; you're going to get to walk for awhile."

Harley stepped down, took the reins and began to scramble up the slope, leading the mule. Wetzel followed, leading the bay horse. For a while, Wetzel eagerly attacked the slope, but before they were halfway out of the canyon his heart was pounding alarmingly in his chest, his thighs were cramping in a different way than when he was on horseback and the thin air at 8,000 feet jerked him down to a halt where he lay on his back on the slope, gasping for breath. Harley waited above, laying underneath the steaming, heaving mule. When the mule and Wetzel's horse looked to have caught their breath he took the reins and resumed his side hill climb up the slope, sometimes on his feet, sometimes on his hands and knees, slipping on the loose pine needles, stepping over or around the blowdowns, always conscious that if he or the mule slipped they would roll to the bottom of the canyon. Approaching the top the slope gentled some and the forest opened up. Harley went to the high side of the mule and stepped on. He spurred the mule and whipped her rump with his hat; she strained, grunted, and heaved and humped herself up the slope, kicking up great gouts of dirt with every lunge to the top. There Harley got down, dropped the reins and started back down the slope. He met Wetzel half way to the bottom. He took the reins of the horse and started back up, climbing with the horse as he had with the mule, to where the slope began to level off and open up. He waited there for Wetzel. With both hands now free to help him climb, Wetzel worked his way up to the guide.

"Come here to the high side of the hill and step on." Harley said.

Very much relieved now to be horseback, Wetzel stepped up on the horse.

"Now use those spurs and take her on up."

Wetzel spurred the veteran mare. Harley got behind and yelled and swatted the horse across the rump with his hat; the mare humped and lunged and dug her way to the top, nearly bucking the hunter off as she topped out.

The hunter, the guide, the horse and the mule were drenched in sweat. Everyone was breathing heavily. The animals stood with their legs spread and their heads dropped and Wetzel was down on his backside, trying to get it back. Harley moved away from the heavy breathing and over the ridge he could hear the sounds of the battle, a thousand feet down in the next canyon. He could tell they had caught the bear. He could hear Geraldine's high pitched squall-chop, Lurk's chopping bark, and the ooooo! ooooo! ooooo! from the Saddleback. He knew there was a running battle going and, listening, he could picture it almost as if he could see it - the bear running, then stopping to snap and lunge at the hounds, the hounds squalling, chopping, booing on the run, then swirling and stinging like a swarm of hornets when the bear stopped to fight. In time Wetzel came over the ridge and joined him.

"Have they treed him yet?"

"No, but they've caught him."

Wetzel listened and then he too could hear the sounds of the battle far below.

"Sounds like they've got him treed."

"That's not a tree bark. And they're moving up the canyon."

"Well if they've caught him he should tree."

"That's a bad bear. He's not going to tree anytime soon. He may not tree at all."

"Well?"

"We ride this ridge, stay above. We may be able to cut him off somewhere. If he trees or they get him bayed up solid, we go to him. But I don't know what that bear's going to do any more than you."

Harley walked back over the ridge and mounted the mule and began to walk the mule along the ridge, getting his direction from the hounds below. When Wetzel caught up he put the mule into a trot. He heard the horse break into a trot behind him and he heard Wetzel say, "Damn!"

They came to a rock outcrop which fingered out over the canyon. Harley stopped there and looked out and down and in an open spot in the canyon below he saw the bear and the three dogs. They were all four very tiny animals from that distance but Harley could still tell the bear by his relative size and the hounds by color. The bear was swinging his forequarters from side to side, occasionally spinning to gather an angle where he could stay head on to the nearest dog. Harley saw Lurk rush in, drawing the bear out; two other dogs came in from either side and grabbed bear; the bear spun on White-eye and made a rush and it looked like he might catch him, but the hound could stay just ahead of the bear and then two more dogs were swarming and stinging and spun the bear back around. The bear feinted another rush, then whirled and broke through the pack with a rapid rolling gate and with surprising speed ran up the canyon to disappear in the brush, the sounds of the pack in pursuit. At the last, Wetzel had been standing with Harley, watching.

"He can't stand those hounds much longer," Wetzel said. "He's got to tree."

"Maybe, maybe not," Harley said. "Right now that bear is starting to climb...you hear it? He'll outrun those dogs going uphill. He's moving, Wetzel, and I'll bet he's going to cross Three Forks Saddle that you can see right over there...see that? We'll rim this mountain and we might cut him down when he tops the saddle."

It was a race to the saddle with the mule and the horse at a lope through the brush, rimming the top of the ridge. The horseman in the lead anticipated the route, reining his mount through the pines, dodging and ducking the limbs, at times leaning off the saddle and down the side of the mule to maintain the pace and then he heard the tell-tale thwack followed by a thud; he reined the mule around and Wetzel was on the ground having landed on his back and he couldn't breath, at all. The branch that cut him loose was still waving in the air. Harley rode back and took the horse's reins and led her back to the rider. Wetzel was bent over now, desperate to get some wind back in his diaphragm. A cut was bleeding profusely on his forehead and a knot was welling up underneath. The race was closer now, much closer, coming at a run up and out of the canyon.

"Let's get it, Wetzel. Bite your lip and climb on; we're gonna see a bear."

The hunter was till working for air as he got to his feet and climbed on the horse. Harley handed him the reins, whirled the mule about and spurred her into a run. The older horse followed, also at a good lope, bringing the hunter along.

Harley arrived at a gallop at the clearing in the ridge where the mountain dipped into the saddle and was greeted by a riot of sound. He could hear the bear crashing through the brush, coming up the slope for the saddle. The hounds were ringing their pursuit off the canyon walls and up through the trees. And then Wetzel was there too, leaning forward on the horse's neck, one hand wrapped around the reins, one hand wrapped around the horn.

"Get down Wetzel! Draw your gun!"

The hunter slid off the horse and his cramped legs failed him and left him on the ground. He regained his feet and went to the scabbard. He reached but could not retrieve the heavy, bolt action scoped rifle from the scabbard; his legs failed him again and he fell. Harley rode over, reached over the saddle and drew Wetzel's rifle and handed it to the hunter as the bear broke in full gallop into view, Lurk chopping not ten yards behind, then Geraldine and White-eye. The hunter dropped to one knee, jacked a cartridge into the chamber and swung on the bear. The big, black bear wasn't twenty yards from the muzzle; the hunter could see nothing with distinction through the scope. Even before the sharp roar of the magnum's report Harley knew Wetzel was way high. The bear and the hounds were over the saddle and disappeared into the trees and down into the next canyon.

"Missed," Harley said.

"FUCK YOU!" and the hunter jacked another round into the chamber. "FUCK YOU SIMMONS!" and he swung the rifle till he held the muzzle on a line with Harley's chest. Harley stood in the right stirrup, pulled his foot out of the left stirrup and swung it over the horn. In this easy seat he reached into his shirt pocket and pulled out a pouch. The sounds of pursuit descended deeper and further into the canyon as he pulled out a chew and loaded his lip.

"Take it easy, Wetzel. The race isn't over."

Slowly, the hunter raised the muzzle of the gun into the air. Then he slumped down on to his injured ass, bleeding at the point of the tail bone through his camo pants. Methodically, he one by one jacked out the remaining cartridges. He put them in a pocket of his camo jacket. Then he dropped the gun and put his face down in the crook of his arm. He said, "My god...oh my god..."

Harley stepped down off the mule, came around and took the rifle, closed the bolt and returned the rifle to the scabbard.

Wetzel said, "I've never...ever... done that."

"Sure you have. We all miss now and then."

Wetzel looked up at Harley. "That's not even funny," he said. "I've never, ever, pointed a gun at a man in my life...not in carelessness, not in fun, certainly not in anger."

"Well, you've done it now. Don't ever do it again. We get close to that bear the next time, you're using my rifle. That contraption of yours is no weapon for this kind of hunt."

The hunter gathered his legs up underneath, limped over and grabbed the horn of the saddle and leaned against the horse. "I'm through, Simmons. Take me out of here. You can come back in tomorrow and get your other horse and pack out the camp."

"And the bear? And the hounds?"

"Fuck the bear. Fuck those dogs. They'll find their way home. You whipped me, Simmons...okay...now you can just get me out of here. I'm paying for this hunt, Simmons."

Harley reached to his shirt pocket and took out the check that Wetzel had written out in down payment of the hunt and handed it to the hunter. "I didn't whip you, Wetzel; the bear did. We jumped a bad bear. Lots of them are bad. That's bear hunting in this country. And it comes down to this: I work for those hounds, not for you. They're going to wear that bear down. And I'm going to be there when they do. And this old horse is going to take you home. You're going to get on this horse and rim around this ridge and you're going to keep your eyes on that bluff over there to the west...you see that?"

The hunter followed the direction of Harley's arm and nodded his head.

"You're going to ride to that bluff, Wetzel, and when you get past it you're going to climb to the south till you top out on the divide. You're going to cross a good horse trail there and turn west. By then this old horse is going to know you're going home and she's going to take you in as good as I ever could."

"How far am I from you're place?"

"Eight hours, with that horse at a walk."

"Eight hours! It'll be dark."

"That horse can see better in the dark than you can right now. You take her to that bluff and she's going to take you to the barn whether you know where you are or not. When you get there just drop the reins and leave the horse and stop at that shack across the creek on your way out. Wake the old woman up if you have to. She doesn't speak much English but you can make her understand where the horse is. She'll take care of the horse."

The hunter came around to the left side of the horse and with a boost from Harley climbed into the saddle. He leaned forward in the stirrups to keep his bloody tailbone off the saddle. His hands were cut by the brush. The knot had welled up real good on his forehead where the limb pummeled him off the saddle and the cut was starting to scab over. He was still breathing with some difficulty from the fall and the climb and the ride. Harley stepped back away from the horse.

"Don't feel bad, Wetzel. You did the best you could...better than most. You're not used to this. Almost nobody is anymore. Now rein that horse around and get started. I've got to catch up to that race."

For a moment, Wetzel looked at Harley like he wished he'd pulled the trigger. Then, without speaking, he reined the horse around and put her into a walk. The horse stepped out like she knew already she was headed for the barn. Harley watched them go and shortly they were out of sight. Harley stepped up on the mule and rode her over to the far side of the saddle and listened for the pack. They were down in Brush Creek; they were moving and would soon be out of hearing, headed up the creek deeper into the labyrinth of Brushy Mountain. There was a way to rim this canyon, too, and stay above the race. Harley reined the mule around, put her into a lope and disappeared into the trees.

~ ~ ~ ~ ~ ~

The sun still shown on the peak of Brushy Mountain; as it had early that morning, it streaked across the higher ridges. But the canyons of Brushy Mountain had been deep in shade for hours and within an hour more, even the peak of Brushy Mountain would lose the last of its light. Harley sat on a carpet of grass in the aspen park, on the north slope just below the summit, by an origin of spring waters, looking off into Brush Creek. With hours of riding, and some climbing on foot, he had gained the headwaters of Brush Creek. He was now ahead of the race. Only it wasn't much of a race anymore. In the canyon below, along Brush Creek, the hounds had badgered the bear to a standstill; the bay, chop, squall and boo of each hound was a very occasional sound now; the bear hadn't moved 100 yards in an hour. All the combatants were wearing down. Harley looked again at the streaks of sunlight coming through the aspens, just now budding out green from winter. He's not going to tree, he thought. Not today, not tonight, not ever. Harley knew he was going to have to go down into Brush Creek to a bear on the ground. He knew too, that the bear would wind him before he got there and that he would find the strength to run from the man scent. If he broke up the steep slopes of the canyon he would outrun the dogs to the top and, for the night at least, the race would be over for Harley. But Harley knew the hounds had fought the bear into a desperately tired state, as tired as the hounds themselves, as tired as Harley and the mule. There was a chance the bear would take the easy route and run back down Brush Creek. The mule had watered at the origins of Brush Creek and had recovered as much as she would without time to feed and a nights rest. Harley went to the mule and drew his rifle from the scabbard and levered a shell into the chamber. He rechecked the safety and returned the gun to the case. Then he drew his revolver from the holster and counted, as he expected, five shells, plus the empty chamber under the hammer. A shell ready to fire would come under the hammer when the gun was cocked. Harley went around to the left side of the mule and footed the stirrup and stepped up into the saddle. He picked up the spring waters of Brush Creek descending into the canyon.

He got closer than he ever could have hoped to the bear; he could see the bear's immense black back through the trees when he heard the bear sound his alarm with a *woof!* - more of a snort than a bark - and then the bear had whirled to gallop down the canyon, away from the man scent, popping the brush and splashing the water out of the creek as he ran. Harley urged the mule ahead at a trot, slowed to go around one blowdown, jumped the mule over a second, then spurred the mule into one last gallop as he watched Lurk pull ahead of the pack with wonderful greyhounding strides to reach, stretch and grab bear butt. The bear spun about and White-eye took him at the neck, right behind the ear. The bear roared and rolled down the creek, splashing water and shedding two hounds only to regain his feet with a third hound, Geraldine, fastened to his haunch. With Harley coming to the catch, the hounds were attacking the bear. And then he was there, firing the revolver from the saddle, placing a shot point blank behind the shoulder, and another, and another, and then again; the gun roared and shot fire in the dim light every time an opening appeared in the swirling fight.

The bear was down. Harley leaped from the saddle and approached the bear with the fifth and final shot. He left it in the gun as the bear slumped into the waters of Brush Creek, his eyes evolving childlike and astonished as the life of him pumped out. Pointing the gun aside, Harley gently released the hammer with his thumb. He set the revolver back in the holster. There came then that sickness that grabbed his stomach and twisted his gut and caught in his throat and he could no longer look at the bear. He turned away and dropped to his knees, folding over on himself, feeling that he must puke, or cry, and knowing he would do neither but for a time must be sick of himself over what he had done. It was very quiet now along Brush Creek. Folded over himself, he listened for some time to the heavy breathing of the mule, and the gurgle of the creek and the hounds licking their wounds. There was no sound from the bear, at all. Then Lurk came over, put his head under Harley's arm, lifted and rolled him over. Harley let himself go onto his back, and Lurk lay down across his chest and tried to lick his face. Harley swatted the hound with his hat, then lay the hat over his own face. "Why do I do this, Lurk?" The hound tried again to lick Harley's face, and again Harley swatted him with his hat. "I know why you do this Lurk, but why do I? Am I so much like you?" The hound whined in a way that was almost a howl, contending with emotions of his own. "Or are you so much like me?" Lurk whined and then really began to howl until Harley cut him off with another swat of his hat. "He was a great one, Lurk; he was one of the best." Then Harley put his hat over his face. He talked up into his hat. "I ought to get a job, Lurk. I'd be home from work already, sitting in a chair with my feet up, watching the evening news, drinking a beer, talking to my boy instead of a hound dog, sharing my supper with someone a lot better looking than you. I'm probably the only person in America is going to spend the night in a cold canyon under a dark mountain with three hound dogs and a mule and a dead bear...you hear me Lurk?" Lurk grabbed Harley's hat away from his face, got to his feet and stepped away with the hat in his mouth. He went and lay down underneath the mule with the hat and began chewing on the hat. Harley did not like laying on his back without the hat to cover his face. And it was getting cold in the canyon. And Lurk wasn't going to listen to any more of this and Harley knew he would need his hat. "Okay Lurk," he said.

First he went and took his hat away from Lurk and he put it on his head. Then he pulled the saddle off the mule, led her downstream and hobbled her out on a good patch of grass. Back at camp he got a fire going, piled on a bunch of dead stuff to make some flame and give some light. Then he got down with the bear and heaved and wrestled and while he couldn't lift the bear he managed to roll it over so it was out of the creek and laying on it's back with its head up the bank. Then Harley drew his knife and by the light of the fire he slit the bear open and then he used his hands and the entrails rolled out steaming in the firelight. Harley reached way up in the cavity and dug out the heart and liver; the hounds came over and gorged on the chunks. Harley used sticks to prop the cavity open to let the carcass air and cool. Then he slit down the inside of one hind leg and peeled the hide back and with the knife he cut crosswise against the grain to take out several large steaks. He went to the fire and cut strips of meat off the steaks and he strung them out on a green stick. Along with matches and a small canteen, he always had some salt in the saddlebags. He salted the meat and roasted it over the fire. He was very hungry now; he could hardly wait for the meat to cook. He began to pull the half cooked strips off the stick and he fed them into his mouth. He cut more strips and put them on the stick and into the flames. He ate his way through two of the steaks and gave the rest to the hounds. Everyone ate till they were drummed out. Then he moved away from the fire and got some dead oak and came back and chunked up the fire. He went and got some more oak for the night. He untied his coat from behind the saddle and put it on. He put the saddle pad on the ground and lay down on the pad with the saddle blanket over his shoulders and with the saddle as a pillow. One by one the hounds came in and curled up around him, hugged by the fire, for the night.

In the morning the hounds one by one got up to move away where they stretched and pissed, leaving Harley suddenly chilled in the frosty canyon; so he got up himself and moved away and, like the hounds, took the time to stretch and piss. He had slept well, the sleep of a tired man. Now he was refreshed and the sun was near the top of the canyon, sunlight creeping down the west wall. Harley fanned at the oak coals with his hat and got the fire going and he threw on some more wood. He went to the creek and put his lips to the creek for a long drink. The water was very cold and some of the best water he'd ever had. He cupped his hands and took water up and splashed his face with the icy water. "God-a-mighty!" he said outloud.

Harley went to the fire and warmed his wet hands till they were dry. Then he went to the bear. He cut off strips of meat for their breakfast, then roasted it over the coals as he had the night before. Following the feast the night before, he wasn't very hungry, but he thought: I'm a twelve hour walk from home and need to eat. He ate a good bait of meat and fed as much to each hound.

Downstream, Ruby had eaten down her patch of grass and was filled out too. Harley removed the hobbles and led her up to camp. He saddled the mule, tightened the cinch, tightened the britching and breast collar, then led her around and drew up the cinch a little more. Then he led her over to the bear. Ruby eyed the bear, rolled her nose and lay her ears back and trembled in an anticipation that clearly did not please her. Harley said, "Ruby, you've never boogered from a bear yet so there's no reason to start now." Ruby wasn't so sure but stood her ground. As a farmer can never have too much baling wire handy, a horseman in the wilderness can never have too much rope. Harley had a lariat and a good stout lead rope tied to the saddle. He took the lariat from the saddle and uncoiled it and looped it around the bear, just under the front legs. He threw the end of the rope over a stout oak limb and then wrapped it around the horn of the saddle. He led Ruby away; she leaned into the weight as she did when pulling a plow and as she walked away the bear came up off the ground. The bear hung there, macabre and grotesque, in the air. "Steady Ruby," and Harley left her with the weight while he removed the lead rope from the saddle and uncoiled it. He made a loop in the rope and encircled the bear with the loop, as he had with the lariat. He threw the end of the lead rope up over the limb and took the end as it came down and wrapped it around the trunk of the oak, taking up all the slack, and tied it. Then he stepped over to Ruby, who held the great bear without apparent effort, and Harley said, "goddamn that's a stout mule," and then he backed Ruby a couple of steps and the lead rope took the weight of the bear as the lariat went slack. Ruby continued to eye the dead bear without love and Harley removed his coat and wrapped it around the mule's head, blinding the mule. He backed the mule three more steps and she was under the bear, the hind legs of the bear hanging just below the top of the saddle. "Steady Ruby," and Ruby trembled but held her ground. Then Harley went to the end of the lead rope and untied it, leaving the wraps around the trunk and holding the end of the lead rope, keeping the wraps tight to the tree. He held the lead rope and took two steps back to the mule. He gave some slack to the lead rope and let the wraps give, bit by bit, and the weight of the great bear took the slack from his hand and the wraps slipped, little by little, from around the tree, and as the bear eased lower he used his other hand to guide it and it rolled over the top of the saddle and Ruby had the weight of the bear across her back. "Steady Ruby," and he worked quickly using both ropes to tie the bear in a rough balance on top of the mule to the D rings in the double cinch and up to the horn, and then he drew everything down tight. He removed his coat from the mule's head, and stepped back. Ruby looked irritable rather than stressed but she knew she was loaded and Harley said, "goddamn that's a stout mule."

They all started down the canyon and one by one the hounds stopped to hunker over a bush and empty out. Soon Harley, too, had the feeling. He dropped the reins and, despite the complete isolation of the locale, went over behind a bush where he loosened his belt, dropped his jeans, squatted, and, like the hounds, shit mightily and heavily, and not without satisfaction.

It was near noon when they got to the game trail that Harley knew the mule could climb to take them out of Brush Creek before its confluence with the Río Jalisco. Harley tied the reins up and turned the mule up the trail. She lowered her head and put her haunches into the climb and Harley followed her great muscley rump up the switch back trail to the mesa above. At the top he took the reins and led the mule away to the west and south and he said, "goddamn that's a stout mule."

At camp he took the time to pack the camp on the roan, staked out on the grass, while Ruby wandered and took up great clumps of grass and watered at the spring. When the camp was loaded Harley went to the mule and said, "Ruby, someday I'd like to find out what your limit is only by then I believe I'd be out of the race." He brought the mule over and tied the roan's lead rope to Ruby's tail and they headed south and west for the divide.

It was well past dark when they all walked into the yard. Harley used Ruby to help him hang the bear from a limb of a cottonwood down by the creek. Then he unsaddled the horse and the mule, rubbed them down, grained them and put them in the pasture with some hay. He let the hounds in the house, to be fed a special meal and to sleep by the fire in the wood stove, what they loved. He fussed over them and fed them and loved them up and built them a fire in the stove. He was well pleased with the hunt, the only discomfiting element being thoughts of Ben Wetzel. Harley had followed the old mare's tracks into the yard, so he knew the hunter had made it in. But Ted had described Wetzel as being "to our uses." Harley left the hounds by the fire and went to the kitchen to make himself some supper, and he thought: if Wetzel bothers to write any story at all, it's not going to be designed to help the cause. It was then that he saw the note on the kitchen table...

Simmons:

Attached please find my check in down payment of $250 (since it wasn't your fault I didn't finish the hunt) and my second check, also for $250 (since I know you got the bear). You're right, the bear took us places I'd have never seen. It's a great country. It's a priceless river. How I will write the story of my own demise, I don't know. But if I get mad - and I'm still plenty pissed - I'll take it out on our common enemies. I'll be back someday Simmons, in shape for the hunt, and I'll beat you to the catch.

Yours,

Wetzel

P.S. In case no one has told you this, there is more to guiding than hunting; you'll never make it as a guide.

*Chapter 11*

A MORNING IN JUNE and it was really beginning to seem like home. Down by the creek, the orchard had blossomed and, blessed with a benevolent spring, had not frozen back. There would be a fruit crop this year. The garden took water regularly and had sprouted green leaves and shoots and the beginnings of a promising crop of vegetables. With the old woman's help, the garden grew in clean green rows, free from weeds. At the house, all the repairs were done; everything worked and held tight. And the old woman came in once a week and cleaned house and straightened up so that his bachelor quarters offered him better living than he deserved. And he had made some changes inside to suit himself. The hides and head mounts the old man had left behind, on the floor and the walls, gave an ambience to the living room that was appropriate and pleased him. And there were new pictures on the wall. The print that Henry Bustos had made for him was now framed and looked as good in Harley's house as it had in the sheriff's office. And an artist with a brush, as talented in his way and as little known for his talent as the sheriff, had contributed a painting to the room. Ted Beeler's "Mountain Man" had a likeness of his father, packing out of the wilderness with his pelts, the work at once alluring, sensitive, understated and accurate to the last detail. This too was framed and now covered a section of one wall that featured an array of fine hounds, tough hunts and old friends. He still had not framed or put up the picture of his own family. There was still time and that time, he was sure, would come. The house, the garden, the whole place was now definitely his own, with the living room in particular offering up especially for him, thoughts, emotions, reminiscences. However, the most awesome thoughts, emotions and reminiscences now emanated not from the trophies, art or photos, but from the calendar on the wall, still open so as to offer the schedule for the month of May. Harley looked at the calendar this day as he had for weeks, knowing he was getting further and further behind. It was now two weeks into June. The month of May offered one notation, that he had made himself, marking that day when school was dismissed for the summer. That was the day he was going to call to claim his son for a weekend. He had not called. Every weekend, it seemed, there was work, business, some outdoor adventure that got in the way. This morning he had made a run to town, ostensibly for some groceries, and hound and horse feed; but in fact to be sure that, if he called, he would not get the wrong voice, to be sure that she would be able to talk. On the way home with the supplies he had swung by Juniper Hills and, yes, her's was the only car at the house. Now, home, the month of May with its single notation loomed with overpowering prominence on the wall. Finally, he reached for the phone and dialed.

"Hello."

"Bonney?"

"Well! I guess we women do have intuition. I knew this week I was going to hear from you. I could feel it."

"I've been back since the funeral."

"I know. I've heard."

"I just decided to stay around."

"I don't know why. It can't be very pleasant for you."

"I have my reasons."

"Well I hope Billy and I are not one of your reasons. I don't want to hurt you, Harley."

"I doubt if you're losing much sleep over that."

"Don't start, Harley."

He waited, unable to speak. Unable to think. So much that he had to say, that he had planned so well to say, had planned for a year to say, was slipping away. He knew he had already lost control of the conversation. And it didn't appear that she was going to bail him out. Finally, he said, "How is he?"

"He's fine."

"Is he doing well in school?"

"Yes."

"Does he have friends, some good friends?"

"Yes, of course."

"He was always so shy. But he always had friends at school...they liked him...such a likeable kid..."

He waited; there was no response, just the ice gripping the line, and all the big things he had to say were clearly inappropriate, would not impress, and he had run out of small talk. And it was certain now she was not going to bail him out.

"Well," he said, "I'll be taking him this weekend."

"Sorry Harley, he's not here."

"Not here?"

"He's at camp for the summer."

"Camp! What camp?"

"I'm not going to tell you. It's up towards Santa Fe, and Taos,...in there; but I'm not going to tell you where."

"Camp! This whole country is a camp. Why would a kid growing up in Del Cobre need to go to camp?"

"That's just the point. Any child deserves to know something more than what Del Cobre has to offer."

"Who taught you to say that?"

"Don't start, Harley. We just felt he ought to have the opportunity to meet some new people."

"Sure. Ageing hippies, *chi chi* shoppers, *gucci* bolsheviks and other birds of paradise. And their offspring. There's nothing new about that, not in northern New Mexico. He should stay here where he can be with folks."

"Harley, sometimes I think you don't even realize how backward you are."

"And what's this *we*?"

"I'm sure you don't want me to go into that. You must know I have a new life now. I have new friends, and I have a new job. I have a job at the bank now. The first decent job I've ever had. I owe that to him, and so much more. And he cares for Billy, just like a father, so naturally he's involved in our decisions."

"Jesus Bonney!"

"Truth is best."

"I don't suppose any of this maneuvering has anything to do with me being back in town."

"Of course not. And it's not maneuvering."

"When is Billy coming back?"

"Never mind...in time for school. Then he'll be busy with school. Harley, just leave us alone."

"You're telling me to leave my own son alone? And what about us?

"Don't start. There is no *us*. It's over. Leave it alone, Harley. Just leave us all alone."

"Bonney...goddamnit..."

"Don't start, Harley. I'm going to hang up now. I don't have to deal with this. I'm going to hang up...now."

## Chapter 12

**TED BEELER** lay deep in his extra large sleeping bag under a full June moon, listening to the stream, and the way things were going he could almost laugh outloud. The gay, exciting feelings that were keeping him awake were happily childlike, and reminiscent of childhood capers that seemed so serious at the time. He had known those same feelings when, just a kid, he'd been up to no good - playing hookie to go fishing, shooting a few squirrels out season, slipping out to meet a girl - and had thought he just might get away with it. Often he didn't get away with it. And then all hell broke loose. But it seldom mattered; it was still fun. And now, an adult on the banks of the Río Jalisco, he felt like the same kid. And he was involved in another caper. Strictly speaking, it was legitimate. He was just doing his job. But he knew that now, as of today, he had the New Mexico River Otter on film, and he knew it was just a matter of time till all hell broke loose. It was going to be fun. Then he heard a loud splash over on the river...

He had been riding this wave of good feelings and fine anticipations since those moments, three nights before, when he had lain in a waterbed and made love with his wife. Earlier, they had discussed the fact

114

that he would be away in the wilderness for a week or more. This worried her, made her both vulnerable and urgent. This brought on an urgency in himself. The fucking and the loving were wonderful. Like old times. Afterwards they had held each other and he had told her, as he always did, not to worry, that there was more danger in the city than in the wilderness. "Harley says," he told her, "you're more likely to get bumped off driving the freeway through Albuquerque than riding through these mountains."

"That sounds like Harley," she said.

And it was true enough, and for the most part she believed him, though she would always *feel* that the wilderness, which she had never known, was more fearsome. Then she had slept close beside him, contented. And contented himself, Ted had lain awake for a time in happiness, a family man in the bosom of a fine family. The woman he wanted was his wife. He had two lovely, mischievous daughters who nonetheless liked to please their father. He had a job he liked, a reasonably good salary, and two bird dogs to hunt and pal around with. According to Harley, the only thing he lacked was his own place in the country and a good mule. "Then you'll be invincible," Harley had said. Ted Beeler had lain awake in happiness, and in anticipation of a week or two in the wilds. There was a certain pleasant anxiety in this thought. It would be, he considered, his first extended trip alone in the wilderness in some time. There was considerable pleasant anxiety thinking about the otters, too. He had never seen an otter in the wild. It was nearly certain that in the next week or two he was going to see an otter, probably a number of them. He was going to get otters on film, and within a month after that the whole state was going to know about it. He was going to deliver the New Mexico River Otter from extirpation and all hell was going to break loose.

Ted Beeler had lain awake in the waterbed for most of the night, anticipating. He left very early in the morning and met Andrews, the Forest Service biologist, at the Ranger Station. The Forest Service was providing the horse and two pack mules and Andrews helped him pack the outfit on the mules - food, grain, camera equipment, tent, tarps to fashion a blind, and everything else he might need, for two weeks if necessary. Andrews was a good packer and between the two of them it didn't take long to get the outfit packed. When they were done Andrews smiled and made reference to a "wild otter chase."

"There's plenty of tracks," Ted said. "I looked at them every way you can. I photographed them. The tracks say otter."

"Tracks are tricky, Ted. Even a good man can make mistakes with tracks. Tracks don't make an otter."

"Harley's seen them."

"Harley's a character."

"He knows this country."

"Harley gets around, all right. The supervisor told me I could ride in next week, give you a hand."

"Harley will probably ride in next week, too."

"Fine, we'll all look for them. If there's otters on that river it's going to raise a ruckus, Ted. You show me an otter and I'll help you raise it."

Ted had left the Ranger Station and had ridden for the divide. He crossed it, spent his first night out, then found the trail Harley recommended and dropped into the canyon. He got to the Meadows in time to set up his camp in under a wonderful grove of Emory Oak, well off the river. Then he took his video camera and still camera with tripod and all the gear he needed to set up and spend his days in a blind. He found a good perch in the rocks above the river, adjacent to the falls and opposite the confluence of Ocotillo Creek. He left the gear secure from the weather under the tarps and walked back to camp where he spent the night. At first light the next morning he was ready in the blind. It didn't take long. His approach and set up had been expertly surreptitious. For along about 8:00 A.M. - about the time most folks were daring the freeway on their way to work - he saw an otter come sliding down Ocotillo Creek, disappear into the big pool, then reappear on the near shore with a small carp in its mouth. He glistened dark brown, almost black, in the sun, with a silvery sheen to the belly fur, as he broke the hide on the still flopping fish and began to feed. Ted had touched the trigger and began to film. Incredibly, the otter had picked up the new sound in the wilderness; he cocked his head and considered this new sound for several minutes. Then he resumed feeding. He left when he was through, still appearing curious but not overly disturbed by the new sound, and disappeared into the pool. He did not come back. But later that morning a female with three kits broke the surface of the pool, came to the beach on the creek side, and frolicked up the creek, the kits skittering along behind their mother, till the bend in the creek and a lush sycamore grove took them from the camera's eye.

That had been enough for Ted for the first day. Wishing he could whoop, shout and otherwise tell the world, he had in fact returned quietly to camp for the day, where he recorded in detail his observations to date.

And now, deep in his sleeping bag under a full June moon, he looked up at the southwestern night and listened to the stream. Then he heard the splash. He lifted himself to an elbow and looked to the sound. He could just see the surface of the river, moving crisply, tinkling and dancing in the moonlight. It must have been an otter, he thought. Then he spoke outloud: "You otters go ahead and carry on. Before we're through, you're going to make a bigger splash than that."

Then he gave a whoop of laughter.

*Chapter 13*

HARLEY knew something was up as he and Lurk drove through town on the morning of an already hot Fourth of July and saw Jim Bo Moreland cross the street in front of them with a look on his face that said he was not all that happy with the state of the nation on this, America's Birthday. Jim Bo had a rolled up newspaper in his right hand and he was tapping it impatiently into the palm of his left hand during his rapid stride like he was fixing to use it to deliver punishment to a bad dog or errant child. Harley slowed to a near stop, because Jim Bo was obviously oblivious to any traffic, and because Jim Bo was headed for City Hall which, on the Fourth of July, ought to be closed? Then Harley noticed that Stan "Bubba" Baer was behind the door of City Hall, and Stew Mayfair, and Dirk Johngood and Morey Solís, and as Jim Bo approached, Harley watched Bubba Baer turn the key, let the worried man in, shut the door and roll the key back around. Harley gradually resumed speed as he watched the occupants disappear into the building. He went down the street, turned up Ballard for the Cafe Luera. At the Cafe Luera he dropped a quarter into the newspaper stand in front of the cafe, took out the one remaining copy of that days' Albuquerque *Times*, and Jim Bo's distress was promptly explained. The headline that keyed the front page below the fold said: REDISCOVERED SPECIES THREATENS WATER PROJECT. Harley went inside the cafe, got himself a cup of coffee, ordered *huevos rancheros*, then sat down with the story in hand...

> SANTA FE - *A senior biologist with the State Department of Wildlife shocked a packed meeting of the State River Commission here Friday with evidence that a species thought extinct in the state is alive and well and in potential conflict with the proposed Río Jalisco Dam.*
>
> *Known as the River Otter, biologist Ted Beeler said the species is about two feet long, weighs up to 30 pounds, and "resembles a large, aquatic weasel." The species once inhabited most of New Mexico's perennial streams, Beeler said, but was extirpated by uncontrolled trapping and habitat destruction. Or so everyone thought.*
>
> *"Officially, the otter has been considered extirpated in the state since 1953," Beeler said. "We had no idea we had a remnant population living in the Río Jalisco."*
>
> *Beeler said his first clue to the otter's presence along a remote portion of the river was during biological survey work last March in conjunction with the proposed dam.*

# HOME IS THE RIVER

*"A local guide suggested that I ought to include the otters in the survey," Beeler said. "I thought he was joking, then I thought he was mistaken, then I found out he was right."*

*Beeler said that during his two week study along the river he identified two breeding pairs of otters, with three and two kits respectively, plus several juvenile animals. He said that based on the guide's information, it appears the otters did not migrate into the area but "have been there all along."*

*Beeler said he had photographed and filmed the otters during his study and he showed a series of slides of the otters to the commission and a map indicating their range along the river and in several tributary streams. The 10 mile stretch of the otter's range is directly upstream from the Río Jalisco Damsite, Beeler said.*

*The proposed Río Jalisco Dam lies in a remote section of the Jalisco National Forest in northern Arthur County. Authorized by Congress a year ago, construction by the Bureau of Reclamation (BOR) is scheduled to begin next year.*

*Commission Chief Sterling Roberts suggested to Beeler that the slow filling of water behind the dam might produce a reservoir "very much to the critter's liking."*

*Beeler said it was his opinion that the otter had survived in the Río Jalisco because the river offered an unregulated perennial flow in a wilderness setting.*

*"You eliminate the habitat and you will certainly eliminate the species," Beeler said.*

*Roberts then asked Beeler if the otter might in any way come under the protection of federal law.*

*"No sir," Beeler said. "The River Otter is rare in New Mexico; it is not rare on a nationwide basis."*

*"Thank you very much," Roberts said.*

*Roberts then said that the point for the Commission to consider was not whether the otters were threatened by the dam but whether the dam was threatened by the otters.*

*"I'm sure the Department of Wildlife will utilize their expertise in mitigating any possible loss of habitat or wildlife that might occur," Roberts said, "but I do not see that the presence of a State Endangered Species should in any way obstruct this commission and the Bureau of Reclamation from enhancing the water supply in*

*southwest New Mexico by prompt completion of the Río Jalisco Dam, as authorized by Congress."*

*Garth Bilker of the Jalisco Rod and Gun Club, a local support group, questioned the timing of the Department of Wildlife in bringing up the otter issue.*

*"Isn't it convenient," Bilker said, "they these biologists have discovered these otters after all these years, just when our dam is ready to be built. It's well known in Del Cobre that the Department of Wildlife is against the project and we expected they would come up with something to try and stop our dam."*

*Sierra Club representative Sylvia Fellows said that the otters presence in the Río Jalisco was a "significant discovery" and pointed up just how little is known about the Jalisco National Forest.*

*"That's terra incognita," Fellows said. "But once New Mexicans realize what a rare gem they have in that portion of the Río Jalisco drainage, it's doubtful they will want any development in that unique area."*

*Fellows added that the Sierra Club would soon do their own survey along the Río Jalisco and would take their case to the public.*

*Public hearings on the pros and cons of the Río Jalisco project will be scheduled for sometime late this year. Hearings will be held in Albuquerque and Del Cobre, a BOR spokesman said.*

## Chapter 14

HAD SHE BEEN AWAKE, the sounds coming from the warm room would have frightened the child. Then she, too, might have been caught up in the fury of their venery. Then she would have heard the lean white stomach slapping sweat against the soft brown belly, the punctuating smacks mounting, building, coming faster, and overlain by the moaning, the grunting, the furious breathing and the unspeakable words. When finally they lay breathing side by side on the bed, the moonlight through the open window caught them glistening and the cooler air from the mountains was coming in. The room had been very warm, but the breeze was bringing it down as it cooled and dried the flesh. Then she said: "I'd better go and check on her. She sleeps so soundly but I want to be sure." He watched her gather herself and leave the surface of the bed, watched again as she returned. "She's fine. Children sleep so heavily; I don't think a fire alarm would wake her up; some mornings I have to hold her for awhile till she comes around."

He said, "It won't be too many years and she'll have thoughts and dreams that won't let her sleep so well. Like us."

"Yes," she said. "Then we'll have to be more careful."

"Then?"

"Of course. Don't you believe we'll always sleep together?"

He lay quietly, feeling the cooler air, and said nothing.

"Well, I do," she said. "I know it's not your dream. But I believe we have a good chance."

He reached to the night stand then, and took the water glass. He drank slowly, carefully; it was good water on a hot night. Then he passed her the water. She sat up and drank the rest of it. Then they both settled again on their backs.

She said, "Can I ask you a very personal question?"

"You can ask it. I don't know if I'll answer it."

"What's she like in bed?"

Again he had no response.

"If I tell you what I imagine she's like, will you tell me if I'm right?"

He wouldn't answer and she took it as acquiescence.

"I sense," she began, "that she doesn't want to so very often and she won't, she just won't, unless she wants to. She decides. And when she decides she comes on very strong and she expects a man will be happy, and ready, to give her pleasure. She takes time, and it must be a certain way, and no disturbances, so she can feel the man but hold on to herself and concentrate. It takes time but if a man gives her that time she is often successful. When she comes she does turn it loose, yet always holding something back. And then she is patient, waiting for the man. *Qué no?*"

He turned away from her, on to his side. She rolled up against him and spoke softly behind him, into the muscles of his back.

"I've hurt you," she said. "I'm sorry, Harley."

"How could you know?"

"With many people, I think you can imagine quite well what they are like when they are naked and are giving themselves away. For years it hurt me, too. I was tormented by those thoughts. I couldn't stop them; I was so jealous. Then I began to realize you were never really satisfied with her."

"It's true."

"But the way it is with her, you're always wanting more, always hoping to break through. So you remain interested."

"I'll admit that."

"Are you satisfied with me?"

"You know the answer to that. What it was, just now, would tell you. And it's always like that with us. You and I were born to fuck."

"Then why aren't I enough?

"It's not as simple as that."

120

"Of course not. But we make love so well, and we sleep together so well. It means something, Harley. It means something more."

"Well, you said it then...I'm always wanting something else, something I don't have. And maybe I can't have it. But I want it. We were happy, for a time, she and I. And I have a son."

She kissed his back and wrapped around him and squeezed him like hugging a big child. "I'm sorry, Harley. *Dispensame.* I shouldn't force you to share all my thoughts."

"You didn't force me."

"I think I pretty much did."

"Well, I guess we all wonder about those things."

"Do you?"

"I wonder sometimes...I have the feeling you're easily satisfied."

"In a way I suppose I am. Making it with a man has seldom been a problem for me. Finding a man I want to make it with is something else. But you're right - we were born to make love together. And I believe we'll always sleep together."

"Can we sleep now?"

"Yes. And sleep well, my friend.. For there is a nice surprise for you tomorrow."

~ ~ ~ ~ ~ ~

The first surprise came somewhat sooner than he expected and wasn't all that pleasant. From somewhere not far away a rooster let loose his first announcement that it was time, in his opinion, for things to start to happen. Harley rolled over and waited with his ears alert to be sure he wasn't dreaming. Pretty soon he heard it again, a very loud, brash rooster indeed, right outside the window, who sounded off as if he were sure the sun would rise because he crowed. Then Harley could see the critter, perched in the Box Elder in the back yard. The rooster was right; it was beginning to get light. He could see Suzie in sleep, the strong profile, featuring her lovely high-priestess nose, just visible. Then he saw that Suzie was awake too, and smiling.

"Isn't he wonderful!" she said. "I just love him. He makes me feel like I'm living in the country, what I always wanted."

Harley said, "When did they unchain him?"

"Just recently. He belonged to one of the neighbors and he just wandered in one day. Jessica was fascinated and I think when I wasn't looking she was feeding him because he started hanging around. I felt he must be returned but the neighbor said, 'keep him; he's a damned nuisance.'"

The rooster let go again.

"Your neighbor is right," Harley said. "My set up is better. The old woman keeps the chickens. I get all the eggs I need, and her roosters are across the creek. I can hear them, but not so goddamned loud."

"We're going to get some chickens. Then he'll have something to crow about. Jessica wants to collect our own eggs. I checked, and it seems there is still no ordinance against it."

"There will be if the wrong sort hears him up close one morning. But get some chickens while you can. Once this place gets so uptown they start legislating against animals, it'll be time to move on."

And the rooster had awakened someone else. In a while Jessica came in to her mother's bedroom, a dark skinned sylph of a girl, with straight black hair and wearing white pajamas. She was carrying a black cat that rode contentedly in her folded arms.

"You guys get up," Jessica said.

"What for?" Harley said.

"Because we need to take my cat for a walk."

"Cats don't go for walks. She's not a puppy dog. She'll wander off and get lost."

"No she won't. You'll see. You guys get up."

Later, Harley and Jessica walked down the street to the neighborhood *tienda* where Harley bought the paper. Jessica was right; the cat followed along down the street like a puppy dog, waited outside while Harley and Jessica were in the store, and followed them back to the house. On the way back Harley and Jessica held hands as they walked along and Harley said, "Jessica, you have trained a cat. No one has ever trained a cat before."

"It's easy," Jessica said.

"It's impossible," Harley said. "It's impossible to train a cat. No one has ever trained a cat to do anything."

"You get a cat, and then I can show you," Jessica said.

"No thanks. One trained cat is enough."

At the house they walked through the front door into the kitchen and Suzie was on the phone, and Harley and Jessica overheard Suzie say: "*Y Gloria me dijo que su esposo ya no puede...*" In the living room Harley said, "Jessica, do you know what your mother is doing?"

"She's talking on the phone."

"She's gossiping. Do you know what gossip is?"

"That's like when you have a secret that you tell to everyone."

"Okay, you got it. Does your mother gossip a lot?"

"Only in Spanish."

Later still, Harley sat on the edge of the couch, reading the paper, aware that there was some mischief going on in the kitchen. Suzie was cooking breakfast and her daughter would tug at her blouse and whisper and then she would peak around the corner at Harley when she thought he wasn't looking. Finally, she approached him with her hands behind her back and a look every now and then over her shoulder at her mother who was in the kitchen nodding approval while she cooked. Then Jessica stopped in front of Harley and said, "How old are you?"

"One year older today than yesterday."

"No good!"

"Roughly thirty."

"Well, okay."

Then she handed him his present. It was sheathed and he promptly drew it out. It was a hunting knife, of a good, handy size, with a simple blade where the beauty was in it's being designed for use. The handle was bone, was elegant, and, like the blade, was obviously done by hand. Harley eyed the knife appreciatively.

"Jessica, how did you know what to get me for my birthday?"

"It's because you are a hunter. And mommy helped. It's from Mexico."

From the kitchen Suzie said, "We made a run to Chihuahua last weekend. There is a knife maker in Janos that my uncle recommended."

"I've heard of him," Harley said. "And I'm proud to own one. Jessica, I know how to burn a brand into this sheath. It's going to say, 'from Jessica.'"

Her eyes got big and she smiled and then she ran into the kitchen to her mother. He followed, for the coffee was on.

## Chapter 15

HE HEARD THE HOUNDS start to howl, the way they did when there was company coming, and then he heard a vehicle in the yard. He lit the fire under the burner, dropped a frozen brick of chili into the pan. He set the pan on the burner as he heard a knock at the door. He went to the door and knew right away this had to be the Río Jalisco Conservation Coalition, that he wasn't expecting till morning.

"Harley Simmons?"

"Uh huh."

"Sylvia Fellows." The woman, to Harley, seemed a bit older than himself, blonde, of a cheerful countenance, and attractive. "We got in town early," she said, "and gave ourselves a tour, got lost, then saw the sign for Gavilán Road. So we decided to come by and get acquainted. I hope we're not intruding."

"You-all come in."

He led them into the kitchen, gathered up four more chairs and promptly had them all seated around the kitchen table.

"Beer?" he asked as he pulled a six pack from the refrigerator and set it on the table. Nobody turned it down. So he twisted off the caps and handed the bottles to Sylvia and Tom and William and Grace. Then he stepped to the stove to check on the chili which was filling the room with it's peculiar, savory odors. "Had supper yet?"

"Oh that's okay," Sylvia said.

"That means you haven't."

Harley went to the back porch, opened the freezer, and brought in two more bricks of frozen chili and put them in the pan. Then he sat down, twisted a cap off a bottle, and considered for a moment Ted's words on the phone the night before: "Try to be a little more accommodating this time!" Harley raised his bottle in a meaningful way, till he had them all with their bottles similarly raised in anticipation, and said: "To the free flow of the Río Jalisco." Relieved, they all drank heartily to that, and Harley thought: I'm going to do all right with this outfit; they're just plain folks.

They began to enjoy beer, and chat, and Sylvia began to talk to Lurk, who was curled up on the kitchen floor. Lurk did not respond.

"Does he bite?" she asked.

"No," Harley said.

"Is he friendly?"

"No. He just ignores most people."

Sylvia reached down and patted Lurk on the head. Then she scratched him behind the ears and said, "nice doggy." He ignored her.

"What a magnificent beast," she said.

"That's accurate," Harley said.

They were well into the third six pack, and all felt well acquainted, when the chili was finally done. With the tortillas on the table he ladled out the steaming stuff into bowls - the wonderful green plant, sectioned for easy eating, the beans and chunks of meat. "It takes a pretty good gringo to eat this stuff," Harley warned. But three of them went into it with relish and after appropriate exclamations - "wow!; my god!; this is the real thing!" - they were tucking it in. Grace was more tentative; when she finally spooned some in she raised her head and sat back in the chair like someone had just slapped her in the face. But she swallowed and after a sip of beer to cool off she went back for more. It wasn't long till she'd caught up with the others and moved her bowl over to the pan for more.

"This meat is different," she said. "What is it...lamb?"

The only person who knew what it was said, "jackrabbit."

Once again you'd have thought someone had slapped her in the face. Then a color rose up from her neck into her face not unlike that of the chili she had been eating. There was no question of a second helping now. The only question was, could she hold the first helping down? She could not.

"The bathroom is there!" Harley said as he quickly got hold of her shoulders and pointed her in the right direction. She was a tall, gawky, horsey woman and she stumbled as she went in reaching for the light and closing the door, but she had the presence of mind to turn on the faucets with force so they were spared the sounds of her regurgitation. Otherwise, following the revelation "jackrabbit," William seemed secure but quit while he was ahead; Sylvia and Tom finished seconds with undiminished relish. They were mopping up the last of it when Grace came back to the kitchen and sat down at the table. Her face was now quite pale, but her bloodshot brown eyes were hot.

"Mr. Simmons," she said.

"Call me Harley."

"Mr. Simmons. I presume you hunted the hare down in order to provide yourself with this chili."

"Well, it wasn't a road kill."

"Why, Mr. Simmons?"

"Why not?"

"I'll tell you why not in just a moment. You tell me why."

"Man does not live by venison alone."

"Very funny...but I'm serious, Mr. Simmons. You'll admit you could survive in our era without killing jackrabbits, or deer. There is chili meat, so named, in any supermarket, even here in Del Cobre, I'm sure. And I've had very good chili that contained no meat at all."

"I haven't. And there's no lack of jackrabbits. They get into my garden, they raise a fit in there. I sit up on the front stoop and roll them over one by one with my single shot .22. That's cheaper and handier than any supermarket, and a good deal more interesting. And jackrabbits' better meat. At least for chili. In New Mexico, real chili always meant jackrabbit, at least until *our era.*"

"I don't think I'm unreasonable on this issue, Mr. Simmons. I do believe in subsistence hunting, where it's a necessary part of life."

"I believe every man, woman and grown child in America ought to be *required* to kill their own meat at least once a year, or go hungry as a consequence...keep hold of our roots."

Tom broke in and said, "What do you say we drink one more to the free flow of the Río Jalisco and call it a night?"

Harley said, "You-all have a room yet?"

"Oh that's okay," Sylvia said.

"That means you haven't. You just as well stay here. Save your money and we'll get an early start in the morning."

Later, the four went out to their vehicle and brought in their sleeping bags. Harley led them into the living room where he turned on the light. The grizzly bear rug on the floor, the hides and head mounts and photographs on the wall, captured the visitors. Sylvia went to the bear rug, lay down spread eagle on it, and commented that she had never felt so small in her life.

"What was he when he was alive?" Tom asked.

"About 800 pounds," Harley said.

William went to the wall, where he focused on Ted's art.

"Harley, did you paint this?"

"I wish. That's Ted's work."

"Ted? Doesn't really surprise me. It's exceptional."

Tom went to the wall where he focused on the old photo of the old man with the wolf slung over his shoulders.

"That's a Timber Wolf, is it not?"

"One of the last. Subspecies, Mondragón Wolf."

Grace said, "I'm not sleeping with a bear."

"Don't have to," Harley said. "The back bedroom is through the door there. There's two beds in there. Whatever's left can sleep on this nice carpeted floor."

"I'll sleep with a bear," Sylvia said, sitting up now on the bearskin.

"Why not?" said Tom.

"Arrange it any way you want," Harley said. "And you know where the bathroom is." Then he went to the wall and took a framed photograph from the wall, the work of Henry Bustos, of the Río Jalisco Canyon, and he handed it to Grace.

"That's where we're going, Grace."

Grace studied the photograph for some time. Then she said, "Did you take this, Mr. Simmons?"

"I'm afraid not."

Grace smiled. "For a second, Mr. Simmons, I thought you'd been hiding an artistic temperament from us."

Tom looked at the photo and said, "Is that it?"

"That's the place; Ocotillo Creek comes in right there."

Grace said, "Mr. Simmons, if you will show me that, I'll forgive you your chili."

"It's a good hike; we'll get an early start in the morning."

~ ~ ~ ~ ~ ~

It was a long pull afoot carrying backpacks and climbing 3,000 feet to the crest of the divide and it was early enough in September that while the early mornings were becoming quite cool, mid-day was still mid-summer hot. It was near noon when they stopped at the crest and removed their packs for the first lengthy rest of the day. They all reclined in the shade with that characteristic blotch of sweat covering their backs and while a canteen was passed around they looked off south over the town, on to the great grasslands stretching away to Mexico, green and lush from summer rains; and north past the river canyon and over the dark mountains of the Mondragón Range where there was no sign of civilization, at all. During the climb, William and Sylvia had lagged behind in places. They were obviously pacing themselves but pacing themselves well and Harley could tell they had done this sort of thing lots of times before. Tom matched Harley stride for stride and was quite obviously hard as nails; he literally took the mountain in stride. Grace huffed and grunted and puffed her way up; you could feel the strain in her climb. But she would not lag. She leaned against a tree now, very red faced, the sweat pouring on to her brow from underneath the curls of her short-cut gray hair. She was a competitor; not as hard as Tom, or as young, but at least as tough.

"I run," Tom said.

"Run?" said Harley.

"Marathons."

"Twenty six miles?"

"Right."

"Where?"

"From the start to the finish, wherever the race is. You run?"

"Not unless I'm chasing something."

Harley led them west off the trail. They bushwacked through the thick aspen and spruce and Douglas Fir on the north slope of Engelmann Mountain to the source spring of Ocotillo Creek. Here in a jungle of northern forest they stopped again. Harley knelt and sucked from the cold spring gurgling out of the ground. The others drank again from canteens.

Slow going, they followed the growing creek down as it picked up half a dozen springs along the way. In places blowdowns lay across the creek. They climbed them, went under or around them, and kept on. The water was perfectly clear and small trout began to appear, flicking into underwater shelters as they passed by. And little by little the jungle opened up as the Canadian Forest gave way to Ponderosa Pine, and the creek began to carve a canyon in its winding route. Late afternoon, summer thunderclouds began to build up and come in from the southwest. Harley dropped his pack underneath an overhanging bluff on the west side of the creek.

"We just as well stop here," he said. "We can get out of the rain under this bluff and if Ocotillo Creek fills with water we're high enough we won't get down to the river a lot faster than we planned."

Then the rains came, midst big booms and wild flashes in the sky. They sat under the bluff, leaning against their packs and watched the show and the creek, which did not noticeably change its flow. Nobody said anything until the storm had passed and the sunset began to slice light through the breaking clouds.

Harley said, "Goddamn it smells good in this country after it rains. I'm going to go catch some trout for supper. There ought to be some semi-dry wood up against the west wall; somebody see if they can gather some up."

Later they fried trout and some dehydrated potatoes that Grace produced that came to life in the pan. They all circled the fire and ate with forks from the pan and when it was gone they quickly fried up another couple of trout and potatoes. Nobody had any complaints, at all. Then Harley brewed some coffee and they stayed by the fire as it got dark. Then as the fire went out they one by one crawled into their bedrolls. The only sound in the canyon was the slight gurgle of the creek...until they all began to hear the unmistakable sound of something alive and large walking down the creek toward camp. It was certainly an animal and it had the ponderous pace of something very large and as it walked its step would squish in the sand or clop on the rocks and every once in a while it would step in the stream and they could hear that too. Harley whispered just loud enough..."You reckon that's a bear?"

They all rose up on elbows from the recline and looked through slivers of moonlight up the canyon. They could see nothing. But it was coming closer.

"I believe that's a bear," Harley said. "What else lives in here could be as big as that? I'll bet it's a big bear. You reckon it's a grizzly?"

"They're extinct," William said.

"That's what they said about those otters. This has got the sound of a bigger bear than I've ever heard...there he is!

A big long-horned *corriente* steer ambled into a moonbeam, winded the humans, snorted, whirled and bawled and bolted back up the canyon, splashing and crashing until he was gone.

"Goddamn I'm glad it wasn't a bear," Harley said.

"Very funny, Mr. Simmons."

They all lay down again. Sylvia said, "Harley, how do you feel about cattle in the wilderness?"

"For me, a coyote or a deer or just about anything that runs here is worth more than a cow. But a cow's just another animal on the land. Too many cows, you've got a problem. Too many coyotes or too many deer and you've got a problem. Too many people and you've got a problem. We can control the number of cows, and deer and coyotes will control themselves. Nobody's figured out yet how to control the number of people, or the things they do. Let's sleep; we'll get an early start in the morning."

~ ~ ~ ~ ~ ~

They came into the deep shade under the sycamore grove along the creek with the pine and the great Emory Oaks in the shade against the bluff where the creek canyon opened up and they could see the confluence with the river up ahead. There was a great array of birds largely hidden in the branches above them and they were all telling the world what a lovely day it was, and William said, "It sounds like a pet shop!"

Tom said, "Just back there we passed the Ocotillo up on the south slope and now here is some ponderosa ...what's the elevation here?"

"About 4500 feet," Harley said.

"Ponderosa doesn't grow at 4500 feet in New Mexico."

"It does along here."

"Right next to Ocotillo Cactus?"

"This is a funny place...hold it Grace! Jesus, you're going to kill an otter track!"

Grace stepped back as Harley knelt down and then they all leaned over the prints in the sand.

"Two of them," Harley said, "right along here they went."

They followed the tracks down to where they went into the river, rather faint inconsequential looking prints made by a now very consequential animal not much bigger than a house cat. Then they stood at the river's edge and looked for a while up and down the canyon. The river was running clear; it tumbled blue/green into the pool coming over the falls. The riparian was leafed out. Everything was lush and plush and alive at the end of a peaceful summer. And the canyon walls towered over everything.

Tom said, "How did we ever miss this mother?"

William reached out and shook Harley's hand.

Grace said, "I want to see an otter."

Sylvia said, "Oh it's so beautiful!" took off all her clothes and descended into the pool.

~ ~ ~ ~ ~ ~

By week's end they had explored the river for many miles upstream and down. They had taken in side canyons and canyons that fingered off the side canyons. They had scaled cliffs, climbed mountains and eaten most of their food. Hiding in the bluffs early one morning, they had watched a family of otters for the better part of an hour and William got the pictures he wanted. The plan the last day was to stay till noon, then pack up and head for the divide. Along about mid-morning Harley was parked in the sun by his fishing rod when William began to tap his fork against his tin cup like he was going to make a speech.

"All right," he said, "this has all been very nice but it's time to consider what we're here for. We've got to make some strategy. Harley, you too."

Harley got up and took a few strides to join the others and sat down.

"Now obviously," William said, "the Río Jalisco Canyon and however many hundred thousand acres around it is deserving of protection. The river must be made a priority of conservationists in the Southwest. The needless, senseless, destructive, fascist development must be stopped. But how? And what is the proper designated protected status once it is stopped?"

Grace said, "The scenic values here, the bird life, the potential for recreation - this would be a wonderful National Park."

"A National Park would have a recreation potential that could divert some commercial interests from the dam," Sylvia said. "We could offer it as a sort of compromise."

"No hunting," Harley said.

"What?"

"There's no hunting in a National Park."

"Mr. Simmons, that's one of the advantages to the National Park designation. At least many think so."

"Many don't. And the only National Park I was ever at had more people, by a lot, than Del Cobre".

"I think," Tom said, "that the park designation might well offer some compromise to the developers, if the dam were stopped, but it might very well split our own ranks. We need unity of opposition to ever hope to stop this dam. We need bird hunters as well as bird watchers. We need horsepackers as well as backpackers. Unity would likely come with a wilderness designation which allows hunting and any other non-mechanized recreation and severely restricts development."

Harley said, "Why designate it anything? You give it a name and it will just draw a crowd. Leave it as it is."

Sylvia said, "Harley, understand that whatever happens, there's going to be some changes. If we don't draw a crowd of interest in this area we're going to lose it. We may lose it anyway. But we have managed to save a number of pristine areas in the Southwest from development. It was always because a lot of people had come to care about those areas."

"Like it or not Mr. Simmons, we are going to have to popularize the Río Jalisco to some extent. But if the wilderness designation will promote unity, I'll support that. Upon reflection, it would be best. Mr. Simmons and his friends can hunt during open seasons, we can watch the birds and go backpacking all year long, and the otters will be spared the crowds that would come with a National Park."

"Good," said William. "But we're getting ahead of ourselves. We've got to stop the damn dam first. And the main problem, as I see it, we have no legal mechanism to do it. This is technically multiple use forest land. There is no protection there. It's an open door to development. And there is no Federally Endangered Species we can go to court with. I think even the threat of that could save this river, if we had the right kind of animal here. But we don't. And Sterling Roberts, among others, knows the weakness in the otter issue. The only avenue of hope is the public forum.

"The public forum...yes," said Sylvia. "And in light of that, why don't we focus on the weakness of the opposition for a moment? Sure, the project is authorized by Congress. But that's not a mandate. Lots of authorized projects have died a natural death. And who supports the project? From what I've seen, and from what Ted and Harley have told us, it has the support of the business community of Del Cobre and a handful of state and federal bureaucrats. That leaves the rest of the state the same place we were a few months ago - we knew very little about the Río Jalisco and so we didn't care. But the potential is out there for significant public opposition."

Grace said, "We need to start a deluge of opposition - petitions, letters, particularly letters, to the Bureau of Reclamation, the Congressional Delegation, and the Governor."

William said, "Garner Greane has about as much sympathy for otters, wild rivers and the like as we have for these incredibly gross developments."

"But," said Tom, "he's a politician. Above all, that's what he is. I'm sure he's made his promises to the local Chamber of Commerce types, but if he starts thinking an unpopular water project is about to scatter some nasty shit on his political career those promises may not be worth the silver tongue that delivered them."

"So," said Sylvia, "we generate a campaign at the people who count. We use meetings, slide shows, direct mailing, phone drives, the usual stuff. We focus on this gorgeous scenery and especially the otters to draw the opposition out. And we have to win the public hearings."

"We'll win in Albuquerque," William said.

Tom said, "We'll drown them in Albuquerque. But winning in Del Cobre would have much more effect. If the project can't draw majority support in the town that's supposed to benefit from its construction, that project is in trouble. We must win in Del Cobre. And that's where you come in, Harley."

They all looked at Harley, who had been silent for some time. Harley had his eye on his fishing rod, parked on a forked stick by the stream not far away. He glanced around at the four of them, then looked back at the river. He said nothing.

"You know the town, Harley," Sylvia said. "You know everyone. You're a big frog in that small pond. We need a catalyst in Del Cobre. What do you say?"

"I'm not a companyman. That's not my field."

Grace drew Harley's attention from the river. She'd been out in the sun all week and her red face had gotten redder and now, talking to Harley, it was getting red hot.

"Mr. Simmons! We've spent the better part of a week together and that's long enough for me to say I've had about enough of you. Never mind your superior airs and your condescending to the rest of us and your teasing me every chance you get. I've come to dislike you, Mr. Simmons, because you're a phony. You're the great man of the wilderness who won't do a thing to save it. You'd have us see you as the last lone wolf, at home here in the wilds and a stumbling dunce once you cross back over the divide and get in sight of town. I'm not buying it. The truth is, you don't care. Not like us. Not like Ted, who's working his ass off and risking his career to save your wilderness."

"I found those otters."

"You didn't find them. You didn't lift a finger. You just happened to be the only one who knew they were here. You *are* at home here, Mr.

Simmons. I probably don't know my way around my own house as well as you know your way around these mountains. We've all learned from you. But where it really counts, the lone wolf is soft."

Harley listened without expression, and he waited a while before he said, "Like I told you, I'm not a companyman. I'm not what you want. But I know who is. He's not like you, or me. He's a businessman, probably the only businessman in town who knows shit from wild honey. He's a savvy guy, and he's on the inside. Folks will listen to him, more than to me or you-all. I'll talk to him. I believe he'll go for it. And the troops will be out for the public hearing. And the opposition won't know where they came from."

Then Harley looked back at the stream as the rod pumped down and bounced up off the forked stick as the line squealed off the drag. Harley left the group and ran over to the river. He picked up the rod, took up the slack, and set the hook. The others came over and watched as the fish took line down river, then as Harley gradually wore it down, worked it back up, and beached it. It was the biggest fish they'd seen in their week in the wilderness - a plug-ugly Flathead Catfish with a grotesque gaping mouth that held Harley's whole fist as he reached in and removed the hook.

"Lunch," Harley said as he thunked the big cat's head against a rock and immediately began to cut into the belly. Then he added, "The thing is..."

"Don't tell me, Mr. Simmons...man does not live by venison alone."

"Grace, before this is all done, you and I are going to understand each other."

"Partly, Mr. Simmons, partly."

### Chapter 16

SITTING OUTSIDE THE MAYOR'S OFFICE, having given his name to the secretary and waiting in line like the rest, was not Harley's idea of how to spend the morning. He didn't like waiting in line to see anyone; there was a vague, perhaps unintentional, yet undeniable subservience to it. In the case of waiting in line to see Jim Bo Moreland, Harley liked it even less. He almost changed his mind and left. Then Jim Bo opened his office door and stepped into the waiting room with Morey Solís and Stan Baer and Dirk Johngood and Garth Bilker close behind. The followers acknowledged Harley as they went by and left City Hall. The two other men seated in the lobby waiting to see Jim Bo were town employees; they were there ahead of Harley but Jim Bo excused them and told them to come back at one o'clock. Then Jim Bo motioned Harley into the inner sanctum. Harley went in and sat down and then Jim Bo came in with the secretary who brought coffee on a tray.

"Cream or sugar, Mr. Simmons?"

132

"No thanks...black."

The secretary left and as she was closing the door Jim Bo said, "no visitors, no calls." Then Jim Bo sat down across the desk from Harley and he fixed his unblinking blue eyes on his visitor and said, "Harley, thanks for coming in...glad you could make it...have you seen the morning paper?"

"Which one?"

"The *Region*."

"No...come to think of it, I haven't seen any of them."

"But you've heard."

"Heard what? I drove in from the homestead and walked straight in here."

"Well, you're getting to be a local hero, just like your dad. That's quite a bear."

Jim Bo handed Harley the morning *Region* hot of the press and Harley read the headline: STATE RECORD BEAR TAKEN BY LOCAL HUNTER. And there in the photo was Harley skinning the bear that Ben Wetzel had missed. There was also a hound in the background, blurred, but Harley could tell in was White-eye.

"Four hundred and three pounds!" Jim Bo said.

"Gutted," Harley said. Then he said, "I suppose you and Garth and the rest are real proud of me."

"Sure we are. A local hero like you is good for tourism, good for business."

"Well, don't thank me. That warden, Beeler, came out that morning - I'd just started skinning - and he said he was sure I had a state record. He took some pictures and talked me into taking it in to weigh it up. Then he helped me skin and butcher and took some of the meat. I'd forgotten all about it."

"Sure. I know. But read on...now they're calling you the last of the mountain men."

"I'll read it later. Anyway, what's a Black Bear? My daddy killed grizzlies twice that size."

"He was the man of his times, Harley, no doubt about that. And you could be the man of your times."

"Right. And I'm real happy that you and the rest of the boys are so pleased with my work."

"Not entirely. In fact, Garth is not pleased with your work at all. I think he's wrong. But we're all real curious about your work, Harley. Since I can tell now you really haven't read the morning paper, check page six."

Harley opened the broad sheet to page six. And page six made it clear why Jim Bo Moreland had handed him that puff about the state record bear. CITIZENS AGAINST THE $HAM was the headline of the full page political advertisement. It went on...*Here's a chance for all residents of Arthur County to get together on something - hunters, fishermen, environmentalists, fiscal conservatives and any businessman who prefers quality in our community to the smell of pork barrel politics can find common cause against the Río Jalisco Dam...* That was enough for Harley. Trying, though not very hard, to suppress a smile, he closed the paper, handed it back to Jim Bo Moreland, and said, "I'll read the rest of that later, too."

"What do you know about it, Harley?"

"More than you, I'll bet. I'm surprised it's out so soon. And I'm surprised that Pennerman would run it at all."

"According to Pennerman, the ad copy arrived with a cashiers check drawn on an Albuquerque Bank and remitted by this so-called Río Jalisco Conservation Coalition. Pennerman sent it back. Then, he says, he gets a call from some guy who represents himself as an attorney. This maybe attorney says there are laws about accepting political ads from some folks and turning them down from others. Pennerman tells me this guy is right about that, attorney or no. So he ran the ad. The question is, where does it come from? Who's behind it? Bubba thinks it's out of town environmentalists trying to influence our situation. The rest of us don't buy that on account of this ad shows too much knowledge of the area and the town and the local scene. There haven't been any of those types down here to my knowledge, and I think I'd know. Dirk thinks it's that local hippie artist, Goodman, the one with the long, stringy blonde hair whose running around with the petition. Garth thinks it's you and further, he thinks you're suckering me with this little understanding we've got. I think it could be Pearlmann. He's been simpering about wilderness protection at the Chamber of Commerce meetings and there's this rumor he's going to run for City Council on a *quality-of-life* ticket, for Christ sake. It may be him but I didn't think he had the balls because he must know he's vulnerable as a businessman if we find out. Anyway, I told the boys I was going to find out in short order because I think you've got the balls to tell me and because of our little understanding."

"What understanding? All that was your idea."

Jim Bo leaned forward. "Well at least when I go out on a limb on an issue I've got the balls to sign my name to it."

"Good for you, Jim Bo."

"So it is you!"

"Suit yourself."

Jim Bo leaned back in his chair and put his feet up on his desk. "Harley, last time we talked I gave you a real good reason to cooperate with me. Now I'm going to give you another one. Solís has been telling me about this certain little love triangle here in town. Very interesting story. A regular soap opera. It's all about you and that fox that works cashier at our bank and that bank officer, Bruce. Word I get is, you'd kill to get that woman and you're boy back. That right?"

For a moment, Harley didn't move. Then he reached for his cup and drank the last of his coffee and put the cup back on Jim Bo's desk. He said nothing.

"Harley, consider that I have called you in here to help you get your mind right. And right now that means getting your attention on my priorities. Now that I've got it, you listen close to what's coming up, because it could make a difference to you. You ever hear of interstate banking?"

"Heard of it."

"It's not public knowledge yet, and I want you to keep this to yourself, but before too long the Arthur County State Bank is going to be part of United Southwest. We will be linked and in cooperation with banks all over the Southwest, plus California. This gives a man like me a lot of options with employees. Now Bruce is the sort any of our banks would want to have. With the data he creates, he can tell us where we're making money, where we're not, and thereby lead us into more intelligent investments. Bonney is an asset, too. She's bright, she learns quick, she's a reliable worker, and the customers like looking at her. We all like looking at her, don't we Harley? The thing is, either or both of those people is in demand, in our bank here, or elsewhere. They could be here in Del Cobre for a long time. Or...they could be transferred to one of our other banks in another state. Or...*one* of them could be transferred. You get my drift yet, Harley?"

"Go ahead, Jim Bo."

"I first met these two nice folks at a barbecue at Morey's. Real nice young people. The kind of young people we need in Del Cobre. We talked for quite a while. And when we weren't talking, I was watching. She is a fox, and she has style, and I was curious on account of all Morey had told me about this love triangle. As for Bruce, he's a genius with computers and has a real head for the banking business. He's a nice guy. He's also a wimp. You can see he's a wimp just like you can see she's a fox. After spending a number of years with you, and then with him, she's got to know that; she's got to see the difference. Now I can't get your woman back for you, but you ought to be man enough to do that. You need to get her leaning your way again, Harley. You do, and that computer man could be a whiz in another bank in another state in one fast hurry. On the other hand, *both* of them, the whole family, could get transferred...oh...anytime. I can work with you Harley, or I can work against you. It's pretty much up to you."

Harley reached for his cup. He had forgotten it was empty. He put the cup back down. After a moment he said, "What do you want me to do, raise the flag for the Río Jalisco dam?"

"Not at all. We've been through that. I want some cooperation. I want someone to run my operation up on that lake. That's to your advantage as much as mine. That foxy wife of yours with all that style isn't going to settle down again with a trapper living hand to mouth on some homestead. You got to offer that woman something, Harley. I can provide a lifestyle that will suit you both. And you might consider that you can do something for your own home town. The future of this town - and it's your home town more than mine, Harley - is dependent on that water project. You're a significant person in this town, Harley. What you say or do matters. You can have a hand in the future of everyone who lives here. That's a lot of people, and good people, too. All I want is a little cooperation. When the time comes, I want your cooperation in this enterprise of mine. Right now I want some cooperation regarding these agitators. There's nothing going to stop this dam. But it's important we not have any delays. Now, what do you know about it, Harley?

"For what it's worth to you, Jim Bo, Bubba is right...it's coming from out of town."

"How do you know?"

"Because I took them out there. They were out there for a week, and I know for fact that after I brought them back they spent several days in Del Cobre. I didn't show them around town but Goodman and several of those other bleeding hearts did. They know enough about this town to write that ad, no problem. But you won't have any influence over them."

"Outsiders. Piss on 'em! I don't need to influence outsiders because they won't have any influence in our town. And nobody pays any attention to the artsy-craftsy people around here. All they'll do is stir each other up. It's a local hero I'm worried about, somebody whose got the influence to make a difference here and get in the way. Someone like you, Harley, or Pearlmann."

"Like you said, Pearlmann hasn't got the balls. And like I said before, I'm not going to take sides with anyone."

"Taking environmentalists out to the woods to see the sights isn't what I'd call cooperation, Harley."

"They paid me, Jim Bo. Paid me pretty good. I'm a businessman, just like you. You pay me, I'll take you out there too."

"I'll see it all when it looks the way I want it to. And what about those goddamn otters? It isn't hard to figure out who discovered them for the Department of Wildlife."

Harley thought for a moment before he had an appropriate response. "I didn't discover them Jim Bo, I just happened to know they were there."

"Well a handful of otters is not going to stop this project. We're not going to sacrifice a whole town for a family of water weasels. Not a chance. All I ask is a little cooperation, Harley. Don't stir things up.

Keep me informed. We get over the hump here and the two of us can work together, and we can make things happen. I can work with you Harley, or I can work against you. It's pretty much up to you."

## Chapter 17

IT WAS A COOL CLEAR NIGHT with the feel of autumn. Harley stepped from cool air into warm air as he entered the lobby of the Copper Palace, turned right, and entered the bar. It was a Friday night and there were a lot of people there but Harley did not expect that one of them would be Ted Beeler, holding up the end of the bar. Harley could recall days when Ted had been a rakehell but those days and those ways had ended when Ted married Sharon and not even Ted had ever seemed to mind. Ted caught Harley's eye and motioned him over and by the time Harley made his way down the bar, greeting a number of the boys along the way, Ted had bought him a beer.

"Been here long?" Harley said.

Ted didn't answer but he had that glassy look in his eyes that told Harley that he'd been here quite a while and then Ted turned his half-full bottle upside down and drained it. He ordered another and then he said, "Sharon's on the rag, has been for weeks, says all I care about is *that river*, and *that dam*, and *those otters* and why don't I relax and enjoy the family anymore?" Ted stopped and drained half a bottle before going on..."She's right of course. But I told her she was just going to have to put up with me like this until these hearings are over and the issue turns the corner one way or another, and that started a fight and don't ever try to argue with Sharon because you'll lose, so I got out. Pretty good crowd here, Harley. And there's more than this on the dance floor. And better than half are women. I got the blinders off tonight, partner."

Harley started to take a long swallow but cut it short thinking that he never was going to catch up with Ted and upon reflection, he didn't want to anyway. Then Ted said, "Let's go where the women are," and Harley followed Ted out of the bar and across the lobby and into the dance hall. Ted paid the cover for them both. Harley found a place along the wall to lean on and look things over. Ted quickly got his hand on a bosomy wild child that Harley knew as Shauna and he pulled her out on to the dance floor. He was a natural athlete, a smooth graceful dancer in spite of his size and how much he'd had to drink. Harley watched as he wrapped Shauna up and swept her along in a swinging two-step while the man at the lead mike sang Merle Haggard's inimitable thoughts about mama and a flight from the law:

"I raised, a lot of Cain, back in my younger days,
while mama daily prayed my crops would fail,

*now I'm, a hunted fugitive, with just two ways,*
*outrun the law or spend my life in jail..."*

Harley watched Ted dancing Shauna off her feet and saw humor in the scene. At the same time it occurred to him that the happily married wildlife officer was bound for a big drunk and maybe some mischief he was going to regret. Harley wasn't bound for a big drunk himself; he didn't do that anymore. He was going to stay sober and he was going to have to watch out for Ted. Indeed, he was sufficiently intent on watching and feeling responsible for a change that for quite a while he didn't realize he was standing in the midst of a replay. Then a woman at a nearby table was smiling at him and he recognized...Ellen! And with her at the table, sure enough, was...Kim! And the parts man! And the guy who sold "western" clothes! And down the wall, spaced by a couple of cowboys, was the big guy who'd banged on his ear! The three guys and the two women were all looking at Harley. Harley smiled and nodded his beer bottle towards the table where four of them sat. But he had a good memory of the last time they were all in the Copper Palace and he was much too sober to want to be any more provocative than a smart-ass smile. Indeed, he considered that a little deference to the situation would be real smart about now. Sidney was helping out behind the bar in an attempt to keep everyone well watered; Harley wandered over to the bar for a visit.

Sidney was wearing a white shirt with suspenders and a red bow tie and a red arm cuff. He looked the part and he was a very fast bartender. He was sloshing glasses, pouring draft beer and mixing drinks as he told Harley that things were "going well," and, "there's a lot of support out there," and, "we're going to surprise a lot of people," and, "how's the fishing?" Harley said the fishing was fine and he had recently guided several competent fishermen to some very nice trout up at the headwaters of the Río Jalisco and he was glad to see Sidney had all the business he could handle. Then, leaving Sidney with all he could handle, Harley went down the wall to the men's room. There was a lineup at the urinals and Harley waited his turn and when it came he stepped up, hung it out, and pissed. He was almost done when he felt the ice cold beer being poured down the back of his shirt and he realized the man standing behind him all the while was the big guy who had banged on his ear. Harley tucked in, buttoned up his Levis and turned around. He looked up at the big man while the beer ran cold and sticky down his back and between the cheeks of his ass. The salesman was behind the big man and the parts man was just inside the door, leaning back against it. At that point there were two other men in the men's room; they saw the scene taking shape and got done and left in a hurry; the parts man let each one out then leaned back against the door to keep anyone else from coming in. The salesman said, "Jimmy here, he wants to break your jaw just like you done him, and me and Butch is gonna help him."

Harley did not like the spot he was in and he liked the odds even less. He said, "It takes three of you cunts to try one man?"

The big man was smiling. He turned to his buddies and then he turned back to Harley and said, "I ain't gonna need any help. I'm gonna beat Harley till he can't stand and then I'm gonna hold him up and give Jimmy a good shot and he'll break Harley's jaw."

The big man tossed the beer bottle in the waste basket and had both hands free as Harley said, "You boys want those two hides, help yourself."

"We ain't worried about the women," the parts man said. "We got the women. And now we got you."

Harley could not see even a sliver of hope in the confines of the men's room. "We settle it here," he said, "Pearlmann will hand us all over to the cops. We all lose. What say we step outside and find out how good shithead here is by hisself."

The big man smiled and turned to the parts man. "You reckon Harley would be a rabbit and run?"

Harley said, "I don't like scum, but I've never run from it. Ya'll will get your chance. Let's step outside and we'll start with shithead."

There was some opportune pounding on the door and the sound of angry voices. Harley stepped by the big man and headed for the door. The parts man opened the door. Harley went out followed closely by three men. He looked for Ted as he went by the dance floor but Ted and Shauna were working each other over in a slow waltz and when Harley got out of the dance hall he went through the lobby, out into the street, and down the street and around the corner with three men stepping close behind him. There wasn't much light down the side street as Harley stopped and turned around, the wall of the building to his left and a line of cars and pickups to his right. The parts man and the salesman took their positions at his flanks and the big man faced him. It was now a cold autumn night and what light there was from the street lights on Main Street showed the breath of four men, tense and ready, as their breathing met the cold night air. Harley considered that he had no more room to maneuver than he had in the men's room. And he considered that he was much too sober to want this. Had he a good buzz on, his blood would be up and he would be eager for "shithead" to make a move. As it was, he could think of a million things he'd rather do.

"You boys might lose those hides while you're worrying about me."

"Those hides aren't going anywhere," the parts man said. "We get them anytime. We've been waiting awhile for you."

There seemed to be nothing else to stall, and Harley said, "Okay shithead, let's see what you've got," as he stepped back to gain space to drop-kick the big man in the belly, and as the big man came forward into the trap something even bigger appeared from around the corner behind him: a Cinnamon Bear. The big man had just time to say "Oh Shit!" as Ted Beeler wrapped him up from behind, spun like a discus thrower, and threw the big man into the side of a pickup. The big man came off the truck with a mighty "ooofff!" and no wind and no idea where he was and into a tremendous fist that dropped him like an out-size sack of horse feed. He came to his knees wavering in disbelief and spluttering blood and feeling with his hands for his face and teeth. The parts man and the salesman came to his aid and the parts man said, "Jesus, Ted, we don't have any quarrel with you."

"You do now. I think you boys best be moving on."

The big man was sobbing in fright over what had happened to his face. The parts man and the salesman of "western" clothes each got under one arm and got the big man up on his feet. They led him like a big babbling child down the street where they hefted him up into the cab of an all-terrain bigun'. Soon the engine turned over and the lights came on and they drove off.

Harley said, "Goddamn, I'm glad you came along. That one ol' kid's about half rough. At least he was till you busted his face."

Ted was glassy eyed and more than a little drunk and he was already thinking of other things. "Sidney saw you-all go out and tipped me off. Let's get back in there. I'm gonna fuck what's her name...Cheryl."

"Shauna."

"That's what it is...Shauna. She's humping my leg. She wants me. She wants to fuck."

"Ted, let's leave all that be tonight. We'll come back to the Copper Palace when things are a little more congenial."

"She's plenty congenial. I'm gonna get laid. When do I ever get out of the house?" Then Ted leaned a little towards Harley and said, "Tell me something...is Shauna good?"

"A rhetorical question I'm sure."

"I figured you had to chouse her a time or two."

"That was a long time ago."

"I knew it. Is she good?"

"She's not that good. Why throw your marriage over for some dirty-leg?"

"Is Shauna one of those?"

"That is one loose horse, I'll guarantee. She's nearly as indiscriminate as I used to be."

"That's terrible. But she's good. Shauna is good, admit it."

"All right, Shauna is good. But she's not that good."

"And she wants me."

"She wants a lot of married men. She's famous for that."

"Well here's the one she'll have tonight," Ted said.

Harley followed Ted back into the dance hall where they found Shauna dancing with a new man. This new man had his hand on Shauna's ass and she was wrapped up on his leg as they stepped more or less with the music.

"That's ol'...Williams," Ted said.

"Wilson."

"That's his name, Wilson. Wilson is an asshole! What's she doing climbing on Wilson?"

"She wants him. And he's married."

"Jesus!" Ted said.

Harley said, "Let's get out of here."

"I need a beer," Ted said. "I'll get us both a beer. Soon as Wilson lets go of her I'm moving back in."

"Wilson is not going to let go. And I've got some free booze in the truck."

"What kind?"

"I don't remember. But I've always got something. Let's rim out and head for the barn."

Harley turned and left and hoped Ted would follow. He was pleased to hear Ted mumbling behind him: "She'll never go home with Wilson. Wilson is an asshole."

"Bet ya'," Harley said.

In Harley's truck Ted sat with a half bottle of red wine in his hand and said, "This is pretty good stuff...nice and cool. Where we going?"

Harley said, "We'll just drive around awhile, then I'll run you home."

"What about my car? I can drive."

"Sure. Wildlife Officer arrested for DWI. I can think of a number of people who would enjoy the hell out of that. You can get you car tomorrow."

Harley drove a rambling route with no destination through town. Ted stayed with the bottle and leaned his head into the cool night air coming in the passenger side window. They both agreed after considerable speculation that involved many graphic details that Shauna was no doubt very good but there must be something wrong with her if she's attracted to Wilson. Then Ted said, "Do you know where that hide lives?"

"Ah Ted..."

"I knew it. Let's go."

"Ted...let's not."

"I tell you she wants me. She's waiting. She's ready."

"You're wasting your time. She's got company."

"Wilson? Wilson is an asshole. Run me over there."

Harley recognized Shauna's house by the car parked in the driveway. Both men recognized the pickup parked out front. It was dark in the house but both men could imagine it was not still.

"That's Wilson's pickup," Ted said. "She's fucking Wilson."

"No doubt."

"What's she doing fucking Wilson? Wilson is an asshole."

"She wants him."

"Jesus!" Ted said.

Harley drove off and began another slow circuitous route that was aimed, eventually, for Ted's house. Ted looked at what remained of the wine, then poured it out the window. Then he slumped down in the seat.

"Jesus," he said.

At Ted's house Harley parked, killed the engine and shut off the lights. It was a dark street and a clear night and looking through the windshield they could see the stars. The air coming through the window was quite cold.

"I've never cheated on my wife," Ted said. "Thanks."

"Don't thank me, thank Wilson."

"Wilson is an asshole." Ted put his head to the window and took in some cold air. Then he said, "How many Harley...how many can say they never cheated on their wife?"

"How many can say they never cheated on their husband?"

"Yeah, in that way, we're a lot the same; it's a horse apiece. You think when they get together and go out and get ripped they talk as rough about us as we do about them?"

"From what I've heard, and overheard, they're not as crude but they're at least as graphic."

"That's terrible. I hope they never get as bad as us. They get as bad as us and we're all in trouble."

"I think they've got more sense than that."

"I hope so. Me, I never think about it, never think about screwing around. I got everything I want. Then once in a blue moon I tie one on and like to boil over. That Shauna didn't help. Shauna is good."

"Forget Shauna. It's not worth it. Never is."

"You would know."

"I would know. Fucking has brought me nothing but trouble."

"Where you going from here...Suzie's?"

"Yes."

"She wants you."

"Hope so."

"She does. Harley, I'm going to do you a favor."

"You already did."

"Those guys? That's nothing. But you straightened me around tonight and I can do the same for you. Harley, give that other up. Some horses, you know, you just can't break. You don't belong with that horse. You keep trying and sooner or later you get your foot caught in the stirrup. Then you get dragged and then you get hurt, bad. The only thing to save yourself is to cut yourself loose. You got yourself caught, partner. Your being dragged. I know it hurts. Cut yourself loose."

"Can't."

"Why not?"

"I don't know. It's not over yet."

"It will be. By then you may have lost everything. Suzie included. But that Suzie...there you have something."

"You don't have to tell me about Suzie. But I'm working on something. I'm going to get that computer whiz out of the way. Nothing illegal. Nothing violent. Just a little strategy."

"Strategy? He's not the problem, Harley. It's you and her. You and Suzie make sense. You and Bonney don't."

Harley rolled down the window, looked out and felt the cold air. "There's things I know Ted, that I just can't do anything about."

"All right. I ought to know better than to mention the word 'Bonney'. What about Billy?"

"I haven't seen him."

"No?"

"When it's time."

"Harley, try this. You're coming down the river, you're in the rapids and there's rocks up ahead. You got to get close enough to see what you're doing, then you have to make a decision...you go for it. If you wait to long, you end up on the rocks."

"Ted, you're trying to tell me something."

"Right."

"Like I said, when it's time."

"All right. All right. When it's time. When it's time it will all sort out and you'll be with Bonney, or Suzie, or nobody at all. And when it's time this dam will be built, or will not be built, and that will sort out too. That's how this all got started tonight - me pushing too hard on everything, the river, the dam, the otters, all the politics, and me leaning on Sharon and now on you. I don't know what for. It's all going to sort out anyway, when it's time. We're all doing the best we can."

"You think so."

"Sure we are."

"Some of us aren't doing our part."

"We all do our part Harley, whatever it is."

"Is it good enough?"

"I used to do a little rock climbing, and winning this one is just a long climb up a high cliff. There's very little to hold on to. But we know what were doing and we've got a hold of whatever's available and we're getting to the top. But still to come, at the top, is our Governor, my boss, Garner Greane. We've still got to deal with him. He's bright, he's cunning, he's slick, and almost no one knows how mean he is. He knows what he likes and he knows what he doesn't like, and mostly what he doesn't like is anything in the natural world that serves no visible economic purpose. It's too bad, because when he's not using his influence against the environment, he can be a pretty good Governor. Anyway, there he stands at the top and we finally get there and all he has to do is step on our fingers and down we go. A half a year of effort and we're dead in seconds. The rally the people are making, from Del Cobre to Santa Fe, is a beautiful thing to see. But that doesn't mean it's going to work. It's hard to feel too confident when a man like Garner Greane still has you by the short hairs."

"How do you keep faith when the killer is still at the top?"

"It's immaterial; you have to make the climb."

Ted got out of the cab. He turned and leaned against the door and looked in on Harley."

"Thanks, partner."

"*Egualmente.*"

"I feel better. But I'm still half on my ass."

"I'd say, walk around the block a couple of times before you risk the house."

"Good idea."

"Tomorrow is another day. By tomorrow night you and Sharon will be right where you want to be."

"Right. Sharon is good."

"Of course she is."

Harley started to drive away. He had just turned the corner when he heard the big voice come booming down the street: "WILSON IS AN ASSHOLE!"

## Chapter 18

HE SAT BELOW THE CREST of the hill with his eye following the fawn roll of the prairie grass on into Mexico and the wind rattled the sharp leaves of the yucca at his back. The mountains, the big timber, the river would be nothing without the desert grasslands, he thought. He spent more time in the mountains, and especially along the river and its streams, but whenever he came to the desert he believed it to be the most wonderful country in the world. And he thought: I wish they boy could see the desert this morning.

He was supposed to be hunting and this was his first stand. But for now he was content to sit relaxed in the lee of the north wind and watch the grass wave in the sun and he was in no hurry to hunt. He took an apple from his coat pocket and bit into it. It was a very hard, crisp, yellow apple and the juice, slightly sour, leaped into his mouth. It had been a good harvest and of course the old woman had helped. She had taken the tomatoes for canning and the beans and chili were dried in the sun at her house. The apples had hung heavy from the trees, more than they could ever use. She had canned some of the apples and sold many boxes at the fall market in town. When all the crop was off he had hitched Ruby to the cultivator, weighted down with stones, and worked the dirt through the fields. The next spring he would plant that half of the field that lay fallow this year. Now he ate a yellow apple in a deliberate way and enjoyed it very much.

He wasn't expecting much from the hunt anyway. The wind had a wild feel to it, as if an early winter storm were behind it. It was exhilarating and made him think of hunting. But game would already be thinking about laying up for the storm; the hunting would be good after the storm had passed. Yet he had felt the need to get out and smell the fall air and watch the grass wave in the wind. And he wanted to check the fur. He knew it would not be prime. The Indian summer had set down in mid-October and stayed and stayed. The nights had been cold though, and now in early November even the lower elevations of the desert were experiencing frost at night. A Gray Fox or a coyote would not be prime on the desert but they would be shimmering with early guard hairs and would not be a waste. This hunt was reconnaissance, and to get the feel of the season.

He ate the apple down to the core and tossed it away. He took a small bottle from his coat pocket and set it upright on the ground and removed the cap. It contained the blood, the solid waste and the urine of a jackrabbit and the rank odor came out of the bottle and wafted downwind, eliminating any man-scent that might be in the air. Then he took the small, wooden call from his shirt pocket. He put the reed to his lips, wrapped his hand around the barrel and over the front to control the sound, and blew the shriek of a dying hare through the call. The shriek came clear and strong then died away in a series of whines as he fluttered his hand into the sound, and the wind took it all quickly away. Every minute for five minutes he did this and then in mild surprise he saw two coyotes loping up the coulee from the south. There was a windmill in a small, runty cottonwood grove a quarter mile away and there they stopped, intent and alert. The suffering hare squealed again in his hand and on they came at a run, sure of a meal. At two hundred yards he raised the rifle from across his knees to his shoulder and began to follow them through the peep sight. The dog stopped 100 yards away; the bitch ran by him, then she stopped too. Through the peep sight he put the white bead just behind the shoulder of the dog and without hesitation squeezed the trigger. The sharp crack of the rifle was soon lost in the wind; the dog twisted up, spun and dropped; the bitch whirled and sprinted south out of the coulee, headed for the next rise. He levered the next shell into the chamber and found the running bitch in the sight. He swung ahead of the sprinting coyote anticipating the point where the bullet and the coyote would meet, then, smiling, he raised his eye off the sight and watched her sail over the rise and disappear. Within seconds she was up and over the next roll in the desert and was gone.

He rolled the carcass and saw a clean kill; the 50 grain solid, loaded down for the hunting of fur, had exited with scarcely more of an opening than the clean *whack* at the point of entry. He ran a hand over and through the fur. The guard hairs were coming in across the shoulders, a little less so down the back and across the hips - good! The pelt was not yet thick with undercoat - not so good! The belly was nearly snow white - very good! He marked a saleable pelt and knew the fur season had begun. He shouldered the coyote and walked to the windmill and nearby he hung the coyote from a cottonwood limb. He skinned it quickly; the pelt came easily off the warm flesh. He rolled up the warm hide and put it in the rucksack, washed his hands in the tank. The wind drying the wetness off his hands was cold and made his fingers ache. He walked back up the coulee and ascended the low hill facing the wind and he could feel it was getting colder as the day advanced. The leaves of the yucca near where he'd sat rattled heavily now in the wind and when he topped the hill and looked north he saw the clouds were heavy and dark over the Mondragón Range. The highest peaks were already white. And shadows under the clouds were taking the sun away from the land as they leaped down over the foothills, coming his way. Before he got back to the truck a dark sky was spitting snow on the desert.

# PART III POLITICS

*"After the making of Eden came a serpent, and after the gorgeous furnishings of the world, a human being. Why the existence of the destroyers? What monstrous folly, think you, ever led Nature to create her one great enemy - man!"*

John C. Van Dyke
*The Desert*

*Chapter 19*

HARLEY SIMMONS stepped out of the weather into Cobre Hall and shook the rain off his hat. The college auditorium was nearly full. He grabbed an aisle seat near the back and watched the remaining seats fill. Then folks took to standing in the back, in the wings, and sitting in the aisle. At the front of the hall, seated behind a long table, were representatives from the Bureau of Reclamation, the State River Commission, the State Department of Wildlife, and the U. S. Fish & Wildlife Service. Harley also noted, in the front row of the auditorium, Del Cobre's "civic leaders," plus the curly head of Rich Pennerman bobbing this way and that as he took quotes, left and right, and put them on his note pad. In time the BOR project planner, Joel Smithers, gavelled the hearing to order and outlined the evening's agenda. The BOR would present in word, graph and pictures the Rio Jalisco Dam proposal, providing cost benefit analysis, the amount of water made available by the project for consumptive use, and the recreation prospectus; the Department of Wildlife would outline in word and pictures the major environmental concerns; citizens would then have the opportunity to make an oral statement·not to exceed five minutes or, if they preferred, could make a written statement of preference on one of the forms provided at the back of the hall. With that, the lights in the hall dimmed, and as Mr. Smithers droned on in a tone of voice one would expect of a man whose work day is inundated by slide rule computations and computer programming, a second BOR employee used a projector to focus a series of charts, graphs, numbers and the occasional photograph on the screen set up on the stage behind the representatives of government. As the project took shape on the screen, Smithers related the graphics to the audience. When his mind wasn't wandering off to more pleasant or seemingly more urgent topics - free-flowing streams, leaping Smallmouth Bass, hounds on the run, prime fur, Bonney's perfectly long white legs, Suzie's magnificent ass, the boy, - Harley heard the gist of the BOR's presentation..."with the recreation benefits factored in, we see a cost benefit analysis of nearly 0.8 to 1; that is, about eighty cents in benefits for each dollar spent...total length of the reservoir when full is 25 miles, with 220,000 acre feet in storage and a gross yield before evaporation to the State of New Mexico of 28,000 acre feet...developed campsites at the dam site and at the Brushy Creek confluence and a full marina and lodge and resort here at the Ocotillo Creek confluence...the reservoir will be periodically stocked with bass, trout and catfish....total project cost is estimated at 112 million dollars..." When Joel Smithers finished his presentation the lights came on to illuminate, momentarily, a pregnant silence. Then Harley saw Jim Bo Moreland seated in the front row set off the applause. This opportune move quickly swelled into a generous endorsement of clapping that Harley judged at a glance to involve about half the people in the room. When the ovation finally subsided Joel Smithers said: "Dr. Beeler, you have the floor."

Ted Beeler stood up by the projection table and quickly substituted a slide projector with a film presentation. He started off with a disclaimer: "The Department of Wildlife takes no formal position for or against the dam. It is merely the intent of this agency to inform the public of possible environmental impacts associated with the proposed construction." Then, with an educated drawl that was about what you'd expect of a good 'ol boy with a Ph.D., he led the audience on a short trip down the Río Jalisco. In fact, Ted didn't say much, just a passing comment here and there to fix the scenes: vermillion cliffs forming a canyon 1,000 feet deep ("some of the finest vistas in the Southwest..."); a fisherman looking a lot like Harley Simmons hooked to a large fish that was taking him downstream ("a naturally reproducing sport fishery that includes two species of trout, Smallmouth Bass, and three kinds of catfish..."); a buck Mule Deer scampering up a side canyon (Mule Deer, Whitetail Deer, elk and Bighorn Sheep are available to the hunter who can find them and pack them out..."); a mixed association of streamside plants ("ninety percent of native riparian habitat has been destroyed in the Southwest..."). When the film came to the confluence of Ocotillo Creek Ted said, "The Department of Wildlife is also concerned about a recently discovered colony of otters, these being the only otters known to exist in the state." Directly, the first otter came out of the pool below the falls with a small carp in its mouth. From that point Ted offered no more commentary to the film. He didn't have to. The otters frolicked on the beach, caught more fish, slid down the banks, appeared and disappeared in the flow, swam in a rush up through the falls and the little ones followed the big ones around. When the film ended with the last otter disappearing without a splash into the pool at Ocotillo Creek the applause began even before the lights went on. When they did go on Harley eye-balled the juxtaposition and figured that, if anything, the no-growth, anti-dam, eco-freaks, had the edge over the boomers and boosters in numbers. Certainly with the shouting, whistling and stomping of feet they made a lot more noise. When the enthusiasm for the presentation by the Department of Wildlife had ended, Joel Smithers regained the microphone and commented dryly, "One can see that the proposed Río Jalisco Dam is living up to is reputation as a highly contentious issue." A careful observer might also have noted that only two people in the hall gave no indication which side they were on. One was Harley Simmons. The other was the sheriff of Arthur County, Henry Bustos.

Joel Smithers went on, "We shall now hear from those who have indicated they would like to make an oral statement. Again we ask that you limit your comments to five minutes or less. And we ask that any sort of response from the audience be withheld until each speaker has finished. I chose at random from the cards...Morey Solís."

Harley was glad he'd brought along a good book as he knew he was in for a couple of hours of polemics, most of which he'd heard before. He drew the paperback from his coat pocket and from time to time turned his ear to catching the highlights of some of the people he knew:

"I'm Morey Solís, chairman of the Arthur County Commission. The future of Del Cobre, the future of Arthur County is dependent on this project - it's as simple as that. I would like to believe that my children, that your children, will have a home here, can find jobs here, that we can initiate new prosperity so they will not have to move away in order to make successful lives. As the Chairman of the Arthur County Commission I say..."

"Garth Bilker."

"I'm Garth Bilker, president of the Jalisco Rod and Gun Club. Where can the average sportsman in southwest New Mexico go to enjoy the out-of-doors? There's too much wilderness here already. All the prime lands are locked up. The dam will provide recreation for the average sportsman, and his family. And isn't it convenient that the Department of Wildlife, with a little help, has suddenly discovered these otters! Everyone knows they're just using the otters to try and stop our dam..."

"Sylvia Fellows."

"Unlike some of the speakers so far I have been to the Río Jalisco Canyon. I spent nearly a week at what I believe is the most beautiful place in the Southwest. To see that river in it's natural beauty, to view an endangered species at home in the wild, this has been the greatest thrill of my life. We should be considering how much we are willing to spend to protect such an area, and such a creature, rather than destroy it. The beauty of it is, the canyon, the river, the wildlife is available to us all, free of charge. We do not need to spend one hundred million dollars to create recreation. We only need the foresight to see the value in what we have..."

"Stewart Mayfair"

"It looks like a coalition of vociferous environmentalists from outside our area have come here in a last ditch effort to stop our dam, and the weak-kneed bureaucrats are playing right into their hands. And all this talk of endangered species! Well I'm here to say, we're an endangered species, too. People are more important than otters..."

"Sidney Pearlmann."

"I feel it is unfortunate that I must differ in opinion from my colleagues in the business community here in Del Cobre, since they above all should realize that long term prosperity is dependent on our maintaining the quality of life characteristics that make our community and our area so desirable. Wilderness is what makes our area unique in the Southwest and the Río Jalisco is the lifeblood of our wilderness. The time has come throughout New Mexico that we begin to view progress in qualitative rather than quantitative terms. In the long run, aesthetics is good business...."

"Jim Bo Moreland."

"First, I would like to congratulate the Bureau of Reclamation and especially the Department of Wildlife for their very informative and excellent presentations. In particular, the wildlife film can be appreciated by all of us who enjoy the great outdoors. None of us who support the dam wish to exterminate the otter or any other wildlife. We're all conservationists at heart. But the otters and other wildlife can be managed. Mitigation procedures are available. And there comes the time when human needs must take precedence. The very highest authority recognizes our dominion on this earth. Our community has languished. The Río Jalisco dam will be our greatest asset once it's built. And the common man supports this project; only the elitist environmentalists support the obstructionist point of view. Are we going to turn the future of southwest New Mexico over to these elitist groups, where the men all have long hair, and the women all have short hair? Doubt that? Just look around this room! Elitism is a hurdle we will shortly overcome. And I can see the day in the not too distant future when our area will rival the White Mountains of Arizona in..."

"Stan Baer."

"My name is Bubba Baer. I've attended a number of these types of gatherings in my life and once again bleeding heart environmentalists who are against growth, progress, and everything that's good about this country are attempting to use some critter which has no commercial value whatever to stop a public project intended for the public good. Are these people even Americans? Or are they against everything America stands for...?"

"Grace Jensen."

"I'm a bleeding heart environmentalist and proud of it. This pork barrel project is both a sham and a shame and I'm going to tell you why. But first I'm going to explain to people like Bubba Baer why the Río Jalisco should be protected, not for recreation, not for long term commercial gain, but as a matter of biotic right. Long before the European settlers began to impact the environment of the Southwest..."

"Ben Wetzel"

"I have come a long way to speak on behalf of the Río Jalisco. To those who would minimize my comments because I am an outsider, I would point out two things. One, please note that I don't have long hair! Second, please consider that I wouldn't travel all the way from New York City if I didn't care about this part of the world. And, I would also point out that the land and water in question is public land...it belongs to all Americans. Now some of you may have already seen the feature in this month's issue of *American Gunner* magazine. But before I summarize the thoughts presented in that article, I want to tell you how I came

152

to want to save the Río Jalisco drainage for wilderness hunting and fishing. Last spring on a bear hunt on Brushy Mountain..."

Harley slid down into his seat as far as his lank frame allowed while Ben Wetzel, the last speaker for the evening, went on for a good deal more than five minutes extolling the manly virtues and All-American values to be derived from hunting bear in the wilderness with, not incidentally, Harley Simmons as your guide. When Wetzel got to the part where he dropped out of the hunt, he managed to be realistic, accurate and self-effacing, without getting too maudlin or self-critical. It was a strong speech by a good speaker but by the time Ben Wetzel finished, folks on both sides had had enough for the evening. Joel Smithers, obviously relieved to be ending his three hours as master of ceremonies, said laconically, "Thank you all for participating in the Federal Public Input Process," and gavelled the meeting to a close. Harley stepped to the back of the hall and stood for a time as the crowed passed by and out the door. From a distance he got a wink from Sidney Pearlmann. Henry Bustos briefly put his hand on Harley's shoulder while looking straight ahead as he left the building. Harley watched Ted. The Wildlife Officer had several of the media gathered around him. Ted was smiling and giving them his, "awh shucks, I'm just a big ol' friendly bear with a Ph.D" routine and then Harley saw Ted look around to the back of the hall and then Harley saw that he was being pointed out to the media. A female reporter followed the directive and Harley could see he'd been spotted. The reporter started to the back of the hall. Harley spotted Ben Wetzel coming up the aisle and said,"Hey Wetzel! Follow me; I'll buy you a beer." Then Harley hid his head under his hat and quickly stepped out into the rain where he was soon lost in retreat.

*Chapter 20*

Dam in Jeopardy?
RIVER OTTERS DRAW SUPPORT

**DEL COBRE** - *Recent public hearings and a write-in campaign directed at the Governor's Office have cast doubt on the proposed Río Jalisco Dam, a Bureau of Reclamation (BOR) engineer said Thursday.*

*Joel Smithers, planning engineer for the Río Jalisco dam, said results of public hearings held earlier this month in Albuquerque and Del Cobre show a clear majority statewide and a slight majority within Arthur County oppose the proposed dam on the Río Jalisco, about 50 miles upstream from the New Mexico/Arizona line.*

*"Overall, counting the public hearings and the mail we've received, input to this agency is running nearly two to one against," Smithers said.*

*Smithers added that it was his understanding that the Office of Governor Garner Greane had also received a recent influx of mail against the project.*

*"I suppose opposition within the state could cause New Mexico to reconsider," Smithers said.*

*Sally Serna, the Governor's press secretary, said Thursday that a large amount of mail had come into the Governor's Office in the past several weeks but declined to give figures as to those for or against the dam.*

*"Some of the letters do not indicate a clear choice and others suggest alternatives," Serna said. "We're getting lots of input from both sides."*

*Smithers said that, despite the protest mail, no new information was presented at the public hearings to prevent the BOR as a federal agency from proceeding with construction of the dam, scheduled to begin this spring.*

*"The project has been authorized by Congress and federal funding is available through the omnibus Southwest Water Bill," Smithers said. "As for the otters, that's New Mexico's decision."*

*Smithers said that much of the recent public opposition to the dam stems from the discovery of a colony of river otters a few miles above the proposed dam site. Smithers said the otters had been thought extinct in the state but their existence has been documented by the State Department of Wildlife following their discovery last spring by "some hunter."*

*That hunter, according to state wildlife biologist Ted Beeler, is Harley Simmons, a Arthur County trapper and guide.*

*"Simmons claims to have seen the otters above the dam site every year for the past dozen years, at least," Beeler said Thursday. "We believe this is true, for his information as to where the otters are living, and their numbers, proved to be accurate."*

*Smithers said the otters have little weight in the issue at the federal level.*

*"A federally endangered species, that would be different," Smithers said. "By the Endangered Species Act, no mitigation is possible for a species listed as endangered. But a species protected by the state is a state concern."*

*Beeler said that while the Department of Wildlife has jurisdiction over the state's wildlife, the State River Commission is the agency that sets water policy for New Mexico.*

*From his office in Santa Fe, State River Commission Chief Sterling Roberts agreed.*

*"By law, the State River Commission will determine if the state wants to proceed with the project," Roberts said. "Personally, I don't see any problem, but the Commission will of course seek direction from the Governor."*

*Serna said that Governor Greane would attend the next meeting of the State River Commission, scheduled for next Tuesday, December 18th.*

~ ~ ~ ~ ~ ~

Harley read through the story a second time. All the while the slim, dark little girl stood behind him on the couch, sometimes leaning over his shoulder, sometimes straightening up to bounce her tiny buns off the back cushion. When Harley had finished reading he handed the newspaper over his shoulder without looking. "You can read it now," he said.

"I already did," she said.

"Oh, what did it say?"

"It says you are the hunter, *el cazador!*"

"What else?"

"It says there will be a dam on the river, and it says the otters will die."

"It doesn't say the otters will die."

"Yes it does. First the dam. Then the otters will die."

"Okay, you got it."

"Why don't you save them?"

"I don't think I can."

"Do you want them to build the dam?"

"I don't know. *No le hace por mi.*"

"How come you speak Spanish like us? *Tu eres un bolillo, qué no?*"

"Yes I am. But I've been to Mexico."

"So have I. Why don't you take us to the river? You could take us fishing, and you could show us the otters."

"Maybe some day."

"Me and mommy are ready now."

"It's winter. You want to go to the river in the winter?"

*"No le hace por mi."*

Debate with this child is futile, he thought. He said, "Why don't you go out back to the *placita* and help your mother make adobe bricks?"

"Why don't you?"

155

"All right. That'll get you out there. Because all you do is follow me around."

"I like following you around."

"What if I put you in my back pocket and took you home with me?"

"If mommy can come too..."

"Maybe some day."

"Me and mommy are ready now."

"I'm sure!"

In the back yard Suzie Navarro had removed the forms and was stacking the dried bricks formed of mud and straw. Other dried bricks were in place; the adobe wall around the court yard was nearly half done. Harley and the little sylph stood side by side, watching. Then Harley said, "We've come to help."

"That's it," Suzie said, stacking the last of the bricks. "I'm ready for lunch."

"Me too," Jessica said.

"You're going down to grandma's for lunch."

"I want to have lunch with Harley, *el cazador*."

"No, you're going to grandma's for the afternoon. I'm having lunch with Harley. Harley's taking me to lunch."

"Oh?" Harley said.

"Yes. You're taking me to lunch. Downtown. Unless of course you have other plans."

"No. No, lunch downtown will be fine." He turned to Jessica. "Next time," he said.

"Next time you take me to lunch," she said. "Downtown."

~ ~ ~ ~ ~ ~

The dry leaves lay scattered across brown lawns, the trees finally barren and still for winter. But it was a bright sunny day that had warmed the winter air so that Suzie was tempted to remove her coat. But it was not quite that warm, so she left her coat on but left it unbuttoned and underneath she wore a dress. He left his own battered hunting coat at her house, feeling comfortable in the middle of the day, and a good deal neater, with a clean wool shirt and new Levis over the long johns he always wore in the winter. She caught him looking at her, peaking through the parted coat, looking at what he could see of her dress, and her figure underneath; she smiled and took him by the hand. He took her hand in his, in a large, tight, uncomfortable grip, but he kept looking at her in that dress and she kept smiling and little by little his hand in hers relaxed. And so they walked through the neighborhood, through the quiet streets and passed the dogs sleeping on brown lawns in the sun, and on down to Main Street to lunch at the Copper Palace.

The Copper Palace Restaurant, since its refurbishment, was known as the "nice" place in town to have lunch, though Harley had always thought they were all "nice" enough. Sidney was there, acting as *maitre d'*. "Well now this is a pleasant surprise," he said, as he showed them to a table, and he held Suzie's chair for her which pleased them all. There were several other couples in the restaurant, as well as several tables with businessmen, who conversed in low important tones. Harley and Suzie knew them all. Everyone nodded or spoke briefly to Harley and Suzie, who nodded in return or offered a brief reply.

Seated, Suzie leaned over to Harley and spoke in low, important tones of her own. "If we're seen here very often," she said, "we'll be known as *a couple*."

"A couple of what?"

"You know what I mean."

"I imagine we already are," he said. "I imagine a lot is known about us. And what isn't known, they can always make it up."

"There probably making up stuff right now," she said. "They're putting us in bed together."

"Sure they are."

"I think it's fun being a couple in a small town," she said. "And we're a nice couple, don't you think?"

"Oh yeah, real nice. Handsome I'd say."

"Thank you," she said.

Suzie ordered a margarita and a chicken móle dish. Harley ordered Tecate Beer and a chicken enchilada plate with green chile and sour cream. The drinks arrived promptly. Suzie sipped at her Margarita, and then she said, "What's going to happen, Harley, on the river?"

"I suppose it could go either way. I was talking to Ted yesterday, on the phone. He's up in Santa Fe working on it, sounds like 24 hours a day. He says the strategy is coming down close to perfect. The press is putting the heat on just like he'd hoped. At the hearing in Albuquerque, the eco-freaks took the boys to the cleaners. They even had the edge here in Del Cobre. And he says they're shelling the Governor's office with letters. A copy of that video slipped out and it's being shown all over the state. That's where a lot of those letters are coming from, Ted said. You read that article this morning in the *Times*."

"Yes. The mysterious hunter had finally been named!"

"The less said about that guy the better. But the key thing, Ted says, is those letters. He says that press aide, Serna, was blowing smoke at the reporter. Ted has a source in the Governor's office and it's not even close. The project is flat unpopular and the son-of-a-bitch knows it. Some of those environmentalists figure Greane is enough of a politician, he might change his mind. I figure he's enough of a politician he'll weasel something out that sounds like he's offering something to everyone. Then he'll go ahead and build that dam."

"What if they build it, Harley?"

"I'm coming to believe, whichever group wins, the life I've had is coming to a close. Anyway you slice it, they're taming the hills."

"You could adjust, draw back a bit."

"I don't want to draw back. I'd like to come to know this country like my daddy did. That river was his home. I'd like to know it like he did, fit it just like that, be a part of it."

"No one living knows that country like you, Harley. You know that's true, and you should be proud."

"I don't know it like he did. That was his home. I want that for myself. But then I want some other things too. What would you want for the river? I always assumed I knew, but I guess I never asked."

"I've never been in the wilderness. Not overnight. I've never had the opportunity to go with anyone who knew the country, and I was afraid to go alone. I don't know if I would like it; I may be just a small town girl. But knowing you makes me want to have that experience. I've always liked knowing our wilderness, our river, is there. What those people are trying to do is very short-sighted. My concern has always been for this town, to preserve what's been here over time. It seems natural to me to want the same for the wilderness and the wildlife, even if that's not part of my life. Jessica is the one who wants to go to the mountains. She talks about it all the time. But I can't take her there, not by myself. She wants to go with you. She loves you, Harley. More than you know."

"Think so?"

"I know it. She was never like this with anyone else, not even her father. You're it, for Jessica."

"Maybeso. She's easy to like. Saucy little outfit. Sharp as a whip. And cute as a little speckled pup under a red wagon."

"I like watching you two together."

"Right. But she's not mine."

"She could be, if you'd let her. We could both be for you, and you could be for us. And I could have more children. I'd like to. I hope to, someday. I like children. I even liked being pregnant, most of the time."

"You make it all sound like a picture postcard."

"Well?"

"Well it doesn't work that way. And I've got my own family to deal with."

"It looks to me like you're not dealing with it at all."

Harley did not respond to this. The food arrived and it was very good and they ate with good appetite. Afterwards, Harley ordered another beer for himself and another margarita for Suzie. Suzie had not forgotten.

"You haven't seen Billy, have you? Or Bonney?"

"I've talked to her on the phone."

"A phone call in ten months! And you haven't talked to Billy at all?"

"No."

"You're afraid of him, Harley."

Harley filled his glass. He squeezed the lime slice along the rim, then dropped the lime into the glass. He sprinkled a bit of salt on the rim. He said, "What do you mean I'm afraid of him?"

"I think you know what I mean. You're afraid you're not his father anymore. You're afraid that he has another allegiance. And you're afraid Bonney has another allegiance too. And you may be right."

"So what do I do?"

"Get it over with, Harley. You're no good to us as you are. You're no good to them, either. You're no good to yourself. Maybe you're not his father anymore. Maybe Bonney is in love with another man. Find out. If you weren't so afraid, that's what you'd do."

They sat in silence then, finishing their drinks. Harley had nothing to say and Suzie worried that she had said too much. They stood and Harley paid and they went out into the street. The bright sunshine shown warmly, though the air was cool, and she leaned against him. He put his left arm around her. Then she reached around with her right arm and put her hand in his back pocket.

"Two margaritas," she said, "and I'm already feeling kind of floozy."

"You feel like a floozy?"

"I'm not a floozy! I said I feel *kind of* floozy."

"Only a floozy can feel like that."

"You think so?"

"I'm sure of it."

They leaned against each other for a time, her hand in his back pocket and then he put his hand in her back pocket. And then he said, "Well, we did it."

"Did what?"

"We went to a fancy place and had lunch. First time for me."

"First time for us. Thank you for lunch."

"*Por nada.*"

"Harley, will you let me take you to dinner some time?"

"Sure. Name it."

"Starting next week I have some time off. How about Tuesday night? You come pick me up at six. And we can see the movie, if it's any good."

"Okay, we'll try it, and see if it's any good."

"Harley?"

"Yes."

"How long has it been since you've been to bed with a floozy?"

"Seems like forever."

They went slowly up the street, towards the neighborhood and home, walking hand in hand.

*Chapter 21*

"BONNEY?"

"It's you!"

"That's right, Bonney, it's me."

"What do you want?"

"I'll be taking Billy this weekend."

"No Harley."

"You'll recall I have certain rights."

"Why now?"

"It's time."

"Is it? From what I've seen, you should have plenty of other interests."

"What have you seen?"

"Never mind!"

"I'll bet he's there. I know school's out for Christmas."

"He's here."

"All right. I'll be over about noon. You don't need to fix him lunch."

"He was planning things with his friends this weekend...he may not want to go."

"Ask him."

He heard her voice with the question, then, in the background, a loud whoop.

"Okay," she said into the phone. "You have him back to me by Sunday evening. What will you-all be doing?"

"I don't know. Something he'll enjoy."

"Well I don't want you doing anything dangerous. No guns."

"No guns."

~ ~ ~ ~ ~ ~

In the morning he was up very early and he let the boy sleep while he saddled the old man's horse and the mule and the gear they would need for a long day. It was still dark when he went back in to the house where he gently held the boy's foot till he came out of a deep sleep. The boy sat up in bed and Harley could tell that for a moment the boy didn't know where he was. Then he said, "What time is it, dad?"

"It's time to get up. By the time we get you in the saddle it will be getting light."

The boy got up and Harley told him to dress warm and then Harley sent him to the bathroom to wash up and brush his teeth. Harley went to the kitchen and poured two cups of hot, black coffee. The boy was awake when he came to the kitchen table and he sat down.

"You want a cup of coffee, son?"

"Mother doesn't let me have coffee."

"You can have some here, if you want some."

The boy watched as Harley set the mug of coffee in front of him. "Okay," the boy said. Then Harley watched as the boy drank his first few sips of black coffee. He could tell the boy had mixed emotions about the taste but the flavor of the event obviously pleased him.

"Where are we going, dad?"

"Over the divide, son, where the country gets bigger the further you go."

"Grandpa used to say, when you go over the divide, the country opens up."

"That's right, that's exactly what it does. And it's a good day for it. It's real cold right now but it's going to warm up. We get an early start and we can cross the divide before noon, catch some trout in Ocotillo Creek, and still be back tonight."

"You never used to take me across the divide."

"You weren't old enough then. You are now."

When they were ready to leave, the boy started out of the house without his hat.

"Don't forget your hat."

The boy brightened up and ran into the bedroom and came back with a new felt cowboy hat.

"Thanks for buying me a cowboy hat, dad. And boots."

"You always want to wear a hat in the winter, or all of you gets cold."

They rode the trail up and up with the early light sifting through the trees and the icy crystals of frost sparkling on the ground. The horse and mule were blowing in the frosty air and tossing their heads; the bits and bridles and curb chains jingled along with spurs and their hooves made their sequential sound on the frozen ground. Until they started talking, these were the only sounds in the perfect stillness of early morning.

"Dad, is that a mountain lion skin hanging on that thing in the barn?"

"That's a bobcat pelt. And that thing is called a stretcher."

"A mountain lion skin would be a lot bigger than that."

"That's right."

"Did you shoot it?"

"Yes. After White-eye and Geraldine treed him."

"What about Lurk?"

"Lurk is a problem."

"I like Lurk; he's my favorite. He's so big. He still likes to knock me down and lick my face."

"Lurk likes you. And he doesn't like many people."

"I wish he was my dog."

"I'd like to give him to you."

"Do you think mother would let me have him?"

"Somehow I don't think Lurk and your mother would get along. You wait on that; we may work something out."

"How come I'm riding this mule?"

"Because she's sure-footed and steady and she's got a good running walk that's smooth and covers the ground. You ride this horse and you'd have to trot to keep up. You have to trot very far and you'll want to go home."

"I don't want to go home. I want to go over the divide."

Near the divide they began to see patches of snow in the shade of the pines but there was little snow on the trail for it followed a ridge and they were still on the south slope. Then they crossed the divide and started down the north slope and for the first 1000 feet of descent the animals stepped through snow that slowed their pace and brought them to a walk. But it got shallower as they descended and it was melting in the late morning sun.

"Dad, how come from town you can't even tell there's snow up here?"

"Because we haven't had a good snow in a month and all that's left is what's in the shady places of the north slopes."

"There's lots of snow here."

"Not so much. In a month you won't be able to cross here, afoot or horseback."

"Then what?"

"Snowshoes."

"Snowshoes?"

"Sure."

"I remember grandpa coming in once with snowshoes. You and mother and I were at grandpa's house and he was coming down this trail into the yard and he had another horse carrying all his stuff..."

"A pack horse."

"Okay, a packhorse, and he had snowshoes tied on top of all the stuff. You remember, dad?"

"I remember. Your grandpa used to go to the high country in the dead of winter because he knew they're wouldn't be anyone around. It never mattered to him what the weather was. He knew the fur wasn't as plentiful up there, and harder to take, but he wanted the best pelts. And he got 'em. Fur primes out awful nice above 8,000 feet."

"Dad, are you as good a hunter as grandpa was?"

"No. I haven't lived long enough to be as good as your grandpa. I don't know if anyone can be that good anymore."

"Why not?"

"Your grandpa lived in another time. The country was bigger and wilder. There were fewer roads, fewer laws, and mostly there were a lot less people. And what your grandpa did was accepted then. Nobody wants to live like that anymore. And nobody wants anyone else too, either. A mountain man is still an American Hero, as long as he's good and dead. As long as he's history. As long as he's not real. Do you see that movie, *Jeremiah Johnson*?"

"Oh sure. That was a good one."

"It was probably the best mountain man movie, ever. It was quite realistic. In real life, Jeremiah Johnson hunted and trapped fur, and lived off the land. The movie didn't make too much of that, but at least they didn't pretend it wasn't so. People still like a mountain man movie, especially if it's a good one. Jeremiah Johnson made people feel something wonderful, about our past, about heritage, here in the West. People didn't mind that he hunted and trapped and sold fur, because it was a movie. It was a fantasy. But try to live like that today, even a little bit, and it's almost against the law."

"You live like that."

"I have. But times are changing and it's getting harder all the time. The wolf is gone. The grizzly is gone. And the wild country is going with them. Wild country never gets any bigger. It only gets smaller, a little here, a lot there, every year. It's being lost. And in the end, it'll be the loss of wild lands and wild rivers that'll drive down a way of life."

"Did Jeremiah Johnson hunt around here?"

"No, his range was the northern Rockies. But there was a mountain man around here who was just as great as Jeremiah Johnson, and he was even meaner."

"Who was that?"

"Jim Kirker."

"Dad, there's this kid named Kirker who sits next to me in music class."

"That would be one of Jim Kirker's great, great, grandsons."

"Really?"

"Sure. There's lots of Kirkers around here. I know just about all of them. They're all descended straight from the mountain man."

"I think that's neat, dad."

Harley was riding ahead and he turned back and looked at the boy who did not yet look uncomfortable in the saddle.

"How are you and Ruby getting along?"

"Oh she's okay, for a mule."

"Did you go on any trail rides last summer?"

"Lots of times. They made us go."

"How was it?"

"It was okay, but not like this."

"Did you do any fishing?"

"Yeah, they made us do that too. We caught some trout."

"What kind?"

"Rainbows."

"Stockers."

"What's that?"

"Trout raised in a hatchery and stocked in a stream."

"What do you call real trout?"

"Trout that are born and raised in the stream are called wild trout."

"Are there wild trout in Ocotillo Creek."

"You bet."

"We'll always hunt in the wilderness and catch wild trout, won't we dad?"

"Sure we will. Even if we have to work up a little make believe along the way."

They came down out of the snow fields and loosened their coats in the warming air and rode off the trail west through a park with some big red pine scattered here and there.

"Son, did you-all lope your horses on those trail rides?"

"They wouldn't let us do that."

"Well, we're going to lope over to that big red pine yonder. Put a little more weight in the stirrups and go with the mule and you can grab the horn if you have to."

Then he put the old horse into an easy lope and the mule ran with the horse and they loped across the park in the sun. He looked over and the boy's eyes were big and wide and blue as he rode with the mule till she came down to a long trot as they approached the big red pine. The boy began to bounce in the saddle and then he lost his stirrups. Harley reached over and caught the reins and slowed the mule but by then the boy was losing his balance over the side, down and down, and when the mule stopped suddenly the boy let go of the horn and dropped to the ground, and there he lay on his back and laughed and laughed just like any goofy kid. When he stopped laughing he sat up and said, "Dad that mule rides like a bucking bronco!...it's more fun than skateboards!"

"Skateboards?"

"Yeah. Only her ears are so long I can't see where I'm going."

Soon they stood on the rim and the boy looked between the mules ears down into the canyon of Ocotillo Creek.

"We'll never make it, dad."

"Yeah we will. You just stay with Ruby."

The mule followed the horse down over the rim and down the slope and when they got to the steep part where the dirt was soft and there was some leftover snow, the animals started to slide, and they set back on their haunches and slide and picked their way down and soon they were drooping their heads and sucking the water from Ocotillo Creek.

"You can climb down now, son; it's time to catch some fish."

The boy stepped down and walked around, trying to regain his legs. Harley hopped over some rocks as he led the horse and mule across the stream where he staked them out on a patch of brown grass. Harley came back across and rigged up his own rod and then helped the boy with his.

"What kind of lure is that?"

"It's called a rooster tail."

"It's pretty."

"It ought to get their attention. Now most of what you read about trout comes from summertime fishing when the water is warm. In the middle of the day the water is too warm for them to feed much and they hood up where it's deep and cool. Then in the evening, as the water cools, they come out to feed. But now it's winter and some of this flow is spring water and some is snow melt and it's all ice cold. It's so cold trout don't feed much. When they do, it's apt to be in the middle of the afternoon when there's been sun on the water to warm it up some. So you change strategy for trout in the winter and you don't expect to catch so many fish but if you're lucky and do things right you can catch some good ones. Below here is a good pool and there will be two or three big trout in there. We need to sneak up on those trout just like we're hunting so when the lure comes to the water they don't know we had anything to do with it."

They walked a quarter mile downstream, around some boulders and down a small waterfall, hopping over the rocks, keeping their feet dry, and stopped ten yards from the pool that ran down narrow and deep and then spread out against a red, rock cliff.

"You see the trout?"

"No."

"Keep looking. Over at the base of that cliff in that patch of sun."

"Oh yeah..."

"You haven't forgotten how to cast?"

"Well..." And the boy rolled the bale on the open-faced reel, caught the line on his finger, and pulled his arm back to cast. "Can we get any closer?"

"Then they'll see us. You can reach them from here."

The boy made a mighty cast and got plenty of distance, so much so the lure cleared the pool and met the cliff were it dropped perfectly in front of the finning trout. There was a belly flash from one of the fish and the fish struck before the boy could close the bale. When he did and started to reel he was into a fish. The trout danced the surface once then went for the depths of the pool. The boy cranked forward, then back, then mostly forward as the rod bent and throbbed and in time the fish came reluctantly up the pool to the beach where he lay below them in the shallows, sleek and sporting flashy spots ringed in red.

"It's a different kind of trout, dad."

"That's a brown, a nice Brown Trout."

"How big is it?"

Harley knelt and made an estimate by flexing the span of his hand.

"Near 18 inches."

"Is that a real big one?"

"That's a wonderful trout in a small stream like this. I guide fly fishermen that would sell off their wives for a wild trout, eighteen inches."

"Do they get bigger?"

"Not much in this stream. But in the river, up above, I've seen trout two feet long."

"Are we going to the river today?"

"No, that's half a day's ride yet."

"Down the creek?"

"You can't get down this creek horseback. You can hike it, but to ride all the way to the river we'd have to rim out and then drop back in down below."

"Can we go all the way to the river some day?"

"We will, when it's warmer, and you're mother will let us stay out for awhile."

"Can we keep my fish?"

"Sure."

"At camp they made us throw them back. They said they weren't safe to eat."

"You get more fishermen than fish and that sort of thing can happen. I'll take care of your fish. You work this pool some more. If they're spooked, work downstream and fish wherever you think it looks good. You don't need to go far. Work all the good water slow and careful. Remember to hunt the fish. And try to keep your feet dry."

"Where are you going?"

"I'm going upstream. I'm going to catch one *almost* as big as yours. I'll take this nice brown and clean him for you and I'll put him in the shade where he'll keep."

In late afternoon he returned to the camp and got a fire going. He boiled coffee and set the small grill over the two rocks and when the boy showed up he took the boy's second catch, a rainbow, smaller, and gutted it and lay it out with the three browns he'd caught over the coals. Then they drank some coffee and when it was time they peeled the crispy fish off the bones and ate them with their fingers as the day began to leave and cool down.

At dusk they mounted and the animals dug in and heaved and lunged and quickly took them out of the canyon. By the time they crossed the park and reached the trail the last of a brilliant Southwest sunset was gone.

"It's dark, dad. I can hardly see this mule's big funny ears."

"We'll have about a half moon pretty soon. And Ruby and Cleo can see a lot better than us in the dark and they know the way home."

By the time they'd climbed to the snow fields the snow had frozen down; it was crunching under their feet as they crossed the divide and then they started down and for a long while the boy, for the first time all weekend, had no questions. When he did finally speak, it was the first question Harley couldn't answer.

"Dad, why don't you ever come and visit us?"

"I don't know what to tell you, son. There are lots of reasons."

"Mother said you came back when grandpa died. That's why we didn't go to the funeral...because she knew you'd be there. We saw you once downtown last summer, at the cafe. We could see you through the window. And one time you were walking into the post office. I saw you first both times and mother said *never mind*, like she does, and she wouldn't stop. You never came to see us and you never even called."

"You're mother and I aren't together any more, son."

"Mother says you're divorced. But you could still come visit us, and I could visit you on the weekends, like now."

"We'll start doing this as often as you're mother will let us."

"Will you come and visit us?"

"You're mother has company, son."

"Sometimes he stays over. But not always. Then you could come visit us."

They rode on through a dark forest. Where there was snow, it shown in the moonlight. And above, pine and spruce and aspen were silhouettes in the night. The horse and mule clicked shod hooves on the frozen ground.

"Mother says you won't come visit us because you have a new girlfriend. She says it's Jessica's mother."

"Jessica's mother and I are friends."

"She's pretty, dad. I seen her at school. She waits for Jessica sometimes. She's almost as pretty as mother."

"Uh huh. Do you know Jessica?"

"Not really. She's only in the third grade.

"I see."

"Will you visit us? Maybe now you and mother wouldn't fight anymore and we could all be together."

"We'll see about that."

At the house the boy slid from the saddle and stood sleepily with his legs bowed like he was still mounted.

"Dad, I don't think I'm a very good rider. Maybe it's because of that mule."

"It's not the mule. It just takes lots of riding. But anyone can learn to ride. It's just that nobody rides enough to really learn anymore. But I think you'll learn."

"I hope so. Only next time I want to ride a horse."

"You get inside now and warm up."

"First I have to say hello to Lurk."

The boy went over to the big dog on the end of the chain and as usual the dog rose up on his hind legs way above the boy, put his paws on his shoulders and knocked him down. The boy squealed and laughed and rolled around while the hound licked him and roughed him up until the boy crawled away.

"Dad, that's the silliest dog there ever was!"

Then the boy hobbled over to the porch steps and into the house. Harley unsaddled the stock, brushed them down, then put them in the horse trap with a block of hay and some grain. He broke the ice on the stock tank and then he went inside. The boy was asleep in the living room chair.

"Wake up son, you're only part way there."

"It's cold in here, dad," the boy said, standing up.

"I'll get the stove going. You get in there and draw the hot water for a bath. There's a heater in there; turn it on.

Harley got the fire going a good blaze. He set the damper partly closed and the heat rapidly filled the room. He put the gear away and put the boy's fish in the freezer. For a while he could hear activity in the bathtub, then for a while he could hear nothing at all. He went in and the boy was asleep in the bathtub.

"Son, you can't sleep here."

The boy woke up in the bright light and once again wasn't sure where he was. Then he said, "I washed up, dad."

"You didn't wash your hair."

"Do I have to?"

"Yes. Here's the shampoo. Wash your hair and then you're going to bed."

The boy came out of the bathroom with his carrot colored hair wet and slicked back from combing and he stood by the stove with the towel wrapped around him. Harley noticed that he was still small-boned and slender but, from the last time he'd seen him, less so, and he was starting to show the physique of young manhood.

"You're coming to be a pretty chuffy little kid."

"Eighty-eight pounds, dad. And I can chin myself ten times."

Then the boy was in bed, around the corner in the dark room while Harley sat up by the stove with only the glow of the fire through the isen-glass windows to light the room.

"Dad?"

"Go to sleep, son."

"Dad, what are we going to do tomorrow?"

"We'll sleep in. Then we'll eat a big breakfast. Then we'll go down to the Copper Palace and watch the Cowboys on the big screen TV."

"That'll be neat. But they won't let a kid in there."

"If you're with me they will."

"Really?"

"Sure."

"Dad?"

"Go to sleep son."

"Dad, next time can we go hunting?"

"We'll see about that. We'll see about a lot of things."

"Dad, if you and mother...?"

"That's enough son. No more questions. Go to sleep."

"Okay dad."

~ ~ ~ ~ ~ ~

He pulled up in front of the house and the boy said, "He's not here, dad. You could talk to mother now."

"Your mother and I will be talking soon. Not now."

"Shall I tell her we went to the bar and watched the football game?"

"We don't have anything to hide, son. You can tell her about the whole weekend. Only when you get to the part about the football game be sure to tell her you drank cokes."

"I will. Thanks for taking me."

"That's fine. Now don't forget your fish."

The boy picked up the large trout wrapped frozen in a recent edition of the Del Cobre *Region* and held it in his lap.

"You go on now, son. I'll see you next time."

The boy stepped down from the cab of the truck and started to run up the walk to the house.

"Mother look what I got! Mother...!"

## *Chapter 22*

HIS MOTHER showed up at his father's house, as his father expected, right after work the following day. Her car was long and low and Harley heard it break the ice and scrape bottom as it crossed the creek. He looked out the window and she was pulling into the yard, drops of creek water flying off the tires. He watched as she got out - nearly as tall as he, tight, styled jeans tucked into needle-nosed boots, legs all the way up to her ass, soft, almost-red hair coiffed perfectly down and over her shoulders and the fur collar of her short suede coat. She came up the steps and opened the door.

"May I come in?"

"Of course."

She stepped in and, quite collected, quickly surveyed the premises.

"It's clean," she said.

"What did you expect?"

"A mess. You're not responsible for this."

"You're right."

"Does your Mexican girlfriend do this for you?"

"It's the old woman who lives across the creek."

169

"I thought as much. Do you have something to drink?"

"Sure."

"A nice red wine? It's so cold."

"I don't know how nice it is, but it's red, and it will warm you up."

"Good. I want some."

He took her coat, then went to the kitchen. He got a beer for himself and he brought the wine in with a glass, all on a tray. She had stepped around the grizzly bear rug and was seated on the couch, waiting. He set the tray on the coffee table in front of the couch. He poured the wine glass full, then went to the wood stove, put in some more wood and gave it a little more air. It seemed plenty warm in the house to him, but he wanted it to be as warm as he knew she would like it. Then he got a chair from the kitchen and brought it to the living room so that when he sat down he faced the woman across the table, sitting on the couch. He noticed that her glass of wine was already half gone. The light in the room was starting to fade with the day.

"I had to see you, Harley."

"Oh?"

"Since you obviously weren't going to come by and see me."

"If there was some signal that you wanted me to, I missed it."

She did not respond to this. Instead, she drank the last half of her glass. He refilled it. He knew her, knew what she liked, and he could tell that she was already starting to feel the wine. He drank slowly from the bottle of beer and he waited. She looked about and said nothing, and he could tell she was no longer quite so collected. And whatever words or thoughts she had brought with her, she couldn't find them. He was ready to help.

"Where's Billy?"

"Don't worry. He's staying with a friend this evening."

"This evening?"

"Tonight. I needed to talk to you alone. I'm picking Billy up tomorrow afternoon."

"And Junior?"

"Junior?"

"You're new boyfriend."

"Bruce. His name is Bruce. He's out of town, on business."

"And when are you picking him up?"

"Tomorrow morning, at the airport."

"Swell."

She ignored this, filled her mouth with wine, swallowed it, and said, "Harley, you can't take him any more."

"Why not?"

"You just can't. You'll hurt him. And you'll ruin everything."

"He had a wonderful time."

"I'm admitting that. I've never known him to be so excited."

"Well?"

"That's just it. He can't go off with you like that and come back all excited, and then just be with us. He's very confused already. He's keeps talking about you and I getting back together."

"Good."

"It's not good. It's leaving him very confused. It will tear him apart. And it will ruin everything."

"You mean for you and Junior."

"Stop that! But yes, it will ruin it for Bruce and I, and for Billy. You'll hurt him, Harley. You must leave us alone."

"He's right, Bonney. He knows it should be you and me. And I know it. What's wrong with you?"

"That's impossible. I didn't come here to talk about that."

"Right."

"Besides, it seems you're pretty well involved yourself...who is she?"

"Suzie Navarro."

"I know her from somewhere."

"You two had a class together some years ago."

"Did we? I know I've seen her before. She's attractive, in her way."

"Yes, she is."

"Anyway, I know more about you two than you think."

"That right?"

"That's right. I've seen you two *in action*."

"In action?"

"Yes. Last week. I was down at City Hall. We had a meeting with Jim Bo. We were waiting to see him and I looked out the window across the street and who should appear but Harley and his Mexican girlfriend. And I watched you two snuggling on the street with your hands in each others back pockets like a couple of horny teenagers. And then you go off up Main Street holding hands..."

"What's wrong with that?"

"Well you never held my hand walking up Main Street! You never held my hand at all, unless you wanted to lead me into the bedroom. But it's fine with that Mexican girl. I never had the privilege. And I don't suppose I even have to imagine what happened when you got her home."

"And I don't suppose I have to guess what will happen as soon as *Bruce* gets in from out of town."

"Well!"

"Well!"

She had finished her second glass of wine. He picked up the wine bottle. She said, "Don't", but he refilled her glass anyway. And once again she filled her mouth with wine. Then she said, "I know what you like to do with women in bed. I suppose that Mexican is raunchy enough for you."

171

"So are you. When you're in the mood, Bonney, nobody likes it any better. Anyway, whatever she and I do, she's not my first choice."

"I've heard that one before. That was your favorite line, after you'd been with someone else. You'll never change, Harley."

"I have changed. I haven't been drunk in nearly a year. I haven't been in a fight in nearly a year. I've been with the same woman for nearly a year. And she's not even the one I want. I've been wanting you to know these things."

"Is it true about the drinking?"

"Yes. I don't need that anymore. And when I'm not drunk, I don't look for fights, or stray women either."

"So you'll do all that for her! You would never do it for me. I begged you Harley."

"I didn't do all that for her. I've been wanting you to know these things. I did it for you."

"It's impossible. We're too different, Harley...the way you like to live. The neighbors still tease me about things, when we were living in the new house...those hounds howling at the moon. And sometimes that mule in the back yard. I still have nightmares...when I would be in the bathroom in the morning, when a woman likes her privacy, and suddenly that big-headed mule staring through the window, looking down at me. I've never been so embarrassed."

"Ruby's forgotten all about that."

"Very funny. That was a residential area, not a ranch."

"They sold them as *ranchettes*."

"That's just a name and you know it. And stop teasing me. You haven't changed about that. You're always showing off that you're different. You want to rub everyone's nose in it."

"I don't want to be different anymore. I want to fit in, with you and Billy."

"Stop putting us all together!"

"It's not too late."

"It is. Too much has happened. Too much hurt. You did some vicious things."

"You said some vicious things."

"What defense did I have? Damn you Harley. Goddamn you!"

"It's not too late."

"It is. You cheated on me. You kept *fucking* other women!"

"You left me. You divorced me."

"You hit me. You broke my fucking nose!"

"You broke my fucking heart!"

He could feel it now himself, the breaking down. And across the table she was losing it. He noted the tears and the flushed face, and the lovely lost eyes of a woman who has had too much to drink. And he noted the wet splotches on her blouse, under each arm; so unlike her,

172

and especially for her not to notice, or even care. He could imagine that the wetness was anxiety, for she must sense that she was losing it. And he could imagine, too, that the wetness was tension, and the tension was sexual. Indeed, he could smell her anxiety, and her sex. And outside the light had largely failed, leaving little more than the glow from the wood stove which crackled gently and pumped out an urgent heat. When he took her by the hand she said, "No Harley," but he knew there was nothing to it. In the bedroom he gently stripped her to perfection. With choice words he flattered her breasts, her ass, her lengthy white legs, till she lay with no defense, athwart the bed. In time his tongue found the incredible wetness between her thighs, parting her lips and almost-red hair. Soon her hips were yielding and heaving with each stroke of his tongue. The way she moved told him where she was, and just before she got there he left off, came up, and rolled her over. She cried out, anticipating new pleasure, as she expertly threw her leg over and mounted his cock. Upright, her pump was steady and unrelenting; he arched and let her do it, knowing what worked. When she was ready he said those things that always shamed her later, but that she had to have at the time, and, as if by order, she made a handful of each breast, caressed herself, and brought herself off. He arched still more, flexed, throbbed, and held it; she just kept coming. And then he let it go...

Always, when it was over, he lay beside her and stroked her back, bringing her down. He did it this time too, knowing what worked.

"Feel lovely?" he said.

"Yes, very lovely. But I'm still drunk."

"Dizzy?"

"No. Just nice and high. But one more glass and it would have been rape."

"Bonney, I want to tell you what I've got arranged for us...Jim Bo has offered me a job."

"Jim Bo?"

"Yes. Your friend and mine. He wants me to run that lodge and marina when the lake goes in."

"What did you tell him?"

"I told him I'd think about it."

"Would you do that?"

"I guess I'd do whatever it takes to get the three of us back together."

"That would be a real job, Harley."

"I know. Steady work. Steady pay. Paid vacations. Insurance benefits...a real job."

"That could be a good job for you. You could do it well, if you wanted to."

"It would be for us."

"You're serious?"

"Yes."

"I almost believe you."

"Believe me."

"Maybe I will...oh...Harley...I'm going to sleep now. Please don't touch me anymore."

He complied, knowing what worked, letting her sleep separate, lying awake himself for a long time, in triumph.

~ ~ ~ ~ ~ ~

When he awoke it was dim light and she was dressing beside the bed.

"Don't rush off; come back to bed."

"I can't Harley. It's getting light. I didn't mean to spend the night. I have to get home, or someone will know."

She went to the bathroom and he dressed and then he walked her to the door. It was getting light enough to see.

"Harley, I need to think about all this."

"Sure. Think."

"I need a few days."

"Fine."

"Then I'll know more."

"I'll be ready when you are. Just don't forget last night."

"I won't. I really have to run now."

"Later, then."

"Yes."

She hugged him briefly and left the house.

## Chapter 23

SHE PUT ON HER COAT and went to the back yard and took out her tension on the big, heavy, adobe bricks, blocking up the wall. She worked hard, worked up a sweat, never stopping until she was good and tired. It all made her feel a little better. And then it was good to come inside and soak under the shower. She stayed until the hot water began to run out. It was her best place, her favorite place, to gather her thoughts, seated in the tub, her head and heavy black hair between her knees, the hot water coming down with softening force from above. The sound and feel of the water, the warmth and steam, put her off in her own world, where she could reconnoiter. If he will just come by, she thought, I will find a way; I won't lose him now. But as much as that thought, she also wanted to hurt him, and knew she might. She thought of ways to do it, of how much he'd earned it. Then she would tell herself to let the anger pass, to work to make things right. Whatever it was, she thought, it doesn't matter much; only the ending will count. And Suzie still felt, in a hoped-for way, that the ending would be hers.

She dressed as she had planned, as if everything was fine. She wore a dress to show herself off, what she knew he liked about herself. When she went to the kitchen to sit and wait it was ten till six and there was still time. Through the kitchen window she watched the street, and in the kitchen she watched the clock. When, finally, she let it all out, she stood and used her arm to take the table cloth, the salt and pepper, the bottle of ketchup and coffee cup half full, off the table and up against the kitchen wall. It all crashed, splashed, and scattered across the floor impressively. Then she sat at the kitchen table and cried. It was just six o'clock. But she knew already he wasn't going to come.

## Chapter 24

HE SADDLED THE ROAN, turned White-eye loose, necked Lurk to Geraldine and started up Gavilán Creek about the time he was supposed to show up at Suzie Navarro's home. They all splashed up the creek, headed for it's source on the south rim of the divide. There were always a few coon along the creek. Chances for Gray Fox and bobcat, too. There was a chance for almost anything along Gavilán Creek. But he wasn't thinking about the hunt so much as recent events. And to his surprise, he almost felt sorry for the guy.

"Lurk," he said outloud to the hound up ahead, "that poor bastard has got the bad news by now. He's second best and now he knows it. He's young yet; he'll get over it. I'm gonna make it Lurk. It's going to be just like I wanted it. White-eye and Geraldine are going to teach you, and we're all going to teach the boy..."

Splashing up the creek in the moonlight, Lurk did not respond. He did not ask Harley how he knew so much about how "that poor bastard" was doing. Nor did Lurk ask Harley about Suzie, whom Harley had not forgotten. He had simply set her aside, not to worry. She knew where his heart was, where his loyalties lay. She knew if he got the chance he was going to go for it. And he knew that, by now, she'd have the bad news too; she'd have figured it out. It wouldn't change a thing if I went by and told her myself, he reasoned; it wouldn't help her a bit. But Harley did not talk about Suzie to Lurk. He didn't say anything about Suzie, at all.

Then White-eye took out on a fresh coon track and the race went so fast White-eye had him treed before Harley could catch and unleash the other two hounds. He stepped off the horse and shined the light up into the bare branches of the big cottonwood. It was a clear night with a good moon. Harley shone the flashlight beam this way and that and one by one the bare limbs came into a direct light. When he found the coon he saw he had rolled himself into a ball like a knot on a limb and he was hiding his eyes from the light. But Harley knew what he saw. He drew the .22 magnum revolver and shot the coon down. He allowed the hounds a grip or two before tying the coon behind the saddle. Then he continued on up the creek.

When next he heard White-eye, the Saddleback was way up ahead and, it turned out, had gone up a side canyon, a dry canyon that narrowed up little by little and soon was nothing but boulders and cliffs. Harley knew it not by name, for it had none, but from past hunts. Harley, Lurk and Geraldine started up the canyon, listening to White-eye, who had something that was not a track. Not yet.

BoooOOO! BoooOOO! Harley rode up on the hound who was sounding intermittently, whipping his tail about, and working around a pile of dirt, sticks and dry leaves. With the light, Harley could see the remains of the buck under the slash. The great cat had killed, fed, and dragged the carcass here, to bury it till hunger brought him back to the kill. He would not be far away. Harley got down and got closer to the kill. It was a very large buck who had wielded a wonderful rack to no avail. He saw where the cat had savaged the neck after he'd struck. Most obvious were the grotesque marks of the cat's jaws and teeth as they'd closed down over the muzzle, now greatly deformed, of the deer. The buck had gone down from suffocation. Backtracking with the light, Harley traced the route of the struggle, from where the cat struck down canyon, to where the buck had gone down and the cat fed first, to where he'd dragged the carcass, now laying partially covered by the slash. White-eye had so much scent, he didn't know where to start. Harley got hold of Lurk and Geraldine and let the older hound work. Eventually, White-eye found a line of scent going up the canyon, then up into the cliffs and rocks on the south wall. BoooOOO!... BoooOOO! Harley followed on foot, holding the two hounds back, shining the light as the Saddleback artfully worked through the rocks on the side of the cliff. And then he struck, finding the place in the rocks where the lion had lain until not too many minutes before. On through the rocks the hound danced, running where he could, scrambling where he couldn't run, till he brought the track back down in the canyon. The hound took the scent off the air and, running with his head up, sprinted up the canyon with his hot-track bay: woooOOO!...woooOOO!...woooOOO! The other two hounds tried to go and Harley had to wrestle them to the ground to get them unhooked. He struggled with the hounds and the clips.

"Goddamnit Lurk! Don't screw it up. We're going for some panther meat, best for you and me. There! Go Lurk! Run you little gyp!"

Harley raced after them on foot; there were rock slides up ahead where a horse couldn't go. He ran where he could, climbed the rock slides, then sprinted ahead with the light in his hands showing the way through the canyon's twists and turns; running, the rocks and cliffs looked almost alive in the light. The canyon twisted and turned; depending on the angle and the distance, he could hear the hounds, and then he couldn't. When he got to them his beam showed they had a mountain lion bayed up on a ledge, fifty feet off the canyon floor.

White-eye had climbed the highest, in an attempt to get to the ledge. He bayed his tree bark and sought a route up. Harley didn't want any of them going any higher. He whistled and Geraldine came down, leaping and dancing and slipping over the rocks. Then Lurk, growing bored with game that was no longer running, came down too. White-eye worked his way a little bit higher. Harley shined his light, cocked his revolver, and waited for a shot. The lion seemed trapped on the ledge; Harley got a glimpse once and at times he could see his long tail hanging over the ledge, but the lion had room up there to stay out of sight of a shot. Then Harley heard Lurk start a running track back down canyon. He heard the race taper off down canyon, then rise up out of the canyon with amazing speed to the mesa above. And he had Geraldine with him. Harley looked back up the bluff; he still had his best hound on the lion. Harley watched as White-eye, despite Harley's whistles and shouts, worked his way up like a canine acrobat till he gained the ledge. The hound disappeared over the ledge and Harley couldn't see but he could hear that White-eye was sounding off in the big cat's face. Harley walked the narrow canyon below, seeking to gain a new angle that would provide sight of the lion and a shot. He could hear the scream of the cat and the bay of the hound. He shined the light up at the ledge, trying all angles; he could not find the cat in the light. He put the light away and started to climb, generally following the route White-eye took, climbing as fast as he dared up the face of the cliff, tense with the height and the near-dark. In time he gained the ledge and put his light on the battle. White-eye had backed the lion around a corner of the ledge, to the brink of the cliff. The lion, who could have killed the hound if he only knew it, coupled up with one paw raised and slashing. Harley drew his gun and crawled closer, tenuous on the ledge, needing an angle to shoot where he wouldn't hit the dog. The hound danced in front of the lion, just out of reach of the slash, sounding off aaaahhh-hoooOOO! aaaahhhhoooOOO! The lion made a move, a short rush, at the hound, then whirled and prepared to leap. Harley knew that White-eye would leap too, and that he wouldn't make it. There was no clear sight for a shot. The lion leaped out into the chasm; Harley dropped the gun and the light and lunged for White-eye. As the lion disappeared into the rocks and the dark, Harley and White-eye went over the side...

Through the night the cold set down hard on the floor of the canyon. It was late in the night, indeed well into morning, when the warm blood on his face, and leg, and the licks of the hound on his face caused him to start to come around. It was Geraldine who had come back and was trying to bring him around. There was no sign of Lurk. There was no sound of baying hounds. But he could hear the whimpers, and the hard, hurtful, strangled breathing not far away. In time he realized it must be White-eye. He got to his knees and wiped blood away from his eyes. He ascertained that his left leg was bleeding profusely, just below the knee, but was not broken. He crawled over to the hound who lay on his side, limp in the rocks. He felt with his hands and touched the head, limbs, then felt the squishy, crumpled rib cage. Gently as he could, he slid the hound off the rocks to bare dirt nearby, all the while saying, "Not you White-eye, not you." But he knew it was White-eye and he knew it was very bad.

Still crawling, he moved about and gathered brush and twigs; he got a fire going; he kept piling on the slash, till the blaze was big, bright and warm. He built as close as he dared to the hound; he wanted to keep the hound warm. Then he removed his coat and lay it over the hound, covering all but the head of White-eye. Then he removed his bandana and wrapped it around his own head. He needed to stop the bleeding from his head. His leg was bleeding too, and was growing stiff. And his head had a terrible ache behind the wound. But it hurt most to look at the hound.

Shortly after sunup, White-eye died. With his hands, Harley pulled out rocks and scraped dirt from a place at the base of the cliff. Still on his hands and knees, he struggled to move the body into the grave. He used his hands to move the loose dirt over the hound and the blood from his head and the tears from his face mixed in with the dirt covering the hound. He worked hard to pile big rocks deep over the grave, that the hound would not be defiled. He rested. Then with one hand on Geraldine's taut back, he raised himself for the first time to his feet. He found a limb for a staff and limped down the canyon, hoping to find his horse.

Down canyon, the roan hadn't moved 50 yards, grazing with his reins on the ground. Harley stepped into the saddle, mounting from the wrong side so he could use his good leg. He wrapped the reins around the horn, giving the horse his head, knowing he would head for the barn. He leaned forward on the horse's neck for support and, followed by the tri-colored hound, started down the canyon.

At the barn he unsaddled the horse and turned him loose in the pasture. By habit, he quickly skinned, scraped and stretched the coon hide, and hung the meat. He started for the house. He did not have good balance. His head retained a terrible ache and the wound was still seeping blood through the bandana. From the ride, the leg had stiffened still more. The sun was well up and the frost was leaving the ground. But he could not seem to get warm. When he got to the front porch he realized that Lurk had been there the whole time, curled up in front of the door, hiding, lurking. "You sorry hound," and Harley tried to kick the dog, but coming off his bad leg the move was clumsy and the hound easily sprang up and out of the way. Then, when Harley opened the front door, the big hound dashed inside, followed by the little gyp. Harley followed them in and got the stove going. He made coffee while he waited for the house to warm. In the bathroom, he found an old bottle of painkillers and took twice the dosage he read off the label. He drank the coffee and it didn't take long and he began to feel the pills. He went to the bedroom. He pulled off his boots and climbed in under the bedspread with his clothes on. The pills came down heavy on his brain and he fell asleep.

He awoke to the sound of a heavy rain on the roof. It was dark outside, the sun leaving early as they approached the shortest day of the year. He went to the bathroom and kept splashing water on his face. He was coming out of the drugs and felt he was beginning to regain a semblance of order in his brain. He looked at himself in the mirror and it occurred to him that he should shower and shave and clean the wound in his head and fix a proper bandage. He did not. His head felt better and had stopped bleeding and, for now, that was enough.

In the living room the hounds slept contentedly in front of the stove. The other hound, White-Eye, was everywhere in the pictures on the wall. Harley could not help but look at these. Especially the recent photo Ted had taken of the big bear, with White-Eye faded, fading out in the background. Harley thought then of another picture which could now go on the wall, a photo that he could look at now, a picture that would make him feel better. He went to the box and got the photo of himself and Bonney and the boy. He already had a place for it and he hung it there. He could enjoy it now, looking at Bonney and the boy. He didn't like the look of himself in the photo. He didn't like himself in that setting, or the faraway look in his eyes. But he didn't care about that. He liked looking at Bonney and the boy. It didn't hurt to look at them now. Now he liked this picture very much. He knew he would go and see her. She had wanted some time. She had had a day and a night and another long day. That was enough. She would be ready now. They could start making plans.

"Lurk! Geraldine! Here now!"

He got his battered stetson and the rough old canvas coat, both freshly blood stained, got the dogs up and out. In the rain the dogs quickly stopped to pee here and there and then they all got into the cab of the truck. He started the engine, let it idle and warm in the yard. Then he started the wipers and drove slowly out of the yard, across the creek, running a little high with the rain, and drove down Gavilán Road. Near town an oncoming vehicle blinked its lights at him and when it went by he saw it was Ted. Harley pulled over as the vehicle turned around behind him. Directly Ted Beeler came in out of the weather, the rain dripping off his hat. Geraldine hopped down to the floor of the cab and Lurk curled up on the seat between the two men. Harley turned the dome light on and Ted said, "Jesus Christ! What happened to you?"

"Ted, I lost White-eye."

"Well damn, Harley."

"We had a big lion up in the bluffs and White-eye went to him. I tried to gather him in. We both had a long fall. White-eye didn't make it."

"He was a great one...Harley, that head wound is bad. You better have that looked at."

"I don't think so...it's coming along."

"Suit yourself. Under the circumstances, I wish I had some good news for you, but I don't. It over, Harley."

Ted opened his jacket and pulled out that day's copy of the Del Cobre *Region*. He handed it to Harley and the headline jumped out:

## DAM WON; PRESERVATIONISTS ZERO!

SANTA FE - *At the urging of Governor Garner Greane, the State River Commission voted unanimously Tuesday to direct the Bureau of Reclamation to proceed with the construction of the Río Jalisco Dam.*

*In a concession to preservationists, the Commission also voted to grant six months grace to the Department of Wildlife for an attempted relocation of several New Mexico River Otters, reportedly living near the damsite.*

*"This is proof that we can have the water development and economic growth we so badly need, and still protect the environment," Greane said.*

*The vote by the Commission put to rest a controversy that had begun last July when the Department of Wildlife and several out of town preservationists attempted to..."*

Harley folded up the newspaper and handed it back to Ted. "That's enough for me," he said. "Cute headline. Pennerman obviously liked writing this one."

"Yeah, he went all the way to Santa Fe to see the kill."

"What are the chances for the otters?"

"Not real good, and you don't need to be a wildlife biologist to see it. The reason those otters are still found in the canyon is, that's the only place where their environment hasn't been greatly altered. Other places, they died off for one reason or another. It will be in one of those other places that we'll try to start them up again."

"Did you mention that at the meeting?"

"I had instructions to say nothing at that meeting unless called upon. Our written reports had been filed, but I doubt any commissioner, or the governor, gave them much of a reading. But after the meeting the press asked me the same thing you did. I said the chances were *problematical* and got out of there before I said anything more."

"You tried, partner."

Ted turned and looked straight ahead, out the windshield into the rain. The truck was running, and the whir of the heater was a soft sound that kept the cab warm. The wipers were slapping a rhythm and moving the rain on the windshield to little avail. "Oh yeah, we all tried," Ted said. "If effort counts, it was a good effort. If results count, it was pretty pathetic. We tried to use politics to influence a politician. Doing that, we were playing his game. And sure enough, he gathered it all up and threw it right back in our face. The man is slick as a wet pane of glass. He endorses a travesty, a consummate pork barrel, and makes a decision strictly on behalf of the boomers who elected him, and he comes out the picture of compromise. You should have heard him ramble on about how awful it would be if we lost those otters. That was right after he got the vote."

"So that's it."

"That is it. I've got the summer to try and get those otters out of there. I'll wait till the kits are old enough that they'll stand some chance, then we'll go in there and see if we can catch some of them. By September, the BOR will be moving the dirt."

Lurk lifted his head briefly, then lay it back down on Harley's knee. The rain beat down on the roof. The wipers rolled and slapped the water off the glass and that quickly the pane was obscured by a fresh sheet of rain. Then Ted said, "Comes time to move those otters, you want to go in there with us?"

"I don't know, Ted. All this may be just as well for me. Bonney and I are getting back together."

Ted looked at Harley. "You and Bonney?" he said.

"Uh huh. I broke the ice. I broke it good. I knew I would, if I got the chance. It's gonna be me and Bonney and the boy. I told her I was going to sign on with Jim Bo. She liked that. So I imagine by spring I'll have to go to work."

Ted was looking straight ahead now, into the rain. "I understand," he said. "Good luck with it."

"I'm on my way over there now."

"Well, I'll let you go. Just wanted to let you know."

"Appreciate it."

Ted kept watching the rain. "By God," he said, "I believe this rain is going to turn to snow." Ted smiled without happiness, pulled his hat down over his forehead, and disappeared into the rain.

Not much later, Harley rounded the corner by the new house he used to live in and saw the big rental truck parked in the driveway, backed up to the garage door. Sick with dread and a load of sudden realizations, he parked across the street and went straight up the walk to the front door. There were lights on inside and as he stepped on the porch the door opened just a crack and he heard her say, "Oh Harley, why did you have to come!"

"What is this, Bonney?"

"I told you I needed some time."

181

"To get away? Open the door."

"I won't. You have no right..."

She got out of the way just in time as he came in against the door and easily broke the chain latch. He stood before her in the open doorway.

"Where's my boy?"

"He's not here."

"Where is he?"

"He's with friends. Don't bother to ask where."

"Not taking any chances, are you?"

"No Harley, we're not taking any chances."

"We had plans Bonney! It's ours now."

"*You* had plans. It's not ours."

"Did you tell the son-of-bitch? I know you did."

"I didn't have to tell him. He knew when I picked him up at the airport. He could tell something had happened. It's like he could smell it on me. I didn't want to tell him. I didn't want to tell you. I don't want to hurt anyone. I didn't want to hurt you, Harley. I thought we would be gone before you even knew."

"That's thoughtful; that's thinking of me."

"What difference does it make? It's over. That's why we're moving, to make sure it's over. We have jobs at a bank in another town. Bruce has been trying for this. He got the job and then that happened, with you and I. Once it came out, we knew we had to leave immediately."

"Jim Bo set ya'll up?"

"He's been very helpful. He'd like us to stay, but he cares enough to help us leave. And he knows all about you and Sidney Pearlmann; you can forget that job."

"That was for us, Bonney!"

"Bullshit; you double-crossed Jim Bo. You told Jim Bo one thing; meanwhile you and that Jew had your little scheme."

"Jim Bo fucked me over!"

"He changed his mind, and I don't blame him."

Harley felt the life going out of him. He was losing it, even his anger. He slumped back against the open door and looked out into the rain.

"Where Bonney? Where are you taking him?"

"Phoenix. And don't bother to ask any more than that."

"Phoenix! What kind of a chance has a kid got in Phoenix?"

"Better than in this jerkwater town!" The wind was bringing cold air, and the rain, into the open door. She was shaking in the cold. "Please leave now Harley, so I can close the door. I'm cold, Harley."

"Too fucking bad."

"You must leave before he comes back."

"I'd like to meet him."

"No trouble, Harley. I'm warning you. We'll put you in jail, buster."

Harley kept looking out into the rain. "What about us Bonney? What about the other night?"

"I made a mistake."

"Simple as that?...a mistake?"

"I was doing okay about you, until I saw you with that woman. I don't know why it affected me so. And then you took Billy for the weekend and he came back and he kept talking about you. And that got me, too. So I came by, to tell you to leave us alone. And I really meant it; that's all I meant to do. And then I got drunk, and I got horny, and there was always that something between us, and I made a mistake. I'm not the first woman who got drunk, and horny, and made a mistake. I knew the next morning it was a mistake. You would have known it too, if you weren't so full of your self-delusions. But I don't care anymore Harley. I don't care what you do with her. I know where I belong."

Harley was looking out into the rain as he listened to this and he saw the car pull up in front of the house. A slim young man got out of the car and started up the walk. He was ducking his head from the rain and did not notice there were two people standing in the doorway, under the porch light, till he was halfway to the porch. When he noticed he stopped and looked up, not sure what he was seeing. He turned around and across the street was an old pickup and a big dark hound was seated in the cab, looking out the window, looking at people. The man looked back to the open door. Then he turned around and walked rapidly back to the car. He got in the car and sat there looking straight ahead, like he hadn't seen a thing. Harley watched him through the rain. And he conjured up all manner of mayhem and destruction he could easily wreak on two people, and their relationship. But he didn't have the life left for any of that. And the rain kept falling, and the cold wind blew it in the door. The right side of his face, that part that was facing the wind and was underneath the wound, was wet. He reached to wipe the wetness from his face and his hand came away with some of the wetness and much of the wetness was blood. And the left side of his face was wet too and he wiped it away. It was neither blood nor rain.

"Bonney?"

"No Harley."

"Bonney, I lost White-eye last night."

"I don't care. I don't want to hear it."

"He was my friend. Do you know what it is to have an animal as a friend?"

"I don't care about any of that. That's just you. Go cry on the shoulder of that Mexican girl."

"I'm sure I've lost that now, too."

"Well too fucking bad."

Harley looked at her. "Bonney?"

"No Harley! No more. You're leaving now." And then she was crying too, and she said, "Oh Harley, if you could just see! If you could just see yourself now. You'll never change, Harley. You'll never be any different than you are. And then one day you and that mule will roll off a mountain and that will be the end of it! Now get out of here, or I'll call the police. You have no right to be here."

There was a long look between them. Then, without looking back, he started off the porch and down the walk. As he passed the car he swept his hat off his head and swatted the hood of the car. As quickly, the man inside reached and pushed both buttons, locking the doors. But Harley never stopped as he limped across the road and got into his truck. He backed the truck around, drove down the street and made the corner. He glanced back and the young man was already climbing the porch steps where he disappeared into the house.

~ ~ ~ ~ ~ ~

Ted was right - the rain was turning to snow. As he drove into the foothills up Gavilán Road it swirled in heavy wet flakes in the headlights and by the time he got to his house it was sticking to the ground. He put Geraldine in the pen and put Lurk on his chain. Then his tracks in the snow went into the house. He went to the stove. There were still some good coals in the bottom but it was due for some wood. But Harley didn't care if the house was warm or cold. He shut the stove door. He did not remove his coat. Reluctantly, yet ineluctably, he was drawn to the pictures on the wall: White-eye; himself and Bonney with little Billy in his arms; his mother with her eyes on the last horizon; pictures of wild country, and the river; his father, who had gotten drunk and died in a snowstorm. He was just as glad he had no pictures of Suzie and little Jessica. But they were gone now, too. It was all gone now for him. He'd seen to that. The urge to smash all the pictures was terrible. But he didn't have the life in him to do it. And he knew he could not make the pictures go away; he'd still have them all in his head. He knew now he only had the life in him to do one thing. One thing only, and it would make the pictures go away. It was the perfect night for it and, suddenly, he couldn't wait.

Harley went to the kitchen and got a bottle of beer. He hadn't eaten in 24 hours and he knew one bottle of beer would get him started. He opened it and chugged it and that quickly he could feel the first liquid of incoherence settle into the outer corners of his brain. He got the wine bottle; she had finished half of it. He poured the other half into his mouth; it disappeared like water down a rat hole. It had been a long time since he'd been hard drunk. But he knew the feeling and those feelings were coming back in a rush. He went to the cabinet and selected a fifth of *Southern Comfort* and put it into the pocket of his coat. He took the cartridge belt, holster and the .357 off the wall and strapped it on.

Outside, under the yard light, Lurk lay almost white, curled up in the snow, but watching, on top of the dog house. "Lurk, get out of the storm you silly hound. Get in your house." Lurk stood up and shook and scattered the snow off his shag coat; the remarkable pelt had a sheen under the yard light and left him as dry and warm as a duck. He kept his eye on Harley.

In the pasture, Harley found the old man's old horse. Harley quickly slipped the bit in her mouth and rolled the head stall over her ears. With his gloved hand he swept the snow off the back of the horse, jumped on bareback and rode to the gate. He leaned over, slipped the latch and rode through, reined the horse around and re-set the latch. Geraldine came out of her dog house and stood at the fence in the falling snow. Lurk stood trembling now in the storm. Harley called out to them, shouting into the weather: "You'll be all right!...You're good hounds!...You'll have a new home!...A good home!...Better than here!...You won't remember me, Lurk!...You'll forget!...You'll be all right...!" Harley started the horse for the next gate and Lurk took one stride and a tremendous leap and put all his weight against the chain. The heavy collar took up around his neck and the heavy chain jerked him onto his back. He came to his feet and howled up into the falling snow. Harley rode to the gate that led into the forest reserve. He opened the gate and rode through as he had before, latching the gate behind him. He kicked the horse into a long trot and headed up the trail for the divide, flush into the black night and white falling snow. He worked the bottle hard. He could feel it. He could already feel it good. He could feel it so good that soon the black of night and the snow in his face and the heave and blow of the horse and Lurk's fading howls were as a dream. No better way than this, he thought. No better way than this.

At the divide the blizzard was so thick and the snow so deep that even the horse was having trouble staying with the trail. Harley gave the horse her head and took out the bottle. There wasn't much left but he wanted to finish it off to be sure when he went down he would never get up. Instinctively, the horse moved in under a tight grouping of Douglas Fir and turned her rump to the wind. The bottle went up and Harley took the last of the sour, peach mash liqueur deep into his gut. It was so good. He wanted it now. He wanted it so bad. He couldn't wait. The horse shifted her weight and Harley felt himself losing his seat. He did not resist. He slid off the slick back and settled comfortably into the soft snow. He curled into a fetal form and waited. He could feel the big, soft flakes settling over him. He could feel the covering, the wonderful covering, enveloping him in white. He did not feel cold. The snow was covering him up and it felt so warm. So wonderful. The alcohol, the liquid incoherence, had now reached every corner of his brain. He could not believe how wonderful it was. He wanted it. He wanted it so bad.

He couldn't wait. No better way than this, he thought. No better way than this...

~ ~ ~ ~ ~ ~

In the morning, when the cloud cover began to break up, the real cold, the true cold, the great cold came down on the land. It was the stinging cold, the dangerous sting of cold in his feet and fingers, that brought him out of it. That and the weight, the great weight on his body, so warm and furry, so pervasive, and breathing slowly in sleep. It was several minutes until his brain came around to where he could figure out why he was still alive.

"Lurk, you son-of-a-bitch."

The great hound began to lick Harley's face. But he would not take his weight off the man.

"Stop that. Goddamnit Lurk. Let me up!"

Harley rolled out from under the hound and struggled to his feet. Nearby, the horse had tromped down the snow under the firs and Harley went there and began to jump up and down on his feet while flexing and working his fingers inside his gloves. He was cold, cold sober now and he didn't want to freeze to death any more. His head hurt, an awful hurt, and for more reasons than one. And it was a terrible pain in his feet and fingers as the circulation came back into the digits. But he could feel the circulation coming back and knew his fingers and toes could not be badly frostbitten, else he would not feel them at all. Off to the side Lurk sat up in the snow and waited patiently...without his collar.

"Lurk, you backed out of your collar. I'm surprised you didn't figure that out before. You tried, Lurk, but it's not going to work."

Harley looked about and quickly figured out where he was. He stepped out from under the fir trees and led the horse up the slope. It was daylight and despite the deep snow he found the trail and the clearing in the saddle where he had camped so many times before. He looked off toward Del Cobre. Groups of heavy clouds still rumbled about below him, spitting snow here and there, but between the clouds he could see portions of the town come and go in the distance. Like the mountains, the town was covered in white. But life and movement and the usual human enterprise was evident. All the reasons that had driven him to a final trip to the mountains still lay below him. There was no reason to go back. He knew where he must go, and what he must do. Only it would be a different proposition, sober.

It was a struggle for the horse going off the north slope of the divide. The snow was very deep, heavy and wet. The forest was all around him and stretched away in the distance, white, expansive, eternal. The trail went in under the evergreens; they hung heavy, brooding with snow. At times, small avalanches of snow came off the boughs, landing in a soft crunch. But the snow gradually lessened in depth as they descended the trail and by the time they reached the rim of the canyon there was more sun than clouds and the sun was almost warm. They went off the rim and worked their way down to the river. Harley raised his legs and held on to the horse's mane as he crossed the stream. Then down river, and then up, up and up, to the north rim. Harley held tight to the horse's mane as the horse lurched up and topped out. It was another mile down river to the clearing and the old fire-scarred juniper. Harley jumped off and slipped the bridle off the horse. He went around behind and slapped the old horse on the rump with the loose reins. The old horse jumped away but didn't go far before she turned and looked with some curiosity at Harley before dropping her head. She began to paw through the snow and pull up clumps of grass. Lurk, of course, would be more difficult. Harley stepped to the edge of the rim. Lurk, seated in the snow near the horse, started over. Harley reached down and picked up a good rock. Lurk stopped, watching warily with his yellow eyes. "You stay Lurk; goddamnit you stay." Lurk took a step forward and Harley raised his arm and feinted a throw; Lurk moved away from the horse and from Harley in a quick dodge; Harley, anticipating, this time let fly. The rock caught Lurk flush on the top of the muzzle. The hound yelped and rolled. Regaining his feet, the blood ran down his bearded face. Then Lurk lay down on his brisket, resting his head in his paws. He kept watching the man and every little bit he licked the blood off his muzzle. "You can't follow, Lurk. When it's over, you and Cleo will go home. Stay goddamnit." Harley stepped over the edge and started down, sliding part of the way in his haste and tossing the bridle off the trail into the brush on the way. The den lay hidden within its place in the rocks. Harley paused there for a last look downstream. Across the canyon, the north facing slope was still well covered with snow. The south facing slope where he stood was melting; already there were dark wet spots where the land and the rocks and the trees shown through the white cover. Far below, the Río Jalisco flowed on, blue-green in the afternoon sun and looking very cold, till it descended into the mountains and disappeared. Harley watched the river flow till his heart ached. And the enormity of the loss, and the sacrilege of what they would do, and the whole broad expanse of his own duplicity came down.

"YOU SONS-A-BITCHES!"

His cry went on down river, echoed back up the canyon, touched the surrounding hills, and ended up...nowhere. That was all. He went then to the mouth of the cave, to the place where, with luck, he would be lost forever. He went to his knees, then to his stomach, and began to worm his way into the mouth of the cave. It was a tight squeeze and there was only blackness as his body blocked the light as he entered. And halfway in the bulk of his coat and the gun at his hip caught him at the mouth of the cave. In the blackness he rested his face on the cold stone and, almost silently, he started to cry. It had seemed so easy, almost pleasant, last night. Last night he could just let it happen. Now he had to do it. He choked off the tears and considered that he might have to back out, remove his coat, his holster and gun, and try again. He did not want to have to face the light of day again. He was into the blackness now and he didn't want to have to look further. It occurred to him that if he saw the light of day again, saw the river in the canyon, he would lose the one resolve he had left. He would twist and squirm and get himself in. He got his elbows underneath and prepared to move. He stared ahead into the blackness, and it occurred to him to question how many rattlesnakes could make this cave their winter home. As quickly, it occurred to him how silly it was that a man who was about to pull the plug on himself with a great blast in a cave should have any worries about rattlesnakes. "Fucking ludicrous," he mumbled. But he nonetheless got one hand free, went to his shirt pocket, got a wooden match, struck it on the floor of the cave and caught the flame. With his arm in a short arc, he slowly illuminated the small room. He didn't see any rattlesnakes. He did see the desiccated skeletons of six wolf puppies, each little more than a handful in size when they'd huddled in a heap to die. "This is a wolf den all right," he said outloud in the cave. Then the light went out.

*Chapter 25*

JESSICA was up early, as she had been for several mornings, kneeling on the couch in her pajamas, playing with her cat and from time to time peering out the window at the street. There was light in the sky but the sun wasn't up yet. Patches of snow still lay in the front yard.

"Jessica. Why are you up so early?"

"Today, mommy. Today he comes."

"Jessica! Do you think you're going to sit there all day, waiting?"

"Yes. Till he comes."

"Well you're not. He's not coming, Jessica. I told you."

Suzie went to her closet and got her robe, then she went to the bathroom. When she came out she went to the kitchen. Through the door, down the step in the living room, she saw Jessica still on the couch, playing with her cat. Jessica made her hand like a spider that crawled with fast fingers all over the couch. This made her cat crouch, swish its tail and pounce. Every little while Jessica gathered up her cat and held it in her lap while she looked out the window into the street.

"Mommy, I heard you crying again last night."

"I just had a bad dream."

"He'll come back, mommy."

"Stop it Jessica! He's not."

"Where is he mommy?"

"I don't know; I told you. No one knows."

Suzie turned away and started some coffee on the stove. She sat at the kitchen table while it perked and she watched her daughter play with her cat and, every little bit, look out the window again. When the coffee was done Suzie poured herself a cup and set it in front of her chair at the kitchen table. Behind her, at the counter, she put two pieces of whole wheat bread in the toaster. She sat down with her coffee while the toast was cooking and when it popped up she turned to the counter and buttered the toast and covered the piece for Jessica with jam. When she turned back to the table with the toast on a small plate, Jessica was standing at the foot of the entry-way, just outside the kitchen, holding her cat in her arms and her big, dark eyes wide with expectation.

"Mommy, Harley *ya viene.*"

Jessica waited and watched. Suzie set the plate down and looked through the window of the front door. She saw his truck, and the two hounds seated in the cab were watching as Harley started up the walk, limping. Jessica watched as her mother went to the counter and poured coffee into Harley's cup, as she always did when she saw him coming up the walk. As always, Harley stepped in without knocking and Jessica watched as her mother took Harley's cup, full of fresh hot coffee, and sent the contents through the air and flush into Harley's face. The cat bailed out of Jessica's arms and disappeared into the back rooms. Jessica stayed to watch as the hot, black stuff splattered, scalded, then dripped off Harley's face, then down on to his coat, shirt, and onto the floor. Then Jessica scampered in retreat to the couch. But she could still peek and listen...

"You bastard!...cut your balls off! Someone ought to."

Suzie turned to the counter and got a dish towel. She came up to Harley and tried to wipe the remnants of the coffee off Harley's face and neck. Harley stood still and waited, red-faced and mute.

"Where have you been?...we've been worried sick."

"It's a long story."

"Well I already know part of it, you tramp."

Suzie tossed the towel back to the counter. Then she refilled Harley's cup and set it on the table in front of the second chair. She leaned back against the counter with her arms crossed in front of her, just below her ample breasts.

"Now sit down, and we'll start over."

"Maybe I should just get on up the road."

"Sit down!"

Harley did what he was told. He sat down and, very carefully, sipped at the coffee through his scalded face. Then he said, "I guess this is a pretty small town."

"Small enough that when Gloria was on her way to work early Tuesday morning she saw your ex-wife coming down Gavilán Road in a real big hurry and a certain look on her face that women know. It wasn't hard to figure out."

"Well, for what it's worth, I came by to apologize."

"Don't bother. You look like a sheep killing dog."

Harley ducked his head a little and sipped at his mug of coffee. Suzie said, "I figured you were on your way to Arizona."

"You heard about that, too?"

"Ted called Thursday evening. He said he'd talked to you Wednesday night and you told him about the hunting accident...how you'd been hurt and about your dog and of your plans with Bonney. He heard the next day that they had all left town...Phoenix maybe. After the storm he went out to your place."

"I saw his tracks when I got back in."

"Well, when he couldn't find you he called me. Of course I didn't have any idea where you were. Naturally, we both started to worry, knowing how you must be taking it. I thought probably you had gone to Phoenix, or wherever they had gone. Ted thought you went into the wilderness, but the storm hadn't left any tracks. He said if you didn't show up today he was going to call Henry and get some riders out there."

Will you call him for me and tell him not to worry?"

"Of course."

"Just tell him I'm fine but I'll be gone for awhile. That's all."

"All right. Did they go to Phoenix?"

"I guess so."

"Is that where you're going now?"

"No."

"Where are you going?"

"I can't say right now."

"Then you must be going after her and Billy, or you would tell me where you are going."

"No, that's not it. That's over. I lost it. I'll be a long way from Phoenix. But I can't talk about it because...Suzie...what I have is a pretty crazy idea. It's crazy enough that if I talk about it, I'll probably talk myself out of it. Or someone else will. And it has to be done. At least I have to try."

"I wish you would at least stay the weekend. You could rest up; you look terrible."

"If I stay even an hour, Suzie, I'll never leave. And there's something has to be done. I'll write to you once I get there, and I'll explain everything. It's nothing for you to worry about. I'll either succeed or I'll fail. Either way, I'll be back."

"Are you leaving like that...what did you do to your head?"

190

"I had a bad fall."

"I know that. I mean that bandage."

"I wrapped it up as best I could."

"Well if I was you I'd say you did a horseshit job. We better clean it up."

"I really need to get going."

"Sit down!"

Harley had started to get up to leave but thought better of it as Suzie went to the bathroom and came back with gauze, scissors, tape and disinfectant. She removed the old bandage ("disgusting!") and spent some time cleaning the wound. She put on the disinfectant and wrapped on a neat, clean bandage. Then she said, "What about you're leg; you're limping." Knowing what was coming next, he got his leg out from under the table and rolled up his pant leg to his knee. She knelt beside the wound and the bandage he had put on his leg. "Chihuahua! I don't know if you're more helpless or hopeless." She cleaned the wound on his leg and wrapped it, too, in a neat clean bandage. "Now," she said, "at least everything has a chance to heal." Then she went to the counter. "Would you like some more coffee?"

"No thanks."

"How about your thermos? Get it and I'll fill it."

"It's full. Thanks."

"I'll make you some sandwiches for the road."

"I packed a bunch of food. But there's one more thing...Jessica! Come here you little ring-tail!"

Jessica came in from the living room and Harley put her on his knee. "Now listen you little skeeziks. You take care of your mother while I'm gone. That's important to me."

"Yes sir."

"And you take care of yourself. That's important to me, too."

"*Sí señor*. When are you coming back to be with us?"

"I'll be back when I finish what I have to do. It won't be so long. As for being with you-all, we'll have to see how your mother feels about that."

"We want you to be with us. She's been crying every night."

"Jessica!"

"Well," Harley said, "there's been all too much of that crying lately, all around. We aren't going to have any more of that."

She hugged him until he loosened her arms and set her down. Then Harley stood up and went to the door. He turned around at the door and Suzie came to him, and she leaned against him and rested her head on his chest. He put one hand to the small of her back and with the other he touched the nape of her neck.

"*Vuelva*, Harley."

"I'll be back in the spring."

## PART IV   THE LONG HUNT

*"The man should have youth and strength who seeks adventure in the wide, waste spaces of the earth, in the marshes, and among the vast mountain masses, in the northern forests, amid the steaming jungles of the tropics, or on the deserts of sand or of snow. He must long greatly for the lonely winds that blow across the wilderness, and for sunrise and sunset over the rim of the empty world."*

Theodore Roosevelt
*The Joy of the Wild*

*Chapter 26*

THE SECOND NIGHT he drove on without sleep, the old truck chugging along easily at fifty-five, on through the great prairies, flat, plowed, barren and white with snow in the moonlight; then he turned east and crossed a great river that flows north; he continued east till the plains suddenly gave way to the forest; and as he stepped from the truck at the pink of dawn he knew he had never felt such a grip of iron cold. Along the forest road the snow scrunched and popped under his feet. He took in air and he felt it stay frigid, deep into his lungs. His piss steamed in an astonishing manner, then quickly froze yellow before his eyes on the road. He could feel the mucous stick in his nostrils. And when the hounds hopped out they yelped and picked up one foot, then another, peeing here and there, as the incredible cold stung their pads.

"My god," he said, "it must be forty below zero. You two are going to have to get used to this. And so am I."

Back in the cab, the heater restored warmth that made the view through the windshield quite pleasant. The land was snow covered. The sun so low, yet coming on with a brilliance that brought pink and yellow tints not only to the sky but to the tops of the endless trees - Jack Pine, Blue Spruce, Black Spruce, the leafless larch or Tamarack, barren aspen and White Birch. These trees grew to the edge of the bar ditch along the road and offered nothing other than themselves as far as he could see - more of a jungle than a forest. A northern, boreal jungle, set in lowlands as flat as the prairie just to the west. Harley looked at the map. He was perhaps a mile off the highway; he could return, go north on the highway and then east and reach the town in a couple of hours. Or he could stay on this forest road, cut another forest road north, the slow road to town. Harley poured a cup of coffee, set it on the dash, and started east down the forest road. He wasn't in any hurry; he had all winter. And he wanted to see if he could cut some sign.

On down the road the first thing of interest was not tracks but a sudden change in terrain. To the south the forest opened up into several thousand acres of slough grass, the tips poking up dead grass brown above the deep snow. Harley had never seen a peat bog but he knew that's what this was; it had to be. Driving even slower he caught something moving way south, where the peat bog abruptly ended and the rim of the forest encircled the slough. It was too far away to identify, yet it must be very large, Harley knew, to show up at all at that distance. He stopped and put the binoculars on the spot and saw his first bull moose, ever. Except for the rack of horns, he looks something like my mule, he thought. "Lurk," he said, "he's even bigger than Ruby; don't ever run one of those." Lurk was curled up on the seat with Geraldine and did not respond. Harley drove on east, deeper into the forest, till he cut the forest road heading north. It, too, had been plowed and he turned and headed north towards town. Along the way he periodically stopped and looked out the window at tracks - coyote tracks, fox tracks, deer tracks, a very large bobcat track (lynx?). Then a medium-sized spidery print that over-stepped itself, back feet in front of front feet, as it loped across the road. "That's got to be a Fisher track," he said to the hounds. "You ever see a Fisher track, Geraldine? Me either. But that's got to be what that is. We'll take a run at one of those before the winter's over, you bet. We've got a lot to learn, boys and girls." But Lurk and Geraldine, as with the other tracks, slept on in the cab, their interest in tracks confined to what they could smell, not see.

They crossed a river. Only there was no water, or none that could be seen; the river was frozen over and covered, like everything else, with snow. They were almost out of the forest, the country opening up a bit, with an admixture of cut-over and burnt-over succession growth of alder and aspen, and the occasional homestead, when Harley stopped for a number of large creatures that had plowed through the snow, crossed the road, and disappeared into the brush and timber to the west. Methodically, controlling a wonderful anticipation, Harley this time stopped the truck, got out, and approached the first set of prints in the snow on the edge of the road. "Christ, look at those feet!" he said. In all he counted nine sets of tracks, some with big feet, some with even bigger feet, crossing the road. The biggest were as large as cougar tracks, only longer and narrower, and with the claws making clear marks in the snow ahead of the pads. They were fresh; a pack had crossed right here, hours before. Harley looked back and Geraldine and Lurk were now up and looking anxiously ahead, steaming up the windshield. "Oh you pups," Harley said, "they're here. But my god look at those feet!"

~ ~ ~ ~ ~ ~

In the sleepy, snowy little town of Winter Road, within view of the Canadian border, Harley stopped at the first cafe he saw. He was very hungry and ate sausage, eggs, drank coffee and buttermilk, and kept ordering toast till he had a good tuck-in. He had stopped having headaches. His leg was still stiff but healing was evident there, too. He was eating again and, except for needing a good ten hour sleep, he was feeling much healthier all around. While finishing the last of the coffee, he took a pen and made a list on a paper napkin. When, after breakfast, he walked down the street and entered the store - Harold's Hardware & Sporting Goods - he felt he was ready.

"What'll it be mister?" The owner of the store stood by the wood stove in his jac shirt, suspenders, dark-rimmed glasses and a grin - a perfect Harold.

Harley looked at his list and said, "One pair pickeral style snowshoes; one wool tractor cap, with earmuffs; one good tight-weave wool coat; one non-resident hunting license, one..."

"Here, give me that goddamn napkin; you've come in here for an outfit!"

Harold, talking a blue streak and a wealth of information, had everything Harley had written down and a few things he hadn't but, sure enough, should have. Finally, the man said, "What about your hands?"

"I've got these good gloves."

"You'll lose your fingers in those goddamn things, unless you spend the winter inside. You need a pair of choppers."

"Choppers?"

"A wool mitten over your hand, a buckskin mitten over the wool. Only way to go in this country...here."

Harley examined his new choppers. Harold kept talking.

"New Mexico, huh?"

"Yup."

"Gonna' hunt some fur?"

"Yup."

"Well, you came to the right place. There's game here, and plenty of fur. This is god's country, especially in the winter when all the tourists leave. Tell me why..."

"Why? Why what?"

"Why all the tourists leave?"

Harley glanced out the window at the big circular thermometer you could see from anywhere in the store and it showed that the mid-day temperature had risen to twelve degrees below zero. "I can't imagine," he said.

"They get cold feet...ha! Get it?"

"Got it, Harold."

"What kind of fur you going to hunt?"

"Fox, some cats, coyote mostly."

"Brush Wolves"

"Brush Wolves?"

"Hardly anybody calls them coyotes around here. A coyote that lives in this country is a Brush Wolf. There's plenty of 'em. But you'll find they're a bigger coyote than what you're used to. You're not going after any of them magnum wolves I hope."

"I wasn't planning on it."

"Better not. 'Course it's against the law now, anyway. But it wasn't that many years ago we could hunt them. One time, I remember this guy came up from Missouri with a pack of twelve hounds. He turned them twelve out on a whole pack of Timber Wolves. The wolves took them off into the bush and began to split off. That scattered the pack. Then the wolves just waited for those dogs. Five of those hounds never came out of the woods. The seven that did was all cut to ribbons. That was a wiser man went home to Missouri. Guess those wolves *showed* him...ha! Get it?"

"Got it...from Missouri."

"Steer clear of those Timber Wolves. They'll chop a hound into little pieces."

"I'll give them plenty of room."

"Say, what about your feet?"

"I've got a pair of Sorels."

"Well you got that right. Only way to go in this country."

"Harold, I need a place to live. Not too fancy. Out in the country so my hounds can howl at the moon."

"You passed that Realty coming in from the west?"

"I came in from the south."

"Go back west, a mile out of town on the north side...Knutsen Brothers Realty. They'll have places to rent. Cheap. You can take your pick. Like I said, the tourists all leave."

Harley went to the counter to pay the man. "Say Harold, how come they call this town Winter Road?"

"You crossed that river coming in?"

"Yeah. It was nothing but snow and ice."

"That's the Winter Road River. It heads up way back in the bush southwest of here. In the old days, no roads, no tractors or snowmobiles, folks skidded logs with horses on that river, and they travelled on it. That river was a road in the winter. Still is, at times."

Harley gathered up a box full of stuff and headed for the door. Harold came around from behind the counter, grinning, and opened the door for Harley.

"Say New Mexico, one more thing..."

"Yeah..."

"Welcome to northern Minnesota."

## Chapter 27

ON A RIDGE above the Winter Road River, 22 miles south and west of town, he found his winter home - an old farm house, cheap, like Harold said. It was furnished, in a sparse sort of way. It had a good wood stove in the basement, a fireplace in the living room, running water, and up the path through the trees was an old dairy barn, long out of use but still sound, which Harley hoped to have a new use for before the winter was over. Harley had asked the Realtor: "Okay if I rig up a pen in here to keep my hounds?" The Realtor had said: "Just mail in your rent on time and don't burn the place down and make yourself to home." It was a good place, and all the better because the nearest neighbor was over a mile away - an old bachelor with a small farm who had an enormous pile of birch wood in the front yard. Harley bought five cords and spent several days splitting it up. He went to town and bought enough groceries and other materiél that, unless he wanted to, he wouldn't have to go to town again for a good long while. Then he went to work on the barn. He sectioned off and framed up a 10 by 20 room and built a large doghouse inside. He filled the dog house with fresh straw. The hounds lay around in the barn while he worked and he said to them when he was through, "If anyone should ask, boys and girls, I built this for you." In fact, Lurk and Geraldine would continue to spend their nights in the house, but Harley knew they could be trusted not to tell anyone the wrong thing. Meanwhile, Christmas came and went. When New Years' Day dawned very clear, very still and very cold, he was ready to begin the pursuit.

"Lurk. Geraldine. Listen up." Harley had passed a coyote track that crossed the road, and the two hounds were sitting up on the seat now; they knew something was up. Harley set a cup of coffee on the dash where it made a small circle of steam on the inside of the windshield. He looked at the hounds. "Now none of this sock-and-shoe scheme of mine is going to work without you two. You two are the key to the whole thing. Lurk, you want to run coyotes, well by god you're going to run them. This is a bigger coyote than you're used to. Brush Wolves, Harold called them. But I know you can catch them. Some of them anyway. And I know you can take them down. I'd like it that you don't kill them till I get there. Just bay them up; when I get there we'll take his hide. Geraldine, it took me two years to break you from running coyotes and now you've got to learn to run them all over again. You'll learn fast because I don't think you ever really forgot. Just go with Lurk; he never did learn not to run them and you can just forget all I ever said about running coyotes. We're going to run them, and fox and bobcat and maybe a few other things, every day the weather permits and ya'll aren't run out. We've got maybe two months to get used to this climate and to learn the country and to get leather tough enough to run down and bay up a couple of Timber Wolves right after the breeding season. You can think of all these small wolves as preparation for two big wolves; that's what we're here for. Meanwhile, we need to take a bunch of fur so we look legitimate and anyway we're going to need the money before we leave here in the spring. I'm kind of looking forward to this Brush Wolf hunting myself. Should be a hell of a race. Remember, we're on a mission; this first race is just the beginning of a long hunt. If we can get it all done without getting killed or caught it will be one of the most beautiful things in the history of dog and man. And it could be the salvation of more than you two could ever understand. All three of us have to work together. We've got to do everything right; there's not much room for any kind of mistakes. And then, we'll still need some luck. Now, you ready?"

Geraldine was leaning against him and she turned her head up and licked his face. Lurk sat and stared straight ahead, trembling and whimpering in anticipation. Harley took the two-ended clasp and necked Geraldine to Lurk. He put the leash on the ring in the center of the clasp and stepped out onto the road with the hounds on the leash. He walked them back to where the track crossed and right away Lurk put his nose in the track in the snow, yelped and looked up at Harley. Harley patted him on the head, then took the snap off the ring in Lurk's collar.

"It's okay Lurk. Take it. He's in there, probably laid up for the day. Hunt him up."

Lurk put his nose back in the track, yelped again, then took the track down off the road, into the bar ditch, up out of the ditch and with just the occasional sounding off began to cold trail the track into the forest. He moved at an intermittent lope, not fast, but easily, at times stopping to snuffle his nose in the snow. He was soon lost from view but now and again the yelping sound he made on the cold trail carried back out of the woods, agitating the little Walker gyp.

"Go girl. Go to him. You've got a better nose than ol' Lurk. You could take him to that Brush Wolf. Go to him girl."

Twice the Walker went in on the trail, expecting to be called back. She was not called back but twice she came back to the road anyway, whining and whimpering and working her tail in confusion. Then Lurk jumped the coyote, rousted him out of his daytime bed in the snow. Harley could hear the trail change that quickly from cold to hot as Lurk broke into his hoarse squall-chop, a frantic squalling cry chopped off abruptly at the end of each squall and that quickly picked up into a squalling-chop again. Geraldine went in on the trail on the run, running silent, going to the other hound while Lurk pushed the track...and then he lost it. He was till booing around in frustration when Geraldine got there and sounded off; directly she worked out the loss and Harley could hear she was running the track. Then she lost it.

For an hour the race was hit or miss. The track was fresh - they had a little wolf running in front of them - but they could not line out on the scent. It was very cold and still and the sounds of their frustration came clear from the woods to the road where Harley waited for the race to develop. He thought: it's the cold; there can be very little scent, even on a fresh track, when it's this cold; their noses have not learned to handle a line at twenty below zero.

Gradually, the trail went north, parallel with the county road, and the hounds grew faint, while the sun, in the low arc of a northern winter, slowly took a bit of the iron cold off the land. It seemed to Harley, straining to follow with his ears, that Geraldine was starting to put some speed on the track when he saw a canine cross the road, way north. It was so far north Harley could not be sure if it was the coyote or one of the dogs. He went to the pickup and got his binoculars and put them on the crossing. It took a while, but first Geraldine and then Lurk crossed the road on the run; the first canine had to be the Brush Wolf.

Harley thought: he's got a long lead, but I think we've got a race. Harley turned the truck around on the road and drove to the crossing tracks in the snow. He got out. He could hear the race well now. They were pushing the track. Lurk had retaken the lead. And the Brush Wolf was running for his life.

Harley went to the pickup and fumbled with the map on the seat of the truck. He was not used to not knowing the country, not knowing where he was or where he was going. Where he knew the country, he could often predict where the game would go. He didn't know this country at all. And he didn't know much about what a north woods coyote, pushed hard by hounds, might do. The map told him the race had entered a section of forest three miles square, bounded by county roads and state forest roads. He thought: a fox will often circle within a square mile of where he's jumped; a coyote should circle too; it would be a bigger circle, but probably not bigger than three miles square. Harley slung the day pack over his shoulders, strapped on his snowshoes, and followed the trail into the woods. Over the snow now, on a cushion of rawhide and ash, he joined the chase.

Five hours later he found it hard to believe they still had a coyote on the run. The air on this still day never moved and the sounds of the chase travelled wonderfully in the cold dry air and Harley knew from the raucous frantic clamor that the hounds were in full stride, run-to-catch pursuit. Yet still the little wolf ran on, running a maze of circles through the aspen, occasional birch and lowland pockets of Black Spruce. The coyote avoided the soft snow, running mostly on the runways laid down by the ubiquitous Snowshoe Hares. From time to time, as he attempted stay within sound of the chase, Harley watched the numerous white-furred bounders leave out ghost-like and quickly disappear in the forest. Though he had spent the better part of the day trying to anticipate the coyote's route, Harley had viewed the race just once. And that once, he was lucky. From far off he heard the race come round and then the squall and chop of the two hounds were coming for him at an astonishing pace. The game trail where Harley stood was the path of pursuit and Harley stepped off the trail and into hiding just in time as the coyote was well ahead of the hounds. And then he was there, flying over snow, his tongue out and his tail held rather low. The view was brief through the trees but Harley was so close he could frame the coyotes head in his view and the coyote appeared relaxed, and light and endless in his stride, and when he was gone Harley wasn't sure if he wanted to catch him or not. Nothing you can run with a hound can run like that, he thought. And then there was Lurk, leaping with power on the track, squalling each time his front feet touched the ground, his head up, for the scent of a running coyote was steaming off the snow. And Geraldine, in turn, no bigger than a Brush Wolf, still in the race and driving with her quick, compact and efficient little stride. And on they went, hour after hour, circling tighter until, seated on a log as the day faded, Harley wondered if they could run him down before dark, or at all.

Harley did not see the catch but he knew his hounds well enough to know what happened. The race had moved back to the west, not far from the truck, and Harley heard it when Lurk's squalling bark abruptly quit. But Geraldine was close and still sounding off, moving the track. Harley knew Lurk had not lost the track; rather, he had run to within sight of the little wolf. Running by sight, pursuing what he could now see, he ran silent and went to the sprint granted him by his part Greyhound blood. Directly, Harley heard the sounds of a struggle and then both hounds went to a chopping bark. "Goddamn, they've got him bayed up!" Harley said. He was already lifting his webs in long strides in the direction of the catch.

The Brush Wolf had found temporary refuge under a blowdown. Harley had drawn his pistol, but when Lurk saw him coming he quit chopping in the coyote's face, went in and grabbed the little wolf. The hound took a slash from the coyote but with Geraldine's help, he pulled him out from under the blowdown.The Walker necked the coyote while Lurk clamped shaggy jaws over the brisket. Harley heard the bones pop; by the time he got there the Brush Wolf was dead. Harley checked his watch. It was seven hours since they'd jumped the coyote and it was an hour from good dark. Harley patted the hounds and rubbed them up with his mittened hands. Then he shouldered the impressive catch and started for the road. The hounds were content to follow the benefit of the trail he made with his webs. "You two caught a bigger coyote than ever lived in New Mexico," he said. "Lurk, looks like you knew what you were doing all along."

## Chapter 28

**THE COUNTRY WAS ALIVE WITH GAME.** And the ever present snow which never felt a thaw and which got deeper as winter closed down like the lid of a box, gave them all away. Harley drove the section line roads and forest roads, and snowshoed through the brush and timber, following the game trails. A fox or coyote track could always be found and, more often than not, Geraldine and Lurk put the maker of the track on the run. Ahead of the hounds, the coyotes ran their big circles in the brush. As the snow piled up through the winter, the coyotes increasingly had to break trail, bucking through the snow, for the hounds. The hounds learned to run single file, pushing the little wolves. The lead hound had an easier time bucking the snow than did the coyote who broke trail ahead of him. The trailing hound had an easier time bucking snow than the hound in the lead. Geraldine and Lurk learned to change leads, the trailing hound almost resting, to push the Brush Wolf harder. More than once Harley watched Lurk, trailing Geraldine, re-gain the lead by running right over his mother's back. And once Harley saw Lurk, faltering in the snow due to his greater weight, get run over by his lighterweight mother. But the coyotes had tricks of their own. Sometimes they ran the same circle so many times the trail packed down, got easier, and they ran better and better as the day wore on. They would double back on their tracks, leaving scent both coming and going and leaving the hounds to wonder which way the race was being run; then the Brush Wolf would strike out at a tangent and leave the hounds in a circle of confusion. Sometimes the Brush Wolf would leave the woods to run the section line roads, forest roads, and the occasional snowmobile track. Then they weren't bucking snow anymore; they were up on their toes, like running bare ground, and they could sprint on equal footing with the hounds. The hounds ran the roads and trails, fol-lowing wherever the race went, and Harley scrambled on foot, or more likely snowshoes, or in the truck to keep up. When the end came, it was always the same: Lurk would finally sight the Brush Wolf, would go silent, and would find the reserve for that awesome leaping stride of death that took him to the coyote. And once he was there it was over; the coyote was put down or bayed up. Whatever, Lurk and Geraldine would wait for Harley, to show him what they had done. January wore on and coyote hides hung in increasing numbers in the basement of the old farm house. But enough north woods Brush Wolves outsmarted and even flat outran Geraldine and Lurk that Harley knew he was in pursuit of the finest game animal he had ever run. Those were the times they would come out of the woods exhausted, well past dark and empty handed as the awful cold set down. And Harley would be exhalted over the loss. "Oh you pups! That was a great one. That was one of the best!"

In the farm country along the Winter Road River the Red Fox were as plentiful as the Brush Wolves. Like the coyotes, they worked the brush and fed extensively on the Snowshoe Hares. And with radar ears they listened for mice under the snow. Cocking their heads and working their ears, the fox focused and pounced unerringly into the snow. They snapped up mice like candy. Some days, Lurk and Geraldine pursued fox. Rarely did they catch one. A forty pound coyote broke trail for the hounds, a 12 pound fox ran over the snow like a rabbit. They never ran the roads like the coyotes, but they knew to double back to obfuscate the scent trail. In desperation, they often knew where to go to ground. On a fox chase, Harley went into the woods with his 20 gauge double, 3 inch magnum shells and BB shot. Blanketed in snow, the winter woods were devoid of bright colors until Harley, listening to the hounds and anticipating the fox's route, saw the red-orange pelt and trailing white-tipped brush in full flight through the trees. Pointing instinctively rather than aiming precisely, he shouldered the gun, swung through and fired in a single motion. He seldom missed and about half the fox tracks started by the hounds yielded a pelt that hung with the Brush Wolf hides back at the homestead.

Fisher were an entirely new challenge and sport to Harley and the hounds. Once the track was found it was trail and tree. In this it was not unlike the pursuit of coon or cats. But the race was not over when the Fisher was treed. Instead, the race continued on, with the Fisher scampering from tree to tree, through the branches high above. The big weasels were more agile than a squirrel, and had the sense to stop from time to time to try and hide in the limbs overhead. Because they kept moving, though they'd climbed, they were the only tree game that could hold Lurk's interest. But Geraldine proved the more adept at keeping them located, once they climbed. And Harley mushed on in pursuit of them all; the shooting of the Fisher with the 20 gauge double was not unlike knocking down a flying bird.

Further south, deeper in the forest, were the cats. Like the coyote, the northern bobcat was larger than his counterpart in the Southwest. The lynx were larger still, easily identified by the huge, hair-padded print they left in the snow. With the cycle of Snowshoe Hare population coming to a peak, the lynx were this season as plentiful as the bobcat in northern Minnesota. Both hounds pursued the first cat that winter; Geraldine pursued the rest. After the first cat was treed, Lurk wandered off in boredom before Harley got to the tree. Lurk was searching for a fox or coyote track. Finding none, he humored himself in futile pursuit of the Snowshoe Hares. Geraldine held the tree and Harley shot the bobcat. He spent the rest of the morning pursuing Lurk. Thereafter, when the track was a cat, Lurk stayed in the back of the truck, or on lead. Hardened on fox and Brush Wolves, Geraldine didn't need any help with a cat. The cats were a lesser sport, and were less plentiful, than the Brush Wolves, but were a greater reward. As with the coyotes and fox, the great cold caused the pelts to fur out lush and gorgeous, and with colors unknown in the Southwest. Fox and coyote pelts were plentiful, and fur buyers could make the hunters and trappers sweat and drive the price down. Harley knew that with the cats he was hanging on the stretchers, he could drive the buyers up.

One afternoon late in the first month of the long hunt Harley and Geraldine came out of the forest with a lynx, nearly as large as a Brush Wolf and thick with fur. Harley knew it was a months wages he tossed in the back of the truck where Lurk sulked with the carcass of a coyote he'd caught that morning. Geraldine scrambled in the back with Lurk. Harley got in the cab, turned the truck around and headed for home. He felt good. He'd been on snowshoes in pursuit since early light and he was tired but, he thought, a good hunt always feels better if it wears you out. He thought too, of the warm fire he would stoke up in the wood stove at home, and the big pot of stew he would soon have simmering on the kitchen stove, while he soaked in a hot tub and nursed a cold beer. He drove at an easy speed, north out of the forest. He passed and waved at the county snow plow, the first person he'd seen all day. The coffee was still warm in the jug and he poured a cup. Out of the forest the county road intersected the forest road and he turned east, then north, up the county road that would take him home. He could see the bridge ahead that crossed the Winter Road River, right by his house, when he became aware of the vehicle close behind him. In the rear view mirror he saw a dark green pickup with a red light on top. The red light wasn't on but the truck was riding his rear bumper and it was clear that the vehicle represented authority and meant for him to stop. Rude bastard, Harley thought. And he thought of the heavy bumper and trailer hitch he had mounted on the back of his pickup, the one that could pull loaded stock trailers, and he thought of what it would do to the front of the dark green pickup if he were to suddenly slam on the brakes. After all, he thought, he wants me to stop. But remembering his mission he merely held his speed long enough that he was sure whomever it was would be steaming a bit, before putting on his right blinker and slowly easing to a stop by the side of the county road. Affecting nonchalance, Harley stepped out and waited by the door, slowing removing a pouch and tucking a quid of looseleaf tobacco into his lip. And he eyed The Law getting out of the dark green pickup...

...The Law was very tall and stood slightly stooped in the green uniformed winter coat and fur-lined cap of the Minnesota Department of Natural Resources; this was not ordinary law; this was a game warden. And the brass nameplate on the green uniformed coat indicated the warden's name was Hilding Thomsen. The Law was ruddy and florid of complexion, blue-eyed, and of a dour countenance, offering no expression or thought that Harley could read. Harley thought: he could be fifty, he could be seventy. The Law came to the back of Harley's pickup, put his foot up on the bumper, removed pen and note pad from his coat pocket and, Harley could tell, began to write down the license plate number. Harley did not go back around the truck to greet The Law. Then The Law's slow deep voice said, "What have you got in back here, Simmons?" as he reached for the handle of the camper shell door and started to lift the lid. There was a roar and the truck started to shake and the game warden shut the door just in time to keep Lurk from coming through the door and all over The Law. Now The Law had expression: he stepped back like someone just hit him in the face. Before The Law could speak, Harley said, "Lurk's pretty territorial. If you've got time, let me open that for you and you can look all you want." Harley came around to the back of the truck. "Steady Lurk, steady," and he lifted the lid. From a distance The Law stooped toward the opening, rather like he expected a bad smell, saw two hounds, a couple of guns, the coyote and the lynx. He stepped back. Harley shut the lid, and The Law got out his pen and pad again and made a few more notes. Harley

203

was waiting to be asked for his hunting license, but saw no reason to volunteer that he had one unless asked. He was also wondering how the warden knew his name was Simmons. The Law finally looked up from his pad and said, "Harold told me there was an out-of-state hunter in the county. I know what you're hunting license says, Simmons; let me see your drivers license." Harley handed over his drivers license and the law put his foot back up on the bumper and placed the license on his knee. He wrote it all down on his note pad. Then he flipped to another page of his note pad and Harley could see he was matching the information from his drivers license with the information he had already collected from his hunting license. The juxtaposition offered no discrepancies. The law handed the drivers license back to Harley and said, "You're a long way from home, Simmons."

Harley thought: that's so obvious, it doesn't deserve a response. Harley said, "Yes, I am."

"What are you doing in northwest Minnesota?"

Harley thought: you've got to be game warden enough to figure that out. Harley said, "Hunting fur with hounds."

The Law said, "Can't you do that in New Mexico?"

Harley thought: typical law; can't find anything wrong so he's going to push and push until he's sure I know I'm dealing with a royal asshole. Harley said, "Of course."

The Law's expression indicated he was not pleased with the answers he was getting. The Law said, "I've been seeing your tracks all over the southern part of Tamarack County."

Harley thought: this has gone on long enough. He put one foot up on the bumper like the warden had done, sent some tobacco juice into the snow, looked at The Law, and waited.

"Well, Simmons?"

"Was that a question?"

"Now look here Simmons, I've got enough trouble with the locals poaching deer and leaving their traplines untended and there's a whole list I could read you, without more trouble coming in from out of state."

"It's a free country, Thomsen, and I've got the right license for what I'm doing...so what's the trouble?"

The warden gave Harley several seconds of that dour, expressionless look, then he put his note pad and pen away and walked to his pickup. He put his hand on the door handle, turned to Harley and said, "Simmons, I'm going to tell you the truth...a man comes all the way up here from New Mexico just to take some fur?...I just can't see it."

The warden started to open the door and Harley thought, it won't hurt to try. Harley said, "That's my place just over the bridge, Thomsen; I'll put the coffee pot on."

For a moment The Law looked like he wouldn't mind. But he caught himself. "I know where you live, Simmons. Maybe some other time."

The Law got in his pickup. Then he rolled down the window and said, "What did you call that hound?"

"Lurk."

The Law gave a slight, dour and expressionless shake of the head and started his truck. He put it into gear and drove off. Harley stood by his truck until The Law was out of sight up the road. Harley thought: I'll bet he's a hound himself when he smells something illegal. Harley said, "Time comes, there won't be any room for mistakes."

## Chapter 29

THERE WERE DAYS when the hunter and the hunting hounds needed rest. Especially the hounds. Two or three days hard running in a row, feet pounding through the cold and snow and ice, left Geraldine's feet tender, sore, cut and swollen. Methodically, attentively, Harley would soak them in a boric acid solution at night, then salve and a warm wrap of gauze. They never had time to really heal, but with the occasional day's rest they were good enough for another race. Lurk's big hairy feet were indestructible. But Harley watched with some concern as the weight went steadily off the great frame of the hound. Harley hauled home meat from the butcher in town and Snowshoe Hares by the half dozen from the woods and fed the best dog food he could find; but he knew Lurk simply ran too hard and burned up too many calories in a long race to ever make it up in one evening meal. So periodically now, they were forced to rest a day and Geraldine nursed her feet and Lurk and Geraldine ate big morning and night and tried to get it back.

But even when they rested they hunted and this was the most important hunt of all. These were the days he would pack them all a lunch and they would load in the truck for a long day - as long as the meager daylight of a northern winter permitted - of scouting around. He knew by now the several forest roads and county roads passable in the winter. From time to time, he'd cross the tracks of the big wolves. He always stopped to look. He noted numbers, direction, and which ones had the biggest feet. He had a map and he noted on the map where they had been, where they were going, looking for patterns; and on the back of the map were his notes of things he did not want to forget about wolves. But he never got out of the truck to leave a man track by a wolf track to allow Hilding Thomsen or anyone else reason to think he had any interest in big wolves. But still he tracked the wolves. Where a wolf or wolves crossed a road into a section of woods, he'd drive around that section, if roads permitted, to see where they went. If there were no roads, he'd track them on snowshoes. He would not go in on the track. He would find a track of a coyote or fox or cat or Fisher to go in on, the hounds necked for control. Then he would circle within the woods till he cut wolf sign. The hounds would snuffle their noses into the big prints.

And they would growl and the hair would raise up on their necks. More intent even than on the scent of the Brush Wolf, but the scent of the Timber Wolf also made them evidence fear. Harley would steady them down and they would track wolves as daylight permitted. Over time, the notes and the scouting around and the tracking formed a lengthy diary and the hieroglyphics were extensive on the map. And the pattern of the various lives of the wolves who lived in the southern half of Tamarack County, northwest Minnesota, presented itself.

Deep in the forest, at the southern county line, a large pack of 13 wolves ranged from the southern county line further south. Most of the time they were further south, in a vast roadless wilderness that Harley did not scout. To know it, he would have to pack in and sleep nights in the black cold. There was no need to do this. North of this pack, closer to home, the nine wolf pack he'd marked his first day in Minnesota hunted a 30 mile circular route. At the northern part of the route they passed every two weeks within three miles of his house. Then they traveled west and, finally, swung south to near the southern county line. Too, there was a lone wolf to the south and east, that lived and stayed in a section of woods two miles square. Harley could tell from his feet that he was very large and he could tell from the sign he left when lifting his leg to pee that he was a male. Harley never saw him, but he suspected he was an old wolf who had been driven from a pack and was living out his years alone. Because this large male wolf lived alone, for a while Harley thought he would be the male wolf he would try to catch. There would remain the great problem of finding a female to make a pair. Harley knew by now there was no female wolf living alone in Tamarack County; she would have to come from the nine wolf pack. Harley kept track of the lone male wolf and for weeks he periodically scouted the sign of the nine wolf pack till he knew them, too. He knew from their tracks and the way they travelled there was a large dominant male, a dominant female, and that the other seven were pups. Five of these pups, judging from their feet, were not full grown and would be the pups from the previous spring. The other two wolves were a male and a female, full grown, but their tracks clearly indicated they did not lead. Harley guessed that these were adolescent wolves, coming two or perhaps three years old. Harley wanted the female adolescent wolf - old enough to breed but as yet unclaimed. He thought to pair her with the old lone wolf. He figured it might work. He hadn't figured how to get her singled out of the pack. The man from Missouri turned loose on the pack and got half his hounds killed. Harley only had two hounds. If either one was killed, the hunt was over. Then, in late February, after a modest warming trend, the temperature began to drop once again below zero day and night. And Harley began to notice, as he expected, that the female coyotes, the female foxes, and the female wolves had begun to piss and drip bright red blood in the snow. The breeding season for wild canines was on. Harley quit hunting small game. He followed the nine wolves by day and he thought and dreamed about them at night. The day he finally saw them, the plan began to take shape.

## Chapter 30

**THEY STOOD ON THE FROZEN LID OF SNOW** far across the wind swept clearing, brought close enough by the binoculars that he could see their magnificent northern pelts ruffle and fluff in the breeze. Between them, they were all the wonderful colors a wolf ought to be. The dominant male, who's eyes had seen the pickup first, was nearly black. One of the yearling pups was nearly white. Among the rest were wolves with fine mixtures of grays, blacks and whites, and they were all looking at him now, motionless, not afraid but intent, magnificent in their demeanor and impervious to the cold. Harley turned off the engine and continued to view them from inside the truck. His reading of the tracks had been correct. He counted nine wolves. The black male was the largest wolf, was leading, and was obviously the dominant animal. A large female showed an ageing face; she would be the mother of the rest of them. The five yearlings were easy to distinguish by their lesser frames. These seven animals were grouped. One hundred yards away was the adolescent male and the adolescent female, large, lank wolves, but neither so awesome as the black. Moving his focus to these two, Harley could answer one question he'd had for several days. He knew two females, the old one and the adolescent one, were bleeding in estrus. But, recently, a third wolf had left blood in the snow, though not from estrus. One wolf had a wound and now Harley saw the dried blood on the ear and neck of the adolescent male. Harley knew what he was seeing. The black doesn't like the competition this time of year, he thought, and he's driving the younger male away. And it looked very much to Harley like the younger bitch was going with him. Harley was no longer interested in the old lone wolf who lived south and east; these two younger wolves belonged together. Harley kept his binoculars on the adolescent wolves as he talked to the two hounds sleeping on the seat beside him. "Pups, I said we'd need some luck, and we're about to get a stroke of it. Those two are leaving out together. Sure enough, they're going to pair off."

## Chapter 31

**THE NIGHTS DROPPED** to 30 or 35 or even 40 below zero. The days warmed up to 12 or 10 or 8 below zero before dipping back down for the night. Harley spent the days on snowshoes, following two wolves who were never far apart. They drifted away from the main pack, which went west and then south on the old route. Harley let the big black and his family go and drifted day by day with the tracks of the young pair, following the larger print of the male and the almost slender print of the bitch. The wolves kept moving west, hunting up the frozen course of the Winter Road River, ever deeper into the bush. Harley saw them twice, once up close as he came in downwind, and they had no idea he was there. The bitch was the palest gray, and as slender and racy built as her track. The dog's pale gray undercoat was overlain with a dark pattern that stood out especially across the shoulders and down the back. His greater frame and bulk shown through the coat. One day Harley tracked their kill. He was on their single file track when it split; the large male track went off into a small, Black Spruce stand, the sort of cover where the deer yard up in the winter. The bitch's track, which Harley followed, went south, then west; then Harley saw where she'd lain in wait in the snow. From that crouch the track proceeded in great bounds through the drifts and soon intersected the bounding course of a deer, and the tracks of the male. Harley followed. The male's tracks were on top of the bitch's, indicating the bitch had led the race. A quarter mile on the blood began to mark the chase; a half mile from where the sprint started the race ended. There Harley found the half eaten carcass of the buck. The early blood sign on the snow was from the slashes he found in the haunch. Part of the haunch had been eaten. All of the viscera - the heart, the lungs, the liver - were gone.

Near the end of the week, deep in the swamp near the source of the river, their wandering ceased. Harley marked the wisdom of their choice. This was country that had never been logged. And no snowmobile could penetrate this frozen swamp. There was a deer herd yarded up not so far away and the Snowshoe Hares were thick. More pertinent to Harley, the bitch's estrus had proceeded from a rich red blood, to a pale red, watery discharge, to a milky yellowish stain in the snow that indicated the mating time. Harley did not seek the den. He would leave them for the time to their housekeeping, giving them a week at least to complete their private act. He would go east and hunt Brush Wolves again. Then he would be back with the hounds. And the first great race would be for the bitch.

*Chapter 32*

HENRY BUSTOS stepped gingerly up the ice covered steps, arriving at work a little late and he was not in pleasant spirits. In twenty years of law enforcement he had faced a series of armed robbers, murderers, smugglers, horse thieves, sexual deviants and a variety of others bent on disrupting society and none of it had ever cost him a night's sleep. But anticipation of appearance in court under cross-examination from certain lawyers could keep him awake all night. This morning he was due in court and would be cross-examined by a defense attorney known throughout New Mexico for his ability to get the most disgraceful people off scot free. This defense attorney could make those he cross-examined feel like they, not the defendant, were on trial. The case this morning involved a violent rapist, guilty as sin and with a long record. This character was sufficiently nefarious that the sheriff himself had led the investigation. But the case, the sheriff knew, was legally weak. The defense attorney would exploit every weak link in the case and the sheriff was afraid he would be one of them. He was not in pleasant spirits.

"Sheriff, don't forget you're due in court at ten o'clock sharp."

"I know Celia, I know."

"Did Terrazas come down from Albuquerque to win this for the defense?"

"I'm afraid so. Mail in?"

"There's a stack on your desk."

The sheriff entered his office, sat down in his swivel chair, put his feet up on the desk and started to sort through the mail. He recognized a variety of official stationary and he tossed these letters aside; he'd let the captain handle it. But the post mark of one letter caught his eye and made him pause. He thought: who do I know in Winter Road, Minnesota? He took out his pocket knife and slit open the letter to find out.

February 25

Sheriff, Arthur County
Del Cobre, New Mexico

Dear Sheriff:

I am writing to you concerning the individual A. Harley Simmons who is listed as a resident of your county. This individual arrived in Tamarack County, Minnesota in late December, ostensibly to hunt fur bearing animals with hounds. This individual is properly licensed and to date has done nothing illegal, so far as I know; however, it continues to strike me as unusual that this individual would travel 2,000 miles from New Mexico just to run some coyotes and cats. Any information you could provide me concerning A. Harley Simmons would be appreciated.

Yours Sincerely,

Hilding Thomsen
District Warden

Henry Bustos looked out the window towards the snowcapped rim of the Mondragón Range and smiled. He thought of the ten page letter he could easily write to the District Warden concerning "the individual A. Harley Simmons." He considered several questionable activities that Harley might entertain during his visit to the northern state. But he was due in court in 12 minutes and he thought: Harley is going to have enough trouble with this game warden without my stirring things up; best stick to the facts. The sheriff put his feet down and swung himself around to the typewriter. He rolled in a sheet of official Arthur County Sheriff stationary and, using two fingers, typed out a strictly accurate response.

February 28

Hilding Thomsen-District Warden
Winter Road, Minnesota

Dear Warden Thomsen:

In regard to your letter of February 25 concerning a one A. (Alvin) Harley Simmons; this individual is well known in southwest New Mexico as a hunter and guide. He is not wanted for anything in this state, nor anywhere else to my knowledge. It does not surprise me that Simmons has gone north to hunt fur for the winter.

Sincerely,

Henry Bustos
Sheriff, Arthur County

The sheriff addressed the envelope, tucked the letter in and sealed it. It was time. He gathered up his notes and court records and headed for the court house. On the way out he handed the letter to his secretary. "Celia, see that this goes out today."

*Chapter 33*

HE SNOWSHOED in from down wind, the hounds necked and leashed, and he got so close to their den he momentarily glimpsed the great gray forms bounding off as they disappeared into the swamp. As soon as he had separate tracks he turned the hounds lose on the bitch. Each hound in turn tested the track, knowing immediately that this was not just a coyote chase; as they roared off the squall, boo and chop was deeper, more frantic, fearful and determined, than anything Harley had heard on the trail.

The bitch fled south, out of the spruce swamp, into a woodland of aspen and birch and the hounds were soon out of hearing. Harley mushed right up the single file track of the three canines, as rapidly as the terrain allowed. An hour from the densite he came to an old logging road, ridden down flat and crusted over by snowmobile tracks. In surprise, Harley saw that the bitch had turned west and was sprinting up the trail. He thought: she feels vulnerable running the deep, soft snow; she's going to try to outsprint the pack. Harley sensed he was coming into another stroke of luck. He could run now himself, lifting and thrusting his snowshoes ahead of him, slapping them ahead on the snow in the peculiar style required, secure at speed on the packed trail. He stopped three times to listen for the hounds, noting on one occasion the long sprint stride of the bitch, the even longer run-to-catch stride of the hound. The third stop he heard them, that chop! chop! chop!; they had already caught the bitch!

Not five miles from the den site, they had her bayed up, just off the trail, the three of them floundering in deep snow as they snarled, snapped and danced away from one another. Cautiously, Harley approached the wolf. She turned to run from the man, but she'd been run down; Geraldine grabbed a back leg; the bitch twisted and snapped and the hound let go in time. Then the bitch leaped at Harley. Lurk took her at the neck, Geraldine grabbed an ear and the two hounds and Harley pinned the bitch, smothered the bitch in the snow. She twisted like a snake. The hounds held on, and Harley had her straddled with all his weight. Harley drew a length of rawhide cord from his coat pocket. It was already a loop at one end and he looped it over her jaws, around her jaws, and drew it up. Like a dog, her jaws had great strength closing down, not much opening up. He drew her jaws closed. He used the rest of the cord and wrapped and wrapped till her jaws were secure. He had plenty of cord and he used another length to hog-tie her front feet. He was hog-tying the back feet when he heard the distant roar of snowmobiles. He thought: goddamn; we don't need that right now. He finished the wrap on the hind feet, slung the trussed wolf over his shoulders, and plodded off into the woods. The machines went by as fast as cars, never pausing, heading west. Harley came out of the woods with the wolf and started east up the trail. He knew the trail, knew it would cross the forest road where he'd left his truck. It was a good distance but he never set the wolf down. She was lank, muscular, but not so heavy as Lurk. When he stopped to rest, he kept her across his shoulders. He didn't want to set her down; he liked the feel of her across his shoulders. As he rested he listened for machines. And he looked and listened to know if he was being followed. The hounds followed Harley, sniffed at the bitch, and, like Harley, every little bit looked back off into the woods...

He came to the plowed drifts along the road. Shy of the road, he turned north off the trail and dumped the wolf in the snow. He rested, briefly, then checked the knots that held the wolf captive. The knots were sound; the wolf eyed him unhappily, but she had long since ceased to struggle; she was a caught wolf. Harley stood and leaned against a tree and considered that it might be best to go home and wait out the day, returning after dark to retrieve the wolf. He didn't like the idea of being on any road in the daytime with a wolf in the back of the truck; not with a warden like Hilding Thomsen patrolling the county. But it was not yet noon; he couldn't leave the bitch untended for six hours. She could draw ravens, which could draw coyotes. Brush Wolves would kill her trussed up and helpless. And ravens could alert another hunter, or a snowmobiler. Or a game warden. Hog-tied like she was, her feet could freeze. He left the bitch in the snow, went to the trail, then descended into the bar ditch along the road, then up and over the snow bank to the road. The forest road ran north and south, straight as a string, mile after mile. He could see his truck, a tiny red dot, parked along the road to the north. There were no other vehicles or signs of life in this part of Tamarack County. He removed his snowshoes and tossed them over the bank into the ditch. Then he started to run up the road to the truck. He worked up to a good stride in his winter clothes and boots, the dogs loping easily alongside. It was well below zero and their running breath - each of them - puffed out visibly into the air. He didn't stop running till he got to the truck. He got in the truck and inserted the key. He said, "Start, you bastard." The old truck turned over and came to life. In ten minutes he had a bitch wolf in the back of his truck and was headed for the barn. He held his breath most of the way, passing a logging truck and one farmer in a pickup, and two snowmobiles, on the road. He arrived without incident in the yard and immediately carried the wolf up the path to the barn. He set her down in the wolf pen and used his knife to cut the cords. Momentarily, the man and the wolf eyed each other, then each bolted to safety. The wolf ducked into the "wolf house" while Harley scampered out the door of the pen and shut it tight. Then he went to his own house and got meat scraps for the bitch and a bucket of water. She was still in her wolf house when he got back. She stared and only moved her nose; she smelled the meat. Harley threw the meat into the middle of the pen and left the water inside the door. He had another bucket ready in the house for when this one froze over - a matter of hours. She would get the best of care. Harley went down the path through the snow to his house. He went in with the hounds and stirred up the fire in the fireplace; the hounds curled up near there. He made three sandwiches, one for each hunter, and heated up a bowl of soup. He could hardly believe his luck - he had left the house at 5 A. M. and was back with a wolf in time for lunch. But he had to believe it. He could allow himself to believe it now. The dogs eyed him with the sad, hopeful eyes of hounds from their curl by the fire. He gave a ham sandwich to each hound. He said, "Pups, it's not a dream anymore."

*Chapter 34*

THE OTHER SIDE OF GOOD LUCK, of course, is bad luck; and though it seems that some are invariably blessed and others always cursed, no one has a permanent clamp on good or bad luck. Harley knew he had had an extraordinary run of good luck in northern Minnesota. He only needed a little bit more. He didn't get it. The next morning - a clear day but some wind and the feel of weather in the air - he got to the point where he'd last heard the hounds and found Lurk slumped in the snow looking very lost, bewildered, his fierce yellow eyes suddenly weak and asking for help. The gash that went down across the neck and deep into the shoulder was half a foot long. A major vessel, severed in there somewhere, was releasing his life into the snow. The steady surge of blood indicated to Harley that it was a vein, not an artery; he forced himself to probe and he looked hard and he found it. At the point of greatest bleeding, he packed his bandana into the gash. Then he removed his wool scarf and wrapped it around and around, finally tying in tight over the wound. The flow was already down to a seep. He looked on up the trail, where the tracks of the big wolf and the little hound disappeared into the swamp. There was no sight nor sound of the little Walker gyp. Harley could only imagine what might have happened, but he couldn't wait to find out. He shouldered Lurk as he had the bitch wolf the day before and began in methodical desperation to trail his snowshoe flow back to the truck. When he got to the road the little gyp was right behind him, unmarked. As always, he cursed the truck to start..."roll over you mother!" It did. He headed for town, the gyp curled up on the floor of the cab, Lurk stretched out across the seat, his head in Harley's lap. The blood seeped gently into Harley's lap and for several miles he drove faster than anyone should ever drive on a snow packed forest road. Gradually, he slowed to a manageable speed. He thought: if I slide into the ditch, we won't get there at all. And he began to think that while the big wolf and his own big dream might be gone, he probably was going to save his friend. Provided the vet was in...

...He was, and he took Lurk ahead of two house cats and one yap dog left waiting in the lobby.

"Jesus Christ!" the vet said as Harley laid the dog out over the examining table. Harley wasn't sure if he meant the wound, or the hound, or maybe both.

"Coyote got him," Harley said. "Big ol' coyote."

"I guess!"

Harley watched carefully. He had taken lots of hounds to lots of vets and he'd known his share of rural vets who were a lot more adept with bloated cattle than with wounded hounds. But this young doctor proceeded with a studied nonchalance that indicated to Harley that he knew what he was doing. The vet quickly had a sedative into a leg vein; that was all he would need to proceed with the surgery and it steadied the shock. Then the assistant came in and Harley got out of the way. Soon the doctor had needle and thread and was probing into the wound. He found the vein and in short order tied it off. Then he cleaned the wound, sewed it up and wrapped it in gauze and bandage. After he washed his hands, the vet touched his finger to the gums of the hound. The gums were pale but some color came back in when the doctor's finger was released.

"You did well, packing it like that. He hasn't lost that much blood. A lot of what has him down is shock. Must have been some Brush Wolf."

"Must have been. Never saw him."

"For the sake of this hound, you better hope you never see him again."

Harley smiled. He felt not so bad now, the way anyone is apt to feel when they realize their bad luck could have been a lot worse. He even began to think that his dream might not be over after all. He began to think ahead.

"Doc, his name is Lurk. He's a Lurk hound, and he never knows when he's overmatched. He's worst with a porcupine. Never has learned about quills. How about some pills so I can work on him next time he gets stupid with a porcupine?"

The vet went over to the cabinet and took out a big bottle of pills. He poured some out on the counter and with a flat stick rolled a couple dozen off into a smaller plastic bottle. He gave the small bottle to Harley.

"For a full-sized hound like him, one of these will make him groggy. Two will put him to sleep. Three and he might not wake up. Got it?"

"Got it. Next time he makes me mad enough, I'll give him three."

Harley drove slowly west then south of Winter Road. Geraldine took her spot on the floor. On the seat, Lurk was coming out of the sedative. He lifted his great shaggy head and looked bleakly around the cab. By the time they got home the wind was already starting to blow dry powdery snow in drifts across the road.

**Chapter 35**

March 4

**DEAR SUZIE:**

We are snowed in. Nothing human could be out in this storm and survive. The crazy thing is, it's not really snowing at all. Everything is white outside the window. But every once in a while the wind will let up for a bit and if it's daytime the sky overhead is pure blue and if it's night the stars are shining. It's all the wind. It's a ground blizzard. It roars and howls and whips around in every direction and it's picking up all the snow that's fallen here in northwestern Minnesota - about 4 feet I'd guess - and it's sailing it someplace else. It has remained below zero, day and night, for fifteen days now and this is a northwest wind, so I don't see any break in the cold. It's late at night here now, the second night of the storm. We're in for a three day blow, at least. We're stuck here but it's okay. We have plenty of wood and the wood stove in the basement keeps the house warm and the fireplace keeps it cheery in the room where I write. Of course, you know how I hate to write. But we're here for awhile and the dogs need the rest and Lurk needs to get well. And you need more than those little notes I've been sending you. So I guess writing you a real letter is the thing to do right now.

I caught the bitch wolf! She's beautiful, Suzie, the most beautiful live thing I've ever seen, at least that was covered with fur (don't get jealous!). The day we caught her, we got so close, I saw her running off through the woods. She was very swift and entirely at home in the woods and the deep snow and she went off like you'd never see her again. But she went to this trail in the woods that's all packed down by those goddamn snowmobiles (you would not believe the noise those things make on the quietist day in the forest, only when they packed that old skid road down they did me a favor). And she went up that snowmobile track and tried to outrun Lurk. She's beautifully built, built to run, long bodied and not too heavy in bone for a wolf with wonderful muscles running down the loin and back legs. She runs so smooth, and if it had been a long race, running into the hours, an endurance race, I don't know if we could have caught her at all. But she went up that hard beat trail and tried to outsprint Lurk and of course she couldn't do that. And she's really not as big as Lurk and he had help from Geraldine so once they caught her they didn't have too much trouble keeping her bayed up. The next day (yesterday) I went in to get the male and if everything had gone like it was supposed to I'd be writing to tell you the hunt was over. The hunt isn't over. The big male wolf ran a ways, then he just waited on those dogs. And he opened Lurk up and I had to take him in to the vet and get him sewn up to save him. He's eating good and coming back and he'll be ready whenever we can get out of here but whether he and Geraldine have got the trick to bring him to bay...well...I just don't know.

For a while, I thought the whole business of going after that male wolf again was, as Ted might say, a moot point. The thing is, with his mate having disappeared, that male wolf has no reason to hang around that den site for very long. He was still there yesterday, when he ran us out of the woods. By supper time yesterday, the storm was in full force. I was pretty discouraged about it all last night. I figured, by the time the storm is over and Lurk is ready to run, he'll be gone, he'll return to

215

the pack. Then today, this evening just before dark, I was sitting here listening to the wind storm and there was this wild howl to the wind. High winds here make the whole house groan and have voices. And there's no telling what kind of sound the wind will make when it blows like this and comes on blowing snow and rushing through the forest, but something about that wild howl wasn't just the wind. So I bundled up and went out in the yard and stood there in the dark and the storm and, you guessed it already, it was him. Now how has he done this? I mean, that den site is 10 miles anyway as the crow flies. If a man lost his mate, why, he'd call the cops, or he'd run an ad in the classifieds, or he'd ask his friends if they'd seen her, or he'd pray to god. But he wouldn't, he couldn't, just *know* where she was. He damn sure wouldn't be able to wander through a storm where you can't see your hand in front of your face and go to the right place and know it was right when he got there. There's a wolf out there right now, somewhere, not a quarter mile from the place, and he *knows*. You never heard such a howl as that wolf. I know I haven't. He's lonely, Suzie. And so am I.

I remember when I was at the University, and my first semester they told me I *had* to live in the dormitory. The next semester they told me I *had* to live elsewhere. You guessed it already - girls in my room. They didn't allow that back then. But I was in the dorm that first semester and there was this guy down the hall and his girl had thrown him over or was slipping away or was slipping out or maybe she was just a long way off, I don't remember. I just remember he had it for her pretty bad and so he wrote her this long letter and before he sent it he asked me to read it to see if it was okay. I don't know why he asked me because I didn't know him that well, but I read it. I told him it was a good one and to go ahead and send it and I hoped it worked. Actually, I was pretty disgusted. I thought: I hope I never get to where I'd write a sappy letter like that to a girl. Well, here goes...

I love you Suzie. I love you so much I don't care anymore who knows it. If it wasn't a storm outside I'd go out there right now and write it in the snow. I'd use my mitten and I'd write it so big you could see it from a plane. I'd write: I LOVE SUZIE. Would you like that? Of course, it's out of the question right now. Anyway, you are the recipient of my first love letter. You are my first love. I've loved dogs, and my son, but as for women, all I ever had was victories and defeats. A lot of early victories and, later, defeats. I always thought it was a matter of strength. Women are attracted to strong men, the story goes. I wanted to attract them, so I acted strong to win them. When it ended, I acted strong to get over them. Of course, it was all just an act. Now I'm in love with you and I have no strength at all. I'm helpless loving you, Suzie. With a word you could squish me like a soft bug. No one has ever made me feel helpless this way. And if they had, I wouldn't have admitted it. Looks like my act is over.

And what will it be like when I come home? It's scary for me to think about seeing you again. I feel like it will be coming to know you all over, in a new way. I can tell you that I have dreams some times. In the night and in the daytime too. I mean dreams about us. Some are sweet, some are raunchy, but even when it's raunchy we're never less than tender, you and I. I want to save it for when we're together to tell you these dreams. I want to tell you everything, all my dreams. And I want to hear yours. It's scary for me Suzie, to feel this way about a woman. I'll need you to help me, to come to know you all over again. In a new way. (I hope all this is not too sappy for you. Believe me, it's not as sappy as the one that guy at the University wrote. I mean!)

Twice I've almost quit and come home. Partly it was because there were times when what I'm trying to do seemed like such a dream, only a dream, and I felt I should quit before I lose my dogs or end up in jail. And partly because this dream is keeping me from you. I really don't know if we can take that wolf. I have to consider there's some chance that wolf cannot be caught and he's going to kill both of my dogs in keeping himself free. Traps are out. I wouldn't know how to make a set in four feet of snow. And he'd probably pull out of a #3. And a #4 would ruin his foot. Hounds are the only way for me to do this. I know my chances would be a lot better if White-eye was here. He was so adept at in-fighting - tough and fast and knew enough not to get caught. Geraldine is all of that but she's so small. Lurk is big enough, but he needs some humility if he's going to stay alive in front of that wolf. Certainly they both know what they're up against now. My guess is they're still willing. I'm still willing. And I know that next to loving you, this is the finest thing I've ever tried to do.

This is a great country, Suzie. I've learned a lot in this country, particularly I've learned a lot from game I've never really run before. I've learned that blending speed and endurance, the coyote is the finest runner in the natural world. It's probably the smartest animal, too. And the most adaptable. The wolf has one thing only on the coyote and that's nobility. In that, I believe the wolf has something on anything else that lives. And I've learned there's nothing prettier running than a Red Fox on snow in the north woods. And a Fisher is as quick, tough and vicious as you'd expect a big weasel to be, and an acrobat in the trees. For pure aesthetics, there's nothing as lovely as the mid-winter pelt of a lynx. And I've often wondered, what is the hunter in pursuit really after? It may be meat. It may be a pelt or hide to wear or sell. It may be the pride that's in any trophy that's well earned. It may be partly challenge. Any thing that's worth hunting has talents that we, as humans, can only marvel at, talents that we lack, and so we find them wondrous - a quail's speed in flight, a coyote's speed afoot, the speed of a Smallmouth Bass in the water. Their talents are beyond us and are portrayed in an alien world and so they are wondrous to us. And so I think in pursuit we're trying to capture some of their cunning, or speed, or grit, or adaptability, or beauty, for ourselves. And maybe to try and come to know their world a little bit. Each and every game has it's particular talents but there's one thing they all have, and that's spirit. They take their world as given and live it without complaint. They take what comes without a whimper. They don't curse God, they don't praise or thank God, and they don't expect a subsidy from the government. It's not that they are passive. They are unyielding in spirit. Their spirit is, I suppose, just their own brand of grit. But it's not just a physical toughness. It's mental and emotional as well. It's spirit. And so I think in pursuit I'm trying to capture some of that spirit for myself. To an extent, I think I have. To the extent that I have, it has helped me with all of my life. That's why I'm here, engaged in this pursuit. During this winter, Lurk and Geraldine and I have been brought to the peak of fitness and drive. I'm a better hunter than I've ever been. Geraldine is a truly superior hound. And I think Lurk has talents that no hound has ever had. And yet, a bunch of coyotes have beaten us, on the run. They did it with speed, endurance, and also with their indomitable wild spirit. We all three have gotten something from that. Something we could not get from any of the catches we've made. I'd like someday to create a breed of dogs like Lurk. If I do, I know there will still be coyotes who will beat us. My creation will never equal the best of natural selection, and I'm glad of that. But I'll always look for the pursuit. I'll always pursue that wild wondrous spirit, and will try to capture some of it for myself. I only hope there will always be places where that spirit can reside. That means wild country and wild rivers, that belong more to the wildlife than to us. Places where that wild indomitable spirit can flourish. Places where a romance with the wilderness is more than fantasy; places where, at least in spirit, it can come true. I've come to believe that what those sons-a-bitches really want, more than anything, is to kill that wild spirit. More than water for consumptive use, or trees for timber, or roads or lakes so they can motor around...more than any of that they want to kill that wild spirit. Just as some of us have an old ancestral wonder of the wilderness, they have an old ancestral fear of it. And so they want to kill it off. I think there's a great deal of foolishness in their thinking. My father used to say, "no animal but man was ever so dumb as to try and change the country he was gifted at birth." I think I'm coming to know what he meant. Here in northwest Minnesota, the Snowshoes Hares are very plentiful right now. If they were to stay this plentiful they'd eat the aspen forest and the second growth, and themselves, into oblivion. But they won't. The foxes, the coyotes, the wolves, the cats and the Fisher; they're all eating these hares. The predators are plentiful and flush now, too. There's a lot of killing going on. In just a few years there will be a lot less hares. In a few more years, there will be a lot fewer predators. Then the cycle, the balance, will begin all over again.

Nothing will ever become too populous for too long. And the country will stay the same. That's the beauty of it. All that killing, all that struggle, all that life and death and wild spirit, and the country is unchanged. It will still provide. Only man can change it. Here in Minnesota, down there in New Mexico, man has changed the country, has depleted it, more in the last hundred years than all the coyotes and wolves, cats and hares, have done in a millennia. They know better. The wolves, I've been reading, have gone a step further in controlling their own numbers. When a wolf pack begins to overpopulate their range, their birth rate abruptly declines, till their numbers are in balance with their range once again. With all our technology and art, with all our smart talk and assumptions, we've yet to learn as simple and wise a thing as that. Without thinking, the natural world knows limits. We can think, but we know no limits. I'm coming to believe that all the answers to our human dilemma can be found in the natural world. But we've insulated ourselves from that world, and so we can't see it. And we're bent on destroying what's left of it, so we will have no place left to even study it. No place left in which to pursue, or observe, and learn. That alone is reason enough to preserve what's left of wild country. And yet, if I can restore the wolf to the Great Southwest, if one small river that still flows free can be saved, that will say something about limits. I'm coming to know something about the natural world. I think, Suzie, I'm even coming to know something about love, or at least loving you. But it's all so much bigger than I am. I just want to be a part of it, and to somehow make a difference. This letter has got to end now. I will seal it up and stamp it and struggle through the drifts and wind to the mail box. The red flag will go up and in a day or two the plow and the mailman in his pickup will break through and my thoughts will be off to you. Hug Jessica for me. Greet Ted for me. Keep yourself safe and warm.

Harley

**Chapter 36**

March 9

DEAR HARLEY:

Do wolves mate for life? Ever since you wrote me, telling me what you're up to, I have been more and more fascinated by your wonderful wolves. So I have been reading about them, too. Everything I've read says they mate for life. Everything you've told me about the wolves you're trying to catch says the same thing. Is it true? I want to know what you think. I want to talk to you about wolves when you get home. I'll tell you what I think right now. I think it is so fine that such a great, primitive creature would be so loyal and sensitive and sensible as to mate for life. In two books I have read so far, they say wolves mate for life because the extended family structure that develops with each pack helps them to hunt and to protect themselves and to survive. I suppose that's all true. But I believe they also stay together for life because they like each other, and enjoy each other, and because they care. Probably not like us. They care like wolves. And so they stay together for life. Of course the male wolf found his mate that you have hidden away at your little farm. He couldn't be without her just because you and that awful storm have interfered. He still cares. And finding her, I expect that's not very difficult for a wolf, though it seems a mystery to us. I think of what he has done to find her, and I hear his howl in the storm, and I think: *el lobo - qué macho!* It seems that wolves have a great deal of knowledge that is beyond our comprehension. In the books, the scientists keep saying that the so-called intelligence of wolves is really just sophisticated animal behavior based on instincts. If that's true, their instincts are still in many ways better than ours. Their behavior, too. If we could only know wolves a little better, think what we could learn!

I saw Ted downtown the other day and of course he asked about you. He always says, "How's Harley doing?" And I always say you're doing fine, "so far as I know." Then he always smiles. He never asks where you are or what you're doing. I'm sure he doesn't know any more than what I tell him, which isn't anything really, but it's obvious from his smile that he knows you're up to something. I get the feeling he understands you very well. He's been very kind to Jessica and I. He calls every now and then to see how we are and last week he and Sharon had us over for dinner. You're lucky, Harley, to have such a fine friend as Ted.

You will be interested in knowing that the dam is very much the talk of the town, the more so as the (anticipated) construction draws nearer. It seems the *Region* has an update on things every few days. Rich Pennerman has had several editorials concerning the "multiple use benefits" that the town will enjoy once roads are built and access that part of the forest. He has also expressed in these editorials a good deal of excitement over mineral deposits that are believed to exist in canyon country along the river. He is sure the development of these mineral reserves by Felps-Dodd will greatly expand and prolong mining in the area, and he's continually upset that the influence of "preservationists" is delaying development. Of course, it's well known that Pennerman is much more enthusiastic about the mining possibilities than the dam itself (Sidney told me that Rich acknowledged to him once in private that the dam was a "pork barrel"). I really think Rich understands more, and could have a broader vision, than the rest of them. But, as usual, he's carrying the concerns and interests of Felps-Dodd to the public through the newspaper's editorials and news "stories" which, as you know, are often cleverly disguised editorials on the front page. All of this editorializing has Jim Bo and Garth and Bubba Baer and Morey at a fever pitch as well. That whole crowd has begun to lobby very hard for road construction to begin. They want the Bureau of Reclamation to immediately subcontract the road construction to Bubba, to begin to widen and pave Gavilán Road and extend it into the forest, over the divide to the dam site. Jim Bo was quoted as saying, "The Reclamation people could have their equipment in there, ready to start, by the time they get those water weasels out of there." I was particularly concerned because if they widen the road it could eliminate the house of La Señora Hidalgo. And Ted's hands are tied. He told me that the entire Department of Wildlife has been instructed by the Governor not to make public comments on the issue and to "get the otters out of there as soon as possible." Then Ted told me, "Those sons-a-bitches" (he calls them the same thing you do!) "are going to have to wait." He said the U. S. Fish & Wildlife Service has taken control of the mitigation plan and has held firm against the Bureau of Reclamation so that nothing will be done on the project until September first. Through all of this, Sidney remains remarkably upbeat. He told me that his business remains good, in spite of the fact that he has been virtually frozen out by the Chamber of Commerce, and the business community. In a letter printed in the *Region* he wrote that he was "cheered" by the local turnout at the public hearing and said: "The right people are here, but the old guard business community has come to believe they *are* the town." According to Sidney, that crowd, the old guard, is merely a "special interest group." He said they should have input on the communities' agenda, but, "they should not be allowed to define it." He plans a run for City Council next fall. He said it's just a matter of time until what he calls a "concern for amenities" becomes a real part of community action. He talks about things like sign ordinances, strict subdivision regulations, historic preservation, open space planning and urban parks, promotion of the arts, and pressuring Felps-Dodd to stop dumping their by-products into our air and water - all anathema to the old guard. "It may be too late to stop the dam, but it's not too late to save the town," - thus sayeth Sir Sidney. I'm going to vote for him!

And now I must tell you about Jessica, that little sneak. You put me in a somewhat difficult position Harley, when you asked me not to tell anyone anything. I don't like lying to my own daughter. But I have. I've been telling her that I don't know where you are but that you will be coming home some day soon and we'll all be together. You can imagine that was not good enough for Jessica. And I didn't know it but one day she found one of your letters and she wrote down the post mark. Later that day I was at the kitchen table and she was in the living room, stretched out on the carpet, and I saw she was going through the road atlas. It didn't take long for her to come prancing up to the table with the map opened out to the state of Minnesota and she said: "That's where he is, mommy!" She was pointing her finger to the town of Winter Road. Jessica is a very smart and independent little girl. She is going to be the devil to handle when she gets to be a teenager and decides she wants to grow up all at once. She is already growing up too fast to suit me. And yet I love her spirit. Anyway, I couldn't lie to her anymore. So now she knows where you are and that you're on a hunting trip, but she doesn't know what you're hunting. And I told her that if she told anyone anything you would be very upset. She thinks so much of you, I knew that was the best way to assure her silence.

What little remains of my life after the mine and Jessica I have been spending "at the wall." There are times when finishing the wall seems as awesome to me as catching the wolves seems to you. The wall must enclose three full lots, with the house being the fourth. The bricks go up just one at a time and I have to make each one myself, from scratch. But I like it. I love it. It's the best therapy for me, for I can work with my hands and work up a sweat even on a cold day. Each block is progress and I find it helps if I don't look at the end, which is still a long way around, but instead focus on the space filled by each brick. My loneliness builds each hour as I drive my truck, and then I work it off with each brick at home, "at the wall." Then I lay in the hot tub and soak and, except for missing you, I'm okay. Nothing can stop me from missing you but working "at the wall" takes the edge away. I'm going to get it done, Harley, and I'm going to do it myself. Except for Jessica, nothing I've ever done has given me such satisfaction. Maybe that's why I did something very daring this week. At least it's very daring for me. Harley, I bought a house! I mean I really bought one, not just acquired one through the family. Do you remember that little run-down adobe two blocks up, at Sonora and Fourth? I know you've seen it because there's an old horse trough out front on the street, one of the last left in town. It's a small house and the edges of the bricks have worn away but it's still sound. The backyard is big and has lots of possibilities but it's all over-grown in weeds and brush. Inside are all these tiny rooms, like a maze. Neat! The place has been empty and for sale forever. I called the owner and asked how much and he said, "Make an offer." That put me on the spot! I quick called my uncle and he said, "Offer him $10,000 cash and he'll run over with the papers before you can change your mind." That sounded like a very good buy to me but I asked my uncle where he thought I would get $10,000 cash. He said he would loan it to me and I could pay it back when I sold it. And he told me whenever I got stuck on fixing it up, he'd help me just like he has here. He said when I got it fixed up to add $5,000 to the sale price and whatever my expenses are and it would sell within six months because he knows I'll have it looking quaint and cute. He was right about the deal; the owner couldn't wait to get the cash and get it all down in writing. So now I have an extra incentive to finish the wall and the *placita* so I can go to work on my new house and make $5,000. Harley, that's what I want to do, when I can break away from the mines. This old town is full of neat old houses, and while everyone is rushing to the subdivisions of Del Cobre, these neat old houses, which have character and are so much more interesting (at least to interesting people), are in decline. I can do with them basically the same thing I've done to my own house here. It could be more than therapy. It could be my living. Do you think I could do it? Would you help me? I don't mean with the work. You have your own work. I mean helping me to believe I could do that. Your support would be important to me. The best part of this town is all the old buildings. I would like to help preserve some of that so it won't be lost forever. What Sidney has done downtown has impressed people; it's catching on. Maybe what I'm doing will catch in the older residential areas.

Now Harley, I want to tell you to never worry about writing me a "sappy" letter, you silly boy. I like all that mushy stuff from you. It's a part of you that you have never given me. But I've always wanted it and now I see it's there and I want you to give it to me. And that's not all I want. Since we are starting anew, I will want to guide your hands so you can come to know me all over again. And you will do the same for me. And I long to hear you when I bring that tremendous stuff pumping up and out of that lovely smooth fascinating thing of yours, every way, again and again. I want some of it to make a baby. I want the rest of it for myself. Do you remember when we went alone, down along the river? Do you think about it like I do? Will you take me there again? Such earthy pleasures there. Only there, with you, have I felt that anything could be done, and that nothing could be hidden. Do you remember how hot it was in the middle of the day, with all the heat from the canyon walls coming down on us! So we lay in the current. I was on you and you were in me. My breasts ached so, I thought they would come. That's where it started. But it didn't stop there. I could feel it coming, in every part of me, until it focused, coming down in a rush all over your prime and urgent cock. And I could never put in print all we did. And yet I wanted to do even more. But it wasn't right. Next time it will be. I can't write about those things. I can't speak of them. I'm all flushed and feeling kind of funny already. But next time will be soon and that's my dream and when it's time nothing will stop us from doing it again.

It's late Harley. By the time you read this your great hunt will be over, one way or another. I can imagine that it's over now. You must know I have been sending you my love and strength every day. But I wonder so, what has happened?

*pensando en tí,*

Suzie

*Chapter 37*

IN THE EARLY MORNING DARKNESS the house was quiet and the wind outside was utterly still. He lay for a time on the bed in the soothing warmth of the sleeping bag, and a part of him wished for the wild winds that had kept him for four days from having to face the long hunt. As it was he had not succeeded. But he had not yet failed, either. It almost would have been easier to lay there, and let one more day go by. And maybe another. But it had to be done.

By the fire, he ensconced himself in clean, long, woolen underwear, then the checked wool shirt, woolen lumberjack pants, wool sweater over the shirt, and the scarf. The Sorrels went on over two pair of wool socks. His stomach was too tight to eat. He put chunks of cheese, the thermos of coffee and other "possibles" into the rucksack. He put on his wool coat, slung the rucksack over his shoulders, took the snowshoes off the wall and stepped out into the yard with the hounds. He shined the flashlight at the thermometer - 14 degrees below zero. It was the warmest six A.M. he'd seen in weeks. "Pups, this cold snap may break yet. You won't have any trouble with the track."

A half mile up the Winter Road River, showshoeing over great billows of perfect white snow, he came to the place where the wolf broke out of the drift where he'd slept, his tracks and great stride heading west and south up the frozen stream. Harley held the light on the tracks, holding the hounds, necked together, with the other. Then he flicked off the light and dropped to his knees.

"Now listen you two. You've got to run him like a bear. Like a big mean bear that won't tree. He's faster and can run farther than any bear but I think you can catch him. He can't possibly run any further than some of the coyotes we've caught. But that's just the beginning. You'll never hold him the first time you catch. You got to sting him and bother him and rattle him and bay in his ear, till he runs again. Then you'll have to catch him again. Lurk, you dummy, if you try to take him down he's gonna tear you up. You've got to understand that by now. You run him and you catch him and then you run and catch him again, till he can't run any more. Then you can hold him. I'll get there, and we'll take him down. Do your job, but don't get yourselves killed."

Harley reached and unsnapped the swivels that held the hounds together. They turned immediately and found the wolf bed and then the wolf track in the dark. They sounded off - they had scent - and Harley could hear the fear and excitement in their voices. Geraldine went off up the river -aaaoooOOO! aaaoooOOO! - with Lurk squalling behind and the race was on.

It was good light when they caught the wolf the first time. Harley had followed the signs of the chase in the snow and the sounds of the chase in the breathless air, running on his webs when terrain permitted, bushwacking through the timber when it didn't, and he suspected as he approached that they had not so much caught the wolf as that the wolf was simply not much afraid of the dogs. Harley got close, but not close enough to see the catch. Then he heard the race run off again. He thought: he's winded me; he knows there's a man in the race now, and he won't stop again until they force him to bay up. Harley mushed on then, hour after hour, lifting and plodding, lifting and running on his webs, always listening to know what was happening ahead, cutting cross country, off the track of the race, to stay within sound, knowing the hunt was over if he lost the pursuit, a zig-zag course that nonetheless went ever west and south, deeper into the Minnesota wilderness, through aspen glades, birch forests, spruce and tamarack swamps and the terrible alder brush, pushing, sweating under his woolens in below zero air, cursing at times and always wishing to Christ they'd catch again, knowing, the further they went, that it was going to be a long, long race. It was mid-afternoon and they had still not made an honest catch when he saw the wolf. Harley stood on the edge of the peat bog, the broad expanse of swale grass entirely covered by snow. He had stopped there, requiring rest and realizing that he must eat. He cut slices of cheese and bolted them down, then poured a cup of coffee from the jug. Eating, and drinking the wonderful black brew, he felt strength coming back, and realized that he should have done so hours before. As always he was listening, sounding in on the race. Lurk led the chase, as he had since the first mile. He still sounded frantic, afraid, strong and determined. Geraldine was back some, but still very much in the race, close enough to help should Lurk overtake the wolf. Then with a swell of rising anticipation, Harley heard the race come round; the zig-zag course of the fleeing wolf was peeling off into its first circle, first signs that pursuit was wearing the prey down. And then the wolf was in the field, crossing at a full gallop in sun brilliant on the snow, bucking the snow into sprays of white fluff each time he landed, splashing a cascade of powdery snow into the air as he leaped ahead; like a great fish he leaped and landed, stride on stride. Lurk had been unable to catch him because the wolf was in his element, at home in the woods and deep snow, powerful in flight, carried on through his homeland by the strength of centuries of unaided survival, and his wild indomitable spirit. And then Lurk, big and dark and rough-coated against the snow; as he drew nearer Harley could see the icicles hanging and tossing from the hounds beard; he heard the squall-chop ring out, one per leap; he was running up the wolf's track with his awesome greyhound leaps; he had a spirit of his own, almost a wolf himself in pursuit. Then the little gyp, nearly lost in the deep snow but still sprightly and strong, half their size but entirely their equal in grit - aaaoooOOO! aaaoooOOO! aaaoooOOO! The hounds would surely gain strength, knowing he was there. He wanted them to know. But he was calling to all of them as he shouted across the snow-covered field: "Run! Goddamnit run! God-damnit run you sons-a-bitches!"

Near dark clouds came in over the forest and it began to snow. Just past dark Lurk caught the wolf. Within seconds, Geraldine was there. Harley was still with the race; he heard the race come to a standoff. He stopped and drew his knife and cut a stout green aspen sapling. Then he approached the wolf. He got close enough, had it been daylight, to see the wolf; then the wolf broke away. He ran two more hours, always circling now, before they could bay him up again. And again Harley approached, and again the wolf broke away and ran. An hour later, it happened again. Then, in less then an hour, it happened again...and again...and again...

Harley flicked on the flashlight and put the beam on his watch. It was past midnight. Ahead, no more than 100 yards, the wolf and two hounds rested in the snow. The race was over, but it was still not clear who had won. The hounds were largely silent now. Harley had not heard Lurk make a sound in hours. He knew from the tracks that the big hound was still there. Occasionally, Geraldine sounded - woooo-woo! - keeping Harley in contact. The wolf would be close to that point of exhaustion that would cause him to yield. Harley thought: he's got to set back in a drift and wait for me this time. But he had thought that for hours, and each time, as the sound or scent of man approached the catch, the wolf found the strength and spirit to break away. Exhausted, still breaking trail for the hounds, he was soon caught. By the time Harley could get there, he was ready to run again. Harley thought: the hounds are too much afraid of him now; now they need to attack. Harley shined the flashlight beam up into the trees. He watched the snow fall through the light. It was snowing quite hard now, the snow falling nearly straight down. And it had gotten warm. Relatively warm. Harley removed his mitten and held his hand in the air. The snow flakes did not feel cold. The air was warmer than any air he had known in Minnesota. The cold snap had broken. Harley flicked off the light and looked again up at the snow falling out of the sky. There was a full moon above the weather and the snow was twirling thickly in the weak light in the sky. He noticed there was a slight drift to the snow; not much, but a trace of breeze, enough to carry sound and scent. Harley thought: I've got to get downwind, then come in on the wolf; if I'm there, they'll jump him; it's time to take him down. Harley marked what breeze there was and drifted with it, moving slowly, with precision, on his webs, trying hard not to make a sound, moving with the wind, circling downwind of where he'd last heard the hound. It was easy to move quietly in the snow, on snowshoes, and there was open forest as he circled and began his approach. He placed each web carefully, using the paltry moonlight to see ahead, keeping the gentle breeze in his face for, it seemed, hours. When next he heard Geraldine, the little gyp nearly stopped his heart - she was right there! He flicked on the light, and so was the wolf! For an instant Harley had the light on the wolf's yellow eyes, and then the wolf whirled and leaped away, leaving his empty form in the snow. Harley whooped and in three bounds Lurk landed on the wolf's back. The wolf was down in the snow, then he was up, twisting, and popping his teeth. Geraldine got him behind the ear, took a bulldog grip as Lurk grabbed a haunch and they strung him out, long enough for Harley, springing forward on his webs, to fall on the wolf and slap the thick green sapling crosswise into the wolf's mouth. The wolf bit deep into the wood but his body largely ceased to struggle as the hounds held their grips and Harley straddled his brisket. Holding the flashlight in his mouth, he drew a rawhide cord from his coat pocket and began to wrap up the open jaws, tight to the stick. He worked and wrapped, then half-hitched and there was no longer any danger from the wolf. Keeping his weight on the wolf, he drew two more cords and hog-tied the front and back feet, as he had the bitch. The race was won.

Harley stood and leaned against a tree to rest in the falling snow. In time, he put the beam of the flashlight on his watch. It was now two o'clock in the morning. He took the time to contemplate the fact that he had no idea where he was. He thought of the old man, his father, who never carried a compass. The old man never carried one because he never needed one, not in a blizzard, not in strange country, not on a moonless night. Deep in the Minnesota bush, lacking that primal sixth sense, Harley wished he had a compass. He checked the snowfall with the beam. The light breeze, the warm air, the wet, heavy snowfall made him think it was all coming out of the southeast. If that were true, he could head at an angle off to the northeast; surely that was the direction home. But this was all guesswork and Harley knew it; he might guess wrong. If he did, he might not see home, he might not see a road, for days. He shined the flashlight at Lurk. The great hound lay curled up tight, exhausted, new white flakes rapidly covering his coat. He lay close to the hapless wolf; you might have thought they were friends. Harley hoped he wasn't going to have to carry Lurk out, too. He shined the flashlight on Geraldine. She sat up in the snow, shivering but alert; she had a lot more left than Lurk, or any of them. She whimpered and walked up to Harley and stood on her hind legs and put her paws up on the front of his coat. She was ready to go home and it occurred to Harley suddenly that she might well know the way. "Go girl. Take us home. Go home girl." The hound dropped down to all fours and without hesitation or any sign of human confusion turned and headed off into the bush. Harley squatted down by the wolf, lifted the animal up and with a lurch of strength lay him across his shoulders. Then he stood up. It was about like hefting Lurk. Harley followed the little hound into the near dark and falling snow. Lurk stepped into Harley's snowshoe flow and came along.

He had to stop. He set the wolf down and stood and flexed and tried to get some of the stiffness and knots of pain out of his legs, back and shoulders. He shined the beam once again on his watch. It was four o'clock in the morning. He shined the flashlight around him and saw what had happened to the terrain. For some time he had seen few trees, very little brush. He thought he was crossing a peat bog. Harley could see now it wasn't a peat bog. The snow he'd been crossing covered ice and the ice covered water. The large white mound not far away, vague in the falling snow, had to be a beaver house. The hound had led them into a big watery swamp, frozen over in winter, perhaps a pond in summer, almost a lake. Harley thought: if she's right, I know where I am. Ahead, Geraldine was already walking out of sight of the light, stepping precisely through the snow, purposeful. Harley went down and shouldered the wolf once again and stepped into the tracks of the hound. Before long, in a marvelous change of terrain, the ice covered swamp funnelled into the winding course of a frozen stream. Of course the Walker dog had known where she was all along. Even Harley could find his way now. She had put him right on the road, the winter road, home.

It was good light when Harley took the final steps up to the barn door. He dropped the wolf in the snow, bent over, and loosened the bindings on his snowshoes. He kicked them off. His legs and back were no worse but there were terrible knots of muscle in his shoulders. It didn't matter; he had the wolf home. He removed his mittens, then reached down and gathered up the defeated carcass in his arms and carried the wolf into the barn. His arms were full but his fingers were free and he flicked on the barn light, loosened the latch and stepped into the wolf pen. The bitch ducked into her wolf house as he dumped the male wolf onto a patch of straw on the floor of the pen. The bitch turned around in the house and when Harley looked up she was watching with immense interest from the door of the house. Her ears were up and her eyes and nose registered recognition as well. But she was too afraid of the man to move. Harley straddled the male wolf and drew his knife. With three quick cuts he released the front feet, the back feet, and then the jaws. Then he jumped to the doorway of the pen. The wolf lay there. Then, showing some life, he used his front paws to loosen the green aspen stick imbedded in his jaws. He rolled to his feet and limped on swollen paws towards a large bed of straw on the far side of the pen. The bitch came out, sprightly, wagged her tail, then went down on her back, exposing herself. He nosed her undersides, wagged weakly, then went to the straw bed and lay down, watching the door where Harley stood. Harley said, "Hard guy, huh? All that howling in the wind and now you play it cool. Lighten up, big boy, you're home."

Harley went to the house and brought a bucket of meat scraps and fresh water to the wolves. Back at the house he got the wood stove go-

228

ing, then he mixed meat scraps and dry dog food and hot water for the hounds. Geraldine stood in the kitchen, waiting eagerly for the meal. Lurk lay on the kitchen floor; he raised his head to smell the food but would not get up. Harley felt of his neck, the wound, felt some swelling, some seepage under the stitches. He raised a lip. The gums were pink, almost red. Lurk was okay. But he was seriously exhausted; more worn down even than Harley, or the wolf. Harley got the big hound to his feet. The big hound ate well enough. Geraldine ate the rest, till she drummed out. Then Harley thought about himself. He had never been so hungry; even the meat scraps and dog food smelled good. He had never needed food and rest so much. Food must come first. He took a frozen steak from the old ice box on the back porch and put it in the skillet. He watched and smelled it thaw and cook. He made a pot of fresh coffee on the stove. When the steak was nearly done, he cracked three eggs into the skillet. They cooked quickly, he rolled them briefly, then all went on the plate with two pieces of hot bread. He ate with great care, savoring everything, never looked up and never thought about anything but eating till he'd sopped up the last and drained the pot. In the living room, the hounds were curled up in front of the fireplace. The wood stove in the basement was pumping good heat into the house but Harley wanted very much for them to have a fire to sleep by. He placed kindling over paper and got the fire going. He placed split birch logs, well cured, over the flames and went to the bedroom and got his sleeping bag and brought it into the living room and lay it out in front of the fire, on the rug, between the big rough-coated hound and the little gyp. He stripped down to his long underwear and worked his way down deep into the bedroll. He lay on his back and he could hear the hounds breathing and the pop and crackle from the fire. He felt sleep coming on. He didn't need to fight exhaustion any more. He let the sleep come. Outside, the benevolent snow fell, straight down, heavy, covering everything in perfect white. Such had the temperature risen, the big white flakes were almost warm.

### Chapter 38

THE CHANGE FROM WINTER TO SPRING in the deep north woods is slow in coming. For those who've had enough of below zero weather and drifts that reach to the window sills (this includes most everyone) it is sometimes agonizingly slow, and there are many setbacks. Premature thaws may be followed by the coldest days of winter with another icy blast and fresh new drifts. March 21st, the first day of spring, may look like winter incarnate. But the change to spring is ineluctable, and once it turns the corner it is profound. All that snow must turn to water; the creeks and rivers fill and flow high and may flood over their banks. Farm fields come up from the snow as giant mud puddles. The woods become swamps. Buds on the trees race to be the first to show; slough grass, swale grass, timothy and alfalfa, wheat and oats, anything that's green and grows comes on green and growing even before the snow is gone. Meanwhile, the very short days of winter are yielding fast to the very long days of summer.

Harley stood in the wet yard in rubber boots. Spring had turned the corner in Tamarack County and Harley Simmons had a bad case of spring fever, another bad case of cabin fever, and a pregnant bitch wolf in the barn. He also had a problem. His season was over. He had come to the north woods to hunt fur and there was no more fur to hunt. In early March the coyote and fox had started to rub and by late March even the early coon, emerging from hibernation, were showing signs they should no longer be taken. And the season on cats was legally over. Harley had no reason to stay any longer, at least none that he could reveal. For himself, he wanted to stay until he had wolf puppies about three to four weeks old. Old enough to travel but young enough to handle. He had a place in mind in New Mexico where he wanted a pair of Timber Wolves and their family to make their home. He wanted all these wolves to stay where he put them. It was a den designed by nature for wolves. A place where wolves would be safe and yet, in another sense, very much in the way. A litter of wolf pups, placed in that wolf den, would cause their parents to set up housekeeping in the perfect place. That was Harley's plan. But to carry it out he had to stay in northern Minnesota well past the fur season, which was about over. He could think of no reason that would keep him in northern Minnesota well past the fur season; no reason that would not arouse suspicion. Especially in the mind of a game warden with a nose like a hound for suspicious behavior. Harley had to think of something. And he knew he had to get out of the house for a few hours. Spring was in the air, the snow was melting, the ice was breaking up and, with the fur season over, he could no longer occupy himself with hunting. Harley had cabin fever and spring fever and he had to think of something so, one evening at the end of March, he got in his truck and headed for town.

There was one honky-tonk in Winter Road, Minnesota, the Municipal Liquor Store, and it was full of people. Harley walked by the bar into the next room where the booths were filled with serious drinkers. The clientele was variegated, but not unusual: businessmen, farmers, farm hands, loggers, red necks, long-hairs, women, lonely hearts, burnt-outs, and the unemployed. One thing Harley didn't expect to find in the Winter Road Municipal Bar was The Law. But when he heard someone behind him calling his name, the voice was alarmingly familiar. For a moment Harley thought, or hoped, he was mistaken. But no...

"Over here, Simmons. Sit down."

Harley turned around. Hilding Thomsen, District Warden, had a booth to himself. He had on the same cap but with the ear muffs tied over the top. Otherwise, he was out of uniform. His long, florid, expressionless face was it's usual ruddy red. Around his blue eyes, the rims were even redder. His long, slightly stooped form hunched over a shot, a beer, and a newspaper. The District Warden was a little bit drunk.

"Don't look so surprised, Simmons. Once in a while the bull gets out of the barn. What'll you have?"

"Grain Belt," Harley said as he slid in the booth opposite The Law.

The warden signaled a waitress who soon brought Harley a bottle of Grain Belt beer. The warden's money was laid out in several bills on the table and he paid. Harley very much needed a drink. He slowly but steadily poured about half the bottle down before he stopped and looked across the table at the warden. The warden was expressionless but was sliding the newspaper across the table for his perusal. "What do you think of that, Simmons?" the warden said.

## WOLVES THREATEN PEAT PROJECT

DULUTH - *A mining proposal for peat gasification that could bring a major industry to a depressed county in northwest Minnesota may fall prey to an endangered species, a recent U. S. Fish & Wildlife Service report indicates.*

*The report, issued from the U. S. Fish & Wildlife Service office here Monday, said, "...the Fish & Wildlife Service does not regard large scale surface mining in Tamarack County as compatible with the critical habitat protection authorized for an endangered species, in this case the Minnesota Timber Wolf."*

*The report further states that, "the proposed re-introduction of the Woodland Caribou would also be adversely affected by development of peat bogs," and, "...should development proceed, full reclamation of affected lands would be required."*

*All this, plus other information and policy guidelines contained in the report, was bad news to James Yardley, president of Peat-Gas Inc. of Minneapolis.*

*"Our prospectus has shown a slim margin of profit at best," Yardley said. "Additional expenditures resulting from environmental hassles with Timber Wolves and other wildlife wouldn't leave us with anything to work with."*

*Plans for peat gasification in northwest Minnesota stem from studies first done in the 1950's by...*

Harley had the jist of it and returned the newspaper to the warden. He really didn't want to talk about Timber Wolves. He said, "I didn't know peat was worth anything."

"It isn't. But you know how people are. If Tamarack County was covered with loon shit some corporation would be after it. I'd say the Service is doing those guys a favor. But how 'bout that, Simmons? When I was growing up, wolves were the enemy. Not twenty years ago there was a bounty on wolves in this state. They paid people to kill them. Now you kill one and you go to jail. I've put two people in jail for it myself. Now the wolf is an *endangered species*. I don't care about that peat project. If I wanted to be close to major industry I'd move to Minneapolis/St. Paul; they've got plenty for the whole state. But ain't that something! You get an endangered species in an area, it seems like everything stops."

"That's what I've heard."

The warden shook his head in disbelief, then raised his shot glass high and turned it upside down in his mouth. He let the whiskey go down and made a sour face. Then he chased it with a long swallow of beer. Harley turned aside, tried to collect himself, and took a long swallow from his own bottle. When he looked back the warden for the first time was not without expression. The warden was smiling at him. The warden's smile was almost impish. In a game warden, that's scary.

"Simmons, I may as well tell you right now...I had you way last winter."

Harley thought: OH SHIT. He fought off the raw grip in the pit of his stomach and said as casually as he could: "How's that, Thomsen?"

"I found your truck one morning along County Road Four. I saw where you and those two hounds went in on a coyote track, headed south. I saw where you crossed the forest road, three miles south, still going. I saw where you and the dogs and that Brush Wolf circled back north and headed into that big birch stand. That's where you got him. Then I saw where you came back out on the county road and I spied you walking down the road back to your truck. You had that Brush Wolf slung over your shoulder, and over your coat you had a revolver and cartridge belt, strapped around your waist. You had two Snowshoe Hares hanging from that cartridge belt. Oh, I had you Simmons. I had you right there."

"I don't get it."

"Simmons, the Snowshoe Hare is a game animal in Minnesota. You can't shoot a game animal in Minnesota with a handgun."

"Why the hell not?"

"Minneapolis/St. Paul, that's why not. The laws of this state are made in Minneapolis/St. Paul. They don't like handguns in Minneapolis/St. Paul. They do whatever they can to discourage their use, statewide. And that's not all."

"Oh?"

You had a lever action rifle in the front seat of your pickup. I'll bet you the next round it was loaded."

"You win."

"Of course. I knew it was loaded. I had you again, Simmons. You can't do that."

"Don't tell me...Minneapolis/St. Paul."

"That's right. They don't like guns of any kind in our wonderful Twin Cities. They'd like them all to go away. They haven't managed that yet so they do what they can to irritate the people who own them."

"Who wants to be shucking shells and reloading every time you're in and out of your truck? Good way for a hunter to shoot himself in the foot."

"Down in Minneapolis/St. Paul, they don't care if you shoot yourself in the foot. They just want you to know that they think guns are bad, bad. They have lots of crime down there. Violent crime. People are robbing and assaulting and shooting each other all the time. You pack that many people into a few square miles, what do they expect? Some of those people are gonna be warped. If I lived down there, pretty soon I'd be warped too. I'd probably want to shoot somebody. Anyway, I had you Simmons."

Harley thought: he wants me to ask why he didn't tag me. Harley wasn't sure he wanted to know. But the warden asked the question for him.

"Bet you're wondering why I didn't write you up?"

"How come?"

"I don't like Minneapolis/St. Paul. I go by the book Simmons, and don't you forget it. But the book is a little different up here. Up here, I've got my own book. As many hares as there are, I don't care if you shoot one with a pistol or hit it with a rock. Take a deer out of season though, leave you're trapline untended, and I'll make you wish you hadn't. Something else. I know what you did to catch that Brush Wolf. You were ten miles, anyway, on snowshoes, following those hounds, running that coyote down. Nobody hunts like that anymore. Hardly any hounds in the country anymore. Those that have them, follow them on snowmobiles. Nobody bushwhacks anymore. You're all right, Simmons. I've got another reason to think you're all right, too. But that's none of your business."

Harley was glad it was none of his business; he really didn't want to know. And Harley thought: the warden sort of did me a favor; how do you thank a game warden? Harley said, "Well, you were right about the loaded gun, Thomsen," and he bought the next round. When the next round came the warden took the shot of rye and, like before, lifted it high and turned it upside down into his mouth and swallowed it, making a face afterwards, all like it was castor oil. Then he chased it with a long

233

swallow of beer. Harley watched the warden. The warden was definitely getting drunk. But Harley recognized the warden as one who would never go over the line. He would drink to a plateau, and stay there. And remember everything the next day. Harley drank his Grain Belt beer without much assurance. He hadn't planned on a social evening with The Law. He was wishing he'd stayed home, even if the warden had done him a favor. Then, as if by order, the district warden did him another favor, and Harley had reason to change his mind about the company.

"You heading out Simmons? Or staying around for the fur sale?"

Harley thought fast. "Well," he said, "I'm homesick for the mountains, and the fur's all started to rub. But tell me about this sale."

"It's a rendezvous. Second week of May, every year, right here in Winter Road. You'll be seeing the signs around town with the date. Usually have it on the football field, right behind the high school. The school board puts it on. Commission is five percent and it goes to the local school system, so it's a worthy cause. Buyers, hunters and trappers from five states and two provinces come in. You've sold fur, Simmons. Generally, it's one buyer and a bunch of sellers. The sellers have to compete and the prices go down. At this sale, there's a bunch of buyers. They have to compete for the fur and the prices go up. Makes a hell of a difference if you've got a load of fur. And I know you took a load of fur this winter. I hope you didn't sell it."

"I had to sell some of it. I needed some grocery money. Sold to one of those itinerant buyers comes through. I've still got most of it."

"Hold on to it. Stay over for the rendezvous. You'll come out on it. Give you a chance to enjoy the country when it's warm. Watch the birch and the popple and the Tamarack leaf out. Everything greens up. Do some fishing. Stick around, Simmons. You'll come out on that fur sale."

"I might do that. Sounds all right."

The warden caught the waitress again, and picked up the next round. And again, the warden made a sour face when he slid a shot of rye down his throat. And again, he chased it with beer. The warden looked across the table at Harley with his blue, red-rimmed eyes. He had definitely reached that plateau. Then, once more, he put Harley on the spot.

"Simmons, how old do you think I am?"

"Hell, I don't know."

"No, but you've wondered. Everyone wonders a little bit, because it's hard to tell. Ain't that right?"

"You're right, Thomsen; it's hard to tell."

"Take a shot at it."

"Sixty-one."

"Not bad. But just between you, me and the gatepost, I'm sixty-nine years old today. How 'bout that?"

"Happy birthday. You're lookin' good, Thomsen."

"I know it. But take a shot at this. When is the mandatory retirement for a game warden in Minnesota?"

"Hell, I don't know that either."

"Take a shot at it."

"Seventy."

"Sixty-five, Simmons. You retire at sixty-five. Now, the plot gets thick, doesn't it?"

"You're such a hell of a game warden, they made an exception."

"The Minnesota Department of Natural Resources is a bureaucracy. A bureaucracy doesn't make exceptions. A bureaucracy makes rules. In case you haven't figured it out yet, I'm breaking one, every day I'm on the job. Now, you've got one on a game warden. Want to hear about it?"

Harley wasn't sure he wanted to hear about it. But it was obvious the warden wanted to tell him. Harley didn't like confessions. But a confession from a game warden was something else. Harley saw a chance to pack something away for safe keeping.

"I always like a good story, Thomsen. Let's hear it, just you, me, and the gatepost."

The warden shifted in his seat and took another long swallow of beer. Then he said, "My career was in Wisconsin. Thirty five years. Then, five years ago today, I turned sixty-four. Wisconsin is the same as Minnesota. I had one year left on the job. I couldn't stand that. I hate poachers. What I like to do is hunt poachers. Wildlife takes a terrible beating from poachers, every year, in every state. There's a certain number of people are greedy; they don't know when to quit; they don't care to know what you mean by *limit*, they don't know to leave something to seed. Hunting poachers makes me feel like I've done something visible for wildlife. Every one I nail leaves that much game to carry on. With all the firepower and machinery poachers have today, they'd kill it all if they could get away with it. I'm real good at hunting poachers. When I don't hunt poachers, I got nothing to do. I haven't hunted animals in years. Got to where I couldn't pull the trigger anymore. I never fished much. I don't have the patience. What would I do without poachers to hunt? When I got the idea I went to my wife for help. At first she wouldn't hear of it. But I talked her into it; made the poor woman an accomplice. I got my file out, quiet like. My wife is a wonderful artist. All we had to do was change the date of birth in a couple of places. The way she did it, you couldn't tell even if you were suspicious, and nobody was looking for it after thirty five years and a perfect record. I resigned from the Wisconsin agency and we moved to Minnesota on a pretense. I sent my resume and application to St. Paul. Told them I was fifty-nine...that's what my file said. They picked me up right away. Made me district warden. I snitched five years from two states. Got one on the bureaucracy. I've got one year left now, Simmons, then I'm sixty-five in Minnesota, too. Then what? What do I do then, Simmons?"

"Move to North Dakota and tell them you're fifty-nine."

The warden grabbed his hat and swatted Harley on the shoulder. "Goddamn Simmons, you're all right! I like that. But it isn't going to work. I'm getting too goddamn old. I know it. It's got to run out sometime. I want to leave with a clean record, even if some of it's phoney. One year from today. That's my last day. And when my work's done, I'll come in here and get drunk. Just like this. I'm not going to fight it anymore. And I have thought of one thing I can do when it's over. I'm going to write a book, Simmons. I'll probably just sort of talk it out and have my wife put it down so it makes sense. She'd enjoy that. I'm going to tell how everything has changed in forty years. When I started out there was a breed of hunters and trappers in the north woods. Not all of them operated legally but there was something to admire in all of them. They didn't cheat. Even when they were illegal, they didn't cheat. They hunted, fished, trapped and bushwhacked like it had been done for hundreds of years. Not anymore. Nobody bushwhacks anymore. The trapper drives around and tends his traps. The deer hunter drives around and hunts deer. The coyote hunter has a snowmobile, the fisherman has a fish finder, the duck hunter motors around in a power boat and hunts ducks. Some of them are legal. But they all cheat. Nobody bushwhacks anymore."

Harley said, "Sounds like a book I'd like to read. Don't forget to include in there how you snitched five years from the bureaucracy. That will make it sell in two states at least."

The warden hauled off and started to laugh. He laughed outloud and he laughed hard and long, till the tears came out of his blue, red-rimmed eyes. When he got it back he wiped the tears off his face and finished his beer. Then he gathered up all his bills but one, leaving a five dollar tip.

"You're all right Simmons. But keep this in mind. Those gun laws they make downstate aren't just for game wardens to enforce. A deputy, a state cop, a town cop; any one of them will check your guns. Drop the clip out of that carbine when you have it in your vehicle. And take that revolver, unload it, and put it under the seat where nobody will see it till you get back to New Mexico."

Harley said, "Sounds like good advice."

"You take care, Simmons," the warden said. "If I don't run into you back in the swamp somewhere, I'll see you at the rendezvous."

The warden stood up. He was a little more stooped than usual, but he was still the tallest person in the room.

"Give you a ride, Thomsen."

"No thanks. I live in town. I walked over here and I can walk home. Do an old man good."

The district warden walked out. Harley felt his heart beat coming back down and the grip go off his stomach. He ordered one more Grain Belt beer. He could enjoy one now.

*Chapter 39*

EACH MORNING he waited with patience and as much quiet as possible outside the door of the wolf pen, listening for pups. Conception would have occurred, as best he could figure, the last week of February. One morning, two months later and right on schedule, he heard the squeaking, whimpering and suckling sounds that told him two Timber Wolves were now a family. He listened with satisfaction for several minutes, then stepped in as he always did to clean the pen. He thought: they may run me out of here now that they have pups. But the door of the pen was at the far end from the wolf house, and that's where the pen needed cleaning. Harley watched the wolves while he completed his short work. The bitch was in the wolf house with the pups; it was a large wolf house and the bitch and pups were well back in it and the pups could not be seen. But Harley could hear the constant activity of wolf pups struggling for food and he could hear the bitch licking pups with her big wolf tongue. The male lay by the door of the wolf house and watched Harley. The male was far enough away that Harley figured, or at least had a confident hope, that he could hop through the pen door and close it if the wolf made a rush in defense. But there was no need. Each morning the male wolf was on guard near the wolf house and each morning Harley and the wolf eyed each other without incident.

At two weeks Harley got to see them. One by one they staggered a short way out of the wolf house, comical on wobbly legs; they tried to tussle and one by one they fell over. When Harley stepped in to clean the pen the wolf pups stopped their ridiculous play, sat up and looked towards the intruder. Their eyes were open now, they were black eyes, and they did not see very well. The pups heard him, and perhaps smelled him, more than they saw him. But they already knew he was there. Later Harley crouched outside the door, peaking through the crack, counting and making mental notes.

There were six puppies. The colors and patterns of their coats would evolve as they matured but already Harley could see what they would be. The largest pup was nearly white. This would likely be a male pup, though not necessarily so; Harley could not tell their sex when they were this age without an examination he was not permitted to give. Harley imagined that this pup was a male; he would mature at close to 100 pounds, as large as his father or perhaps a bit more, but coated the palest grey, like his mother. He thought: I will call this pup Blanco. There was a small pup that was a shiny black. This was easily the smallest pup in the litter, almost a runt. Harley imagined that this was a female and that she would keep her dark coat; taking color to the forests of the great Southwest very much like her grandfather, the huge black male that led a pack in Tamarack County. Harley was not worried about this small pup. Though small she - if it was a she - was already very aggressive and clearly more agile than her larger brothers and sisters. She was very bold and explored the pen ahead of any of them. She held her own in tussles with her littermates and Harley was confident she held her own at the food faucets, too. Harley imagined that she would one day bear pups who would carry her talents to the remote regions of the Southwest, and he called her Fiesta. Four other puppies were darker grey wolves, nearly identical in color and size, and colored not unlike their father. Three of these Harley had trouble telling apart, they were so alike. One was identifiable because he tended to keep to himself. He didn't care to play as the others did, and when he did play he tended to lose his temper, growling rather ferociously for a tyke who was just up on his feet, then going off by himself. He was an outcast; he cast himself out. Harley thought: if he was a kid, they'd have to send him to a special school. He appeared as healthy, if not as happy, as the others; Harley called him Lonesome and figured he would grow up to be a lone wolf and did not worry about his lack of social graces. Harley did not worry about any of these puppies. They all appeared healthy and sound, their mother, who played with them now and fed them outside the wolf house, had plenty of milk, and Harley provided both parents with as much meat, much of it freshly killed Snowshoe Hare, as they could eat. And then one morning during their third week of life Harley found the big Blanco puppy dead.

He was a male puppy and he had been cast off with the waste at the far end of the pen. Harley had raised a lot of puppies. As often as not, one or more pups did not survive. But usually, death or at least weakness was evident in the first few days of life. This had been a perfect pup. Harley took the body of this nearly white pup out of the barn into the sunshine of a warm spring day. He felt with great care over the entire body for signs of injury. He examined the nose and mouth for signs of congestion or disease. There was no apparent reason for this puppy's death and because this was a wolf puppy, no professional pathology could be employed. Harley placed the puppy in the grass outside the barn. He removed the large red bandana from his back pocket and spread it out, covering death. Then he went back into the barn, concerned for all his wolves. He watched for most of an hour. There was no sign of weakness or disease or anything but continued good health in the remaining pups, and their parents. Harley left the barn. He got the shovel and took the pup to the ridge along the Winter Road River west of the house. Here he dug the grave, wrapped the pup carefully in the bright print cloth, and buried the pup. He got a large smooth stone from the river and placed it over the grave. Harley sat by the grave, overlooking the river, while the stone, wet from the river, dried in the sun. Below, in the river flush with snow melt, Northern Pike, some of great size, were rushing upstream in their spring migration to their breeding grounds. They were not stream fish. Their haunt was the nearby inland sea, the great Lake of the Woods of Minnesota, Manitoba, and Ontario. Only in spring would Northern Pike work the strong currents, pushing up to the more settled sloughs near the headwaters to breed. Harley sat in the sun on the ridge and watched them through the day. They swam with purpose; they would not be stopped.

## Chapter 40

**HARLEY** could not remember when he had seen nicer fur. One by one the stretched, dried and cured-out pelts - coyote, red fox, coon, Fisher, bobcat and lynx - went into the tub of warm water, shampoo, and then, conditioner. Gently he washed and rinsed each pelt, then hung them to dry. When they had dried he carefully combed, then brushed them out, till they fluffed and were shiny in the sun. When all were done he hung them on the wall of the barn. None of them would grade out less than good, many were excellent, and more than a few were absolutely prime. He ran his fingers through these prime pelts, that no synthetic could match in look, in feel, in the quality of natural warmth. Then Harley crossed the yard from the barn to the house and entered the kitchen. He took fresh hamburger from the refrigerator and packed two handfuls of fresh meat into two baseball-sized pieces. He took one of the tranquilizer pills and inserted it into one piece of meat, and he put two pills into the other piece of meat. The wolves were hungry and out at the barn Harley tossed the meat with one pill to the bitch and the meat with two pills to the male. Each bolted the meat down with a gulp. He went to the barn wall and removed all the pelts and packed them into the back of the truck. Then he went back to the wolf pen. The male was nearly asleep and the bitch was groggy enough that Harley could gather up the pups. He put them in a wooden flat-topped box, made special for their journey to a new home. He would keep them from the bitch whenever he had to set her down with pills, limiting the amount of any chemicals that could pass to them in her milk. He had to chase them down to catch them in the wolf pen and Lonesome and Fiesta growled in their small way and fought. But he got them in the wooden box and closed the lid. They could poke their heads out the top but that was all, and then he left them and went to town.

~ ~ ~ ~ ~ ~

It was a lovely Minnesota day, blue and sunny with warm, soft air; the aspen were leafing out along the road and in town the grass was green on the football field where the rendezvous was in full swing. Harley drove in the parking lot and saw license plates from Minnesota,

North and South Dakota, Iowa, Wisconsin, Ontario and Manitoba. He registered and got a table on which to display his furs. It took him several trips and by the time he got all his fur to his table a buyer was already giving both the fur and their owner the eye. Also there was the district warden, Hilding Thomsen. Harley and the warden made some small talk while the buyer went through the fur. He ran his finger through guard hairs, checked for any sign of rubbing, of fur taken too late. He checked the hide side of the fur for any signs of pelts having been sewn up, and worked his fingers through the pelts and tugged here and there to see that the pelts had been properly scraped and that the fur was sound in the hide. He worked rapidly and selected carefully; he didn't check every pelt for quality but he checked samples and he counted them all. Harley could tell the buyer liked the pelts and that he knew right away they were all good to prime and that they had received meticulous care. The buyer did not want to appear too eager and Harley knew much of the survey was for show. He also determined that this buyer wanted to make a deal before some other buyer got into the act.

"You've got some pretty good fur here," the buyer said finally.

The warden cut in, "Those are top quality pelts and you know it, Jason."

The buyer went on like he hadn't heard the warden. He said, "A few of them were shot and you've sewn them up."

"They were sewn up right," Harley said, "You can't take much off for a few stitches."

Again, the buyer went on like he hadn't heard the response. "I count 31 coyotes, 13 Red Fox, 7 Fisher, 11 coon, 5 bobcats and 3 lynx cats."

"That's right," Harley said.

"All right. I'm going to give you forty each for the Brush Wolves, forty five for the fox, sixty for the Fisher, twenty for the coon, one hundred for the bobcats and one hundred fifty each for those lynx cats."

Harley liked the prices. He knew the buyer was low on the cats but the prices were still better in all ways than he'd received earlier from the itinerant buyer. Harley figured he wouldn't be cheated too bad if he just said yes, but he'd sold enough fur to know that horse trading was mandatory and that only an ignorant buyer would allow his best prices on the first offer. This was not an ignorant buyer. Again, the warden cut in.

"Oh shit, Jason. You want us to call one of those other buyers over here for this boy to get a fair price? Or maybe he'll just pack it all back to New Mexico. They'd fight over this northern fur down there."

Harley added, "If you can't make a big jump on those cats you can quit lookin' at 'em."

The buyer never looked at either man but made a show of going through the fur one more time.

"All right. I'm going to give you fifty each for these coyotes, fifty-five for the fox, eighty for the Fisher, twenty-five for the coon, one hundred fifty for the bobcat and two hundred fifty each for these three lynx cats 'cause they're prime and there ain't a dozen of them here today. If that's not good enough, you can take them to New Mexico for all I care."

The buyer never looked up as he spoke. He kept fondling the fur and so he didn't see the warden wink, but Harley did.

"Write the check," Harley said.

The buyer wrote the check for four thousand six hundred dollars. Harley in turn paid five percent commission out of that amount to the school board that put on the fur sale. At his truck he bid farewell to the warden.

"Simmons, you come back."

"I probably will, Thomsen. Someday I probably will."

"Well don't wait too long; I'm not going to be fit for the woods forever. Come up next winter. I'll put on my snowshoes and go with."

"I might just do that. You take care, and stay young."

"I feel great. I feel five years younger than I really am! You take care Simmons; you're all right."

Harley drove through Winter Road and stopped at the bank where he cashed his check. Then he went out to the homestead. The first thing he did was rake all the straw and the wolf hair and other debris out of the barn and he set it on fire. He got a hammer and he banged away till he'd knocked down the frame walls of the wolf pen. He left the plywood walls piled neatly for whoever lived there next. Then he took the wolf house and he slid it into the back of the truck. He broke a bale of straw and spread some of it out in the back of the truck and he put some in the wolf house. He left several flakes in the corner of the bed of the truck so he could change straw when he needed. Then he took the box full of wolf puppies and put it in the back of the truck. The little black Fiesta pup stuck her head out of the box and yapped at him. They were all wanting out. Their father seemed twice as heavy limp and asleep, but Harley heaved him up into the bed of the truck. The bitch was lying down but was not asleep and Harley was leery of her. He came around behind her with his coat held like a cape and he came down on her and wrapped her head up in his coat. Then he lifted her into the back of the truck. He put a pan of water in the back, pulled the curtains on the windows of the camper shell and shut the door to the camper. Then he went inside the house. He was packed and ready. He made one trip to put his duffle with all his gear in the truck. Then he went back in the kitchen and got his thermos, full of coffee, and let the dogs out. They ran around the yard and pissed and emptied out while Harley checked to make sure he hadn't left anything in the house or barn. Then he locked the door and put the key on the nail under the porch. He went to the truck and opened the door and Geraldine and Lurk leaped into the cab. Harley took one last look at a home he would not forget, then he got in the cab of the truck. He inserted the key and turned it and said, "Be there!" The truck coughed and rumbled to life. Harley put the truck in gear and slowly drove out of the yard and on to the county road where he turned, headed south and west.

~ ~ ~ ~ ~ ~

It was springtime in America. Heading south and west through the boreal forest, the north country flowers lined the forest roads and the aspen and birch displayed their pale green young leaves that would darken through the summer and crisp and yellow in the fall, but these were tender young spring leaves, pale green, and Harley liked the looks of them, fleshing out in the spring; as the pickup sped past on the forest road, it made a breeze that sucked in the limbs and caused the leaves to wave at his passing; and then they were out on the eastern edge of the Great Plains, all the stubble had been plowed under and worked down in the fall and, looking out across the black dirt as he went by, Harley here and there waved at a farmer making one last pass with the cultivator, or spinning out a shower of white nitrogen from the spreader, or drilling oats or spring wheat; then across the Red River and south through the Dakotas; crops were further along and increasingly the black dirt sported narrow rows of green sprouts; he stopped briefly when he needed to buy food or fill the jug with coffee, to piss or stretch and run up and down a side road with the dogs, to clean out the old straw and spread out new fresh and clean, and early on he opened the wooden box and released the hungry, eager, squirmers to their mother who was no longer tranquilized and was heavy with milk; then in the dark through Nebraska and Kansas, and the panhandles of Oklahoma and Texas where crops grew under sprinklers that walked in circles and spread artificial rain; in eastern New Mexico he was on the western edge of the Great Plains and the sun was high and some natural spring rain had greened the range lands; no crops here but prairie grass that rolled on to the last horizon and the truck purred on west into the setting sun; Albuquerque was bright lights at dusk as he descended the twisting canyon highway into the valley and then south on the interstate, following the river; he was in a desert state now but he knew there were cottonwoods along the Río Grande and he wished he could have seen them as he passed in the night; and then he was headed west again, climbing and climbing on into a mountain state; there was a good moon and as he topped out at the pass he could see the silhouettes of the Sierra Negra; it had been two thousand miles since he'd left a piece of the remnant American Wilderness and now he stopped in the chill and dark to smell the mountain air and look of to the great dark humps that rose and fell away in myriad peaks and declinations to the west of the Sierra Negra, another piece of American Wilderness, the Mondragón Range; Del Cobre was quiet and largely asleep at midnight as he rolled in on the strip and turned up Gavilán Road, then left by the old widow's house, across the creek and into the yard; it was midnight and he hadn't slept since the north woods but he still faced a long day this springtime in America.

~ ~ ~ ~ ~ ~

First he tossed a piece of meat with one pill to the hungry bitch. Then he tossed a piece of meat with two pills to the male. He left them in the back of the truck to dope off while he put Geraldine in the pen. He tightened down Lurk's collar a notch and put him on the chain. In the horse trap Ruby and the two horses were sleeping on their feet. They were not shod but with the flashlight Harley noticed that someone - the old woman, Ted maybe - had trimmed their feet. Harley put a lead rope on the mule and the old man's mare and led them to the barn. He put his saddle on the horse first. Then he threw a pack saddle on the mule, cinched her up, adjusted the breast collar and britching, and then he hung one of the big canvas panniers over the forks. They had been the old man's panniers and the old man had made them himself, extra big, to haul out elk quarters and the like, not knowing they'd also be big enough to pack a live wolf. Harley cut leg holes, front and back, in the heavy canvas ducking. Then he went and opened the back of the truck. "Okay big boy," he said, "you're first." Big boy was conked. Harley gathered him up and carried him into the barn to the mule. Ruby flexed her nostrils and rolled her nose at a strange smell she didn't like and when Harley started to lift the wolf up into the pannier he noticed her flex her back and cock her back leg for a forward kick. She hadn't been packed or ridden in months and was inclined to be rank. Harley stepped back and hauled off and kicked her in the stomach. "Cut that out you silly fool!" That took the kink out of her leg and the flex out of her back and he lifted the wolf into the pannier, fitting his legs through the holes, and latched the flap. Then he went to the bitch. She was three sheets to the wind and Harley gathered her up and carried her over to the mule and lifted her into the pannier on the other side. He closed the flap down and then tied his coat and his rifle and other gear on her side to balance the load with the heavier male. He went and got the box full of pups and set it between the forks of the pack saddle, right in the middle on top, and lashed it down. Then he led the stock out of the barn and over to the forest trail gate. He went through the gate, closed it, and stepped up on the horse. He wrapped the lead rope from the mule around the saddle horn and started up the trail at a walk. That was the pace he would have to use all the way. But he didn't plan to stop till he was done.

*Chapter 41*

OUTSIDE OF HIS OFFICE THE SHERIFF was standing at the counter looking at the police blotter, and when the officer in charge of the night shift went by on his way home the sheriff said; "You get that warehouse burglar?"

"Sure did," the officer said. "They'd put a dog in there since the last burglary, just like you said they should. Loomis came by and heard the dog barking. Pretty soon there's our man, climbing out a window on the north wall. Loomis was waiting there as the guy dropped to the ground. Guy's pant leg was torn; the dog got him pretty good."

"Luján? Didn't he used to work there?"

"Sure did sheriff. He was packing a grudge 'cause they fired him. Seems like he kept stealing stuff out of there, little by little, just for spite."

"Good work. Anything else?"

"Well, it wasn't worth putting on the blotter, but guess who's back in town?"

"*Tu me dices.*"

"Our old friend Harley."

"Yeah?"

"I was coming in west on the strip and there's this old pickup up ahead that I hadn't seen around town in months. I didn't see who was driving but it turned up Gavilán Road. Had to be crazy Harley. Wonder what he's up to this time?"

"You never know with crazy Harley."

"Crazy ol' Harley. Well, I'm out of here."

"Good work, Luis."

The sheriff got a cup of coffee and went to his office and while he sat at his desk drinking his cup of wake-up he thought about Crazy Ol' Harley. The fur season was well past, so it was not surprising that Harley Simmons had returned to Del Cobre from Minnesota. But still...?

"Celia, is the captain in yet?"

"No sir; I expect him any time."

"Tell him to watch the shop till I get back. I've got my eye on a couple of marijuana plots back in the woods. Might take a little ride. Just tell the captain to watch the shop."

"Yes sir."

The sheriff took his squad car and drove through town and turned north up Gavilán Road. He turned west by the widow's house, across the creek and up into the yard, parking right behind the old truck. He got out and went to the door, noting a hound in the pen, a hound on a chain, and one horse in the horse trap. He knocked on the door and got no answer. He started for the barn and then he noted the boot prints of one man, and the tracks of one unshod mule and one unshod horse, headed for the gap in the fence. He followed the tracks through the gap and for a hundred yards up the trail. Then he turned and walked back, went through the gap, and back to his car. He drove out across the creek and stopped at the widow Hidalgo's house. The widow Hidalgo was in the back yard feeding a flock of noisy, colorful chickens.

"*Buenos dias, Señora.*"

"*Buenos dias, Enrique. Que tal?*"

"*Muy bién, gracias. Y Harley, cuando llega?*"

"*No sé. En la noche, pero ya se fué con los caballos.*"

"*Sí, yo sé. Bueno, no diga nada de esta.*"

"*Sí, Señor.*"

The sheriff drove out Gavilán Road and headed west through town, then north up Nogal Road. Near the end of Nogal Road he turned into his own place. He went to the shed and scooped some oats into the bucket and took a bridle off the wall. He walked out and noted that the horse trailer was still hitched to the pickup; that would save some time. He stepped into the corral and began to swish the oats around in the bucket. The sleepy-eyed sorrel mare over by the trough perked up, turned and looked, rolled her nose and began a good head-nodding walk over to the bucket. The sheriff let her get a couple of mouthfuls then lifted her head and he was just slipping the bit into her mouth when his son appeared on the back porch.

"What are you doing home, dad?"

The sheriff called back over his shoulder as he rolled the headstall over the mare's ears. "Get my saddle, son...*Andele!*"

## Chapter 42

HARLEY STOPPED BY THE FIRE-SCARRED JUNIPER. It was hot in the late afternoon in May and with the sun and breeze he was almost dry; and the first thing he did was cut the cords that held the fat doe across the saddle. Then he pulled the doe off the saddle and he immediately dragged her over to the rim and started down the slope. He dragged her down to the rock bluff where he pulled her through the slot in the boulders and lay her in front of the den. He drew his knife and slit her gut to the brisket and the gut and the stomach and the liver and all the rest of the viscera, intact and bloody and rich in smells, rolled out. Then he hurried back up the slope. At the mule, Fiesta had her prick-eared head poking out of the hole in the box and she and the rest of them were crying for mother and milk. They had not fed since he removed them from the truck and they were seriously hungry but they would now have plenty of time to catch up. Harley lifted the box off the packsaddle and carried it down the slope to the den. He opened the box and took the squirmers out one by one and placed them well back in the cave. One by one they started back out but the bright sunshine, the strange visceral smells, and Harley himself caused them to retreat to darkness and safety where they screamed pathetically for milk. Harley ran back up the slope and opened the flap of the pannier on the bitch. He had pushed one more pill down her throat early in the day and had tied a stout limb crosswise in her mouth. She was just about recovered from the tranquilizer and could struggle mightily so he left the stick in her mouth. He wrestled her out of the pannier and put a rope on her and held her, kicking, as he took her down the slope to the den. She was very heavy with milk and needed to nurse as badly as the pups need to feed. She heard their screaming. As soon as Harley cut the cord that held the stick, and removed the rope, he let her go. She ducked into the cave. Harley heard the screams stop suddenly and he could hear them scrambling for the faucets and then he heard them suckling vigorously. The only whimpers were the faint sounds of satisfaction and no one was left out. Again Harley scrambled up the slope. It was mid-morning since the male had been tranquilized but he had received two pills and he was still half in the bag. Harley opened the flap and rolled the big male out. He gathered him up and carried and dragged him down the slope to the den. He laid him out in front of the den not far from the dead deer. The wolf got himself up on his front legs. His back legs wouldn't support him yet and he dropped down to his elbows and looked at Harley, an arms length away. Harley looked at the wolf and on past. The sun would be gone in a couple of hours and from where Harley looked, lights and shadows and the colors of a wilderness canyon were all there as they had always been, with the Río Jalisco deep and blue/green in the canyon and the heart and the life of it all. Nearby he could hear the pups suckling lustily, and the female wolf licking and making a fuss over her brood. Harley sat down right there, leaned back against a rock, took out his pouch, got a good chew under his lip, and then he addressed the wolf:

"Now listen here, big boy. We both know none of this was your idea. You had a good set up there in Tamarack County and now there's this big change in plans and there was nothing you could do about it. But goddamnit, if a wolf can't make a go of it in this country, there's something wrong with him. You'll like the climate. There's a perfect change of seasons but no season is severe compared to where you come from. There's more snakes, some you have to watch for, but there's no mosquitos or horseflies to drive you to ground on a hot summer day. You'll have to learn to run the hills but there's plenty of game. There are some people around that will want you gone when they find out you're here. But don't worry about that. I know a big guy with a badge and a gun will guard you with his life, so you just take a run at being what you are, a wolf, and make this country your own. This is wolf country. It was wolf country for millions of years and it's still wolf country, thanks to you. Take care of your family. They'll need you. We all need you, in ways you can't understand and no one will ever be able to put into words. Take care of yourself, be a wolf, don't play both ends against the middle, and I'll see you around some day."

The wolf looked on warily, seemingly uncomprehending, but his eyes were brighter and more alert all the time and then he rose up on his front legs. Harley thought: I'd better get the hell out of here. He tipped his hat at the wolf, stood up, turned, and wound his way through the rocks and scrambled up the slope. He tied the lead rope from the mule back to the packsaddle. They were going home now and Ruby would know it and there was no need to lead her. Harley stepped up in the saddle and reined the horse around. He rode down the rim till he cut the trail descending and they picked their way down to the river. They swam the river again, swollen with the last of the snow melt, and ascended the trail on the south side, rimming out, picking their way to the top. It was dusk when they cut the trail leading south to the divide and home. Harley put the horse into a trot and then something caught his eye and he stopped. There was just enough light left that he could read the tracks in the trail. A shod horse had come down the trail on top of the tracks he'd made coming in, earlier in the day. That same shod horse had gone out, on top of everyone's tracks, including it's own. Harley eyed this shod track as he continued on south, towards the divide. At the fork, the shod horse went out the way it had come in, headed west now on the Gunsight Trail. Harley continued on south. He was curious about the shod horse, but not worried. He thought: some cowboy, making a round. And he no longer felt like riding home at a trot. It was nearly dark now and there was no hurry. There was no hurry about anything anymore. It was done. He had done it. There was absolutely no hurry and suddenly he realized how tired he was. He wrapped the reins around the horn, gave the horse his head at a walk, the mule stepping steadily behind. Long before he reached the divide he was dozing off in the saddle.

## Chapter 43

THE STRIP OF NEGATIVES hung from the wire in front of the window and one by one the sheriff eyed them through the monocle and he thought: it's amazing what you can see with a 500 mm lens. Step by step the numbered negatives told the story. The first frame showed a man in a cowboy hat descending the steep canyon slope. He was on foot and he led, first, a horse that carried a doe mule deer tied across the saddle. A second animal, an enormous mule, carried two canvas panniers on either side of a pack saddle and a large flat-topped box between the forks. The picture showed the legs of a large animal sticking out of the bottom of the pannier nearest the camera. Further along the strip was a frame the sheriff eyed through his monocle for some time. The man had just come out on the bank after swimming the river. The horse, too, was on the river bank, while the mule was coming up out of the flow. The sheriff focused his eye on the box on top of the mule. A little fox-eared head was poking out a hole in the top of the box. It was little and it was from a distance but the 500 mm lens brought it amazingly close. The magnifying monocle brought it even closer. The remaining pictures told the rest of the story - a shot of the man dragging the deer carcass down the slope on the far side of the canyon; the man carrying the flat-topped box down the slope; the man carrying and dragging, first, one large wolf-like animal, then a second down the slope. The large wolf-like animals were clearly alive and every time he descended the slope, the man disappeared into a pile of boulders, then reappeared and scrambled up the slope. Frame by frame the pictures told the story. The sheriff turned away and took the monocle out of his eye and thought: it really is amazing what you can see with a 500 mm lens. The sheriff put his monocle down and went and got a cup of coffee. Back at his desk, he had coffee in one hand and he was smoking his pipe with the other. His eyes went past the negatives and out the window to the blue/black rim of the Mondragón Range. There was no sign of snow on the south slope, but the sheriff knew that good drifts remained in places on the north slopes and that all over the Río Jalisco drainage these drifts were feeding the river with the last of the spring run-off. The run-off was sufficient that a man, a horse and a mule had to swim it to get across. It was a good run-off. The sheriff's pipe went out and he reached into his shirt pocket for a wooden match. He set his coffee down and struck the match with his fingernail and watched the flame flare at the tip, then catch the wood. In one motion he set his pipe down and stood up; he took two steps towards the window and set the flame underneath the strip of negatives. Smoothly, expertly, he began to draw the flame up the strip, scorching and crisping all the negatives, frame by frame, into oblivion. The sheriff's office door was seldom closed and deputy Jenks stuck his head in.

"Sheriff?"

"Uh huh."

"I thought I ought to tell you, that burglar that Loomis caught the other night was complaining about his leg and it was swelling up pretty bad so we took him over to the hospital just in case."

"Good. Watch him. And don't bring him back till he's well."

The deputy stayed and watched as the last of the flame shriveled the last frame on the strip. Then he watched as Henry Bustos blew out the match and took the shriveled strip off the wire and dropped it into the empty waste basket.

"You sure are fussy about your pictures, sheriff."

"I only keep the ones I like."

## Chapter 44

HE STOOD in the living room with the phone to his ear. The phone was ringing and he was watching Suzie Navarro, through the doorway, in the kitchen. Her backside was to him, she was wearing her coveralls for work, and her hands were busy at the counter, making her lunch.

"Ted?"

"Harley! You old son-of-a-bitch. Where you at?"

"In town. Here at Suzie's."

"What have you been doing? I kept expecting to get a postcard from Acapulco or someplace like that. Figured you'd said goodbye to this hard old country for good."

"No, nothing like that. I just needed a little down time, and a change of scenery. Have you caught those otters yet?"

"No, I'm just now starting to get a crew together. We're going in first of next month. Everyone is wishing us well, even Jim Bo Moreland."

"I'll bet. Say Ted, before you get too far along with that otter crew, there's something you might want to check out. I got in a couple of days ago and I got to thinking I ought to take one last look at the Río Jalisco, before she's gone. So, just between you, me and the gatepost, I rode in there just to look around and pay my respects and Ted, you're not going to believe this, but I think there's a family of Timber Wolves making a home in that old den in the bluffs above the Ocotillo confluence."

"Oh Jesus, Harley!"

"'Course, I'm not for sure; I'm no wildlife biologist, but they sure looked like wolves to me."

"Jesus Christ, Harley!"

"I figured you might want to ride in there and take a look."

"Uh huh."

"Being a wildlife biologist, you'd know if they're wolves or not."

"Right."

"I figure, if they are wolves, you'll know what to do."

"I'll know what to do."

"It's probably just like those otters; I mean, they were probably there all along, only no one ever knew it."

"Right."

"Make a nice video."

"I'm way ahead of you, Harley. And Harley?"

"Yeah."

"You stay away from that goddamn wolf den. I'll take it from here."

"It's all yours Ted..."

Harley hung up the phone and stepped into the kitchen. She turned around and they wrapped each other up like they would never let go. She spoke her words quietly and close to his ear.

"Harley, you look exhausted."

"Nothing ten hours of sleep on your couch won't cure."

"And you feel so skinny. When I get home from work I'll make us enchiladas and I'll feed you good."

"Yes. And then we'll lay around on the floor and listen to some salsa music and maybe get a little drunk."

"And then we'll go to bed. I'd give anything if I didn't have to go to work right now."

"It's okay. We'll have lots of time. Only you be careful. I worry about you on that job...all that heavy equipment."

"I'll be careful."

"I'm sorry I missed that little skeeziks."

"She'll come walking home from mother's and she'll see your truck and she'll start running."

"Come the weekend, we'll all take the dogs and go picnic by the river. The cottonwoods are greening up and the catfish will be biting."

"Yes," she said. Then, slowly, reluctantly, they let go of each other, and she said, "Harley, what you've done...can it work?"

"It could. But it's only the beginning. We'll need more wolves in time, to put some flex in that gene pool. And then there's the matter of the Grizzly Bear, and getting some protection for that river. What these wolves will do is put some spirit back in the wilderness; people all over the country will feel it. And the wolves will give us some time. That's mostly what we need. The slash-and-burn boys can't run this country forever. I don't guess we're going to change the world, but wouldn't it be nice if we could save some of the romance?"

"Yes!" she said. Then she kissed him. And then she turned back to the counter where she picked up her lunch box and put her hard hat under her arm and stepped to the door. And there she turned around.

"Harley, will you promise to be here when I come back?"

"Will you promise to come back?"

"I'll come back."

"I'll be here."

250